PENGUIN BOOKS

A GOOD MAN IN AFRICA

William Boyd was born in 1952 in Accra, Ghana, and grew ere and in Nigeria. His first novel, *A Good Man in Africa* (1981), won the Whitbread First Novel Award and the Somerset Maugham Prize. His other novels are *An Ice-Cream War* (1982, shortlisted for the 1982 Booker Prize and winner of the John Llewellyn Rhys Prize), *Stars and Bars* (1984), *The New Confessions* (1987), *Brazzaville Beach* (1990, winner of the McVitie Prize and the James Tait Black Memorial Prize), *The Blue Afternoon* (1993, winner of the 1993 Sunday Express Book of the Year Award), *Armadillo* (1998) and *Any Human Heart* (2002, winner of the Prix Jean Monnet). His latest novel, *Restless* (2006), won the Costa Novel of the Year Award. He is also the author of four collections of short stories: *On the Yankee Station* (1981), *The Destiny of Nathalie 'X'* (1995), *Fascination* (2004) and *The Dream Lover* (2008). He is married and divides his time between London and South West France.

WILLIAM BOYD

A GOOD MAN IN
AFRICA

PENGUIN BOOKS

PENGUIN BOOKS

Published by the Penguin Group
Penguin Books Ltd, 80 Strand, London WC2R 0RL, England
Penguin Group (USA) Inc., 375 Hudson Street, New York, New York 10014, USA
Penguin Group (Canada), 90 Eglinton Avenue East, Suite 700, Toronto, Ontario, Canada M4P 2Y3
(a division of Pearson Penguin Canada Inc.)
Penguin Ireland, 25 St Stephen's Green, Dublin 2, Ireland (a division of Penguin Books Ltd)
Penguin Group (Australia), 250 Camberwell Road, Camberwell, Victoria 3124, Australia
(a division of Pearson Australia Group Pty Ltd)
Penguin Books India Pvt Ltd, 11 Community Centre, Panchsheel Park, New Delhi – 110 017, India
Penguin Group (NZ), 67 Apollo Drive, Rosedale, North Shore 0632, New Zealand
(a division of Pearson New Zealand Ltd)
Penguin Books (South Africa) (Pty) Ltd, 24 Sturdee Avenue, Rosebank,
Johannesburg 2196, South Africa

Penguin Books Ltd, Registered Offices: 80 Strand, London WC2R 0RL, England

www.penguin.com

First published in Great Britain by Hamish Hamilton 1981
First published in the United States of America by William Morrow & Company, Inc. 1982
Published in Penguin Books 1982
Reissued in this edition 2010

005

Copyright © William Boyd, 1981
All rights reserved

The moral right of the author has been asserted

Printed in England by Clays Ltd, St Ives plc

ISBN: 978-0-141-04689-1

www.greenpenguin.co.uk

MIX
Paper from
responsible sources
FSC
www.fsc.org   FSC™ C018179

Penguin Books is committed to a sustainable
future for our business, our readers and our planet.
This book is made from Forest Stewardship
Council™ certified paper.

The author wishes to acknowledge
the kind assistance of the Southern Arts Association.

For Susan

Somewhere a strange and shrewd tomorrow goes
    to bed,
Planning a test for men from Europe; no one guesses
Who will be most ashamed, who richer, and who dead.

W. H. AUDEN

PART ONE

Chapter 1

'Good man,' said Dalmire, gratefully accepting the gin Morgan Leafy offered him, 'Oh good man.' He presents his eager male friendship like a gift, thought Morgan; he's like a dog who wants me to throw a stick for him to chase. If he had a tail he'd be wagging it.

Morgan smiled and raised his own glass. I hate you, you smug bastard! he screamed inwardly. You shit, you little turd, you've ruined my life! But all he said was, 'Congratulations. She's a fabulous girl. Lovely. Lucky chap.'

Dalmire rose to his feet and went to the window that looked over the Deputy High Commission's front drive. Heat vibrated up from the parked cars, and a dusty even light lay over the view. It was late afternoon, the temperature was in the low nineties, Christmas was less than a week away.

Morgan watched in disgust as Dalmire tugged and eased his sweaty trouser seat. Oh Priscilla, Priscilla, he asked himself, why him? Why Dalmire? Why not me?

'When's the great day then?' he asked, his face all polite curiosity.

'Not for a while,' Dalmire replied. 'Old Ma Fanshawe seems set on a spring wedding. So's Pris. But I'm easy.' He gestured at the sombre bank of clouds which loomed over the rusty sprawling mass that was the town of Nkongsamba, state capital of the Mid-Western region, Kinjanja, West Africa. 'Looks like we're in for a shower.'

Morgan thought about replacing the gin in his filing cabinet, decided against it and poured himself another stiff three-fingers. He waved the green bottle at Dalmire who threw up his hands in mock horror.

'Lord no, Morgan, couldn't take another. Better let the sun hit the yard-arm.'

Morgan shouted for Kojo, his secretary. The man promptly emerged from the outer office. He was small, neat and dapper with a starched white shirt, tie, blue flannels and black shoes loose on his feet. Every time he was in Kojo's presence Morgan felt like a slob.

'Ah, Kojo. Tonic, tonic. More tonic,' he said, trying to keep himself in check.

'Comin', sah.' Kojo turned to go.

'Hold on. What's that you've got?' Kojo held several looping strands of paper-chain.

'Christmas dec'rations, sah. For your office. I thought maybe this year . . .'

Morgan rolled his eyes heavenwards. 'No,' he shouted. 'Never, none of it in here.' A merry bloody Christmas I'm having, he thought bitterly. Then, aware of the startled look on Dalmire's face he said more reasonably, 'Nevah bring 'im for here – you sabi dis ting. I nevah like 'im for dis place.'

Kojo smiled, ignoring the pidgin English. Morgan scrutinized the little man's features for signs of resentment or contempt but found no trace. He felt ashamed of his boorishness: it wasn't Kojo's fault that Dalmire and Priscilla were engaged.

'Of course not, sah,' Kojo said politely. 'It will be as usual. Tonic comin' up.' He left.

'Good man?' Dalmire asked, eyebrows raised.

'Yes, he is actually,' Morgan said, as though surprised by the thought. 'You know: bloody efficient.' He wished Dalmire would go. The news was too depressing for him to maintain his conviviality for much longer. He cursed himself futilely for not paying more attention to Priscilla these last weeks, but they had been impossible, amongst the worst he had ever experienced in his generally fraught existence in this stinking hot frustrating shit-hole of a country. Don't think about it, he told himself, it'll only seem worse. Think about Hazel instead – the new flat. Go to the barbecue at the club tonight. Do anything other than dwell on golden opportunities missed.

He looked at Dalmire, his subordinate, Secondary Secretary. He thought now that, in fact, he had really disliked him all along. From the day of his arrival. Something about his unreflecting Oxbridge assuredness; something about the way Fanshawe had instantly taken to him. Fanshawe was the Deputy High Commissioner in Nkongsamba, Priscilla was his daughter.

'Glad you had a chance to have a chat with Morgan, Dickie,' Fanshawe had said to Dalmire. 'Old Nkongsamba hand is Morgan. Been here, oh, getting on for three years now, isn't that right, Morgan? Part of the furniture almost, eh? Ha Ha. Good man though, Dickie. Finger on the pulse. Got great things planned, haven't we Morgan, eh?'

Morgan had smiled broadly throughout the whole harangue, a brief but foul chant of rage running through his brain.

He looked at Dalmire now as he stood by the window. He was wearing a white shirt, white shorts, beige knee socks and well-polished, brown brogue shoes. That, Morgan decided, was another thing he despised about him: his affected old-colonial attire. Ghastly wide shorts, billowing Aertex shirts and his college tie, thin and discreetly banded. Morgan himself sported flared, light-coloured flannels, bright shirts and these new wide ties with fist-sized Windsor knots which, so his sister assured him, were the latest fashion back home. But when he met with Fanshawe, Dalmire, and Jones, the Commission's accountant, they made him feel cheap and flashy, like some travelling salesman. Even Jones had taken up shorts since Dalmire's arrival. Morgan detested the sight of his fat little Welsh knees peeking out between the hem of his shorts and the top of his socks like two bald, wrinkled babies' heads.

Morgan wearily dragged his attention back to Dalmire who was saying something while still dreamily staring out of the window.

'. . . the whole fate thing, gosh. Priscilla was just saying how extraordinary it was that my very first posting should be here.'

Morgan felt a sudden desire to weep hot tears of frustration. How dare he throw fate in his face? When it could so easily have been *him* standing there, the new fiancé, if Hazel had only kept . . . if Priscilla hadn't . . . if Dalmire had never come . . . if Murray . . . Murray. He stopped the runaway car at the edge of the cliff. Yes, Murray. Fate had been working overtime.

Dalmire was still talking. 'Don't you agree, Morgan? Astonishing how these things happen?'

'Quite,' Morgan said, looking intently at the Annigoni reproduction of Her Majesty on his office wall. 'Absolutely. No question.' He sighed quietly. He cast a glance at Dalmire who was shaking his head in wonder at the miraculous nature of things. What was so remarkable about Dalmire? he wondered to himself. Mild, reasonably pleasant features, thick brown hair with a straight well-defined parting, slim, fit-looking build. In strong contrast to himself he had reluctantly to admit, but beyond that nothing but unexceptionable blandness. And, in truth, he had to concede also that Dalmire had always been amicable and subservient; there was no evident cause for the poisonous hate he now nurtured in his breast.

But he knew he hated Dalmire abstractly, *sub specie aeternitatis*, so to speak. He hated him because his life was so easy and his attitude, far from one of abject and astonished gratefulness that this should be so, seemed rather to indicate that this was as fixed and natural a state of affairs as the planetary orbits going on invisibly above their heads. He wasn't even particularly clever. Checking up his A-level and degree results in his personal file Morgan had been amazed to discover how much worse Dalmire had done than he. And yet, and yet *he* had gone to Oxford, while Morgan went to some concrete and plate-glass building site in the Midlands. He *already* owned a house – in Brighton, legacy of some distant aunt – while Morgan's UK base was his mother's cramped semi-detached. And yet Dalmire had been posted abroad as soon as his training was over while Morgan had sweated three years in an overheated office off Kingsway. Dalmire's parents lived in Gloucestershire, his father was a Lieutenant-Colonel. Morgan's lived in Feltham, his father had been a catering manager at Heathrow . . . He could go on and on. It just wasn't *fair*, he moaned to himself, and now he's got Priscilla too. He wanted something harsh, cruel and inexplicable to happen to Dalmire; something shocking and arbitrary, just to put him in touch with real life again. But no, the final insult from a bourgeois, ex-public school God had allowed Priscilla to be swept off her feet within weeks of Dalmire's arrival.

His thoughts were interrupted by a knock on the door and Denzil Jones, the accountant, poked his head round it.

'Excuse me, Morgan. Ah, there you are, Dickie. See you at the club. Five-ish?'

'Fine,' Dalmire said. 'Think you can cope with eighteen holes, Denzil?'

Jones laughed. 'If you can, boyo, so can I. See you there, OK? Tara, Morgan.' Jones left.

Morgan reflected that of all the accents he disliked, the Welsh was the most irritating. Except possibly Australian . . . or perhaps Geordie come to that . . .

'Good little golfer is Denzil,' Dalmire volunteered amiably.

Morgan looked astonished. '*Him?* Golf? You must be kidding. With a gut like that?' He sucked in his own. 'I'm surprised he can see the ball.'

Dalmire screwed up his face in polite disagreement. 'There's more to Denzil than meets the eye. You'd be surprised. Handicap of seven. It's all I can do to beat him.' He paused, 'Talking of golf I heard you used to play a bit. What about joining us?'

'No thanks,' Morgan said. 'I've given up golf. It was ruining my mental equilibrium.' He suddenly remembered something. 'Tell me,' he asked. 'Do you ever see Murray on the course?'

'Dr Murray?'

7

'That's the one. The Scottish chap. Doctor for the university.'

'Yes, I see him down there at some point during the week. He's quite good for an oldish fellow. I think he's teaching his son to play at the moment – he's usually been with a young kid the last week or so. Why?'

'Just curious,' Morgan said. 'I wanted a word with him. Perhaps I'll catch him at the club.' He looked thoughtful.

'How well do you know Murray then?' Dalmire asked.

'I only know him professionally,' Morgan said evasively. 'I had to see him for a while about a couple of months ago for . . . I wasn't feeling so good. Just before you arrived in fact.' Morgan's face coloured as he remembered the most achingly embarrassing moments of his life, and he said with some venom, 'Actually I can't stand the man. Sanctimonious, Calvinistic so-and-so. Totally unsympathetic – can't think why he became a doctor – hectoring, bullying – sort of moral storm-trooper.'

Dalmire looked surprised. 'Funny. I've heard he's very well liked. Bit stern maybe – but then I don't know him at all. They say he holds that university health service together. Been out here for ages, hasn't he?'

'I think so.' Morgan felt a bit of a fool; he hadn't meant his attack to be quite so vigorous, but Murray had that effect on him. 'I suppose we just didn't hit it off,' he said. 'Personality clash. The nature of the illness and so on.' He left it at that.

He didn't want to go on about Murray because he regarded the man as a wholly unwelcome and intensely annoying presence in his life. For some reason he seemed to stray across his path repeatedly; no matter what he did he seemed to run into Murray somewhere along the line. In fact, now he thought about it, in a way Murray had cost him Priscilla; indirectly, Murray was responsible for this latest disastrous piece of news that Dalmire had so smilingly brought him. He stiffened involuntarily with anger. Yes, he remembered, if Murray hadn't told him that night . . . He stopped himself: he saw the if-clauses stretching away to the crack of doom. It was pointless, he told himself in a sudden chill of rationality, Murray – like young Dalmire – was simply a handy scapegoat, a useful objective correlative for his own stupid mistakes, his fervent pursuit of the cock-up, the banal farce he was so industriously trying to turn his life into: Morgan SNAFU Leafy, R.I.P.

He looked pointedly at his watch, then interrupted Dalmire's reverie. 'Look, Richard,' – he couldn't bring himself to call Dalmire Dickie, not even now – 'I've got a hell of a lot of work to do . . .'

Dalmire looked at his feet and pushed both his palms forward, as if to support a toppling bookshelf. 'Far be it from me, old man,' he said mock-abjectly. 'No no. You plug on.' He walked to the door swishing an imaginary golf club. 'Sure you don't fancy a round this afternoon? Threesome?'

Morgan was sorely tried by the way Dalmire persistently accompanied his conversational remarks with visual analogues, as if he were a presenter on a TV show for the under-fives. So in response Morgan exaggeratedly shook his head and histrionically indicated towering reams of bumf in his in-tray. Dalmire flashed him a thumbs-up sign and slipped out of the door.

Morgan sat back in pained relief and gazed at the motionless fan set in the ceiling. He sat and listened to the hum of his air-conditioner. How, he asked himself with a smile of sad incredulity on his face, how could a demure, refined . . . *sweet* girl like Priscilla marry that crass nonentity, that ignorant scion of the English upper-middle classes? He pinched the top of his nose in heart-rending disbelief. She knew that I loved her, he told himself, *why* couldn't she have seen . . . He checked the progress of his thoughts for the third time. He should stop deluding himself this way: he knew why.

He stood up and walked round his desk to the window. Dalmire had been right about the storm. There was a fuming cliff-edge of dense purple-grey clouds looming to the west of Nkongsamba. It would probably rain tonight; there invariably were a few thunderstorms at Christmas time. He stared out over the provincial capital. What a dead-end place, he thought, as he always did when he contemplated this view. The only large town in a small state in a not-very-significant West African country: the diplomatic posting of a lifetime! He sneered — you couldn't even call it a backwater. He felt miserable: the irony wasn't working for him today. Sometimes he panicked, imagining that the records of his posting had been lost, deep in some bottomless Whitehall file, and that nobody even remembered he was here. The thought made his scalp crawl.

Like Rome, Nkongsamba was built on seven hills, but there all similarity ended. Set in undulating tropical rain forest, from the air it resembled nothing so much as a giant pool of crapulous vomit on somebody's expansive unmown lawn. Every building was roofed with corrugated iron in various advanced stages of rusty erosion, and from the window of the Commission — established nobly on a hill above the town — Morgan could see the roofs stretch before him, an ochrous tin checker-board, a bilious metallic sea, the paranoiac vision of a mad town planner. Apart from a single rearing skyscraper at the town's centre, a bank, the modern studios of Kinjanjan Television and the large Kingsway general stores, few buildings reached higher than three storeys and most were crumbling mud-walled houses randomly clustered and packed alongside narrow pot-holed streets lined with deep purulent drains. Morgan liked to imagine the town as some immense yeast culture, left in a damp cupboard by an absent-minded lab technician, festering uncontrolled, running rampant in the ideal growing conditions.

Apart from the claustrophobic proximity of the buildings to one another, and the noisome cloying stench of rubbish and assorted decomposing matter, it was the heaving manifestation of organic life in all its forms that most struck Morgan about Nkongsamba. Entire generations of families sprawled outside the mud huts like auditioning extras for a 'Four Ages of Man' documentary, from wizened flat-breasted grandmothers to pot-bellied pikkins frowning with concentration as they peed into the gutters. Hens, goats and dogs scavenged every rubbish pile and accessible drain-bed in search of edible scraps, and the flow of pedestrians, treading a cautious path between the mad honking traffic and the crumbling edges of the storm-ditches, never ceased.

Among the brightly-clad swarming crowds were alarmingly deformed leprous beggars, with knobbled blunt limbs, who staggered, hopped and crawled along, occasionally, if in a particularly dire condition, propelling themselves about on little wooden trolleys. There were lissom motor-park touts escorting big-buttocked shop assistants; small boys selling trayfuls of biros, combs, orange dusters, coathangers, sunglasses and cheap Russian watches; huge-humped white cows driven by solemn, thin-faced Fulanis from the North. Sometimes dusty, dirt-mantled lunatics from the forests could be seen weaving their nervous way among the throng in crazed incomprehension. One day Morgan had come across one standing at a busy road junction. He wore a filthy loin cloth and his hair was dyed mud-orange. He stood with wide unblinking eyes gazing at the Sargasso of humanity that passed before him, from time to time screaming shrill insults or curses, shuffling his feet in a token spell-casting dance. The crowd laughed or just ignored him – the mad are happily tolerated in Africa – content to let him gibber harmlessly on the pavement. For some reason Morgan had felt a sudden powerful bond of sympathy with this guileless fool in his hideously alien environment – he seemed to share and understand his point of view – and spontaneously he had thrust a pound note into his calloused hand as he edged past. The madman turned his yellow eyes on him for a brief moment before stuffing the note into his wide moist mouth where he chewed it up with a salivating relish.

Morgan thought shamefacedly of the episode as he surveyed the town. Depending on his mood Nkongsamba either invigorated or depressed him. Of late – or at least for the last three months – it had cast him into a scathing misanthropy, so profound that had he possessed a spare nuclear bomb or Polaris missile he would gladly have retargeted it here. Blitzed the seven hills in one second. Cleared the ground. Let the jungle creep back in.

For an instant he visualized the mushroom cloud. BOOM. The dust slowly falling and along with it a timeless weighty peace. But inside him he suspected it was probably futile. There was just too much raw, brutal life in the place to allow itself to be obliterated that easily. He thought it would be rather like that cockroach he had tried to kill at home the other night. He had been lost in some lurid paperback when out of the corner of his eye he'd seen a real monster – two inches long, brown and shiny like a tin toy, with two quivering whiskers – scuttling across the concrete floor of his sitting room. He had enveloped it in a noxious cloud of fly-spray, swatted it with his paperback, stamped on it, leapt up and down on the revolting creature like some demented Rumplestiltskin, but to no avail. Although it had been trailing a transparent ooze, its whiskers were buckled, it had lost a couple of legs and was only groggily keeping on course, it had nonetheless made the shelter of the skirting board.

He turned away from the view and the faint noise of tooting cars that came through the firmly closed windows. The rain would be nice, he thought, dampen the dust, provide a bit of coolness for an hour or so. It was important to keep cool, he said to himself, especially now. He felt fine in his office, he had his air-conditioner turned up high, but outside his enemy the sun lay in wait eager for battle to recommence. He had decided that his low heat threshold was something to do with his complexion: pale and creamy and well supported by a thick layer of subcutaneous fat. He had been in Africa for nearly three years and still hadn't developed anything you could call a real tan. Just more freckles, zillions of them. He held his forearms up for scrutiny; from a distance he looked as though he was quite brown but as you drew closer the illusion was exposed. He was like some animated *pointilliste* painting. Still, he reflected, if his calculations were right, in another year all the freckles should merge together to form a continuous bronzed sheen, and then he wouldn't need to sunbathe ever again.

In another year! He laughed harshly to himself; the way his life was currently going it would be a miracle if he lasted beyond Christmas and the elections. The mad implausibility of this last event made his head spin every time he thought about it. Only in Kinjanja, he thought, only in Kinjanja would they hold elections between Christmas and the New Year. Not just any old elections either, the Yuletide poll had all the signs of being the most important yet held in this benighted country's short history. These thoughts brought him reluctantly back to his work and he moved away from the window, warily circling his desk as if it were wired to explode. Cautiously he sat down and opened the green file that lay to one side of his blotting pad. He read the familiar heading: KNP. The Kinjanjan National Party. He opened it and the still more familiar features of its Mid-West representative, Professor Chief Sam Adekunle smiled out at him from beneath the celebrated handlebar moustache and mutton-chop whiskers. Numbly he riffled through the pages, his eyes dully flitting over the projections and assessments, the graphs, demographic surveys, breakdown of manifestos and confidential analyses of the party's political leanings. It was a good, capable piece of work: thorough, painstaking and professionally put together. And all done by him. He turned to the last page and read his final memorandum to the effect that the KNP and Adekunle were the most pro-British of the assorted rag-bag of political parties contesting the future elections and the one whose victory would be most likely to ensure the safety of UK investment – heavy, and heavily profitable – and to encourage its maintenance and expansion in the coming years. He remembered with little satisfaction now how pleased Fanshawe had been with his work, how the telex had buzzed and clattered between Nkongsamba and the capital on the coast, between Nkongsamba and London. Great work, Morgan, Fanshawe had said, keep it up, keep it up.

Morgan cursed his efficiency, his acuity, his confident evaluations. Fate sticking her oar in again, he thought grimly; why hadn't he chosen the People's Party of Kinjanja, or the Kinjanjan People's Progress Party or even the United Party of Kinjanjan People? Because he was too bloody keen, he told himself, too effing smart, that's why. Because for once in his life he'd wanted to do a good job, wanted some acclaim, wanted to get out. He slammed the file shut with a snarl of impotent anger. And now, he accused himself mercilessly, now Adekunle's got you by the short and curlies, hasn't he? Strung up and dangling.

Blackmail, so the detective novels he read informed him, was a nasty word, and he was surprised that he could pronounce it in such close association with his own name and suffer only minor qualms. Adekunle was blackmailing him – that much was clear – but perhaps his comparative equanimity stemmed from the bizarre nature of his blackmail task. However unpleasant it was it couldn't be described as onerous, in fact he hadn't done a thing about it in the ten days since it had been delivered. Adekunle could have asked for anything – the contents of the Commission's filing cabinets, the names up for New Year honours, an OBE himself, free access to the diplomatic bag – and Morgan would have gladly complied, so desperate was he to keep his job. But Adekunle had made one simple request; simple as far as he was concerned: nightmarish for Morgan. Get to know Dr Murray, Adekunle had said. That's all, become his friend.

Morgan felt his brain slow to idle of its own accord, a kind of fail-safe device when it became dangerously overloaded. Murray. That bloody man again. Why, why did Adekunle want him to befriend Murray? What on earth could two such utterly different men as Murray and Adekunle have in common that would be of interest to either one? He hadn't the faintest idea.

He shook his head violently, like a man with water stuck in his ear. He put the file away in its drawer and dispiritedly turned the key in the lock. He must have seemed like a gift of heaven to Adekunle, he decided; a fat white man joyfully offering himself for sacrifice . . . At this point he rolled down the reinforced titanium steel blinds around his imagination, a mental trick he had perfected: he didn't want to think about the future and resolutely ordered his mind to ignore that forbidding dimension. He could achieve the same effect of solitary confinement, a sort of cerebral Coventry, with other recalcitrant faculties like memory or conscience which could be irritating, nagging things in certain circumstances. If they didn't behave they didn't get spoken to. He closed his eyes, leant back, took deep breaths and allowed only the monotonous hum of the air-conditioning unit to fill his head.

He was on the point of dozing off when he heard a rap on his door and, squinting through his eyelashes, saw Kojo enter.

'Oh Christ,' he said impatiently. 'Yes, what is it?'

Kojo approached his desk, unaffected by his hostility. 'The letters, sah. For signing.'

Muttering complaints under his breath Morgan went through the outgoing mail. Three negative RSVPs to semi-official functions; invitations to prominent Britons inviting them to a Boxing Day buffet lunch to celebrate the honoured visit of the Duchess of Ripon to Nkongsamba; the usual visa acknowledgements, though here was one rejection for a so-called minister of the Non-Denominational Methodist Brethren's Church of Kinjanja who wanted to visit a sister mission in Liverpool. Finally there was a note to the British Council in the capital saying yes, they could put up an itinerant poet for a couple of days while he partook in a festival of Anglo-Kinjanjan culture at the University of Nkongsamba. Morgan re-read the poet's name: Greg Bilbow. He had never heard of him. He signed all the mail quickly, confident in Kojo's immaculate typing. Keeping the Union Jack flying, he thought, making the world safe for Democracy. But then he checked his sneers. From one point of view it had been the mindless, pettifogging boredom of his work and the consequent desire to escape it that had made him attack the KNP dossier with such patriotic zest – and look at the can of worms that had turned out to be, he admonished himself ruefully.

He handed the letters back to Kojo and looked at his watch.

'You off home now?' he asked, trying to sound interested.

Kojo smiled. 'Yes, sah.'

'How's the wife . . . and baby? Boy, isn't it?'

'She is well, sah. But . . . I have three children,' Kojo reminded him gently.

'Oh yes. Of course. Silly of me. All well, are they?' He stood up and walked with Kojo to the door. The little man's woolly head came up to Morgan's armpit. Morgan peered into Kojo's office: it was festooned with decorations, ablaze with cheap paper streamers.

'You like Christmas, don't you, Kojo?'

Kojo laughed. 'Oh yes, sah. Very much. The birth of our Lord Jesus.' Morgan remembered now that Kojo was a Catholic, he also recalled seeing him with his family – a tiny wife in splendid lace costume and three minute children all identically dressed in gleaming white shirts and red shorts outside the Catholic church on the way in to town a few Sundays ago.

Morgan looked at his diminutive secretary with uncon-cealed curiosity.

'Everything OK, Kojo?' he asked. 'I mean, no problems, no major worries?'

'I beg pardon, sah?' Kojo replied, genuinely puzzled.

Morgan went on, not really sure what answer he was trying to elicit. 'You're quite . . . happy are you? Everything going swimmingly, nothing bothering you?'

Kojo recognized 'happy'. He laughed a high wheezy infectious chuckle. 'Oh yes. I am a very happy man.' As he walked back to his desk Morgan could see Kojo's thin shoulders still shaking with merriment. Kojo probably thought he was mad, Morgan concluded. A not unreasonable diagnosis under the circumstances, he had to admit.

He took up his position again at the window and looked down at the driveway, trying not to think about Priscilla and Dalmire. He saw Peter, the imbecilic and homicidal Commission driver polishing Fanshawe's long black Austin Princess. He saw Jones walking out to his Volkswagen with the unrelentingly cheery Mrs Bryce, wife of a geologist from the university, who acted as Fanshawe's secretary. There were a couple of expatriate wives who did part-time clerical and secretarial work around the Commission, but Mrs Bryce was the only regular one. She was very tall and thin and the calves of her legs were always covered with shilling-sized, angry red mosquito bites. Podgy Jones waddled along beside her. They stood for a moment next to Mrs Bryce's mobylette and chatted earnestly. No doubt, Morgan thought sourly, she's telling Jones she's 'the happiest woman in Nkongsamba', how she never grumbles and how everything is really 'nice' if only you think about it in the proper way. Seeing how friendly Jones was being, Morgan half-heartedly wondered if they might be having an affair. In anywhere else but West Africa that notion would have raised shouts of incredulous laughter, but Morgan had known stranger couplings. Feeling vaguely grubby as he did so, he tried to imagine Jones and Mrs Bryce making the beast with two backs, but the incompatibility of their respective physiques defeated his best endeavours. He turned away from his window wondering why he always ended up thinking about sex. Was it normal, and were other people similarly preoccupied? It made him depressed.

If Mrs Bryce was on her way home, he reasoned, trying to shake the mood from his shoulders, then Fanshawe must have packed up for the day, and he had every intention of following suit. He was in the process of unslinging his lightweight tropical jacket from the hanger on the back of his office door when the internal phone on his desk rang. He picked it up.

'Leafy,' he barked aggressively into the instrument.

'Ah, Morgan,' said a plummy, cultured feminine voice on the other end, 'Chloe here.'

For a couple of desperate seconds Morgan was convinced he knew no Chloe, until he suddenly linked the name with the person who was Fanshawe's wife: Mrs Chloe Fanshawe, wife to the Deputy High Commissioner in Nkongsamba. The mental lapse came about because Morgan never thought of her as Chloe, and only seldom as Mrs Fanshawe. Usually the kindest epithets were the Fat Bitch, or the Old Bag. The problem was that they hated each other. There had been no overt hostility, no bitter confrontation, no single act that set off the conflict. It was an understanding that they had both seemed to reach quite spontaneously, entirely natural and unsurprising, as if it were some unique genetic accident that had brought about this animosity. Morgan sometimes thought it was quite mature of them tacitly to acknowledge it in this unfussy way: it made co-existence less complex. For example, he knew instantly that this pointed exchange of Christian names in fact meant that she wanted something of him; so, guardedly, he replied: 'Hello . . . ah, yes, Chloe,' testing the name on his tongue.

'Not busy are you, Morgan?' Ostensibly a question, it clearly functioned as a statement: no response was required. 'Care to pop over for a sherry? Five minutes? See you then. 'Bye.' The line clicked.

Morgan thought. For a brief moment an unfamiliar elation bloomed in his chest as he considered that it might have something to do with Priscilla, solitary offspring of the Fanshawe loins, but the sensation died as abruptly as it had arisen: Dalmire had been crowing in his office not twenty minutes ago – nothing could have changed that quickly.

Wondering what she wanted, Morgan pulled on his jacket and walked through Kojo's office and down the stairs. The sudden transit from air-conditioned chill to late-afternoon heat and humidity affected him as shockingly as it always did. His eyes began to water slightly, he was suddenly aware of the contact between his flesh and the material of his clothing and the wide tops of his thighs chafed uncomfortably together beneath his damp groin. By the time he reached the foot of the main stairs and had walked through the entrance vestibule and out of the front door, all the benefits of his afternoon's cool comfort had disappeared. The sun hung low over Nkongsamba making the storm clouds menacingly dark and its glare struck him full in the face. The sun shone large and red through the dust haze of the Harmattan – a hot dry mistral off the Sahara that visited West Africa every year at this time, and that cut the humidity by a negligible few percent, filled the air and every crevice with fine sandy dust, and cracked and warped wood and plastic like some invisible force-field.

Morgan turned around the side of the Commission and walked down the gravelled path towards Fanshawe's official residence some hundred yards away in the spacious grounds. The Harmattan had withered every blade of grass to a uniform brown against which the clumps of hibiscus and thickets of bouganvillea stood out like oases in a desert. To his left behind a straggling line of nim trees were the Commission's servants' quarters, two low concrete blocks that faced each other across a bald laterite square. Morgan could see, set up around the smoke-blackened verandahs of the quarters, the traders' stalls bright with fruit and vegetables, and he could hear the singing of women as they pounded clothes at the concrete wash-place at the top end of the compound, the crying of children and the clucking of mangy hens. There were officially six dwelling units for the Commission's staff but lean-tos had sprouted, grass shelters were erected, cousins, odd-job gardeners and nomadic relations had turned up, and on the last count forty-three people were living there. Fanshawe had asked Morgan to evict all unauthorized inhabitants, claiming that the noise level was becoming intolerable and that the rubbish dump behind the quarters was unsightly and encroaching on the main road. Morgan had yet to do anything about this, and he doubted strongly if he ever would.

He cut across the lawn to the front of Fanshawe's house. He looked for Priscilla's small Fiat and his heart leapt when he saw its rear poking out of the garage to the right of the house. She was at home then, he thought, unless Dalmire had taken her golfing. Self-consciously he adjusted the knot of his tie.

The Deputy High Commissioner's residence in Nkong-samba was an imposing two-storeyed building. There was a porticoed entrance above steps which led up to a long stoop with a row of French windows running the length of it. Inside were high-ceilinged airy reception rooms, and the back of the house looked down upon one of the more select suburbs to the south-east of Nkongsamba. The sun was about to sink into the thunder clouds to the west and was casting dramatic beams onto the whitewashed façade.

Morgan was on the point of climbing up the steps when Fanshawe leaned over the stoop balustrade. He was wearing a lurid blue Chinese shirt with a round collar that was dotted with purple ideograms.

'Evening, Morgan,' he said briskly. 'Anything I can do?'

Obviously he knew nothing of his wife's phone call. This was a bad sign, Morgan felt worry tremors shiver through his body.

'Chloe . . . Mrs Fanshawe asked me to look in,' he explained.

'Really?' Fanshawe said as if unable to comprehend this aberration on his wife's part. 'Well, you'd better come on in.'

Morgan walked up the steps. Fanshawe stood beside a red plastic watering can. 'Watering the plants,' he said conversationally, nodding towards several crude black earthenware pots overflowing with fecund greenery. With an outspread palm he indicated the open door. Morgan went in and sat down.

He found it hard to fix or even identify his feelings about Fanshawe: they wavered between the three poles of nostril-wrinkling contempt, total indifference and temple-throbbing irritation like one of those executive toys where a wire-suspended ball vacillates between three magnets. He was a thin ascetic-looking man with balding grey hair brushed straight back from his forehead. He had a tiny, meticulously pruned moustache which maintained an exact horizontal line equidistant between his nose and upper lip. Its obliviousness of facial contours made him look as if he was always about to break into a smile even when he was at his most earnestly pro-British. Consequently Morgan found it almost impossible to take him seriously. Fanshawe was a Far East man and had spent his working life in consulates and embassies in such exotic places as Sumatra, Hong Kong, Saigon and Singapore. Nkongsamba was his last posting before his retirement and he interpreted it as a definite slight. He had almost two years left to serve and the prospect of eking them out as a Deputy High Commissioner in such a God-forsaken, insignificant spot was something his professional pride would not let him take easily. He nurtured a secret dream of a dramatic last posting, a brilliant finale to an uninspired career. This brought about periods of evangelical zeal in his administration of the Nkongsamba Commission, like a model prisoner on death-row hoping his good behaviour will bring him a last-minute reprieve. It also made him very depressed about living in Africa, particularly in a spot so comparatively uncivilized as Kinjanja. 'Culture shock,' he had mournfully told Morgan on several occasions, referring to his arrival on the dark continent. 'Like a blow between the eyes. I don't think Chloe will ever recover.' Both Fanshawes were given to lyrical outbursts about the grace and dignity of the East, they would talk ecstatically about the centuries, the eons of culture and disciplined development the East had enjoyed. 'Far more civilized than us, old man,' Fanshawe would intone. 'And the African, well, what can I say?' Here would come a knowing smile and a cocked eyebrow. 'A beautiful, elegant person, your Oriental. Harmony you know, that's at the back of it all. Yin and Yang, that's right isn't it darling? Yin and Yang,' he would call unselfconsciously across a crowded cocktail party to his embarrassed wife. Fanshawe had forced himself to believe all this, Morgan had come to realize, and like all zealots was incapable of even recognizing that any other point of view existed, and so Morgan had reluctantly given up trying to draw him into discussions about the grace and harmony of Gengis Khan, Changi Jail and Pearl Harbour. Fanshawe may have convinced himself, but as far as his wife was concerned Morgan knew instantly it was sheer affectation.

For example the Commission residence itself was got up like a cross between some makeshift Buddhist temple and a Chinese restaurant. There were carved wooden screens, paper lanterns, impossibly low furniture, stark driftwood flower arrangements, silk paintings and an immense brass gong in one corner hanging from a pole supported by two half life-size gilded wooden figures. Returning home with Priscilla one night (it seemed like years ago now, they had only just begun 'going out') Morgan, emboldened by the romance and drink, had seized the padded gong beater and effected a languid slow-motion swing at the gong, crying out in basso profundo over his shoulder 'J. Arthur Rank presents'. It had not gone down well: the shocked, unlaughing expressions of the family, the heretical implications suffusing the strained silent atmosphere, the fumbling tense seconds as he nervously strove to replace the gong-beater on its tiny impractical hook . . . He shivered slightly as he remembered it now, seeing the gong reposing brassily in the corner, and wondered what the old bag wanted him for.

Fanshawe, as if reading his thoughts, said, 'I imagine Chloe'll be down any moment,' and, equally on cue, his wife stepped sedately down the stairs that led up to the first floor. Before he had met this one, Morgan had assumed that people called Chloe were either the neurotic brilliant daughters of Oxbridge dons or else silly screaming debutantes. Mrs Fanshawe was neither of these and Morgan had had to revise his Chloe-category considerably to fit her in. She was tall and palely fleshy, a moderately 'handsome' woman gone to fat, with short, dyed black hair swept back in a dramatic wave from her face and held immovably in position by a fearsomely strong lacquer; even in the most intemperate breezes Morgan had never seen a single hair stir from the solid lapidary mass of her coiffed head. She had a chest like an opera singer too, a single wedge of heavily trussed and boned undergarmentry from which the rest of her body tapered gradually into surprisingly small and elegant feet; too small, Morgan always thought, to support the impressive disequilibrium of her bosom. She held herself in a manner that encouraged this conclusion: poised, feet slightly apart, thighs braced, head canted back as if she felt she was about to crash forward onto her face. She ventured into the sun rarely, maintaining her unexercised pallor like a memsahib from the Raj by means of this reticence and also with the aid of unsparing applications from her powder compact, which she wielded often, and in public. Her other favourite cosmetic tool was a bright scarlet lipstick, which only served to emphasize the thinness of her lips.

'Ah, here you are at last, Morgan,' she said (as if she were the one who had been kept waiting), sweeping across the room and cautiously lowering herself into a squat armchair. 'Sherry I think, Arthur,' she said to Fanshawe, who duly presented everyone with a pale Amontillado.

'Well,' Mrs Fanshawe exhaled, raising her glass. She then said something that, to Morgan's ears, sounded very like *Nakanahishana*. 'A Siamese toast,' she added in condescending explanation.

'Erm, *nakahish*. . . um, cheers,' Morgan responded, taking a grudging sip at his warm cloying sherry and feeling sweat prickle all over his body. Nobody drank sherry in Africa, he fumed inwardly, and certainly not at this time of day when what your body craved for was something long, clinking with ice and possessing a kick like a mule. Morgan looked at Mrs Fanshawe's pale knees as she resettled the hem of her Thai silk dress around them. Nobody, he was acutely aware, had so much as breathed the name of Priscilla, so he resolutely took the bull by the horns.

'Marvellous news about Priscilla and . . . mmm, very pleased,' he said feebly, raising his sticky glass to toast the couple for the second time that day.

'Oh you've heard,' Mrs Fanshawe enthused. 'I'm so glad. Did Dickie tell you? We're terribly pleased, aren't we Arthur? He's got such good prospects . . . Dickie, that is.' It all came out in a rush and was followed by an awkward silence as the implied comparison was swiftly picked up and inwardly digested.

'Priscilla will be down in a minute,' Mrs Fanshawe continued, her pale skin refusing to colour. 'She'll be glad to see you.'

Sherry made Morgan depressed and this lie deepened the gloom that was settling on him as inevitably as night. He stared morosely at the dragon-patterned rugs on the Fanshawes' floor as they filled him in on the details of Dickie and Priscilla's good fortune and the excellent connections of her future in-laws.

'. . . and, amazingly, it seems Dickie's a family friend of the Duchess of Ripon. What do you think of that for a coincidence?' Morgan looked up sharply. The request would be due soon; he had an infallible ear for topics being bodily dragged in. 'Which is actually what I wanted to have a chat about, Morgan,' she said predictably, running her hands beneath her buttocks, smoothing out the silk creases. 'Have you got a cigarette there, Arthur?' she asked her husband.

Fanshawe offered her a rosewood box inlaid with a mother-of-pearl Hokusai landscape. She took a cigarette from it which she screwed into a holder. Morgan waved the box away when it was presented to him. 'Given up,' he said. 'Mustn't tempt me, tut-tut.' Why did he have to sound quite so cretinous? he wondered, as Mrs Fanshawe smiled at him through clenched teeth. She lit her cigarette. I know why she uses a holder, thought Morgan: she likes to bite things. The creases in Mrs Fanshawe's soft throat disappeared momentarily as she threw her head back to blow smoke at the rotating ceiling fan.

'Yes,' she said, as if replying to a question, 'the Duchess'll be spending Christmas night here, arriving at some point on Christmas Day. She's very graciously agreed to officiate at a children's party in the afternoon at the club.' She left it like that, vague and up in the air. Oh no, Morgan thought miserably; the games, she wants me to run the games. He set his features in a firm mask. He was going to refuse, he didn't care how they pressured him, he was *not* going to spend Christmas trying to organize hordes of screaming brats.

Mrs Fanshawe tipped ash from her cigarette. 'The Duchess,' she continued airily, 'is giving small presents to all the expatriate children, and,' here she turned and beamed at Morgan, 'we were hoping to get you in on this.'

Morgan was confused. 'I'm afraid I don't quite understand.'

Fanshawe broke in. 'Christmas spirit, all that.' Morgan was no wiser, but he felt apprehension hollow his chest.

'Exactly,' Mrs Fanshawe crowed as if everything was clear and above board. 'We thought, didn't we Arthur? that as *we* are the Duchess's hosts it would be fitting if a senior member of the Commission were . . . were in some way involved with her own very generous act.'

Morgan was flustered. 'You mean you want me to distribute the presents?'

'Precisely,' Mrs Fanshawe said. 'We want you to be Father Christmas.'

Morgan felt the anger and outrage boil up inside him. He gripped the sides of his armchair and tried to control his voice. 'Let me get this straight,' he said slowly. 'You want me to *dress up* as Father Christmas?' He felt his top lip quiver with fury at the effrontery of their suggestion. Just who the hell did they think he was – court jester?

'What's this, Morgan?' came a voice from the stairs. 'Are you going to be Father Christmas?' It was Priscilla. She wore white flared slacks and a powder-blue T-shirt. Morgan's jumping heart lifted him to his feet. Priscilla. Those breasts . . .

He caught himself. 'We-ll,' he said, making the word two syllables, the better to illustrate his reluctant refusal.

'But that's *mar*vellous!' Priscilla squealed, sitting herself down on the arm of a sofa. 'You'll make a super Santa. How clever of you, Mummy.'

Morgan felt even more confused: how could anyone mis-understand such a crude vocal inflection? But at the same time he was pleased: pleased she was pleased.

'I don't know,' Morgan continued hesitantly, 'I thought Dalm . . . Dickie would . . .'

A peal of laughter greeted this half-suggestion. 'Oh Morgan, don't be such a silly,' Priscilla exclaimed, 'Dickie's much too thin. Oops . . .' She pulled down her bottom lip with her forefinger in mock-apology. 'Oh God, sorry, Morgan.' Everybody grinned, though, including him. He hated himself.

'*Go* on,' Priscilla said leaning back, pointing her breasts at him. 'You'll be fantastic.'

At that moment he would have done anything for her. 'All right,' he said, fully aware that he would probably regret this decision for the rest of his life. 'Glad to.'

'Good man,' Fanshawe said, approaching with the sherry decanter. 'Top you up, shall I?'

Priscilla left at the same time as Morgan. She was going down to the club to meet Dalmire after his golf. Morgan walked with her to her car. His depression had deepened, he had a buzzing, incipient headache.

'By the way,' he said, 'I meant to mention it: congratulations. He's a nice chap, um, Dickie. Lucky man,' he added, with what he hoped was a grin of wry defeat.

Priscilla gazed dreamily at the Commission. Her eyes swept round to the storm clouds behind which the sun had now sunk, rimming the purple cliffs with burning orange. 'Thanks, Morgan,' she said, then: 'Look.' She wriggled her hand at him. 'Like it?'

Morgan gingerly took the offered finger and looked at the diamond ring. 'Nice,' he said, then added in an American accent, 'A lat of racks.'

'It's his grandma's' Priscilla told him. 'He had it sent out in the diplomatic bag when he knew he was going to propose. Isn't he sweet?'

'Mmm. Isn't he,' Morgan agreed, thinking: the conniving, covert little bastard.

Priscilla took her finger away and polished the stone against her left breast. Morgan felt his tongue swell to block his throat. She seemed to have forgotten everything that had happened between him and her, erased it completely from her memory, like cleaning condensation from a window, everything gone, even that night. He gulped: that night. The night she'd unzipped his flies . . . best to forget too, he supposed. He looked at her round plump face, her thick dark hair, cut boyishly short with a fringe that seemed to rest on her eyelashes. She was very nearly a pretty girl in a typically unambitious English Home Counties sort of way, but she was prevented from achieving this modest beauty by her nose. It was long and thin and turned up sharply at the end like a ski-jump. Even the most partisan observer, the most besotted lover, would have to admit it was a dominant feature which even overcame, ultimately, the potent distractions of her fabulous body. Morgan remembered an afternoon's sunbathing with her when his eyes would run irresistibly up her slim legs, past her neat crutch, swoop over those impossible breasts to alight fixedly on that curious nose. She had a flawless complexion, her lips were, unlike her mother's, generous and soft, her hair was shiny and lustrous. But . . .

Morgan of course didn't give, or hadn't given, a fart about her nose, but in a spirit of pure aesthetic objectivity he had to admit it was a prominent landmark. Perhaps after a decade or so across the breakfast table it might have begun to get on his nerves, he said to himself sour-grapily, feeling only marginally compensated.

They stood silently together for a moment, Morgan looking at a soldier-ant gamely negotiating the interminable mountain range of the driveway gravel, Priscilla holding up her ring to catch a fleeting shaft of sunlight.

'Looks like it's going to be a real storm,' she remarked.

Morgan couldn't stand it any longer. 'Pris,' he said feelingly, 'About that night, about *us* . . .'

She turned on him a smile of uncomprehending candour. '*Do* let's *not* talk about it please, Morgan. It's over now.' She paused. 'Dickie'll be waiting for me down at the club. Can I give you a lift?' She opened the door of her car and got in.

Morgan crouched down and looked in the window. He put on a serious face. 'I know things have been bad lately,

Pris, but I can explain. There are,' he smiled faintly, 'convincing reasons for everything, believe me.' He thought for a second before deciding to add, 'I think we should talk.' It sounded good: mature, seasoned, unhysterical.

Priscilla had been fiddling with the key in the ignition. She flashed the same smile at him again: the one that said you can talk all you want but I can't hear a thing.

'Coming to the barbecue?' she asked blithely.

'What?'

'Tonight. At the club.'

It was no use. 'Yes, I expect so.'

'See you there then,' she said. She switched on the engine, backed out of the garage and headed off down the drive. Morgan watched it go. How could she treat him like this?

'You bitch,' he uttered softly at the departing car. 'Selfish, unfeeling bitch.'

Chapter 2

Morgan walked morosely back to the Commission. He looked at his watch: half past five. He had told Hazel he'd be at the flat before five. He could smell smoke from the charcoal braziers in the servants' quarters: dinner time, the Commission would be closed. He went in to the staff car park and saw his car was the only one remaining, his cream Peugeot 404, or 'Peejott' as they were known locally. He had bought it in the summer when everyone else was to leave. Hazel had suggested a Peugeot, they carried a lot of status in Kinjanja. By his car shall ye know him. Mercedes Benzes came at the top of the list; you hadn't arrived until you did in a Mercedes. They were for heads of state, important government officials, high-ranking soldiers, very successful businessmen and chiefs. Next came the Peugeot, for the professional man: lawyers, senior civil servants, doctors, university heads of department. It spelt respectability. Citroens, grade three, were for young men on the make, pushy executives, lecturers, *arrivistes* of all kinds. Morgan publicly scoffed at such overt status symbols and justified buying a Peugeot for sound engineering reasons, but nonetheless, he enjoyed the appraising looks it received, felt vaguely flattered by the open weighing-up people subjected him to when he stepped out of the car: not important enough for a Merc, but a man of some quality just the same. It was too bad for Hazel that he only drove her about under cover of darkness; none of her friends had ever seen her in it.

He headed the car down to the main gate, saluted the night watchman and turned left down the long straight road into town. The Commission lay off the main road between the town of Nkongsamba and the state university campus. It was a two-mile drive down a gentle slope into the town. The Commission was placed atop a ridge of low hills that overlooked Nkongsamba from the north-east. One and a half miles further up the road lay the university campus where a significant portion of the expatriate British population of the Mid-West lived and worked.

Morgan considered going home for a shower but then abandoned the idea. Home was on an enclosed residential estate prosaically called New Reservation (he sometimes felt like an American Indian when he gave his address), which was about twenty minutes away from the Commission on the major highway north out of Nkongsamba. He had told his servants Moses and Friday to expect him back but he could always ring them from the club. It would keep the idle bastards on their toes, he thought savagely.

The road was lined with flamboyant trees on the point of bursting into radiant scarlet bloom. The rain, if it came tonight, would bring all the flowers out. He drove past the sawmill where Muller the saw-mill manager and West German chargé d'affaires lived. There was a French agronomist at a nearby agricultural research station who looked after the interests of the few French people in the state, but between them and the Commission they made up the official diplomatic presence in Nkongsamba. All the big embassies and consulates were concentrated in the capital on the coast, a four-hour drive away on a deathtrap road.

He began to approach the outskirts of town. The verges widened, dusty and bare of grass; empty stalls and cleared rickety tables of day-time traders lined the route. He passed an AGIP filling station, a shoe factory and a vehicle park and then suddenly he was in the town, busy and bustling as people and cars made their laborious way home after work. There were some larger concrete buildings on the outskirts, covered in wrought-iron work and standing in their own low-walled gardens. Strange sweet burning smells were wafted into the car's interior through the open window.

He slowed the car to walking pace as the streets narrowed and joined the creeping honking procession of cars that clogged Nkongsamba eighteen hours out of twenty-four. He let his hand dangle out of the window and thought aimlessly about the day and the massed ranks of his current problems. He asked himself if he was really that bothered about Priscilla and Dalmire, if it really affected him that much. He got no clear answer: there was too much bruised masculine pride obscuring the view. He drove on past the swarming mud huts set a little below the level of the road, past the blue neon-lit barber shops, soft drink hoardings, the ubiquitous Coke signs, the open-air garages, furniture shops, tailors sewing furiously on clacking foot-powered machines. He saw the looming flood-lit façade of the Hotel de Executive and his heart sank as it had become used to these past two months, as the memories of his first confidential meeting with Adekunle – held within its walls – hurried into his mind. Tin advertisements glittered around its door, reflecting the lights that were going on now dusk was settling on the town. He heard the raucous blare of American soul-music emanating from within its courtyard-cum-dance floor. 'Tonite!!' proclaimed a blackboard propped outside the entrance. 'Africa Jungle Beats. JOSE GBOYE and his top dandies band!!!! Fans! Be There!' Morgan wondered if Josy Gboye had been playing that fateful evening.

He turned off the main road and went bumping over potholes up a steep street that led past the Sheila Cinema, which was offering Michèle Morgan and Paul Hubschmid in *Tell me Whom to Kill* and *Neela Akash*, billed as a 'sizzling and smashing Indian film'. He drove by the cinema and pulled the Peugeot into the forecourt of a chemist's shop. He tipped the attendant a few coins and walked along the road ignoring the small boys running and chanting by his side. They were shouting 'Oyibo, Oyibo' which meant white man. It was something every Kinjanjan child did almost as a·matter of course; it didn't bother him, it was just a persistent reminder that he was a stranger in their country. He shook off his escort and two minutes' brisk walking brought him to a newish row of shops. There was an optician's, a Lebanese boutique and a shoe shop; above them were three flats. Hazel lived – courtesy of Morgan – above the boutique.

He looked quickly about him before running up the steps at the side of the building to the first floor communal passage-way at the back. He took out his key and opened the door. The first thing he noticed was the smell of cigarette smoke and his tetchy mood sparked into anger as he had expressly banned Hazel from smoking now that he had given it up himself. The room was also dark as the shutters were closed. He groped for the light switch and flicked it down. Nothing happened.

'Nevah powah for heah,' said a voice.

Morgan jumped, alarm making his heart pound. 'Who the hell is that?' he demanded angrily, peering in the direction of the voice, and, as his eyes became accustomed to the murk, made out a figure sitting at the table. 'And where's Hazel for God's sake?' he continued in the same outraged tone, stamping across the room and throwing open the shutters.

He turned round. The unexpected visitor was a lanky black youth wearing a yellow shirt open to the waist and disgustingly tight grey trousers. He was also smoking a cigarette and wearing sunglasses. He raised a pale brown hand in Morgan's direction.

'Howdy,' he said. 'I'm Sonny.'

'Oh yes?' Morgan said, still fuming. He opened the door of the bedroom. Hazel's cheap clothes lay scattered everywhere. He heard the sounds of splashing from the small bathroom. 'It's me!' he bellowed and shut the door.

Sonny had risen to his feet. He was very tall and slim and he stared moodily down at the street below, smoke curling from his cigarette. He was wearing, Morgan noticed, very pointed brown shoes.

'Pleased to meet you,' Sonny drawled, the mid-Atlantic tones grating on Morgan's ear. 'Nice place you got for Hazel.' Morgan made no comment: Hazel had some explaining to do. Sonny glanced at his watch face on the inside of his wrist. 'Ah-ah,' he said, dropping his pose, 'six o'clock done come. I must go.' He loped to the door. 'Thanks for the beer,' he said, 'so long,' and he slipped out.

Morgan noticed two empty bottles of Star beer on the table. He strode to the kitchen and slammed open the fridge door. One bottle left. He calmed down slightly. If that bitch had given Sonny-boy all the beer, he told himself, he'd have strangled her. Then his face darkened. He asked himself what the bloody hell that lanky spiv had been doing in his flat anyway? Drinking his beer while Hazel washed. Muttering threateningly he poured himself a glass from the remaining bottle and went back to the bedroom door. 'Hurry up,' he shouted. He sat down on the plastic settee and stretched his legs out in front of him. He took a long draught of the beer and its chill briefly made his temples ache. He gazed possessively round the room. It had cost him a lot, but it was worth it to get Hazel out of the rancid hotels she had lived in previously. He wanted her away from the bars and the clubs, somewhere he knew she'd be, somewhere discreet where he could get hold of her when he wanted. Selim, the Lebanese boutique owner from whom he rented the flat could be trusted to keep what little he knew, or guessed, to himself.

The flat was small and crudely finished to the normal standards of Kinjanjan masonry and housefitting. Bare concrete walls with loose, fizzing light switches and waist-high electric points; angled door and window frames with sophisticated jamming potential, tapered skirting boards and so on, but at least it was a home of sorts. Hazel had placed a purple rush mat on the terrazzo flooring but that was her sole contribution to the decor. Apart from the settee upon which he was now sitting the only other furniture Selim had supplied was a formica table with spavined aluminium legs and two steel-tube and canvas chairs of the sort that are normally seen stacked against the walls of assembly halls. The cramped kitchenette at one end of the main room contained a sink, a Calor-gas stove and a fridge. The only item Morgan had contributed to his love nest was a large standard fan which normally stood in the bedroom, gently rotating to and fro, blasting a steady stream of cool air onto the bed. Suddenly the lights went on, the fridge shuddered and started to grumble softly away.

Hazel walked into the room. She wore a threadbare pink towel wrapped around her body and secured beneath her armpits. She was without her wig and her short woolly cap of hair glistened with water droplets. She was a pretty girl with a light brown face and pointed chin. Her lips were large and her nose small and wide, only her eyes marred the classic negroid aspect of her features. They were thin and almond shaped and gave her a strange uncertain suspicious look. She was small with heavy breasts and hips and thin-calved legs. Her toes were bunched and buckled from the fashionable shoes she crammed her broad feet into. In the interests of gaudy sophistication she had plucked her eyebrows away to tiny apostrophe marks. In his less charitable moments Morgan accused her of being flighty and unashamedly venal – she had two illegitimate children who lived with her family back in her native village and of whom she rarely talked. She spoke instead of clothes and status, her two main interests in life, and Morgan fully realized that a white lover and this flat represented a leap of several rungs on this unpredictable ladder.

He had met her at a party at the university where she told him that at one time she'd been a primary school teacher, a career which he suspected she'd abandoned for casual prostitution, though he recognized that the term carried little opprobrium out here, as was witnessed by the unconcern over her two bastards. For all his cynical evaluation Hazel was necessary to him, more so now than ever, he realized, as a boost to his tottering ego and a source of reliable uncomplicated sex. At least, that was the plan, and he treated her selfishly and imperiously in the pursuance of it. But, somehow, it had never really worked out; the expected satisfaction had not materialized and he was faced with the growing suspicion these days that things were in reality running along some subtle scheme of Hazel's devising and that it was *he* not her who was being exploited; a feeling that the unexplained presence of people like Sonny in his life only served to emphasize.

He noticed that she was holding an unlighted cigarette in her hand.

'Can you give me a light?' she asked as if he were a stranger.

Morgan sighed inwardly. He'd have to put a stop to this now. He stood up. 'Look, I told you, no smoking.'

The cigarette drooped between her lips. 'You have never come for three days,' she said sulkily. 'What am I supposed to do? And then you tell my guest to go,' she added accusingly.

'I didn't tell him, he just went,' Morgan said, then, wondering why he felt he had to defend himself, burst out: 'Anyway,

35

I don't give a good God damn. When I give up smoking you do too, and no questions asked. What do you think it's like for me to kiss you?'

She looked coy at this.

'And,' Morgan went on, 'who was your "guest" anyway? Sonny or whatever.'

She put the cigarette down on the table and secured the tuck in her towel. 'It was my brother,' she said flatly. Morgan felt his indignation seeping away. He tried to keep his eyes off the way her large breasts splayed beneath the towel, tried to ignore the tickle in his groin; he had to see this out first.

'I thought you said you had no brothers.'

'Yes, from my mother. This is same father different mother.' She looked at him unperturbed. Morgan considered the veracity of her story: there was no way he could compete under these circumstances.

'All right,' he said grudgingly, 'but I don't want him to come here again, OK?'

Morgan dropped the condom in the tin waste-paper basket under the sink in the bathroom. He was still being cautious. Murray had told him to 'use the sheath at all times'. It was typical of Murray to call it a sheath, he thought; he could still hear the man's dry Scottish accent. It was typical also, he reflected bitterly, how Murray's influence reached into the most private areas of his life. He shook his head in resigned disbelief, it was uncanny how it happened. But also he was still not entirely happy with Hazel's explanation of Sonny's presence and he didn't feel like taking any chances. He always expected Hazel to make a fuss about him using contraceptives and the implications they had, especially as he had forced her to go on the pill a couple of months ago, but she had made no visible sign or comment as he had laboriously rolled it down over his flagging erection. The fan had been turned up to full and had swept the bed with cool draughts, drying the sweat on his buttocks and back.

Afterwards, he found he could still taste the Fanshawes' sherry in his mouth for some reason, and had sent a protesting Hazel out for some more beer to wash it away. 'If you hadn't given it to bloody Sonny-boy you wouldn't have to go, would you?' he had satisfyingly rebuked her.

While she was away he had decided to run a bath. This simple act was equally unreliable and ridden with pitfalls. He turned on the cold tap and for a full minute all he heard was a muted whistle of air, then the tap juddered, gave a couple of metallic snorts and a low-pressure stream haltingly flowed out for a while, filling the bath with two inches of water, before it was reduced to an ineffectual dribble. Morgan carefully lowered his sweaty body into this, gasping as his genitals were immersed. He soaped himself as best he could and splashed the lather off. Hazel brought him his beer and he sat for ten minutes or so in the bath sipping direct from the bottle. Presently a benign alcoholic haze began to fog all his undesirable memories. He turned on the tap again, found the pressure had built up and washed his hair.

When he stepped out of the bath he saw Hazel sitting in her bra and pants painting her fingernails. Morgan drained his beer bottle. There were two good things about living in Africa, he told himself convivially: just two. Beer and sex. Sex and beer. He wasn't sure in what order he'd place them – he was indifferent really – but they were the only things in his life that didn't consistently let him down. They sometimes did, but not in the randomly cruel and arbitrary way that the other features of the world conspired to confuse and frustrate him. They were as reliable as anything in this dreadful country, he thought, and, he reflected smugly, feeling more buoyant and pleased with himself all of a sudden, he was certainly getting enough of both.

He dried himself leisurely. Hazel had switched on her

transistor radio and low monotonous soul-music issued from the crackling loud-speaker. Morgan thought about ordering it silenced but decided to be obliging and refrain. Hazel was reliable too, he thought kindly: well, almost, in her own bizarre way. He was grateful to her.

Standing rigidly to attention and craning his head forward Morgan could just see the tip of his penis beyond the burgeoning swell of his pot-belly. Beer and sex, he thought. When he couldn't see it any more he'd go on a diet. He continued to pass the towel regularly over his body but it was no longer having any effect: he wasn't wet exactly, but remained distinctly moist. He padded through to the bedroom and stood in front of the standard fan. He took a large tin of talcum powder from Hazel's crowded dressing table and liberally dusted his armpits and groin. When his pubic hairs had turned a ghostly white he pulled on his underpants – pale blue billowing boxer shorts. This had been another of Murray's recommendations. There was the man again, Morgan seethed, but he had to admit it made sense, and it was comfortable. Kinjanja's humid clime was not suited for tight, genital-bunching hipster briefs: you had to let the air get to those dark dank places.

He caught a glimpse of a section of his torso in Hazel's dressing-table mirror. Fat lapped over the waist band of his boxer shorts. He was particularly distressed by the two pads that had seemingly clamped themselves immovably to his back – like tenacious alien parasites – in the region of his kidneys. He was getting too large: fifteen and a half stone at the last weigh-in. He winced at the memory. He had always been on the biggish side; in his beefy adolescence his mother had tactfully described him as 'big-boned', though 'burly' was how he now liked to see himself. He was of average height, around five foot nine or ten, and had always cut a stocky figure but in his getting-on-for-three years in Nkongsamba he had put on almost two stones and his silhouette seemed to bulk larger every week.

He crouched down and peered over Hazel's shoulder at his face in the mirror. He fingered his jaw-line. Christ, he thought with some alarm, the bone is half an inch below the surface. He stretched his neck from side to side, turning his head and squinting at his profile. He had a broad face, it could carry the extra flesh not too badly, he reckoned. He smiled at himself, his strong smile, showing all his teeth. There was something vaguely Brandoish about him, he felt. Hazel looked up from her nail painting, thought he was smiling at her and smiled back.

Standing up he inflated his chest, sucked in his gut and flexed his buttocks. He didn't really look thirty-four, he decided, that is, if you ignored his hair. His hair was the bane of his life: it was fine and wispy, pale reddish-brown and falling out. His temples took over more of his head every month. Somehow his widow's peak held on, a hirsute promontory in an expanding sea of forehead. If his bloody receding didn't stop soon, he reflected, he'd end up looking like a Huron Indian or one of those demented American Marines, currently wasting the inhabitants of South-East Asia, who shaved their heads leaving only a prickly stripe running down the centre. Gently, with all ten finger tips, he teased the soft hair across his brow: it was too sad really.

Back in his clothes he returned his attention to Hazel. She was spending a long time preparing herself for something, and it wasn't for him. He looked around the room and its tawdriness set his spirits in the now familiar slide: the frame metal bed with its thin dunlopillo mattress, the cheap local furnishings, the bright ceiling light with its buzzing corona of flying insects and Hazel's garish mini-skirts and shifts cast around the room as haphazardly as seaweed on a beach.

'Can't you keep this bloody place tidy?' he said complainingly. Then: 'And where are you going tonight?'

Hazel was struggling into a tight pink cotton mini-dress and she was wobbly on high-heeled patent-leather shoes. 'I can't stay here all night,' she said, not unreasonably. 'I am going to the Executive. Josy Gboye is starring there.'

Morgan laughed sardonically. 'Oh yeah? And I suppose you're going alone.'

Hazel adjusted her wig, a heavily back-combed straight-haired black one modelled after the hair style of a British pop-singer. 'Of course not,' she said simply, 'I am going with my brother.' She fastened on her gold earrings. Morgan thought she looked like a tart, lurid and sexual, and deeply attractive. He realized he was jealous; he would have liked to be going to the Executive with her, but it functioned as an unofficial campaign headquarters for Adekunle's party workers, and it would not be wise for him to be spotted there with the elections just a week away. Besides, the last person in the world he wanted to see at the moment was Adekunle. The barbecue at the club would be safer: safe and dull.

Hazel saw his smouldering look and came over to him. She put her arms round his waist.

'I want to go with you,' she said, nuzzling his chest. The stiff nylon hairs of the wig tickled Morgan's nose making him want to sneeze. 'But if you won't allow me, what can I do?'

Confronted by this logic he decided to be unreasonable.

'All right,' he said. 'All right. But be back here by 10:30. I think I'll look in later.' He thought this highly improbable but he didn't like being taken for granted.

He bent down and touched his lips to her neck. Her skin was smooth and dry. He smelt 'Amby' – a skin lightening agent most Kinjanjan girls used – talcum powder and a thin acidic whiff of fresh perspiration. He suddenly felt very aroused. He never failed to register amazement at the swiftness of his erections – and their subsidence – in Africa. He pressed himself against Hazel, and she backed off laughing, her almond eyes creased thinner with amusement. She gave her infectious, high-pitched laugh.

'Dis man,' she said in pidgin-English. 'Dis man 'e nevah

done satisfy, ah-ah!' She clapped her hands in delighted mirth.

For some reason Morgan found himself smiling bashfully, a schoolboy blush spreading slowly across his face.

Chapter 3

Morgan parked his Peugeot in the club car park. He got out and gazed across the warm roofs of the other cars at the club building. It was a dark night and the gathering rainclouds had obscured the stars. A coolish breeze blew from the west and Morgan smelt the damp-earth odour of impending rain.

The club was situated to the north of the city in one of the more seemly purlieus. Nearby stood a dusty racecourse and polo ground and the only Nkongsamban cinema regularly frequented by Europeans. The club itself was a large sprawling building which had been added to many times in the last half century and its haphazard design illustrated a variety of solid colonial architectural styles. It boasted also half a dozen red clay tennis courts, a sizeable swimming pool and a piebald eighteen-hole golf course. Inside were a couple of bars, a billiard room, a function suite of sorts that doubled as a discotheque and a large lounge-area filled with rickety under-stuffed armchairs which on festive occasions was cleared to provide space for dances, tombola and amateur dramatics or, should any crisis arise, acted as an assembly point for anxious expatriates.

It was a seedy-looking building, over-used, always seeming in need of a fresh coat of paint, but it was, by virtue of the poverty of alternatives, a popular place and Morgan, when he didn't detest it as a repository for all the worst values of smug colonial British middle-classdom, often found himself savouring its atmosphere: the wide eaves providing ample shade for the long verandahs, the whirling roof fans rustling the tissue-thin airmail editions of *The Times*, the barefoot waiters in their white gold-buttoned uniforms clicking across the loose parquet flooring as they brought another tall green frosted bottle of beer to your chair.

But it wasn't always shrouded in this nostalgic fog for him: there were bar-flies and bores, lounge-lizards and lechers. Adulterers and cuckolds brushed shoulders in the billiard room, idle wives played bridge or tennis or sunbathed round the pool, their children in the care of nannies, their housework undertaken by stewards, their husbands earning comfortable salaries all day. They gossiped and bitched, thought about having affairs and sometimes did, and the dangerous languor that infected their hot cloudless days set many a time-bomb ticking beneath their cosy, united nuclear families.

So Morgan changed his mind about the club from time to time. It had provided him with a few sexual partners – the hard, thin-faced wife of a civil engineer with five children, the large, moustachioed energetic spouse of the Italian Fiat representative in Nkongsamba – and for this he was duly grateful. He like the pool too, when it was free of the wives and their screaming brats, and he happily took advantage of the tennis courts and golf course when he felt so inclined. What he didn't like so much was the deadening familiarity of the place after three years: the same tiresome old bachelors, the sun-wrinkled, gin-sodden couples with their endless dinner invitations and impoverished conversations. Being First Secretary at the Commission made him something of a social catch, and anyone who thought they might have a remote chance of landing an OBE or MBE shamelessly sought his company, plied him with drinks and meals and with remarkable lack of subtlety would tell him of their years of unstinting service in Kinjanja, what they had achieved and sacrificed for Britain. After three years of this Morgan was beginning to think *he* deserved some sort of reward himself for the hours of his young life he had sacrified listening to sententious political analyses and dreary racist diatribes.

There was another club up at the university where he was an honorary member and which he sometimes patronized. It had a swimming pool and tennis courts but no golf course, was newer and smaller and the intellectual levels of its members marginally higher. These two places, the cinema and private dinner parties represented all the social outlets available to the expatriate population of Nkongsamba. It's no wonder, Morgan thought as he made his way through the parked cars towards the fairy-lit club façade and the jangling sound of pop-music, that we're such a desperate lot.

He walked into the colonnaded entrance porch of the club house. A large noticeboard was covered with club rules, minutes of meetings and announcements of forthcoming events. His jaundiced eye swiftly surveyed what was on offer: XMAS GALA PARTY, he read, TO BE ATTENDED BY HER GRACE THE DUCHESS OF RIPON. He shuddered, wondering what had possessed him to agree to be Father Christmas. Next to that was the golf club's GRAND BOXING DAY COMPE-TITION, *all welcome, prizes for everyone, sign below.* He turned away in despair. Outside the main door was a newsagent's kiosk that sold European newspapers and magazines. Tucked away amongst the display of heat-blanched copies of *Newsweek, Marie-Claire* and *Bunte* Morgan knew there were a few issues of American sex-magazines. He was surreptitiously leafing through one entitled *Over-40* – it was not a publication for gerontophiles, the number referred not to the models' age but to their mammary development – when he heard footsteps on the concrete path behind him. Snatching up a copy of *Reader's Digest* he looked round guiltily and saw Dr Murray approaching, accompanied by a young boy.

Morgan felt contrasting emotions stampede through his body: hatred, reluctant admiration, fear and embarrassment. He did his utmost to affect nonchalance.

43

'Evening, Doctor,' he said with wide-eyed jocularity, indicating with one twirling hand the vague source of the pop-music. 'Dancing tonight?'

Murray looked at him as if he were slightly mad, but said politely enough, 'Not for me, I'm just dropping my son off here.' He introduced Morgan: 'This is Mr Leafy, from the Commission.' The boy seemed about fourteen, tall and slim with a look of brown hair falling across his forehead. He had a distinct look of his father about him. He said hello as politely too, but Morgan thought he detected a look of suspicious recognition in his eyes, as if somewhere, in unsavoury circumstances, they had met before.

Murray was about fifty and also was tall and slim. He was wearing baggy dark flannels and a crisp white short-sleeved shirt; indeed, Morgan had never seen him in anything else. Murray had a strong sun-battered face with deep deltas of laugh lines around his eyes and short, wavy, pepper-and-salt hair. His nose seemed a little too small for his face, and his blue eyes sometimes had a humorous glint to them, but more often than not they were probing and unforgiving. Morgan knew the look well.

'You go on in,' Murray told his son. 'Phone when you're ready to come home.'

'OK, Dad,' said the boy looking a bit nervous, and he went into the club. Murray turned to go.

'Holidays?' Morgan asked, desperately keen to keep the conversation going, remembering with real anguish what Adekunle had ordered him to do.

Murray stopped. 'Yes. All the family together now, my son arrived about a week ago.'

'Uh-uh,' Morgan said, his head a sudden echoing void. 'Yes, I see, must be nice having him out here,' he said fatuously.

The penetrating look had returned to Murray's eyes. 'Is everything all right?' he asked. 'No recurrence, everything functioning normally?'

Morgan felt his face going hot. 'Oh yes,' he said hastily, 'fine there. Absolutely.' He paused. 'Listen,' he said in horribly inept bonhomie, 'what about a game of golf? Must have a game sometime.' Why did Murray bring out the arsehole in him? he wondered, appalled at his lack of finesse.

Surprise registered for a moment on Murray's face. 'Well . . . yes, then. I didn't know you were a golfer, Mr Leafy?'

'Morgan, please.' Murray didn't take up the friendly invitation. 'Yes, I'm quite keen,' Morgan lied. 'Funny we've never met on the course. When are you free?'

Murray shrugged. 'Whenever suits you. Look, I must be going, my daughters are in the car. We're off to the cinema,' he added in explanation. '*The Ten Commandments*.'

'Fine,' Morgan said, relief flooding his voice, at last he had some success to report to Adekunle. 'Shall we say this Thursday afternoon. Four?'

'Good,' Murray agreed. 'See you then, first tee.' He said goodnight and walked back to the car park. Morgan watched him go, he suddenly felt weak from the tension. You bastard, he thought, if you only knew what you are putting me through.

He went shakily into the club, which was busy and, he noted with Scrooge-like displeasure, manifesting signs of Christmas everywhere you looked. The streamers, the baubles, the ruffled bells reminded him once again of his foolish undertaking to personify the spirit of this season himself and for a full minute he raged inwardly against the Fanshawes, mother and daughter. Outside in the club's garden, spotlights lit up the barbecue. White-jacketed stewards gathered around three huge bath-sized grills made from oil-drums divided longitudinally. These were filled with glowing charcoal and above this hundreds of kebabs sizzled on wire netting laid across the drums. Morgan noticed Lee Wan, a Malay biochemist from the university ladling out punch. A cheerful friendly little man who organized pantomimes and children's parties. He was also a seasoned reprobate, and, under his tutelage, Morgan had been introduced to Nkongsamba's club-brothels some two months after his arrival in the country. He thought about joining the queue for the kebabs but his appetite had left him and he was beginning to wish he hadn't come, the bustle and the seasonal gaiety were too overpowering in his present mood.

His eye caught a noticeboard with an arrow-shaped sign on it saying 'Teenage disco, this way'. Morgan sighed, a mixture of longing and exasperation. With the advent of the Xmas holidays the expatriate population of Nkongsamba was sizeably increased by the arrival of all the sons and daughters from boarding-school in Britain and Europe. For a month the tennis courts and the swimming pool were taken over by these youthful hedonists. They would lie in groups around the pool's edge, like basking seals, smoking and drinking, gambolling sexily in the water and occasionally kissing with shameless abandon. Late one evening he had wandered into one of the club's teenage discos – some of the girls were breathtakingly attractive – and had found the room in total darkness. Three couples swayed on the dance floor in a position of vertical copulation and the perimeter armchairs were occupied by hunched and entwined combinations of two. Morgan had never, *never* been to a party like that in his life, far less when he was their age, and the unjustness of it all made him tremble with inarticulate envy.

A few of these teenagers wandered about the club now, casually dressed in jeans and T-shirts, laughing and joking. Morgan caught a glimpse of Murray's son standing on his own, friendless apparently, eating a kebab. He gave him a wave but the boy didn't react. Little creep, thought Morgan, as he turned and headed for the bar. He wanted a drink badly.

The expatriate community needed little excuse to come out in their droves to celebrate and the 'Bumper Xmas Barbecue' was no exception. Morgan responded to the smiles and nods of recognition as he threaded his way through the press around the bar. The noise of conversation was intense and people had a flushed excited look. There were a few Kinjanjans among the predominantly European crowd, but not that many. The club was fully integrated but its black members seemed to keep away on the whole. They had better places to go, thought Morgan, wondering what was going on at the Hotel de Executive. He looked at his watch: just after nine – he would give Hazel a ring to make sure she complied with his 10.30 curfew. Then he remembered there was no phone in the flat; there was nothing to stop her staying out all night for all he'd know about it. He felt a violent rage building up inside him: calm down, he told himself, calm down. Just because he was being blackmailed by an unscrupulous politician, just because the girl he wanted to marry had got engaged to his subordinate, just because his mistress was out getting up to God knew what with her 'brother', there was no reason for him to lose his rag, was there? Come on, he said to himself with withering scorn, be reasonable, it could be worse, couldn't it?

He ordered a large whisky from the steward and asked for the telephone. This was placed on the end of the bar for him and he edged his way round to it, stealing a sip from his glass, and dialled his home number.

'Allo?' It was Friday, Morgan's house boy. He came from Dahomey and spoke French; his command of English was erratic.

'Friday,' Morgan said, 'it's master here.'

'Masta 'e no day. 'E nevah come home yet.'

Morgan turned his face away from the crowd, the anarchic fury exploding in his head caused him to squeeze his eyes shut as tightly as he could manage.

'Listen, you stupid bugger, it's me,' he rasped into the receiver. '*C'est moi, ton maître.*'

'Ah–ah.' Friday exclaimed, 'Sorry-oh, masta. *Désolé.*' He went on with a stream of apologies.

'Never mind, never mind,' Morgan rapped out. 'I'll be home at ten. Tell Moses I want an omelette. Yes, when I come in – a cheese omelette.' That should make them sick, he thought with evil satisfaction.

'Excuse, masta, can I go? My brother he . . .'

'No you bloody well can't,' Morgan shouted, slamming down the phone. To his surprise he felt his hands shaking. Make them wait in for me, he thought blackly, they'll just watch my television, eat my food and drink my booze. It was a full-time job getting your own back on the world, he reasoned, you couldn't afford to weaken.

He heard someone call his name, and looked up. To his dismay he saw the grinning faces of Dalmire and Jones at the other end of the bar. They were beckoning him over. 'Over here, Leafy,' he heard Jones shout beerily. It sounded like 'Woava yur, Leefi.' God, he thought, that Welsh accent's got to go. He pushed his way sullenly round to where they stood. Dalmire and Jones were a little tipsy. They were still in their golfing clothes and had obviously been drinking since the end of their game. Morgan thought they were like a couple of schoolboys who'd slipped away from an outing and dodged into a pub.

'Hello there, Morgan old man,' Dalmire said heartily, resting a hand on Morgan's shoulder. His speech was a little slurred, his normally even features slackened by the alcohol. 'What'll it be?'

'I'll have another whisky please,' Morgan said, trying to drive the coldness from his voice. He emptied his glass and put it on the bar. 'Large, if you don't mind.'

'A pleasure, squire,' Dalmire averred.

'Bloody 'ell,' Jones said, shaking his round dark head in admiration. 'You can certainly put 'em away.' He giggled stupidly. Morgan noticed beer froth on his upper lip. Dalmire slapped Morgan powerfully on the back.

'He's a good man, is Morgan,' he said thickly. Morgan wished he wouldn't use that ghastly rugger-club expression. 'Bloody good man,' he continued challengingly. 'Fed me gin at half past three this afternoon. Bugger keeps it in his filing cabinet.' There was an explosion of laughter at this from Jones. Morgan glowered.

Jones grinned conspiratorially. 'Quiet celebration eh? Great news about Dickie and Pris, what do you say, Morgan? Marvellous.' He slipped his arm round Morgan's shoulders. 'Better not let Arthur catch you though,' he breathed into Morgan's ear.

Morgan was about to describe in graphic detail what he would do to Fanshawe with the said gin bottle if the former tried to tick him off about it when he realized that the Deputy High Commissioner was Dalmire's prospective father-in-law, and so kept it to himself. He contented himself with smiling knowingly and tapping the side of his nose with his forefinger. This sent his two companions off into another attack of chuckles.

'God, aren't you a fly one though,' Jones wheezed. 'Yur, let's have another round. Boy,' he called to the barman, 'same again.'

Morgan looked resentfully at them: Dalmire, in his mid-twenties flushed with drink like any adolescent: Jones, shiny fat face with puffy blue jowls married to a pale sickly wife with two pale sickly kids. It made you think, he said to himself, they certainly sent the dross out here. But then he realized he had included himself in the general condemnation, a thought which depressed him deeply for a moment before his pride told him he was different from the others, special, the exception to the rule. The self-evidence of this evaluation didn't strike home with the convincing justness he had expected, so he changed the subject.

'Where's Priscilla?' he asked Dalmire. 'I thought she was coming down to meet you.'

'She's off with Geraldine and the kids,' Dalmire told him. Geraldine was Jones's wife. 'Getting some kebabs. You eating here?' Dalmire asked. 'Why don't you join us?'

Jones seconded this suggestion. They both seemed genuine. The thought came to Morgan, as it had done a few times in the past when faced with similar unprompted invitations, that they actually liked him, wanted his company, found him intriguing and amusing. He was always a little nonplussed on these occasions too, sentiments of humble gratitude spontaneously rising up within him. However it annoyed him to feel grateful to people like Dalmire and Jones, it seemed demeaning in a way, so he made a point of ruthlessly expunging such emotions when they occurred.

'Ah . . . no thanks,' he said tapping the side of his nose again, playing out the role of rake, hell-raiser and debauchee they had created for him. 'Must be going soon. Got a date.'

This initiated a series of throaty laughs, mutual rib-digging and low cries of 'Wor-hor-hor.' Morgan wondered why he did it. His musings were interrupted by the arrival of Priscilla and Geraldine. Geraldine Jones was wearing a green . . . frock was the only suitable word, that hung limply from her thin shoulders and displayed the top half of her wash-board chest. She had big eyes in a small face, like some potto or lemur, and short indeterminately brown hair.

'Hello you lot,' she said with forced cheeriness. 'Hello Morgan, nice to see you. What's all this laughter about?'

Morgan knew instantly the kind of response Jones would make to this question and watched with mounting horror as the little Welshman fashioned a crude leer out of his plump features, tilted his body forward confidentially and said in his sing-song voice, 'Ow-er Mor-gan's got a ro-man-tic ass-ig-na-tion.'

As the red mist of virulent wrath dimmed his view, Morgan felt like plucking the eyes from Jones's face, stamping his head to a pulp, ramming all types of fiendishly blunt uneven instruments into his various orifices, but instead, by a ruthless act of self-control, he managed a twisted, white-lipped smile, acutely conscious of Priscilla stiffening perceptibly beside him. While his heart sank to his shoes, the mildly comforting thought came to him that this indicated she was not entirely indifferent as to how or with whom he spent his evenings. Nevertheless she moved round to stand by Dalmire, whose eyes were beginning to look distinctly glazed, and gave him a loving little peck on the forehead. Dalmire put his arm round her and patted her haunch. She looked Morgan in the eye: he thought he could read triumph there. Before she could speak Morgan blurted out the first innocuous thing that came into his head.

'Met Dr Murray's son tonight. Spit and image of his father.' He craned his neck as though searching the room for him. As expected this got everybody following suit.

'I'm sure I saw him out by the barbecue,' Geraldine remarked. 'Quiet boy, on his own. Shame.'

'Marvellous doctor, that Murray,' Jones affirmed importantly. 'I don't know what we'd have done without him, or what would have happened to Gareth and Bronwyn. It's difficult, this country, for our two.'

Everybody looked serious for a moment, reflecting on this.

'He could do with a dash of the old milk of human kindness I reckon,' Morgan commented, inserting the knife half an inch.

Geraldine looked astonished. 'Oh no, do you think so? I found him ever so nice and helpful.'

'Depends what's wrong with you I expect,' Priscilla interjected. 'There are so many hypochondriacs out here. I think Murray can spot them a mile off.' There was more general agreement. Morgan didn't like the sound of this one bit: what exactly did Priscilla know? he wondered uneasily.

One of Jones's children ran up. It was the little girl Bronwyn and she was holding a red balloon. 'Daddy, daddy, look what I've got,' she piped. Jones picked her up and in a mood of bibulous fatherly love nuzzled her neck saying, 'Oo's a clever likkle girl en? Eh? Oo's daddy's likkle clever girlie? Brrrr,' and so on until she screamed in panic to be put down. Whereupon everyone except Morgan leaned over her to admire the red balloon, commenting on its rare and exotic beauty and Bronwyn's Nobel Prize-winning intelligence in acquiring it. Amongst the hullabaloo Morgan noticed Dalmire's hand slide from Priscilla's hip round to cup and squeeze her buttock. The green-eyed monster ruled in Morgan's heart. Its reign, however, was shortly terminated by the arrival of a steward bearing a note. Bronwyn had now been joined by her brother Gareth, also clutching a balloon – only this time a yellow one – and also demanding acclaim and admiration so Morgan had plenty of undisturbed time to accept the note, thank the steward, look puzzled and read it. It said:

'I am in the small bar. Why don't you come and join me. Sam Adekunle.'

Morgan thought he was going to be sick, he even felt a bit unsteady on his feet. He thrust the note into his pocket and thought furiously. His deep concentration eventually impinged on the consciousness of the others present and they stopped talking and looked curiously at him.

'Is everything all right?' Priscilla asked.

'Not bad news, is it?' Jones laughed nervously. 'Been stood up by the girlfriend?'

Morgan forced a smile. 'God no.' He played for time. 'Worse than that.' He said the first remotely plausible lie that came into his head. 'Apparently some British Council poet we're meant to be putting up has gone and got himself lost. Bloody artist, typical.' He left it vague. 'Ah well, duty calls.' People commiserated, their conversation resumed. Morgan drained the last inch of his whisky, shuddered, and moved round the side of the group to put it on the bar.

He felt Priscilla's hand on his arm. 'Everything *is* all right, isn't it, Morgan?' She sounded concerned, and he was touched. He shot a glance at Dalmire, who was chatting to Jones, and looked back at Priscilla, taking in the shiny fringe, the silly nose, the fabulous breasts as if for the first time. Love bloomed like a napalm blast in his heart: a stupid, irrational drink-induced love that had little to do with the emotion spelt with a capital L. He thought: if only he could *have* her, somehow, before she and Dalmire got married then, well, everything would seem fairer, more even and proper. Her hand was still on his arm, Morgan laid his on top of hers.

'Everything's fine, Pris,' he said softly, noble in defeat, trying to convey also that she was making a terrible mistake but ah well there you go. 'Under the circumstances,' he added wryly. He removed his hand to expose her engagement ring. Priscilla snatched it away, as if his arm had suddenly turned blazing hot, and tucked it in the pocket of her jeans. She looked down at her feet in confusion.

Morgan leaned forward. 'You don't want to listen to Denzil's nonsense about me having a date,' he whispered. 'It's just his curious Welsh sense of humour.' He patted her reassuringly on the shoulder, then raised his voice. 'Bye everyone,' he called. 'See you anon.' He strode off, exulting momentarily at this superb turning of the tables until he recalled suddenly where he was striding to. His step faltered and he looked back longingly at the small circle of people he'd just left. He felt a terrible sense of isolation descend on him. Adekunle was waiting.

Chapter 4

The small bar was the name given to the club room that overlooked the eighteenth hole. Normally it was occupied by perspiring golfers downing pints of shandy but at this time of night it was deserted. A sleepy steward slumped on the bar; Morgan wondered where Adekunle was, thankful for his discretion.

He heard his name called from the stoop. Walking out on to it he saw Adekunle's bulk at the far end, the tip of his cigarette glowing in the darkness.

'Ah, Mr Leafy,' Adekunle said again, coming to meet him with his arm outstretched. 'I think we will have rain tonight.' Morgan shook hands with him and concurred nervously. Adekunle was a big man with bulging apple-cheeks and a well-padded jowl. He was a distinctive figure; images of his moustachioed face currently regaled hoardings throughout the Mid-West. Tonight he looked even larger than usual as he was in his full traditional costume, an embroidered, loose, knee-length cream tunic with prodigious wide sleeves that were folded back over his shoulders, matching cream pyjama trousers that tapered to the ankle and a black velvet, gold-threaded tarboosh that, in the Kinjanjan fashion, was crushed lopsidedly down on his head. The evident wealth and splendour of his outfit, plus his considerable girth made him seem like some all-powerful native potentate, an African Henry VIII.

'Forgive the paraphernalia,' he said. His voice was deep and educated, with a near-perfect English accent modulated by hints of American tones he'd picked up while studying at the Harvard Business School. 'But I'm going on to a party rally.'

'I didn't expect you back so soon,' Morgan ventured, his voice sounding unnaturally husky and at least two registers higher. 'Did you have a good trip?'

Adekunle smiled broadly. 'An excellent trip, thank you, most fruitful. London was cold and very crowded.' Adekunle paused, and when he continued the genial note was missing from his voice. 'I wanted to see you . . . urgently. So you can imagine how delighted I was to spy you out here. I am the bringer of bad news I am afraid,' he puffed cigarette smoke out into the night. 'As I feared we have a problem. A problem with Dr Murray.'

'I'm glad,' Morgan cleared the catch from his throat. 'I mean I'm glad you were so discreet. My colleagues are out there.'

'Don't mention it,' Adekunle said urbanely. 'I fully understand your position.'

'Listen,' Morgan croaked, 'would you mind if I got another drink?' He paused, unsure if he could form the following words. 'Before I hear your problem.' He went into the bar, shook the steward awake and was given another whisky. He took a large gulp and rejoined Adekunle on the stoop. Adekunle lit another cigarette and asked in his unperturbed, sonorous voice, 'Talking of Murray, how is your friendship with him progressing? Is everything going as planned?'

Morgan swallowed, he was glad at least to report some success. 'Going quite well,' he said weakly. 'As you suggested I've been trying to mix with him socially which is . . . a little difficult as he's not the most sociable man. However, I *am* playing golf with him later this week.'

'Golf,' Adekunle said reflectively. 'Excellent. Just you and Murray?'

'Yes . . . at least, I assume so.'

'Good, Keep it that way.'

'I hope you don't mind me asking,' Morgan said plaintively, 'but what's this all about? I'm afraid I don't understand anything. Why is it so important for me to become friendly with Murray? What exactly do you expect me to do?'

Adekunle looked quizzically at Morgan. 'I suppose I can tell you now,' he said. 'It is not unreasonable. Yes.' He paused, and then said quite quickly as though it were the most natural thing in the world, 'I want you to get to know Murray because I want you to bribe him.'

Morgan wasn't at all sure he'd heard this correctly. 'What?' he said haltingly. 'Murray? A bribe? You must be joking.'

'I'm not joking, my friend,' Adekunle said in a tone that effectively removed any doubt on that point from Morgan's mind. He suddenly felt nauseous: a nightmare vision of the future was forming in his muddled brain; unrelated events in the past fell into their allotted places in the dreadful pattern; ambiguous remarks and attitudes suddenly became menacingly explicable. With some effort he managed to speak.

'You want me to bribe Murray,' he said faintly. 'To do what?'

Adekunle took him by the arm and led him to the far end of the stoop. The bar lights cast a faint glow on them. In the darkness somewhere beyond the pool of light the fairways stretched out into the forest. 'Let me explain,' Adekunle said reasonably. 'There is a building project at our university here in Nkongsamba in which I have a very great interest – not just because of my, ah, professorial connections with the university but for other reasons as well. You see,' he went on, 'the university is expanding and they want to build a new 500-room hall of residence and cafeteria. The land that they want to build the hall on belongs to me. I have been expecting to sell that land for some months now but there have been hold-ups.' He held up his hand for silence as Morgan was about to interrupt. 'There is also a university committee called the Buildings, Works and Sites Committee. Its job is to investigate and consider the viability of all new university building projects from the point of view of hygiene, social and environmental concerns and report its conclusions to the university senate. It is an important committee, in fact it carries a veto on all building projects and its chairman . . .'

'Is Dr Alex Murray,' Morgan gulped.

'Precisely,' Adekunle congratulated. 'You are, as the saying goes, catching on.' He plucked at the embroidery on his gown. 'I became aware of the problem some time ago through certain contacts I have. But yesterday, on my return from London, I was informed by my sources that my worst fears have been realized. Dr Murray,' there was a hint of annoyance as Adekunle pronounced the man's name; Morgan knew how he felt, 'Dr Murray intends to file a negative report on the proposed site. If he goes through with this the land will not be bought and there will be no sale.' Adekunle smiled grimly. 'I feared as much,' he said. 'I had to make preparations, which is why I . . . decided to, ah, how would you say? engage your services in this delicate matter of persuasion.'

'You want me . . .'

'I want you to persuade Dr Murray to change his mind.'

'Oh my God,' Morgan said feebly, suffering from an attack of neurotic clairvoyance. 'I'm not sure . . .'

'Please,' Adekunle said silkily, squeezing Morgan's arm. 'Let us not talk of defeat.'

'But what's the problem?' Morgan asked. 'Why is he saying no?'

Adekunle flicked the stub of his cigarette out into the night. 'There were certain objections to be expected: the proximity of Ondo village, the inconvenient course of the nearby river, but these were not major, they could be overcome without difficulty. Villagers can be persuaded to resettle, rivers can be diverted.' He sighed with exasperation. 'Unfortunately for all of us Dr Murray is very thorough. A very thorough man.' He took a cigarette pack from a pocket in his robe. 'Perhaps you know,' he said, lighting a cigarette from it, 'that my family are tribal chiefs in this part of the world. In fact we own a great deal of the land around Nkongsamba. But, alas, the expenses of political life are very considerable, and so two years ago I was obliged to sell some of my family's land. Some land which now borders the proposed site for the new hall of residence.' Adekunle smiled emptily. 'I was chairman of the Nkongsamba Chamber of Commerce at the time and so it was, shall we say, convenient for me to sell it to the Nkongsamba Town Council. They own that land now.'

Morgan frowned. He wondered if in his naivety he was missing something very obvious. He still couldn't see how it all tied in. Perhaps Adekunle's ponderous euphemisms were a code he should have picked up on immediately. 'Does Murray know you own the land?' he asked.

'No,' said Adekunle. 'No, no. I am sure of that. None of these transactions occur under my own name,' he said condescendingly, as if suppressing his frustration at Morgan's slowness. 'I don't think,' he went on, 'that the University of Nkongsamba would spend hundreds of thousands of pounds if they knew it was going to their own Professor of Economics and Business Management. No,' he continued, 'the problem lies with the Town Council. The land I sold two years ago is today the new Nkongsamba municipal rubbish dump.'

'Oh,' Morgan said, suddenly seeing. 'I see.'

'They started dumping there about six months ago. At present the dump is still fairly small and insignificant and at some distance from the proposed hall site. However in another year it will be most obvious, in fact if they continue at this rate the rubbish will be pressing against the walls of the buildings. But if by then,' he said fake-sadly, 'construction is underway it will be too late to find a new site.' Morgan was impressed by his concern for his students' welfare. 'Nobody,' Adekunle said emphatically, 'nobody could know this now. Unless they consulted the town planning records.'

'And Murray has consulted the . . . yes.'

'You have it, my friend. A very thorough man, as I said.'

'But can't you get them to move the dump or something?' Morgan asked hopelessly.

Adekunle gave a scornful laugh at the impracticability of this suggestion. 'And where will you put thousands of tons of decaying rubbish? Besides,' he added, 'since entering politics I have been obliged to abandon my more influential positions within the council for the sake of, what shall we say, probity.' The word seemed to leave a sour taste in his mouth. 'I am sorry, my friend, but there is no other way. And in any case it is vital that this deal goes through now. I cannot afford to wait.' He spread his hands. 'Election expenses. And when, I mean if, we win I will need substantial reserves. No, Murray must change his report. Without Murray there would be no problem, the land would have been sold already.' He looked at Morgan. 'You are a white man, a representative of Her Majesty the Queen's Diplomatic Service and a friend of his. I am counting on you to change his mind.'

Morgan gazed bleakly heavenwards. He felt the weight and menace of the invisible black rainclouds above him as a personal threat, a final vindictive rebuff from a surly and spiteful God. The Canutian impossibility of the task Adekunle had set him made him want to laugh hysterically; the sheer audacity of the suggestion made him want to weep with helpless despair. Did the man know nothing of Murray? he wondered. Could he not see in those stern features the moral rectitude of a latter-day John Knox?

Morgan began, gently, to explain. 'If you knew Dr Murray as well as I do, you would see the impossibility of . . .'

Adekunle interrupted. 'Please, I do know Murray. He is a man, Mr Leafy, just an ordinary man like you and me. He is not a god, he is not some kind of heroic figure as I think you imagine him to be.' Adekunle wagged an admonitory finger. 'Don't forget that,' he cautioned, 'in any of your dealings, with whoever it may be. Dr Murray is just a hard-working man, he has three children, schools in England are expensive.' He smiled. 'You didn't think I was going to ask you to rely only on your . . . your powers of rhetoric. You can offer him ten thousand pounds sterling,' he said flatly. 'In any bank: Switzerland, Jersey, Guatemala – wherever.'

Morgan said nothing. He was thinking about ten thousand pounds.

'Everybody, as the saying goes, has their price. I think ten thousand pounds will be sufficient for a poor man like Dr Murray.'

Morgan was rocked by the munificence of the bribe. Even Murray . . . Evil possibilities and vile scenarios began to swarm in Morgan's head like blow-flies round rotting meat. Uppermost among them was the exquisite irony of seducing that severe self-righteous man. Just to be there, he thought, and watch the corruption spread through him like a stain. Adekunle's broad lips were parted in a slight smile as he watched Morgan pondering.

'You may be right,' Morgan admitted. You may just be right.'

'We don't have a great deal of time,' Adekunle warned. 'This must be settled before the elections, certainly before the next meeting of the Buildings, Works and Sites Committee which is early in the new year.' He looked at his watch. 'Ah,' he said. 'I must leave. I will go round the back way.' He crossed the stoop to the steps that led down to the golf course. At the top of the steps he halted and turned to face Morgan.

'I don't like to remind you of your, let us say, obligation to me, Mr Leafy,' he said. 'And I don't think I need remind you of possible unpleasant consequences either. But you can of course – when this matter is settled – rely on my absolute discretion, and,' he smiled, preparing his final circumlocution, 'shall we say my continued support in your line of work as long as you remain in my country?' He turned and walked off into the dark.

Chapter 5

When Morgan arrived home the first fat heavy drops of rain were spattering on his windscreen. He drove the Peugeot into the garage and got out. The pale grey dust of his driveway turned to black mud in front of his eyes as the torrent from the swollen clouds in the darkness above him unleashed itself upon the earth. He watched the force of the rain battering down, clattering tinnily on the corrugated iron of the garage roof, drowning the sound of the strong wind that thrashed through the bushes and trees in the garden.

The light was on above his front door but there was no other sign of life in the house. Where the hell were Friday and Moses? he wondered angrily. It was only a matter of thirty yards from the garage to the front door but in this rain he'd be soaked in seconds.

'UMBRELLA!' he bellowed in the direction of the house, hoping his voice would carry above the noise of the downpour. There was a brilliant flash of lightning, as if in sarcastic response to his faint cry, illuminating his garden in harsh monochrome for a brief instant, followed some moments later by a hill-cracking peal of thunder. Morgan restrained himself from shaking his fist at the dark sky as he sprinted splashily towards his house, leaping over the burbling stream that already gushed around the doorstep, and flinging himself panting onto the verandah.

His house was a long squat bungalow, set in a generous garden dotted with small groves of frangipani and avocado trees and presided over by several towering casuerina pines. Only half the house – the two bedrooms and his study – was mosquito proofed. The other half, consisting of an airy dining/sitting room, kitchen and pantry, was fronted by the usual wide verandah upon which he now damply paced. The inundating rainstorm thundered on the roof and poured off the eaves in an extended sheet of water, turning the gravel gutters that surrounded the house into rushing streams that flowed across the wasted grass of the lawn to collect in an ever-widening pool at the bottom of the garden near the perimeter hedge of poinsettia. In the frequent flashes of sheet lightning Morgan could clearly see the silently expanding mini-lake, its surface tin-tacked by the heavy raindrops.

He slowly regained his breath, mildly alarmed that a thirty yard dash should leave him panting this way, kicked off his sodden shoes and went through to the kitchen in search of his servants. There, he found Friday asleep, sitting with his head pillowed on his arms at the scrubbed wooden table in the centre of the room. Leaving the light off he walked past him silently and looked out of the open kitchen door at the back garden. Beside the steps that led down from the kitchen stood an old table and, as he had expected, he saw his aged cook Moses sitting upon it – quite protected from the downpour by the eaves that projected a good six feet. Moses was sitting with his long shanks drawn up beneath him staring out at the curtain of rain. He was puffing away on his foul-smelling pipe and by his side there was a grimy calabash and a glass full of cloudy, pale green palm wine. Thunder barrages bracketed the sky overhead and the scene again flickered into ghostly life from the lightning. The weight of water falling on the earth seemed to have transformed the surface of the garden into a slow-moving, treacle-like tide. Water flowed, stopped, inched forward again; pools formed and broke, leaves and grass were transported short distances and dumped, and still the rain came down. It was a hell of a storm, Morgan thought.

Moses belched softly, turned to top up his glass and saw Morgan standing there with his hands on his hips. He threw down his pipe and leapt to his feet.

'Ah-ah. De rain sah. I nevah go hear you one time, masta,' he said and ducked up the steps past Morgan, switching on the kitchen light and shaking Friday awake who immediately began a long explanation of his extreme tiredness.

'Shut up, Friday,' Morgan ordered. 'One cheese omelette please, Moses. And Friday, switch on my air-conditioner and bring me one bottle of beer.' He went into the sitting room and switched on the lights and the roof fan, happy to have caught his servants napping.

He was halfway through his bottle of beer when Friday brought him his omelette and placed it on a side-table in front of him.

'*Ça va*, masta?' he asked cheerfully.

'No it doesn't,' Morgan said. 'I need a bloody *fourchette* and bloody *couteau*, don't I?' He shouted after Friday who'd dashed back to the kitchen, 'Salt and pepper too!'

Friday was a very small, powerfully-built man in his early twenties who had come over from his French colony in search of work. Morgan had felt smart and cosmopolitan when he'd employed him – the nearest thing to a French maid in Kinjanja he'd wittily bragged – but the little man was hopelessly inept, had never got to grips with the English language, and was cordially detested by Moses, Morgan's cook. Moses, in contrast, was thin and lanky and really quite old. No one knew his exact age – including Moses – but he had a wrinkled grizzled face and there were many grey spirals in his hair which probably meant he was well over sixty. He was a sly old man who filched professionally from Morgan and refused to let the demands of his job interfere unduly with his easy-going life. He could cook omelettes, fish cakes, a kind of stew, chicken curry, make rhubarb crumble and sherry trifle and that was it. Everyday the palm wine seller called at the kitchen door and Moses would buy a pint or two of the powerful drink. He cut up his own strong tobacco which he bought in moist strips like blackened bacon rinds and which he smoked in a tiny-bowled pipe that he always produced whenever he sat down to a tumbler of cloudy palm wine. What he could cook he cooked well however, and Morgan found that he tired of the diet less frequently than he might have supposed. It was enlivened from time to time by dinner invitations and, whenever the mood took him or whenever the prospect of fish cakes palled, he would eat at one of the clubs, in town or at the university, or at some of the Lebanese or Syrian restaurants whose kitchens were generally held to conform to minimal standards of hygiene.

When he had finished his omelette Morgan walked out to the verandah and peered into the night. The rain seemed to be abating, the thunder and lightning heading eastwards. He could hear the croaking of frogs and toads coming from the blackness.

He decided to go to bed. He knew what it was like after rain: every insect sprouted wings and took to the air in mad untrained flight. He told Friday and Moses to lock up and go home. He snibbed the corridor door behind him, hearing as he did so the rumble of the glass doors of the living room being slid shut, and walked up the passageway to his bedroom.

He had a quick shower and dried himself off. He sat on the edge of the bath and thought about Murray. How would he approach the man? How would he introduce the idea of the bribe? How would Murray react? He suddenly felt appalled that he, an official of Her Majesty's Government's Diplomatic Service, should be casually plotting in such a corrupt and criminal way, that his filthy luck had placed him in such vile and unhappy circumstances. In search of some solace he switched his mind to the sex he had enjoyed with Hazel earlier that evening. It distracted him for a minute or two, but slowly and inevitably a not wholly unpleasant sense of melancholy began to descend on him as it often did at such times. The house was quiet apart from the comforting hum of his air-conditioner, the rain appeared to have stopped, only the eaves still dripped into the gravel gutter-beds. He fancied he could hear the crickets starting up outside, brr-brr, brrr-brrr, telling the world how cold they felt.

His thoughts turned, appropriately for a moody exile, to home. He thought about his mother in Feltham, a kindly fun-loving widow who, so she had hinted in her last letter, might really, finally, be marrying Reg, her boyfriend of many years. Reg was a newsagent, a nice man; Morgan had known him all his life. He was quite bald but was one of that deluded crew who think that a damp lock of hair bisecting the gleaming pate from ear to ear will effectively persuade people otherwise. Reg was all right, Morgan thought warmly: he was friendly, liked a drink, got on well with his mother. So were Jill and Tony, he added, his sister and brother-in-law. Yes, they were all nice; they rubbed along very happily whenever he went back home on leave.

But then a sudden anger flared up. They were all so bloody *ordinary*, he told himself ruthlessly, so depressingly unremarkable, so inoffensive. He thought of his father – an indistinct enigmatic figure to him now – who had died when Morgan was fifteen. Keeled over from a coronary while helping a workman install a new dishwashing unit in a Heathrow cafeteria. Morgan occasionally gazed at his parents' smiling posed faces in the family snapshot album and wondered how on earth he had developed the way he had: selfish, fat and misanthropic.

He gloomily heaved himself to his feet, his backside sore from the unyielding bath-edge. He went disconsolately through to the bedroom and flung himself on the bed. Everything was going wrong. He shut his eyes and thought about his day: averagely disastrous. First Priscilla's engagement, next the Father Christmas fiasco underway, then Adekunle's 'bad news'. Now all he had to do was bribe Murray: he was doing well. He turned round abruptly and pulled a pillow over his head. Good God, he thought, what a can of worms, what a fucking snake pit. Murray too. Somehow everything came back to Murray. The man had marched into his life with all the tact of an invading army. Three months ago he hardly knew him, was only barely aware of what he looked like, and now he had to bribe him to help a devious politician pay for a crooked campaign. For an awful moment he thought he was going to cry mawkish, vinegary tears of self-pity, so he rudely sat himself upright, pounding pillows into shape with angry fists and snatched up a paperback. He glanced at the title. *Hell comes Tomorrow!* it screamed at him in vulgar red capitals. In a wave of premonitory disgust he flung it at the wall.

He switched out the bedside lamp and settled himself down, trying to get to sleep. He took uneasy, faltering stock of his day. Had he done anything he could be remotely proud of? Had he done anything good? Had he done anything thoughtful, unselfish or unmotivated? Had there been any event that wasn't directed towards the sole end of furthering the material, physical and spiritual well-being of Morgan Leafy Esq.? Well . . . no. He had to admit it: a definite, unqualified no. Thinking back he ruefully acknowledged that he'd been rude, sulky, bullying, selfish, unpleasant, hypocritical, cowardly, conceited, fascist etc. etc. A normal sort of day. But, he thought. Yes, but. Was he any different from anyone else in this stinking country, in this wide swarming world? Again, as far as he could see, as far as his experience had dictated, no. No was the only honest answer. As usual this brutal analysis did not bring with it much comfort. Unsettled and unhappy he turned over, closed his eyes and called on sleep.

Chapter 6

The phone rang. It was beside his bed and its ring was, at this hour, loud and brain-curdling. As he picked up the receiver he glanced at the alarm clock. Twenty past twelve. He couldn't have been asleep for more than ten minutes.

'Hullo, Leafy here,' he mumbled into the mouthpiece.

'Hello, Morgan? Sorry to bother you at this hour. It's Arthur Fanshawe here.' Fanshawe's voice was tense but solicitous.

'Arthur,' Morgan said. 'Anything wrong?'

'Yes,' Fanshawe replied straightforwardly. 'Something of a bugger actually. Can you get out here?'

'What? Now?' Morgan allowed more protest to creep into his tone than was wise.

'If you don't mind.' Fanshawe was suddenly clipped, offended.

Morgan sat hunched on the edge of his bed. He rubbed his eyes. 'Look, can you tell me what it is? I mean . . . are you sure I . . . ?' Fanshawe's tingling silence on the other end was eloquent. 'I'll be there in about fifteen minutes. 'Bye.' Morgan put the phone down. The stupid mad shit, he thought wrathfully, what the hell's going on? As far as he could remember he wasn't even on standby duty. It was Dalmire tonight: had they disturbed Dickie's beauty sleep?

Grumbling his doubt about this to himself, Morgan pulled on the clothes he had been wearing that day and splashed his face with water. Outside the rain had stopped and the dark moist night was dyspeptic with noises and mumblings. Toads burped, crickets trilled, bats swooped and beeped. As he walked across his verandah he saw squadrons of moths and flying ants battering around the front door light. Underfoot, his shoes crunched on the twitching drifts of myriads of exhausted insects, who had unfolded new wings at the onset of the rain and taken to the air for a brief joyous flight, lured by the glow of the hot bulb. His feet squelched on the mud of his garden path and driveway as he walked out towards his garage. Overhead the sky had cleared and the familiar wide canopy of stars shone down. You always saw more stars in Africa than you did back home, he thought.

The road to the Commission was quiet, a few taxis returning, late-night revellers and one enormous articulated lorry thundering heedlessly down the road south, piled high with ground-nut sacks. As he turned into the Commission's car park he was annoyed to find it empty. Dalmire had clearly not been disturbed. If this problem was so all-fired important, he asked himself testily, where were the other members of staff? The Commission building appeared deserted too, with no lights shining.

Morgan parked his car and headed briskly across the dark

garden to the Fanshawes' residence which, as he approached, he could see was lit up like a liner on both floors. He guessed the problem was a domestic one and rolled his eyes heavenwards. Again he noticed no other cars in the driveway. Morgan ascended the steps and rapped on the glass door of the sitting room. Through it he could see Mrs Fanshawe and Priscilla sitting on one of the sofas. Priscilla had her arm round her mother's broad shoulders. At Morgan's cheery knock they both looked up in alarm, and Priscilla jumped to her feet and skipped across the room to open the door.

'Oh Morgan,' she said with relief in her voice, 'I'm so glad you've come.'

The genuineness of her expression so astonished him that he almost failed to appreciate her trim beauty, her ruffled hair and the skimpiness of the Japanese housecoat she was wearing, the bottom of which stopped half way down her thighs.

'Hello, Morgan.' It was Mrs Fanshawe. Morgan noticed that her eyes were red. Had she been crying? he wondered, never having seen her face register any of the softer emotions. 'It's so dreadful,' she whimpered, remaining hunched on the sofa, a handkerchief balled in her hand, her large body quite disguised by a massive pale blue candlewick dressing-gown.

'Drink?' Priscilla asked.

'Well . . .' Morgan spun on his heel to survey the bottles on a shiny mahogany cabinet, rubbing his hands together as if he were cold.

'The coffee will be ready now,' Mrs Fanshawe intoned listlessly.

'Coffee will be lovely,' he said, a grin stamped across his face. 'Milk and three sugars, please.' He looked admiringly at Priscilla's legs as she walked out of the sitting room to the kitchen. 'Where's Arthur?' he asked, conscious of his superior's absence. 'Nothing's happened to Arthur, has it?' he asked again, realizing too late how unconcerned he sounded.

'Of course not,' Mrs Fanshawe snapped back in irritation.

That's more like it, Morgan observed to himself, she's coming round. 'No,' Mrs Fanshawe went on, 'he's outside,' she waved at the darkness, 'seeing if there's anything he can do.'

The mystery was beginning to get on Morgan's nerves. What in Christ's name had they pulled him out of his bed for? 'Um, what exactly's happened?' he inquired politely.

'It's Innocence,' Mrs Fanshawe said sadly.

'Innocence?' Morgan was frankly puzzled. Was this some obscure jibe at him because of his failure to divine what the problem was?

'My maid,' she explained crabbily. 'My maid Innocence. She's dead.'

'Oh.' Is that all? he screamed inwardly at her. Why am *I* bloody here then? He was about to pursue this line of enquiry with more vigour when he saw Fanshawe climbing the front steps.

'Morgan,' Fanshawe said wearily. 'Glad you're here.' He looked most strange, Morgan thought. He was wearing a green silk Chinese dressing-gown with large orange lotus-type blossoms on it. A pair of striped Viyella pyjama bottoms clashed uneasily with this opulence. Fanshawe's face was pale and his normally sleek grey hair stood up in fine wispy tufts.

'Bloody awful problem we've got here,' he admitted, shaking his head sorrowfully. 'Thought you'd be the chap to deal with it.' He looked Morgan in the eye. 'Can't understand these Africans at all,' he said hopelessly, like a criminal confessing his guilt. 'Just can't make head nor tail of them, can't figure out how the Kinjanjan mind works. Closed book to me. Now, if this were the East . . .' he let the implied comment go unfinished. Morgan wondered why Fanshawe thought he'd be the 'chap' to deal with these unfathomable mysteries. Meanwhile Mrs Fanshawe had risen to her feet and was belting her dressing-gown tightly about her waist, thereby crudely accentuating the bodyforms which bulked beneath the candlewick shroud. Morgan inwardly remarked on the prodigious humps that defined her chest and how, curiously, they wobbled transversely as she marched over to her husband.

'Come on, Arthur,' she commanded. 'Leave it to Morgan. He knows these people better than we.'

'Just a sec,' Morgan interrupted, before Fanshawe could be led off to bed. 'I'm afraid I haven't quite got the full picture yet. Innocence is dead, sure, but I don't see where I fit in.'

'Sorry,' Fanshawe brushed his forehead absentmindedly with his palm. 'Sorry I didn't explain, it's all been a bit of a shock. Innocence's over at the servants' quarters. She was struck by lightning during the storm, died instantly I believe. I called the police – a constable's just arrived – but apparently there's some ghastly mystical, what do they call it? juju problem. Magical hocus pocus, you know, couldn't work out what they were talking about. Thought you were the man for that.' He paused. 'Can't tell you anything else, I'm afraid. You'll have to see if you can make any more sense of it. See if you can get the whole thing sorted out tonight.' The Fanshawes moved to the foot of the stairs. 'I think,' said Fanshawe wearily, 'it's something to do with disposing of the body, I don't know. Anyway Morgan, do your best, see you in the morning.'

Morgan said goodnight and the Fanshawes went off to their beds. He was about to make for the drinks, feeling sorely in need of one, when Priscilla returned with a cup of coffee for him. He took it from her, their fingertips touching briefly. He wondered what she was wearing under her robe. To his surprise she prodded Morgan's stomach with a forefinger. 'Yes, I thought so,' she said. 'Three sugars, no wonder. Must be like drinking syrup.' She didn't seem too worried about Innocence's death, Morgan thought, in fact she was being very familiar. Was it a good sign?

'By the way,' Priscilla said. 'Did you find that poet chap?'

'Poet?' Morgan's mind went blank. Then he remembered his excuse from earlier in the evening. 'Oh, that poet.'

'Are there some more around?'

'No, oh no. And . . . ah we never found the other one.' He thought suddenly that he should be taking advantage of their being alone together. 'Listen, Priscilla, can I . . . ?'

'Never mind,' she interrupted brightly. 'I'm sure he'll turn up.'

'What? Oh yes . . . but I . . .' It was too late, she was already at the stairs.

'Probably won't see you in the morning,' she said. 'Isn't it *too* awful about Innocence? 'Night.'

She was gone, a flash of brown legs. This family, Morgan thought grimly, are not treating me right; they're taking me too much for granted. First I'm Father Christmas, now I'm a bloody undertaker. He poured a slug of brandy into his coffee, stirred it up and drank it down. Right, he said to himself, let's see what all the fuss is about.

The Commission's servants' quarters consisted of two low mud-brick blocks facing each other across a well-trodden patch of laterite, down the middle of which ran a concrete sanitary lane. At one end of the square was a stand pipe and wash-place, a large concrete basin beneath a corrugated-iron roof supported by thick wooden poles. A large cotton tree stood by the wash-place. Around the two dwelling-units were many small lean-tos, traders' stalls and shelters made from sticks, packing cases and palm fronds. Between the main road and the block furthest away from the Commission a sizeable dump had grown up over the years, on which sat two wheelless car chassis and which provided the main source of nourishment for the various goats, dogs and chickens that roamed about it unhindered.

As Morgan approached the quarters he became aware of the sounds of muted commotion. He could hear the babble of excited voices and a soft chanting wail of lamenting women. He began to feel a little nervous, considering for the first time what exactly he was going to meet. He was about to come up against death, after all, something he hadn't done before. The death of Innocence. The improbable symbolic portentousness of this did not bring a smile to his lips. He walked round the corner of the nearest block and dimly made out a crowd of approximately thirty people gathered around the far end of the laterite compound near the base of the cotton tree. He walked across the compound carefully stepping over the sanitary ditch. He felt a slight twinge of alarm. He noticed some mothers with younger children sitting around lanterns on the small verandahs that ran the length of the blocks. As he approached the large group by the tree a figure detached itself from it and came towards him. It was, he soon saw, the policeman, dressed in immaculately starched khaki uniform of shirt, shorts and knee socks. In the starlight Morgan could see his black boots gleaming. He carried a torch and there was a long truncheon slung at his belt.

'Evening, constable,' Morgan said, all calm authority. 'I'm Mr Leafy from the Commission. What exactly's going on?'

'Ah. The woman is dead, sah. Lightning done kill her one time.' He turned and shone his torch. The crowd was not clustered around the body as Morgan had thought but was standing in appalled silence a safe ten yards away. The torch beam flicked across the black mass of Innocence's body and there were appreciative gasps from the onlookers. Innocence had been struck down in the gap between the end of one of the blocks and the rough concrete base of the wash-place.

Morgan swallowed. 'I suppose we'd better have a closer look.' He didn't know why he supposed this, but it was all he could think of doing. 'May I?' He took the constable's torch and advanced towards the body. There was a collective intake of breath and much shifting about from the crowd as he did so. Morgan realized, with some alarm, as he approached that this – Innocence – was the first dead person he had ever encountered and he wasn't quite sure what precisely he was expecting to see or how he would react.

Before he could get close enough however, someone ran out of the crowd and tugged at his sleeve. It was Isaac, Morgan saw on turning round, one of the Commission's doormen and general factotum. He was a solemn-looking man with a Hitlerian toothbrush moustache.

'Mr Leafy sah,' he said. 'I go beg you, sah. Don't totch her. Make you nevah totch her, sah.' His voice was serious.

Morgan looked at him in surprise. 'Don't worry Isaac,' he said. 'I've no intention of touching her.'

'Be careful, sah, I beg you.' Isaac's eyes were wide with warning. 'Dis he be Shango killing. Nevah totch the body.'

'Sorry?' Morgan said, keeping his torch beam well away from the inert dark lump that was Innocence's body. 'A Shango killing? Who the hell is Shango?'

Isaac pointed skywards. Morgan looked up at the stars. 'Shango is God,' Isaac said piously. 'Shango is God for lightning.' He illustrated this with a jagged sweep of his arm. 'Shango done kill this woman. You cannot totch her. No person can totch her.'

Oh my sweet bloody Christ, Morgan thought sourly to himself, no wonder that sly bastard Fanshawe backed out of this one. Sweet effing Jesus. 'OK, Isaac,' he said resignedly. 'I won't touch, but I have to look.' He walked up to Innocence's body and squatted on his haunches about three feet away. Clenching his jaw muscles he brought the torch beam up to play on Innocence's face. He remembered her well, a fat jolly woman who was always in attendance at the Fanshawes' functions. Now she lay dead on her side, the top half of her body twisted round so that her face blankly contemplated the sky whence the fatal lightning shaft had come. Not far from her body lay a galvanized steel bucket and scattered wrung bundles of washed clothes. Morgan imagined what must have happened. Washing some clothes when the storm broke, throw them into the bucket, prop bucket on head or shoulder and waddle-dash across the short distance from the wash-place to the shelter of the verandah. But she'd never made it. Morgan found himself wondering if lightning made a whooshing noise, if there was a crack, smoke . . .

He was quite emotionless as the beam hit Innocence's face, only a taut, stretched feeling in his body. Her eyes and mouth were wide open, as if frozen in mid-yell. On her right shoulder and down the right side of her face was a curious scorch or burn mark, an oozing weal purple against her chocolaty skin. The rest of her body appeared quite untouched and solid in its ungainly repose. Her clothes were sodden – a cheap nylon short-sleeved blouse, a native cloth wrapper-skirt – drenched by the downpour. Her right hand was held out along the still damp ground, pale palm uppermost, fingers slightly curled.

Poor Innocence, he thought, what a way to go.

He rose to his feet and walked back towards Isaac, who had been joined by the constable. Morgan returned the torch to him.

'Look, Isaac,' Morgan said. 'We have to move her.' He felt a little unsteady on his feet. 'We can't just leave her lying there for Christ's sake. Where's her house?' Isaac indicated a doorway in the middle of the block. 'Has she any family?' Morgan asked.

'There is one daughter. Maria,' Isaac told him. Morgan remembered her too, a slim teenage girl who also worked for the Fanshawes. She was only fourteen or fifteen. He sighed.

'Right,' he said. 'Isaac, will you and Ezekiel', he mentioned the Commission porter, 'help me move her into her house until we can get an undertaker to come? Ezekiel?' he called into the crowd and Ezekiel emerged, a large bow-legged man with a pot-belly. He joined them a little unwillingly.

'Constable,' Morgan instructed, 'if you take the arms with me, and you – Isaac – with Ezekiel take the legs. OK? Come on then.'

Nobody moved. There followed a brief impassioned burst of conversation in native dialect. Then Isaac spoke:

'We cannot totch her, sah. Please, I beg you once more. Ifin you totch her before, you will bring yourself trouble. Bringing everyone wahallah. You no go die well,' he finished up solemnly.

Ezekiel nodded in glum agreement. 'Plenty wahallah sah, for every people.'

The constable drew Morgan to one side. 'Excuse, sah. This people are believing for Shango. They think that ifin they move this dead woman, they go die themselves one time.' The constable smiled condescendingly. 'They think Shango is angry with them. They have to make big juju here. Bring one fetish priest before.'

Wahallah, juju, fetish priest, lightning gods . . . Morgan stood in the dark compound, smelling the damp warm night, listening to its noises all around him, his eyes fixed on the body of the dead woman, wondering if it was all some frightful dream he was having. He massaged his temples with both hands. 'Constable,' he said conspiratorially, 'will *you* help me move her – get her out of the way at least. The two of us should manage.'

'Ah.' The constable spread his hands. 'I cannot. If I move the body before they make juju they will think I make Shango angry. They will not like it.' He shrugged his shoulders in apology. 'I must go. I will make my report.' He saluted, turned and walked out of the compound.

Morgan felt waves of panic break in his mind. He thought hard. The crowd showed no signs of dispersing, they stood patiently in their group beneath the cotton tree, as though awaiting the arrival of some VIP, obsessed by this sign of Shango's displeasure that the god had dropped in their back yard. Morgan called Isaac over. 'Isaac,' he said gently. 'It is against the law to leave a body in the open like this. I *have* to call an undertaker. Now, will you let them remove the body?'

'They will not,' Isaac said equably.

'Pardon?'

'When they see that Shango has strock this woman. They will nevah lift her.'

Morgan smiled. 'Well,' he said. 'We'll just have to take our chances on that.'

An hour later Morgan sat disconsolately on the concrete surround of the wash-place. Innocence still lay untouched half a dozen yards from his feet. He had phoned the police, who claimed that as no crime had been committed it was nothing to do with them. Then he had phoned a firm of undertakers in Nkongsamba, who said they would be out within the hour.

They had just left. Isaac and Ezekiel had spoken to them and the two undertakers, lugubriously dressed exactly like their European counterparts, had flatly refused to disturb the body until the fetish had been done. They even became quite angry for a while, accusing Morgan of trying to hoodwink them into offending Shango.

In the east the tree tops were silhouetted against a thin gash of pale lemon. It was ten to four. Innocence would be stiffening up now, he thought queasily, her eyes and mouth for ever open, her body permanently twisted round. He had tried to appeal to the servants' Christianity – they were all Christians, this was no pocket of paganism – but their polite and uncon-cerned references to tribal protocol, the required summoning of the fetish priest, the various necessary rites, the obligatory slaughter of a goat, only confirmed to Morgan what he'd always expected: that they could shed their Christianity as easily as a pair of trousers. He stood up and went over to stare down at Innocence. Her death stirred nothing in him now. The fact that he was standing looking down at a dead person, someone who he had known, raised no emotions in him. She wasn't a person anymore, she was an object – a thing – effectively reified by that lightning bolt: a thing, moreover, that was turning into a bloody great problem.

He felt very tired and rubbed his jaw, rasping the bristles

on his face. It was still quite dark but through the nim trees he could see the corner of Fanshawe's house. He pictured the family: father, mother and daughter sleeping soundly in their beds. While he stalked about this gloomy compound like some demon insisting on the body that was due to him. It made him sick, he hated every fucking one of them, their stinking bourgeois affectations, their ghastly fake chinoiserie, their prim enclosed little minds . . . He felt his face going hot. This was no good, he told himself, there was no point inveighing against the Fanshawes now, calm down, he advised, calm down. He walked over to the cotton tree. Only half a dozen maintained their vigil now, sitting on the high tangled roots that spread out from the base of the trunk like grotesque varicose veins.

'Isaac?' Morgan said hopefully.

A tall stooped figure rose up. 'I am Joseph, sah. Joseph the cleaner. Isaac 'e done go for sleep.'

Wise man, Morgan thought. 'OK Joseph,' he said firmly – it was like dealing with a gang of Old Testament prophets. 'You savvy dis fetish thing?'

Joseph nodded. He had a shaven skull and was very black, almost Nubian in appearance. In the crepuscular light he looked two-dimensional, a hole cut out of the environment. 'Yes, sah,' he said. 'I go savvy am.'

'Fine,' Morgan said, maintaining his businesslike tone. 'Great. Go and get the juju man and we'll do the fetish.'

'Please, sah. I no fit do it,' Joseph said simply. 'The family of this dead woman must do it.'

Oh bloody hell, swore Morgan despairingly, there's always another hitch. 'All right, you'd better get Maria,' he said. Maybe there would be some way of ending this morbid farce after all. Soon Maria was brought, weeping and swollen-eyed and supported by two women. She was clutching a rosary in her hands. If it wasn't so serious, Morgan thought to himself, it would be bloody funny.

'Maria,' he began gently, acutely conscious of his terminal

fatigue, his frayed nerves and the massed forces of frustration hemming him in. 'Maria, you know that before anyone will . . . move your mother, we have to get a fetish priest along?' She weakly nodded her assent. 'Well,' he continued, 'it seems that only you can make this possible. You have to get the priest.' At this point Maria let out a great wail of dismay and collapsed into the arms of the two women. Morgan backed off in alarm. 'Joseph,' he called out. 'Go and see what the matter is.'

Joseph returned shortly with the necessary information. 'She is weeping, sah, because she says she has no money.'

'Money?' Morgan said in astonishment. 'What does she want money for?'

'To pay for the priest,' Joseph said.

'Well for Christ's sake I'll lend her a few bob,' Morgan offered impatiently, reaching into his pockets. 'How much does she need?'

Joseph did some mental calculations. 'She need forty pound. No, but then she must purchase one goat and some beer.' He shrugged, 'I think fifty pound, maybe sixty. But there is funeral as well. For Shango killing you must have special funeral. She is crying because she only has fifteen pounds about.'

Morgan's heart sank at this latest setback. Fifteen pounds was a reasonable monthly wage by Kinjanjan standards. He turned away and roamed the compound wildly, trying to coax his tired brain to come up with more alternatives. A faint greyness of coming dawn now charged the atmosphere. Time was running out for him. Fanshawe would be expecting some results after a night's work, where in fact things hadn't advanced one bit, he might as well have ignored Fanshawe's summons for all the good he'd done. It wasn't just what Fanshawe would say, though; there was the more serious problem of the effect of the African sun on Innocence's body . . . He felt like tearing his hair out. What he needed was an organization not staffed with frigging Shango worshippers, some normal, ordinary people who did an efficient, orthodox job, who'd pick her up and stow her in a morgue somewhere until a funeral could be arranged. He'd done enough pussyfooting around pagan sensibilities, he decided, the time had surely come for some forthright energetic roughshod-riding.

As he thought about the options and courses open to him the answer came with a slow inevitability, like a tune in his head whose title he'd soon guess, given enough time. An efficient organization, unaffected by the Shango cult: there was only one in and around Nkongsamba which fitted that description and was suitable for the delicate task in hand. Only one. Murray. Murray and his University Health Service. Murray, with his loyal, well-drilled staff and his gleaming white ambulance. They could drive here, pick up Innocence and whisk her away before anyone had a chance to get hot under the collar.

The inevitability of the choice didn't dispel all his doubts, however, nor the vaguely shaming irony of calling on the man he planned to bribe to help get him out of a sticky situation. As he strode through the dew-slicked grass back towards the Fanshawes' house he tried to convince himself that he was doing the right thing, silence that warning bell which was persistently ringing somewhere at the back of his head. If you couldn't ring a doctor about a death, he argued, what could you ring one about? And besides Murray wasn't just a doctor, he was *his* doctor. What was more he was a white man, and white men in black Africa helped other white men in need. Damn it, Murray was practically a friend he told himself, weren't they playing golf next Thursday? He felt a sudden warm glow of friendship towards the doctor, which he assiduously stoked up. Murray was a firm, unbending sort of man but the remarkable thing about him was that you knew where you stood. You took him as he was and that was how he took you. Yes, for all his unyielding ways he was a decent honest man. All inconvenient thoughts of the impending bribe were banished from his head as, buoyant with fellow feeling and sympathy and happily confident that this dreadful state of affairs would soon be a thing of the past, he leapt up the front door steps and quietly let himself in to the Fanshawes' sitting room. He leafed through the telephone directory until he found the university exchange's number. He dialled.

'Hello,' he said. 'Will you put me through to Dr Murray's house, please?' He heard the clicks of the connection being made. The phone rang. And rang. He was about to ask the exchange to check if they had the right number when he heard the receiver being lifted.

'Yes!' The gruff venom in the voice disturbed Morgan.

'Erm, Dr Murray?' he inquired tentatively.

'Yes.'

'Oh good. Morgan . . . Morgan Leafy here. From the Commission. I've got a problem here and I . . .'

'Medical?' Murray's terse Scottish voice had lost none of its hostility despite the fact that Morgan had identified himself. He was a little surprised at this and made a further effort to quell powerful second thoughts that suddenly rose in his mind. It was too late for them now, he had to go on.

'Why yes. You don't think I'd ring you if I . . .'

'Have you phoned the university clinic?' There was a note of resigned fatigue in Murray's voice as he interrupted for the second time. It made Morgan feel a fool, cretinous.

'Well no. But this is an emergency.'

'The clinic is fully equipped to deal with an emergency,' Murray said patiently. 'My staff then make the decision whether to call me or not – it allows me to get a full night's sleep from time to time. Ask the switchboard for the number. Goodbye.'

'Just a moment,' Morgan said, beginning to get angry himself at such peremptory treatment: the man was a doctor for God's sake. 'If you'd let me explain . . . I've got a dead woman on my hands and I . . . I need your help.' Morgan could swear he heard Murray's muffled oaths in the background.

'Did you say dead?'

'Yes.'

'I take it it's not Mrs or Miss Fanshawe.'

'God no,' Morgan said, surprised. 'It's a Commission servant actually. Why do you ask?'

'Because Mrs Fanshawe and her daughter are the only women at the Commission entitled to call on the University Health Service. We are forbidden to treat non-members of staff. We are *expressly* forbidden to operate outside the university boundaries apart from the British members of the Deputy High Commission. The duty sister at my clinic could have told you that, Mr Leafy. Now perhaps you'll let me get some sleep.' Murray's Scottish accent imparted real harshness into his last words.

Morgan felt his frayed nerves begin to send off sparks. 'For God's sake,' he exclaimed. 'I don't give a hoot about your rules and regulations, I'm asking you to help us out of a jam. This woman's been struck by lightning, she's quite dead but nobody'll touch her because of some bloody mumbo-jumbo about some Shango-god or something.' Morgan paused, this new upset was too dreadful to contemplate. He saw his last option disappearing as a result of Murray's ridiculous intransigence. He felt desperation building up inside him. 'It's an appalling problem. I need you to take the body away. No one else will.'

'Jesus Christ,' he heard Murray expostulate. '(a) it's five o'clock in the morning, (b) as I've told you I can do nothing for anyone who's not a member of the university and (c) I do not run my health service on the basis of private favours. You're asking me to violate the statutes of the University of Nkongsamba and betray official undertakings made to the City of Nkongsamba Health Authority on the grounds of so-called personal friendship. No, Mr Leafy. It is your problem, there is *no* way you can make it mine. Contact the proper authorities, that's what they are there for. Now kindly leave me alone!'

Morgan sat shivering in his chair during this hectoring tirade. The enormous strains of the last twenty-four hours finally proved too much for him and without for a second thinking of the consequences he burst out, 'And what about the fucking Hippocratic Oath eh? You're a fucking doctor, aren't you, you sanctimonious Scottish bastard . . .'

Murray slammed the phone down. Morgan tailed off, still muttering racist imprecations. The unmoving, the stubborn, the beam-headed . . . He threw back his head and bared his teeth in a silent scream of pent-up anger, frustration and hostility at the universe.

He staggered towards Fanshawe's drinks cabinet and poured himself half a tumbler of gin. He walked out on to the back verandah and took a mouthful. His eyes streamed with tears and he shuddered as it went down. His view of the southern precincts of Nkongsamba bathed in a peachy matinal light shivered and went soft at the edges. He set down his glass with a rattle on the concrete balustrade at the edge of the stoop. He shook his head fiercely; a manic, berserk anger seemed to be rampaging there, like a lunatic in a padded cell. The bastard, he breathed out acid rancorous bile at the dawn, the dirty rotten filthy bastard! He went on, giving his imagination free rein. It seemed to help, at least minimally. He sensed overloaded systems responding to gentle tender hands at control. He felt like a skilled pilot nursing a grievously stricken airliner into a crash-landing. But as his anger began to subside and ratiocination asserted its dominance over the passions once more the consequences of his fury slowly brought themselves to his shocked attention. Oh no, he said haltingly to himself, oh no, *the golf.* That was away now. Gone, irretrievable. And Adekunle, he thought too, what would Adekunle say? He contemplated Adekunle's wrath and shivered. How could he bribe Murray now? he asked himself. And Fanshawe? The body was still there. What was Fanshawe going to do when he found Innocence baking in the morning sun?

He threw the rest of the gin into a flowerbed. He felt sick, exhausted and grimy; it seemed as though some malicious person had prised apart his eyelids, lifted them up and emptied small phials of fine sand there. He'd handled everything so badly, misjudged and miscalculated all round. Par for the course, he thought cynically, no point in breaking the pattern. He knew in his heart that shit creek had claimed him this time. Full fathom five. He looked up through the brown water hoping for a flicker of sun. But it was all murk.

The new day burst cool over Nkongsamba with its usual display of crisp breathtaking beauty. Motionless smoke-threads rose from a thousand charcoal fires into pale blue skies. The green of the trees tested the gold of the kind morning sun like a bride discovering her trousseau. Ectoplasmic wisps of mist clung possessively to the meandering paths of creeks and streams and shrouded the taller hills. Africa at her most gloriously seductive.

But Morgan knew that Innocence lay not two hundred yards away. The jelly of her eyeballs dry and opaque. Her pink tongue contracting in her gaping mouth, mites and insects patrolling her body for moisture, her blood stagnant and pooling, her muscles and limbs stiff and unpliant.

He gazed blankly at the progress of the new day, indifferent to its splendour. Murray *could* have helped him if he had wanted to, he realized; if he had an iota of concern, a jot of feeling for him. But he didn't give a fuck, that much was plain, he was more worried about his rule book, observing the letter of the law. Morgan squinted at the landscape watching its contours blur and elide. He was on his own as usual. He knew then that he wanted to bribe Murray, tarnish his gleaming image, foul his perfect reputation more than anything else in the world. More than he wanted rid of Innocence; more than

83

he wanted to marry Priscilla; more than he wanted to sleep with any number of beautiful women. He felt quite weak with the power of his desire. Something drastic had to happen to that man's conception of himself: it was long overdue, and he, Morgan Leafy, would make it his business to see that it occurred, especially now that Murray had deliberately struck him down in this way. So brutally – almost as Shango had felled Innocence.

It was all Murray's fault, he said to himself quietly and calmly. Everything was Murray's fault.

PART TWO

Chapter 1

Morgan well remembered the first occasion he had met Dr Murray. At the time he hardly knew him. Murray never came to the Commission cocktail parties, even though his name was often mentioned as most of the British in the university had fallen sick — or their children had at one time or another — and had therefore called on Murray's services. Morgan had heard nothing but good: the three university clinics functioned more efficiently than ever, rabid dogs had been cleared from the campus thanks to the registration and inoculation schemes he had introduced, everyone was satisfied. Murray was held to be — despite a certain formality of manner — a fine doctor whose diagnoses were invariably correct and whose cures were effective. Morgan had taken scant notice of this sort of cocktail party chit-chat. He was not interested in the doctor or his clinics, he had enjoyed robust good health since his arrival in Kinjanja, apart from the odd upset tummy or septic mosquito bite and had never needed to utilize the University Health Service, to which the white members of the Commission staff were officially attached.

One morning, shortly after Morgan's relationship with Hazel had begun, he was discussing the thorny problems of efficient contraception in Africa with Lee Wan at the bar of the university club. Lee Wan was sitting on a bar stool, a considerable portion of his brown leathery pot-belly visible through the straining gaps in his olive green shirt.

'Listen, my boy,' he said, swirling the ice cubes in his pink gin with a brown finger. 'You want to get that popsy on to these contraceptive pills, p.d.q. Forget your rubber johnnies, your FL's — unless you can get a pal to bring you some out from the UK.' Lee Wan was a naturalized British citizen, and spiced his speech with a curious mixture of archaic slang and what he considered were bona fide English expressions. He had studiously lost all trace of a Malay accent. 'Don't use the local rubbish for Christ's sake,' he went on, dropping his voice for the sake of the two ladies sitting near the bar. 'It's like poking through a glove.' He wheezed with laughter at his simile and slapped Morgan on the arm. 'A bloody sheepskin glove,' he choked. He wiped his eyes. 'My God,' he gasped with hilarity, 'My dear God . . . Simeon,' he called to the barman. 'Let's have another two gins here.'

Morgan had smiled at Lee Wan's joke but not too widely. Sometimes he thought the tubby Malay as vile and disgusting a creature as he had ever met and felt guilty for enjoying his company. He was mildly repulsed by the turn the conversation had taken and he looked out onto the bright pool terrace from the cool shade of the ground floor bar. Outside, water splashed over a modern cuboid fountain and two tiny children shrieked and played on the concrete surround. Nearby their mother took advantage of the burst of sunshine to augment her tan.

It was mid-September. Most of Nkongsamba's expatriates had been away in Europe on leave and were gradually returning to take up their work again after the summer's break, which coincided with Kinjanja's rainy season. Morgan had taken his last leave back in March and with Fanshawe and Jones back in Britain he had been alone in the Commission for the last two months. He had found time heavy on his hands, what with the slack volume of work, the daily steaming downpour and the clubs quiet and torpid. He had been fairly happy to renew his friendship with Lee Wan and had soon been roped in to bar-crawls round Nkongsamba, perilous boozing sessions in Lee Wan's campus bungalow and gut-expanding curry lunches on Sundays. It had been, on reflection, an unpleasant period of debauch that left him buried for short periods under heaps of recriminations. Still, he thought, it had seen him through the rainy season, the worst part of the Kinjanjan year, and he had met Hazel.

Morgan looked at his watch. The Fanshawes were arriving after lunch at Nkongsamba's small airport, flying up from the capital, and he was due to meet them there with the official Commission car. An advance letter from Fanshawe had informed him that their daughter was coming out with them to stay for a while. Morgan wondered vaguely what the daughter of Arthur and Chloe Fanshawe would look like. Jones had returned a week ago from his holiday in Swansea or Aberystwyth or somewhere Welsh; the rains had finished too. Life, he thought, would perhaps crank itself to its feet and try to be a little more tolerable.

Morgan accepted a new gin from Simeon and topped it up with tonic. He decided to make this his last: it wouldn't do to turn up at the airport and breathe alcohol all over the Fanshawes. He leant back against the bar and idly enjoyed the sparkle of sun on the pool water, finding the splashing of the fountain pleasantly soothing. It wasn't such a bad life, he thought, sipping the chill drink: the weather was fine, he had status in the community, a reasonable salary, big house, servants and, he smiled with self-satisfaction, he had a black girlfriend with fabulous breasts. This brought him back to the recent topic under discussion.

'It's all very well for you,' he remarked to Lee Wan, 'but I can hardly ask for a gross of Durex Fetherlite to be brought in with the diplomatic bag.' Lee Wan spluttered into his gin and pounded his knee with mirth. Morgan smiled: he wasn't such a bad old chap was old Lee, he thought, revising his earlier uncharitable opinion. Real colonial character, good value, good man to have around.

'Anyway,' Morgan said. 'Where do you get these contraceptive pills from?'

'Send her to a doctor,' Lee Wan advised.

'Mmm . . .' he countered, 'but how much is that going to set me back? Can't you get them at a chemist?'

Lee Wan found this funny too. 'God, you lazy crumpetmerchant,' he said admiringly to Morgan. 'You're shafting yourself stupid and you don't want to spend a penny. Christ Almighty, man.' He thought for a moment and then suggested, 'You could try Murray perhaps. He might let you have some. All the white wives out here are on oral contraceptives and Librium. Ha ha,' he gave a little laugh. 'That's Africa for you, eh? trouble-free sex and tranquillizers. What do they call it? Post-pill paradise or something. Load of nonsense. Never seen a more neurotic, glum bunch in my life.'

'Do you think that Murray might give me some?' Morgan mused. 'I mean, do you know him well? Is he that sort of chap?'

'Oh yes,' Lee Wan said expansively. 'My old friend Alex Murray? Tell him you're a chum of mine.'

'Might just do that,' Morgan said. 'I'll drop into his clinic on the way to the airport. Here,' he said, clinking his glass against Lee Wan's, 'drink up. I've just got time for another before lunch. Simeon? Two gins here, chop-chop.'

Morgan drove through the university campus following Lee Wan's directions to Murray's clinic. The Federal University of Nkongsamba was the largest in the country and was set in an expansive well-appointed campus on which everything was contained including houses for the senior staff and a village for the junior staff and servants. All told there were upward of 20,000 people within its boundaries. Morgan drove easily along pretty tree-lined roads towards the administrative centre of the university. On either side of him were the fecund gardens and sprawling bungalows inhabited by the senior staff. The pale asbestos roofs seemed to be flattened under the weight of the midday sun, driving the walls inch by inch into the hard ground. Morgan had eaten at the club restaurant: a rather stringy roast chicken and half a bottle of wine which, on top of the gins, had combined to give him a slight nagging headache.

He passed the new and splendid university bookshop. A

workman was painting out a graffito which read OTE KNP. Ah yes, Morgan smiled to himself, the elections: they should be good for a laugh. Beyond the bookshop lay the university administrative offices, the central assembly hall, the arts theatre, the senate building and a wide piazza dominated by a high clocktower. Between this complex and the main gate a mile off, was a broad straight swathe of tree-lined dual carriageway. It was an impressive piece of landscaping and was known to the expatriate university staff as the Champs-Elysées. Morgan turned off it and drove down a narrow road to Murray's clinic. It was composed of two senior staff bungalows linked into one. Behind it stood a square two-storey sick-bay containing two wards with a dozen beds in total. Serious cases had to be despatched to the capital where there was a large American-financed teaching hospital.

The car park was busy with cars. Squatting in the shade of the verandah were three African mothers with sick children. Morgan walked uneasily past these tiny wracked faces and went into the main waiting room. On the wall was a prominent notice detailing hours for students (7–10), junior staff (10–12), and senior staff (12–2). Morgan checked his watch – five to two – he had just made it but he couldn't afford to hang around: the Fanshawes were due to arrive at a quarter to three. The rows of black plastic chairs were occupied by various senior staff and Morgan smiled at a couple of faces he recognized. The building was clean and functional and the familiar brain-pickling smell of hospital disinfectant pervaded the atmosphere. In the far wall was a hatchway with the sign 'reception' written above it. Behind a glass window sat a dapper little clerk. Morgan approached the *guichet*. It was like a bank or a railway station.

'Good afternoon, sah,' the clerk greeted him.

Morgan leant on the narrow counter. 'I'd like to see Dr Murray please,' he said. 'As soon as possible.' He glanced at his watch to indicate pressing time.

'Dr Obayemi and Dr Rathmanatathan are on surgery today. Please take a seat, your name will be called.'

Morgan wasn't used to this non-preferential treatment, but he'd met this bureaucratic self-importance many times before and he knew how to handle it. 'Is Dr Murray actually here?' he asked inoffensively.

'Yes, sah,' said the clerk. 'But he is not taking surgery.'

Morgan smiled icily. 'Will you tell him that Mr Leafy from the Commission is here. Mr Leafy. The Commission. Yes. Go on. You can tell him.' Morgan thrust his hands into his trouser pockets. These little men, he said to himself, you just have to know how to treat them.

The clerk came back in two minutes. 'Dr Murray will be here soon,' he said peevishly. 'Please take a seat.'

Morgan allowed triumph briefly to light up his face, then sat down. Various doors and a passageway led off the waiting room, the floor was terrazzo tiling, there were no paintings or posters on the walls, just a clock, and no magazines to read. The afternoon heat outside made the room warm and muggy.

Five minutes later Murray appeared down the passageway. Morgan rose to his feet expectantly but Murray didn't beckon him forward. Instead he came on in to the room. Morgan vaguely recognized him: he appeared to be around fifty, was tall and slim wearing grey tropical-weight flannels, a white shirt and blue tie. He had short wavy grey-brown hair and a weather-beaten freckled look to his face. He held out his hand. Morgan shook it. It was cool and felt dry and clean. Morgan was conscious of his own sweaty palm and the fact that his fingernails needed cutting.

Murray introduced himself. 'I'm Alex Murray,' he said. His gaze was direct and evaluating. 'I don't think we've met before.'

'Morgan Leafy,' Morgan said. 'I'm First Secretary at the Commission.'

'What can I do for you, Mr Leafy?' Murray had a noticeable

Scottish accent, plain and unlocatable. Morgan took half a step closer to him.

'Actually I'd like to see you about something,' he said, a little discomfited at having to explain in mid-waiting room. He sensed people's attentions turning towards him.

'Oh,' Murray said. 'A health matter. I thought this was Commission business – the way you had my clerk introduce you.'

'No,' Morgan admitted. 'It's a personal matter.' Murray eyed the clock which had ticked on past two. Morgan interpreted his glance and added, 'I *was* here before two.'

'What are your objections to my colleagues?'

'I beg your pardon?'

'I take it you have some objections to seeing the two doctors who are on surgery today. I'm not,' he concluded pointedly.

This was going a bit far, Morgan thought, he was becoming tired with this grilling. Who did Murray think he was talking to? Some lead-swinging undergraduate? It was time to throw a little weight about.

'I've been at the Commission a couple of years now,' he said with a confident smile. 'As we haven't had the pleasure of meeting and as this is my first visit to the clinic I thought I might mix business . . . with business. If you see what I mean?' He paused to allow his genial authoritative tones to sink in. 'I've absolutely no objection to Dr Obayemi or Dr Rathna . . . math . . . what's-his-name . . .'

'Dr Rathmanatathan. What's-*her*-name.'

'Yes, quite. But they aren't British – I assume – and you are. And as I haven't seen you up at any of our Commission do's or get-togethers I thought it might be, you know, nice.' That should do the trick, he thought, though he resented having to invent a reason in public. Murray made no apologies.

'Come this way,' was all he said and led Morgan down the passage to his consulting room. It was large, uncluttered and bare of decoration, containing a desk, two chairs, a high examining couch and a folding screen. The bottom half of the windows were painted white. Through the top half Morgan could see a bough of a tree and a corner of the sick-bay. An air-conditioner was set into the wall; the cool was delicious. They both sat down.

'Marvellous machines,' said Morgan amicably, 'saved Africa for the European, mnah-ha,' he gave a brief chuckle. After the guarded, slightly frosty nature of their exchange outside, and remembering what he was in fact there for, he was concerned to establish a more amenable atmosphere.

Murray, however, seemed not prepared to indulge in any preliminaries. He went straight to the point. 'What exactly is the problem?' he asked.

Morgan was surprised at this. 'Well,' he said, somewhat flustered. 'It was Lee Wan who suggested I come and see you. About my little difficulty.' He smiled in the way that lets the listener know he's about to hear an intimacy of sorts – a trifle silly, but only too understandable between men of the world.

'Yes,' Murray said curtly. 'Go on.'

'Oh. Right. I've, ah, got this girlfriend, you see.'

'Is she pregnant?'

This was all wrong, Morgan thought, it shouldn't be going this way. Murray had screwed up his eyes slightly as if a bright beam of light were shining in them.

'Lord no,' Morgan tried laughter again, but to his ears it sounded uneasy, almost perverse. 'No no. That's what I'm interested in preventing. You see I was hoping you could prescribe the pill for her, the contraceptive . . . Lee Wan suggested that you . . . that it might be possible.' To his dismay Morgan felt his ears beginning to warm with the onset of a blush.

Murray leant forward. His eyes were cold. 'Let's get a couple of things clear before we go any further, Mr Leafy,' he said evenly. 'First Mr Lee Wan doesn't run this clinic so his

94

knowledge of the services we offer is not to be relied on.'

'Gracious,' Morgan protested. 'I wasn't trying to suggest . . .'

'Second,' Murray went on regardless, 'if this "girlfriend" of yours is a member of the university send her along at the relevant time and we'll see what we can do. If she's not, then I'm sorry. She'll have to go elsewhere.'

'Well, she isn't actually,' Morgan said apologetically. 'She's a young, ah, girl I met – from the town . . . I just thought . . .' He felt a complete fool.

Murray sat back in his chair and pointed a biro at Morgan. 'Mr Leafy,' he said in a more reasonable voice. 'You can't honestly expect me to provide oral contraceptives for all the girlfriends of my patients.' He smiled. 'Every tart in Nkong-samba would be queueing up outside the door.' He got to his feet, the meeting was over. Morgan pushed back his chair as Murray came round his desk. 'Take her to a doctor in town. Shouldn't cost you too much.' He put his hand on the door-knob. 'Can I give you a word of advice, Mr Leafy?' Murray said. 'I've been in Africa over twenty years now and I've seen a lot of young men in here, very like you, enjoying certain freedoms that the life out here offers.' He paused, as though debating whether to go on. 'I'll be frank. If you're having sex regularly with a girl . . . from town, it's a good idea to use the sheath. It's a barrier of sorts against infection. It can save a lot of trouble and embarrassment.'

Morgan felt outraged; it was like being lectured to by your headmaster on the perils of masturbation. He tried to make his voice as icy as possible. 'I don't think that will be necessary. This girl doesn't live in a brothel you know, she's perfectly respectable.'

'Good,' said Murray. He seemed quite unconcerned. 'It's just something I point out, as a matter of course. A piece of advice, that's all.'

★

Fine, Morgan thought blackly, well you can stick your advice up your tight Scottish arse. He couldn't believe it, British people just didn't speak to the Commission staff like that, they were respectful, deferential. He'd never been so humiliated, so disgracefully spoken down to, so . . .

He crunched the gears and drove off with gravel spattering from his rear wheels. It was incredible, he told himself as he roared out of the university gates, Murray just *assumed* he was screwing some tart, took it for granted she was black, it went without saying she'd be diseased. The fact that he was right on two counts at least didn't matter a damn. He smiled cynically to himself: Lee Wan was an appalling judge of character.

He was still fulminating as he pulled into Nkongsamba's small airport. He saw Peter, the Commission's driver, standing beside the official gleaming black Austin Princess. Morgan parked his car and walked over to join him. The heat was intense and Morgan felt the sun burn through his thin hair, roasting his scalp. The haze rising off the apron in front of the low airport building made the tarmac look as though it was on fire, about to burst into flames. His eyes were dazzled by flaring spangles of light exploding off the chrome fenders and glasswork of the parked cars. The Kinjanjan flag hung limply down the flagpole beside the squat control tower. Morgan took his sunglasses out of his breast pocket and put them on. Everything calmed down; the colours looked less bleached, the windscreens were striped and speckled like mackerel.

'Plane on time, Peter?' he asked the driver.

Peter saluted. 'Ten minutes delay, sah,' he said, grinning, exposing the prodigious gaps between his teeth.

'Oh bloody hell,' Morgan said angrily. He inspected the car, the polished sides reflecting his body back, crushing him like a concertina, making him look like a walking box. He ran a finger round his sweaty collar and straightened his tie.

He strolled across the car park to the airport building, a modern prefabricated structure. Inside it was only marginally cooler. An African family sat at a table in front of a small refreshment bar. A military policeman dozed by the arrivals door. Outside on the tarmac stood an ancient Dakota in the Kinjanjan Airways livery, one engine nacelle draped with a tarpaulin. In the shade cast by the fuselage two mechanics slept on straw mats.

Morgan hoped everyone was awake in the control tower. He went over to the refreshment bar. Beside it stood a revolving rack of well-thumbed magazines. He selected a two-month old *Life* and flicked through it. Muddy terrified GIs in Vietnam; mind-boggling shots of the Earth, seen from a space-probe; a centre-spread feature on a movie-star's Bel Air chateau. Life.

The family at the table were all wearing their best clothes. The husband sported yellow and purple robes, the young wife, her face paled with powder, was in silvery lace, a massive knotted head-scarf towering on her head, the two little boys in scarlet pyjama-suits. They were probably meeting an important relative. The little boys were noisily draining soft drinks. It seemed like a good idea to Morgan, especially as above the front of the bar it enticingly advertised 'Coca-Cola. Ice Cold.'

Morgan looked over the bar. A sulky girl in a tight faded dress sat on a beer crate. 'I'll have a Coke, please,' Morgan said. She slowly rose to her feet and walked across to the bottle cooler. Lassitude certainly ruled here, he remarked to himself, wiping a bead of sweat from his eyebrow. He knew that his pale blue shirt, fresh this morning, would now have two soup-plate sized dark navy stains at either armpit, and possibly an intermittent streak down his spine. He should have worn a white one, he thought angrily, it was going to look marvellous when he greeted the Fanshawes' daughter, as if he were the 'before' sequence of an underarm deodorant advert. He'd just have to keep his hands pinned to his sides.

The girl behind the bar idly searched through the bottles in the cooler. She had powerfully muscled buttocks that caused the dress to bunch in tight creases across the small of her back.

She selected a bottle and brought it over to the bar. Her eyes were blank with boredom and fatigue. She was about to lever the top from the bottle when Morgan noticed it was a Fanta Orange. 'Hold it,' he said. 'Wait. I ask for Coca-Cola,' he dropped naturally into pidgin English, unconsciously adopting its thick-tongued, nasal accents.

'No Coke,' the girl said, and flipped the top off the bottle with her opener. She chose a straw and dropped it in. 'One shilling,' she demanded.

Morgan felt the ribbed bottle. Warm. 'Why he nevah cold?' he asked.

'Machine done broke,' she said, shuffling back to her seat with the shilling.

'OK,' he said. 'Make you give me one Seven-Up instead.' Warm lemonade would be more bearable than warm sweet orange, just.

The girl looked at him as if to say don't fight it, mac. 'Only Fanta,' she flatly pronounced.

Bloody typical, Morgan thought as he took a reluctant sip at the cloying warm liquid, bloody typical. His headache was getting worse.

The Fanshawes' plane – a Fokker Friendship – proved to be forty-five minutes late. Morgan watched it turn and bank over Nkongsamba, the sun flashing on its wings, and straighten up for its approach to the runway. He called Peter into the arrivals hall to help carry the luggage. The plane landed and taxi-ed onto the apron, coming to a halt beside the Dakota. The sleeping mechanics did not stir. Steps were wheeled out and a trolley trundled over to collect the cases. The Fanshawes were first to appear: Mrs in a creased pink dress and matching turban, Fanshawe himself looking hot in a brown suit. But it was the daughter that engaged Morgan's attention. She was far more attractive than a knowledge of her parents could have ever led him to expect: mid-twenties, he calculated, wearing a short white dress with a pattern of red dice all over it, her face shadowed by a white straw hat with a very large floppy brim. Morgan informed the sleepy MP that this was the Deputy High Commissioner arriving and he snapped out a salute as Fanshawe came through the door.

'Morgan,' Fanshawe said. 'Glad to see you. Been waiting long?'

'Not at all, not at all,' Morgan lied, anxious to please. 'Enjoy your leave?' he asked Mrs Fanshawe, who looked tired and sweaty. Morgan noticed she was limping, her feet, swollen from the flight, bulging out of high-heeled shoes. She managed a weak smile of assent.

'Priscilla darling,' she called to her daughter who was selecting a red vanity case from the pile of luggage that had been deposited in the arrivals hall. 'Come and meet Mr Leafy.'

Priscilla came over, taking off her stupid hat. Morgan saw firm legs, a trace of hockey-player's calves, slimmish body and unimaginably sharply pointed breasts, or sharply pointed bra, perk beneath the cotton material. He looked into the face below the fringe and saw the supercilious plucked eyebrows and privileged, lazy eyes. He saw too the unfortunate ski-jump nose. But he ignored all this, he didn't care, he was thinking elatedly: she is for me, she is more than I could have hoped for, beyond my wildest dreams, this girl is the one I have been waiting for.

'Phew,' she said. 'Terribly hot!' The accent was gratingly posh. Morgan wondered if this was oblique comment on the widening stains beneath his armpits. For a panicky moment he debated whether – not daring to look down – the damp circles had spread across his chest to meet beneath his tie.

'Priscilla,' said her mother, putting an end to further speculation. 'This is Mr Leafy, our First Secretary.'

'How do you do, Mr Leafy,' she said, shaking hands with him.

'Morgan, please.' He smiled his most winning smile.

The ladies were shortly ensconced in the over of the waiting car. There were yelps of discomfort as thighs and buttocks made contact with the burning leather upholstery.

'Good Lord, it's hot,' Fanshawe exclaimed, as he and Morgan stood supervising Peter loading luggage into the boot. 'Nothing but heavy frost and fog our last week home.'

'Sounds sublime,' Morgan ventured enviously.

Fanshawe rubbed his hands together, looking speculatively around the airport car park. 'Very interesting few months ahead, Morgan, very. Bags to discuss,' he added keenly.

'Have we?' Morgan said. He couldn't think what Fanshawe was referring to.

'The elections,' he enthused. 'At Christmas. Oh yes yes. Very important.' He paused. 'I've been briefed of course. Unofficially mind you, but its clear what has to be done.' His eyes were alight with excitement. 'It's a golden opportunity.'

Morgan, still baffled, raised his eyebrows. 'Really?' he said.

'Oh yes. Astonishing stroke of luck. For us that is.' He laughed to himself quietly. 'They're even flying us out a new expat. staff member, take over routine duties, leave our hands more free. Should be here in a couple of weeks.'

'*Our* hands?'

Before Fanshawe could enlarge on his cryptic fervour his wife stuck her pink moist face out of the rear window. 'Arthur,' she exclaimed angrily, 'we're roasting in here.'

As Fanshawe climbed into the car he said conspiratorially over his shoulder, 'see you tomorrow. We've got a Royal visit too, well, semi-Royal. Christmas, it's all happening then.'

As the car drove off Morgan thought the girl gave him a little wave. Just in case she had, he waved back.

Chapter 2

Fanshawe called Morgan into his office the next day and explained matters in greater detail. It seemed that some people he had seen at the Foreign Office while he was on leave were concerned about the coming elections in Kinjanja. Kinjanja's recently discovered oil reserves showed every sign of being more substantial than was at first estimated, and as a result the question of who won the next election had assumed a far greater importance within the unstable sphere of West African politics. Some preliminary sounding-out had already been done on the major parties in the country and one had emerged as being potentially more pro-British than the others. This party also stood a reasonable chance of unseating the present unpopular government and accordingly all four Deputy High Commissioners had been enjoined by the FO cautiously to evaluate the regional power bases of this party, calculate its true motives and alliances and assess its potential as a possible friend to Britain, one who would secure, maintain or even encourage her interests. Fanshawe related this quickly as if it were official gospel. But then his agitation became noticeably more visible. 'The party in question,' he said, 'as you've probably guessed, is the Kinjanjan National Party, the KNP.' Morgan hadn't guessed; he had made a big effort to learn as little as possible about the coming elections. But he nodded sagely all the same. 'Anyway,' Fanshawe continued, 'its nominal leader is some old Emir from the north – an established religious and tribal figurehead, but who's respected and has a loyal following. What's more important as far as we are concerned are its two young Turks – so to speak.' Morgan forced, then wedged, his slackening features into a semblance of passionate interest, which involved knitting his brow into a gnarled frown and taking his bottom lip between his teeth. 'Yes,' Fanshawe went on, 'one of them is a lawyer – Gunlayo or something – based in the capital, who's their legal brain and constitutional expert but the other one, the one with responsibility for foreign policy and international affairs is . . . guess who?'

Morgan hadn't the faintest. He went 'ah' and 'mmm' a few times and scratched his head, eventually admitting that Fanshawe had got him there.

'Well,' Fanshawe said triumphantly. 'Wait for it . . . Sam Adekunle,' he announced. 'Our very own Sam Adekunle, Professor of Economics and Business Management at the University of Nkongsamba.' Morgan wondered why this was so significant, but he felt sure that Fanshawe would eventually get round to enlightening him. 'Marvellous stroke of luck,' Fanshawe insisted. 'Here we are stuck miles up country, a quiet little backwater and it turns out we've got this political bigwig on our doorstep.'

'Yes,' Morgan said slowly, 'Extraordinary luck.' He shifted in his seat, rubbed his chin thoughtfully, nodded a few times and repeated the word extraordinary.

'You see what this means,' Fanshawe pressed on, leaving his desk and going to stand by the window. He clasped his hands behind his back and raised himself up and down on tiptoe. 'Our analysis and evaluation is going to be of key importance.' He whirled round suddenly to face Morgan, who gave a little jump of alarm at the unexpected movement. 'We're in the best position to find out what makes the KNP tick, what it thinks, what its ambitions are. What we tell the FO is going to carry a lot of weight. A lot of weight,' he repeated. 'Adekunle's position in the party makes him, from the UK's point of view, the most interesting man in the KNP. And,' the glee in his voice was unmistakeable, 'the man's right bang on our doorstep!'

Morgan's brain was sluggish that morning, he just couldn't concentrate. 'That's marvellous news for you, Arthur,' he said distractedly. 'What do you propose to do exactly?'

'Oh no,' Fanshawe said. 'Not me.'

Morgan smiled. 'Sorry?' he said pleasantly.

'Not me,' Fanshawe said. 'You.'

'*Me?*' Morgan suddenly woke up.

'Of course. I can't possibly start investigating or encouraging Kinjanjan political parties, can I?'

Morgan wondered what he meant by encouraging. 'I suppose not,' he said, his voice heavy with trepidation. 'But I don't exactly see what I can do . . . I mean, I've got a hell of a lot on already and . . .'

'Why do you think we're getting a new member of staff?' Fanshawe interrupted. 'To relieve you of the daily routine, give you a free hand, let you really get to work.' He gazed at Morgan as if entranced. 'This is what it's all about, Morgan, *real* work. Real diplomacy. Not this endless socializing, mindless official business. No, you can really do something positive here, something creative. For your country.'

Morgan had bowed his head from acute painful embarrassment as this tirade had progressed and was screwing the knuckles of each forefinger into his temples. What in hell's name, he asked himself, was the old goat bleating on about? 'For your country', something creative for his country; give him a cocktail party any day. 'Excuse me, Arthur,' he said. 'But what did you mean just then by "encouraging"?'

'Coming to that,' Fanshawe said. 'The way I see it, your mission' – there was a tremor in his voice as he said this word – 'is to try to get to know Adekunle personally if possible. Mix with him socially. Try to find out everything you can. Not the usual guff they fill their manifestos with but the – what do they call it? – "realpolitik". You know,' he seemed to be growing frustrated at Morgan's lack of enthusiasm, 'realities, hard facts that we can pass on. I want you to write everything up in a report, anything you can get on Adekunle and the KNP. I'll take it from there, liaise with the Commissioner in the capital, get the gist back to Whitehall.'

Oh yes? thought Morgan, I don't like the sound of that. Fanshawe seemed to sense this and hastily countered. 'Of course, I can tell you confidentially, Morgan, that a really top class piece of work here could, well, do us – our, ah, careers – no harm. Let's face it, I think we both agree Nkongsamba's not a major posting, not exactly the summit of our ambitions . . . I think I'm not going too far to say that both of us wouldn't object to moving on somewhere a little more exalted. When there's Washington, Paris, Tokyo, Caracas out there, Nkongsamba doesn't . . . well, you know what I mean.' He fiddled with the knot of his tie, touched the neat bristles of his moustache and frowned. Morgan was perplexed: he had never heard Fanshawe speak so openly and intimately before. 'We've known each other for a good while now,' he continued, 'and I don't think I'd be giving any family secrets away if I told you that Chloe and I had always hoped that the final years of my diplomatic service would end, well, somewhere . . . *not* Nkongsamba. The same goes for you I'm sure. You're a young man with . . . with ability – you have to be looking ahead.'

The subdued flattery fell soothingly on Morgan's ears, and for an instant he felt sorry for Fanshawe, an ageing failure with his dreams unfulfilled, but he still realized he'd be doing most of the work.

'What exactly do you want me to do?' he asked hesitantly, keen to move the subject away from these awkward and uncomfortable personal revelations.

'Try to meet Adekunle for a start. He's an urbane sort of chap, modern tastes, English wife, children at prep school in the UK, that sort of thing. Shouldn't be a great effort for you to get into his particular social circle in the university. You know a few people there, don't you? Shouldn't be impossible. Then gently let him know that we're on his side.'

'I'm not sure,' Morgan said. 'I do know who Adekunle is but I don't see him around much socially at all. Seems to keep to his own kind as it were.' To his surprise he found his interest quickening as he considered the possibilities. 'I'll tell you what,' he said, enthusiasm creeping into his voice. 'The next big jamboree we have here, let's invite all the local political people. That way I might gain some sort of entrée.'

'First class idea,' Fanshawe congratulated, obviously thrilled. 'We'll think up some excuse for a do. Duke of York's birthday or something.' He chuckled at his own waggishness. 'Yes. You'll keep me in touch? Every move?'

'Naturally,' Morgan said.

'Good,' Fanshawe said. 'Excellent. We can work this one out together, Morgan. Soon have something solid to show them.'

Morgan suddenly had an idea. 'What's this Royal visit you mentioned? Is it coming up soon? We could use that as an excuse.'

'No,' Fanshawe looked crestfallen. 'She's coming out at Xmas. Not really a Royal either: someone called the Duchess of Ripon, third cousin twice removed to the Queen or something equally distant. She's representing Her Majesty at the Independence celebrations. Tenth anniversary on New Year's Eve you know. She's doing a whistle-stop tour of the country – should be with us for a couple of days – finishing up in the capital for the big celebrations.'

'And the elections,' Morgan added.

'Yes,' Fanshawe mused. 'Tell you what, I'll get Chloe to organize some party or other. She enjoys these functions. Priscilla can give her a hand.' Fanshawe stroked his little moustache thoughtfully. 'Speaking of which,' he said, 'I wonder if I could ask a little favour of you.'

'Fire away,' Morgan said amicably; he wasn't averse to doing any favours connected however remotely to Priscilla Fanshawe.

'Chloe would murder me if she knew I was telling you this,' he said sadly. 'But it's better if you're fully in the picture.' He paused. 'Priscilla's had a bit of a sticky time lately, you see.

She was engaged to a young chap in the Army – Marines – known him for ages, met him while we were in KL. Well, this summer he suddenly ups and offs back to Malaya, calls off the engagement, resigns his commission and marries a Chinese girl. Living out there now, working for her father.' Fanshawe's features registered tragic disbelief. 'Can't understand it. Such an appalling waste. Well brought-up young chap too, good family and all that. Quite inexplicable.'

Morgan said nothing. Since he'd started sleeping regularly with Hazel miscegenation had become a sensitive topic.

'I was wondering if,' Fanshawe cleared his throat, 'if you could perhaps pop round from time to time. Show her round the place maybe. Cheer her up if you can as she's naturally been down in the dumps rather since it all fell apart. I'd be most grateful.'

'Don't mention it,' Morgan said. 'I'd be glad to. My pleasure entirely.'

Chapter 3

Morgan tried to thrust his tongue into Priscilla Fanshawe's mouth, but its flickering tip met only the immovable enamel barrier of her teeth. Resignedly he contented himself with another lingering dry Hollywood-style kiss until his lips began to hurt from their being continually pursed. He allowed his hand to drop from her forearm onto her hip and felt her body stiffen. He let it rest there for a couple of seconds before obligingly returning it to her unerogenous arm. He hadn't indulged in such discreet inoffensive foreplay, such diffident tactical petting since the early days of his adolescence, but the nostalgic Proustian memory-glow had soon worn off and he was rapidly becoming bored with the game.

They were sitting in the front seat of Morgan's Peugeot which was parked in a dark corner of the Ambassador Hotel's car park. It was about half past ten at night. The Ambassador was Nkongsamba's most exclusive and elite hotel. It sat proudly on a hill about two miles north of the city. It was a modern six-storey block with a reputedly international restaurant, a swimming pool and a casino. The food in the restaurant was appalling, the service disgracefully slovenly and the swimming pool grew green algae despite being so heavily chlorinated that you could practically see the gas rising from its surface. The casino, on the other hand, was the one place in Nkongsamba where tacky mediocrity wasn't the watchword and a dash of sophistication had gained a precarious foothold. It was run by a Syrian entrepreneur who had imported two plump girl croupiers from Beirut and was patronized almost exclusively by fellow Middle-Easterners. Morgan and Priscilla had just passed a giddy hour in its dimly plush interior at the roulette and baccarat tables and Morgan had steadily lost twenty-three pounds, before prudence told him that Priscilla was unlikely to be impressed by a flawless capacity to back the wrong numbers.

It was turning out to be an expensive evening – the second he had spent in Priscilla's company. They had started out at the university club's restaurant, where Morgan had bought their priciest wine, a sweetish highly-scented Piesporter, and from there had proceeded to drinks in the 'Embassy' bar at the Ambassador where they had shared a joke at the curious aptness of the venue. When Priscilla informed him that she'd never been in a casino, Morgan offered to show her how one functioned.

He had planned that the evening should end this way. He had sought her hand as they sauntered from the casino entrance towards the car park. It was accepted, fingers were linked, they both turned wordlessly to face each other, smiled and squeezed. They sat in the car, maintaining the silence, looking out at the view of Nkongsamba's glimmering lights before commenting huskily on its magnificence. Steadily a 'mood' was established, a tingling awareness of their warm breathing bodies close to one another in the enclosed unobserved darkness of the car. Priscilla had run both hands through her hair causing her sharp breasts to rise beneath the cream satin blouse she was wearing.

'It's been a marvellous evening,' she had breathed. Morgan had leant across, his left elbow on the back of the car seat and whispered 'Priscilla . . .' her head turned and their lips touched, exactly as they knew they would.

And here they still were.

Now Morgan applied his mouth to Priscilla's again; gently at first, tenderly, sensitively – she had nice soft lips. Then he started breathing quickly through his nose – in-out, in-out – in simulated passion, wriggling his head around energetically as if their lips were stuck fast and he was trying, vainly, to wrench them apart. Priscilla responded in muted kind, eyes shut, shoulders alternately heaving. Thus encouraged, Morgan slid his hand off her upper arm and on to her left breast. Priscilla's eyes immediately shot open and she clawed herself upright with the help of the dashboard.

'Morgan, please,' she said in half-hurt reproach.

He almost burst out in uproarious laughter at this display of coy restraint. Here he was, he said scornfully to himself, with a highly-sexed compliant black mistress in a down-town hotel – and he was putting himself through this obstacle course. Patience, he thought to himself, and said 'I'm . . . I'm sorry, Priscilla,' sticking manfully to the required formula. 'I shouldn't have, but, well, you're to blame,' he touched her face as though to emblematize her provocative beauty, smiling at her helplessly. She smiled too and lowered her gaze. He started the car engine. 'We'd better get you home,' he said.

During the silent drive back he asked himself why he was

bothering, and offer up as he might reasons of boredom, masculine challenge, sex and so forth, he knew instinctively it was really because he had always wanted to – he searched for a word – go out, be linked, associated with, wanted by, even married to a girl like Priscilla Fanshawe. He had never ever so much as been acquainted with anyone like her before, so even a chaste and tiring ten-minute embrace and the milli-second's impression of an impossibly firm breast beneath his palm represented a considerable triumph in the deprived scale of his life, a positive move up in his impoverished world. And although he felt a little ashamed to admit it he knew that if he could keep things as they were, gradually work on improving them, immense gains in self-esteem and personal kudos would ensue. Perhaps even a giant leap in social mobility, leaving his tawdry past unrecognized far behind him.

The ruthlessness of this desire for Priscilla, and the things she represented for him, surprised him rather when he objectively considered that aspects of her physiognomy and character were off-putting to say the least. There was her voice and her nose and the attitudes they seemed to embody: a profound incuriosity about any world other than her own, a bland superficiality in all her personal relations: always pleasant and charming – as if an evil, bitchy or hurtful thought never passed through her largely empty head – or, if it did, it was dressed up in rib-digging, simpering innuendo. Paradoxically, for they were attitudes he otherwise affected to loathe and deprecate, he found he slotted himself into those brainless behaviour patterns with a quisling's ease. Everything became super or dreadful, shades of grey were not admitted. People were either 'sweet', 'really sweet' or 'awfully sweet' unless they overtly conspired against you. Human endeavour and general ami-ability were held to be in plentiful supply among the right sort of people, and with pluck, courage and good fellowship all sorts of grubby little problems could be seen off.

Accordingly, Morgan moved his birthplace nearer the

Thames to Kingston, gave himself a scholarship to a minor public school, promoted his father to personnel manager, provided his mother with a private income and, to his surprise, even found himself saying 'yah' instead of yes.

They drove past the saw mill and he shot a glance at Priscilla. 'Nearly there,' he said. But as the gates of the Commission approached Priscilla suddenly called out 'Stop!' and Morgan obligingly pulled into the verge.

'I don't feel like going home yet,' Priscilla said turning to face him. 'It's early, can we go somewhere else?'

Morgan thought quickly. 'We could go back to my place . . . For a cup of coffee,' he added promptly. 'It's not far away and it'll be easy to get you back here before it gets too late.' Kindly disinterested tones highlighted his voice. He felt so noble, so upright. So hypocritical.

Priscilla placed her hand on his which was resting on the steering wheel. 'That'd be lovely,' she said.

Morgan and Priscilla sat side by side on Morgan's settee. They were watching a TV programme in which a man with a battered suitcase and a cigarette jammed in his mouth solved problems the CIA and MI5 couldn't cope with. It ended with the hero removing his cigarette to kiss the beautiful daughter of an American diplomat. In his contented mood Morgan interpreted this as a favourable omen. Priscilla had kicked off her sling-back shoes and had tucked her feet up beneath her. She was leaning against him and had lodged her head in the angle formed by his neck and shoulder.

'More coffee?' he asked. 'Another brandy?' Moses and Friday were away for the night.

'Gosh no,' Priscilla giggled, 'I'll be peeing all night.' As if this mildest of improprieties were a signal Morgan bent his head round to kiss her. In the last half hour she had relaxed sufficiently to allow gentle tongue probing and the infrequent squeeze of a breast. Morgan kissed her neck, it was moist and tasted vaguely salty. He noted that her short black skirt had ridden pleasingly up her thighs.

'Morgan,' she said in a small voice, 'do you know why I came out here. To Nkongsamba?'

'Haven't the faintest,' he lied, nuzzling her ear while he undid a button on her blouse. He slid his hand beneath the satin and inched it along her chest until he met the abrupt gradient of her breast and the lacy reinforcement of her bra. Try as he might, and short of using his other hand as a lever, he could not prise his fingers under it.

'I just wanted to say thank you,' she said. Morgan withdrew his hand and looked at her in some astonishment.

'What on earth for?' he asked.

She pecked him on the cheek. 'For not storming off in a rage because I wasn't . . . relaxed.'

'Don't be silly,' he admonished.

'It's just that I'm not very sure of myself . . . I'm a bit "uptight" as I believe the current expression goes.' She picked up Morgan's right hand and examined it minutely as if it were some mysterious and rare artefact. 'Which is why I've come out here.'

'Oh,' Morgan said, carefully non-committal.

'You see I used to be almost engaged to this chap Charles, only we had a terrific bust-up. The whole thing was getting fairly serious, I . . . I had practically moved into his flat.' Morgan stored this piece of information away. 'When I suddenly realized he just wasn't the right sort of person for me. Just one day, no particular reason, I saw it was completely wrong. Hopeless.' She paused. 'Charles was a sweetie, but not for me, if you know what I mean.' She looked at him for support. 'You can't, you shouldn't let things go on under those sort of circumstances. It's better to make a break.'

'Oh yes. You're right,' Morgan agreed. 'Absolutely. Yah.' He looked serious, intensely understanding.

She cuddled up to him. 'It was pretty gruesome. Shouting

and crying. He was terribly upset. But I knew I had to do it.'
Morgan smoothed the hair on her head. 'Which is why I'm
a bit, you know, stiff and cautious. Emotionally bruised,
Mummy calls it. You understand.'

Morgan nodded. 'A case of once bitten.'

'Exactly,' she affirmed. 'Exactly,' squeezing him with
gratitude.

Morgan deposited a kiss on the flipped-up end of her nose.
'We'd better get you home,' he said.

They enjoyed the final and the most passionate embrace of
the evening in the dark driveway of the Fanshawes' house. As
he drove home Morgan was glowing with self-congratulation,
attributing the persistent dull ache in his groin to an unrelieved
night-long erection. Later, lying back in his bed, he lazily
contemplated the vivid memories of Priscilla's strong smooth
legs and tried to imagine what her breasts looked like, gently
releasing his frustration into a wad of toilet paper. As the
tingling pleasure seeped along his legs and out of his toes it
was replaced by a slight but uncomfortable burning, scorching
sensation at the tip of his penis. Further examination established
that there was a slight rawness there which was effectively
soothed by the application of some Nivea cream. He assumed
that it had been caused by the rubbing of his buckled hard-on
against the zip of his trousers or raised hem of his Y-fronts, a
small price to pay, he reflected, for such a well-conceived and
executed evening's wooing.

Before he fell asleep he thought about Priscilla's lie: He
scoffed briefly at the illusions people erected around themselves
in desperate pretence before he realized that he himself wasn't
exactly in a strong position to deride this form of behaviour.
Priscilla's version of her falling-out with Charles made her the
agent; moreover, a mature and sensible one, demanding overall
a mutually fulfilling relationship and, by the by, just letting
him know she was no virgin. Morgan smiled to himself: one
gift he was blessed with, he considered, was the ability to see

through people, to size them up, see what they really were beneath public pose: an invaluable talent.

As he thought on, it occurred to him that maybe this gift of Priscilla – young, unattached, not ignorant of his charms – meant that his luck was on the turn. Those drab years as an executive officer in overlit, overheated civil service offices in the South of England, the disastrous interviews and repeated failings of Foreign Office exams before the eventual scrape-through. The shaming training period, the snobbishness, the cold shoulders of his colleagues, the prolonged wait in some Whitehall cul-de-sac, the fifth-grade overseas posting to Nkongsamba where he'd already languished eighteen months longer than he should have, perhaps, perhaps all this had been arranged by someone just so he could meet Priscilla. Fate, Destiny, Big G – he offered up a prayer of thanks just in case – who knows? For the only time in his life he was the right man in the right place at the right time. He could feel a warmth welling up in his heart, a languor suffusing his body; he sensed his muscles bulge and flex, he spread his arms across the bed, stretching his fingers wide. He knew what it was; he felt pleased with himself, and, better still, he was sure he was falling in love with Priscilla.

Chapter 4

The lawn of the Commission was bathed in a yellow glow from the high-powered floodlights strategically placed at first-floor windows. A hundred or more people, blacks and whites, swarmed around the cold buffet tables and the two bars. Over to the left was a large cinema screen with rows of seats ranged in front of it. Morgan looked down on the throng from one of the back windows, invisible behind the glare of the floodlights. He had been unable to spot Adekunle on the ground and had moved up here to get a better view. He saw many faces he recognized among the cream of Nkongsamba society who had been lured here tonight by the prospect of free booze and food and who were, because of this bait, prepared to suffer the private screening of yet another film on the Royal Family. That, Morgan had to admit, had been a stroke of genius on Fanshawe's part. This film, billed as an 'intimate portrait', had been despatched recently to all the British High Commissions and embassies throughout the world as part of a large-scale diplomatic publicity stunt. It had not been scheduled to reach Nkongsamba for many months yet but some judicious pressure by Fanshawe had managed to get it sent up prematurely from the capital. A private viewing was duly arranged and official invitations hastily sent out. It was to be an excuse for a jingoistic explosion of self-admiration for the expatriate Britons, and the anticipated regular shots of splendid castles, historic artefacts, beaming Royalty and endless immaculate parades would surely provide a gentle but potent reminder to all the non-British present of precisely just what it was they didn't possess and why, therefore, they just weren't quite such special people. Normally these sorts of occasion had the same effect on Morgan as weddings: they were awash with false sincerity, hypocrisy and a dreadful backslapping bonhomie that always made him sweat with embarrassment.

Tonight, however, was different. To his surprise he had found himself looking forward to it, and now as he peered down on the assorted heads beneath him – blond, brunette and balding, woolly peppercorn and towering head-ties – he felt an unmistakable surge of excitement. This was a set-up, he reminded himself; he was working – yes, *undercover* – for his government. It was a small job perhaps, merely the securing of information on a foreign country's political party, fairly low-priority stuff, but such jobs, he told himself, were the broad base of intelligence, the firm foundations of global diplomatic gestures, the unnoticed background to those head-lined ministerial initiatives.

Morgan had to confess that Fanshawe's enthusiasm for their plan had been infectious. He had behaved like an excited schoolboy playing at spies; he had given a drawer of a filing cabinet over to the project, to which only he and Morgan had the key. He had even gone so far as to bestow a code name on the operation: he called it 'Project Kingpin', after Adekunle's party's initials – KNP. 'We'd better have a Kingpin meeting,' he would say cautiously to Morgan in the passageway, or, 'This is material for the Kingpin file,' or, 'Any progress on Kingpin?' Morgan had thought at first that it was all a bit sad really, but had happily gone along with it anyway as he was reaping the benefits of this new alliance with Priscilla's father. 'You know,' Priscilla had said to him during one of their latest meetings, 'Daddy's been terribly impressed with you recently – singing your praises night and day. What are you two up to?'

'Nothing really,' he had said modestly. 'Routine stuff, that's all.'

Earlier on in the evening Morgan had been remarking on the excellence of the punch to the overweight wife of an engineering contractor when Fanshawe had sidled up and muttered in his ear 'Kingpin's arrived,' and had glided off dramatically, like a courtier informing a prince of a plot against his life.

Now, looking down on the herd of loyal subjects, Morgan saw Adekunle standing by the beer bar with a white woman he took to be the politician's wife. Adekunle was wearing native dress and was carrying a carved ebony stick. His wife, Morgan thought, looked unhappy and incongruous in a loose yoke-necked blouse, a wrap-around cloth skirt and bulky headscarf. As he watched, Morgan noticed the way people came up and paid court to Adekunle almost as if he were the host. Scanning the faces Morgan recognized two other political leaders keeping as widely separated from each other as possible. There was Femi Robinson, an angry little Marxist who was the local representative of the People's Party of Kinjanja, and there was Chief Mabegun, governor of the Mid-West state and head of the Mid-West branch of the ruling United Party of Kinjanjan People. Widespread popular discontent over its bloated members and the inefficient lean years Kinjanja had suffered while it was in power had brought about the approaching general election. Mabegun, Morgan thought, looked like he was running on the graft and corruption ticket again. He was a vastly fat man who seemed to be implying by his own comfortable obesity that power had been good to him so a vote cast in his favour might, possibly, provide everybody with similar benefits.

But both Robinson and Mabegun were, Morgan accepted, small fry beside Adekunle. The main leaders of the PPK and the UPKP were in the capital; the Mid-West representatives were only minor luminaries, with little or no influence outside their own small state. Adekunle, on the other hand, was in a different league. He was a respected academic who had spoken at the last meeting of the Organization of African Unity. From the information Morgan had gathered thus far, Adekunle seemed to spend more time flying round the globe to various third-world conferences or UN special committees than he did giving lectures or, as dean, administering his faculty. There was also talk, Morgan had established, that he might be the next vice-chancellor of the university.

As Morgan watched, he saw Fanshawe and his wife go up and chat to Adekunle who smiled and beamed at them with urbane geniality. He saw Fanshawe, in response to some remark of Adekunle's, laugh uneasily and shoot a quick glance over his shoulder up at the first-floor windows. Morgan swiftly pulled himself back behind the wall though he was fairly sure he couldn't be seen. Typical Fanshawe, he fumed inwardly, the man clearly wasn't suited for this covert work if he revealed the positions of his confederates so thoughtlessly. It was time, he decided, that he went down and sorted things out.

As he slowly descended the stairs on his way to meet Adekunle, he felt his pulse quicken and a tight ball of pressure establish itself securely behind his sternum. He stepped out of the back entrance of the Commission and on to the crowded lawn.

As he weaved his way through the groups of people towards Adekunle, he could feel his palms moistening and his mouth drying. Adekunle was a large man. He was going steadily to fat as all successful Kinjanjans seemed inevitably to do – as if it were a generic concomitant of power and esteem – and he had about him an aura of self confidence as unshakable as a force-field. He was talking sternly and in a low voice to his wife who looked sullen beneath her headdress and who was smoking a cigarette, nervously staring down at the trampled grass. As Morgan drew near they both looked up smiling suddenly in a well-practised insincere way.

'Professor Adekunle,' Morgan said. 'How do you do? I'm Morgan Leafy, First Secretary here at the Commission. I think we met once briefly before.' This was not true, they had only been in the same room, but it was his favourite introductory device, often throwing people into confusion as they racked their brains trying to remember the occasion. It had no such effect on Adekunle. He smiled beneath his wide moustache.

'Did we? I'm afraid I don't recall, but how do you do anyway.' He shook Morgan's hand. 'This is my wife Celia.'

'Hello,' Celia Adekunle said in a demure voice. She kept her eyes on Morgan's face. As with all direct looks that he received he found this one somewhat disconcerting; he suspected they stirred vast untapped reservoirs of guilt deep within him. He returned to Adekunle.

'Very good of you to invite us here,' Adekunle said, before Morgan could speak, in tones of thinly disguised sarcasm. 'I see my distinguished rivals are present too.'

Morgan smiled. 'All in the interests of balance,' he laughed. 'Talking about which . . .'

'And to see a film of your wonderful Royal Family,' Adekunle continued regardless. 'Most thoughtful. Most uplifting.'

'Well, between you and me,' Morgan said confidentially, 'any excuse for a bunfight, if you see what I mean.'

'Ulterior motives. Now I understand. Devious people, you diplomats.' Adekunle signalled over a waiter who was carrying a tray of drinks and helped himself to an orange juice. Morgan was distressed by the note of hostility and sardonic displeasure that still coloured Adekunle's voice. He decided to be direct.

'How's the campaign going?' he asked as innocently as he knew how. 'Well, I hope.'

Adekunle affected surprise. 'My campaign? Why on earth should the British be interested in my campaign? Why don't you ask my opponents, Mr Leafy? I'm sure they can judge its effects better than I.'

'Ah now, professor, let's not be naïve,' Morgan chuckled knowingly. 'I think it's fairly common knowledge that the British government would naturally be very interested in the outcome of the elections.'

'*Very* interested?'

Morgan looked around and became aware again of Celia Adekunle's intense gaze. 'Well yes, I think you could say that.'

'How interested?'

'Just a moment, professor,' Morgan said quickly, realizing that the conversation was going further and faster than he'd intended. 'We can hardly discuss such matters here.' He flashed a nervous smile.

'I don't see why not,' Adekunle insisted obstinately. 'If you invite representatives of the three major parties to a function such as this you must expect politics to show her face, as the saying goes. Isn't that so, Celia?' Morgan couldn't tell if this was banter or a serious point.

'It shows its face everywhere else,' Celia Adekunle said drily. 'Why make an exception in this case?'

Alarmingly, Morgan noticed that Femi Robinson was edging closer to them.

'Commissioner Fanshawe seemed most interested in my campaign too,' Adekunle observed further.

'Did he?' Morgan said with as much unconcern as he could muster, thinking that Fanshawe was a stupid meddling old berk: he had probably got Adekunle's back up. 'He's just returned from leave,' Morgan said in explanation. 'He's probably catching up.'

'You haven't briefed him then?' Adekunle asked.

Morgan felt his bow tie tighten round his throat. This just wasn't going as he'd expected. Adekunle was being most aggressive. 'I think we should change the subject,' he said looking appealingly at Celia Adekunle and smiling broadly.

'I think the film's about to start,' she said. Morgan looked round in astonishment to see Fanshawe clapping his hands and herding people towards the rows of seats. The stupid shit! Morgan swore inwardly, Fanshawe was meant to wait for his sign, couldn't he see that he and Adekunle were still talking?

Adekunle meanwhile had deposited his untouched orange juice on the nearby bar. 'At last,' he said, rubbing his hands together. 'This is the icing on the cake, as the saying goes. Nice to meet you, Mr Leafy.' He moved off towards the seats accompanied by his wife. Morgan was about to follow him when he felt a tug on his sleeve, he looked round to see Femi Robinson, the Marxist, his patchily bearded face by Morgan's shoulder.

'Mr Leafy?' he said, 'May I have a word with you?'

'What?' He wondered how Robinson knew his name. He looked back and saw Adekunle about to sit down. 'No,' he said with more force than he meant and snatched his jacket cuff from Robinson's still clutching fingers. He ran after Adekunle. 'Professor,' he called desperately.

'Ah, Mr Leafy, yet again. Always turning up like a bad penny, yes?'

Morgan kept his voice low. 'It would, I think, be a good idea if we had a talk.'

'Oh yes?' Adekunle said sceptically. He turned to his wife. 'This will do fine, Celia.' He looked back at Morgan. 'A talk, Mr Leafy? What could we have to discuss?' He sat down beside his wife. His seat was on the end of a row next to the centre aisle. Morgan grew aware that most people had secured their places by now.

He leant forward, bringing himself into Celia Adekunle's unflinching stare. 'Well,' he said, 'we could talk about . . . interest and balance, er, that sort of thing.'

Adekunle smiled, his muttonchop whiskers raised by his bulging cheeks. 'No, Mr Leafy,' he said finally. 'I don't really think they're attractive topics. And by the way, I think you're obstructing the projector.'

Morgan looked round. Jones, who was supervising the film, waved him aside impatiently. He heard Fanshawe call his name and saw him pointing to an empty seat in the front row between Mrs Fanshawe and Chief Mabegun. Priscilla was three places away beside the Jones children. There was a sudden whirr and a blinding light struck him on one side of his face, silhouetting his round head and thin hair sharply against the screen. There were a few high-spirited whistles and calls of 'Get your head down.' He crouched low and scurried back up the aisle towards the projector. He was emphatically not going to sit for an hour and ten minutes beside Mrs Fanshawe. He felt angry and frustrated at the unsatisfactory way his conversation with Adekunle had gone, and his mood was not helped by Jones who hissed as he went past: 'What are you bloody playing at, Morgan?'

Shut up you stupid Welsh git, Morgan swore under his breath, otherwise ignoring him, standing for a moment behind the final row of chairs watching the credits roll over a huge royal crest. What a disaster, he thought, contemplating his talk with Adekunle. And what a cynical bastard he was too, leading him on like that. He felt ashamed of his ineptitude, his clumsy inability even to set up another meeting. Had he been too subtle? he wondered, or was it the other way round? He shook his head in despair. So much for covert diplomacy, he thought scathingly. The entire audience must have seen him trotting after Adekunle like some importunate salesman determined to make his pitch. He gritted his teeth with shame and embarrassment.

Slowly he became aware of the presence of figures in the dark around him. On both sides of him the Commission servants had quietly gathered and were gazing entranced at the film in open-mouthed wonder, their faces ghoulishly illuminated by the reflected light. Morgan turned to the screen. The Royal Family were engaged in setting up and enjoying a picnic in a stereotypical Scottish setting. They wore kilts, tweed jackets or thick woolly jerseys. In the background was a small loch and further off were purply-green hills and pine woods. It was a cloudy day with small patches of intense blue among the clouds, hurried on by a gusty wind that billowed kilts and blew strands of hair across Royal faces. The young princes ran about in childish abandon but the elders were agonizingly conscious of the camera crew's presence and the conversation was *sotto voce* and bland. Occasionally a remark of mild humour was passed – 'Three sausages! You greedy thing!' – and the audience would scream with uproarious laughter.

Morgan looked about him. Above, the stars shone, all round the crickets chirruped, the air was hot and damp and the formal clothes on the arrayed guests were heavy and uncomfortable. The beam of light emanating from the projector was alive with fluttering moths and insects casting their tiny shadows onto the Scottish countryside. From time to time a bat would dive-bomb the flickering insects, a darker more solid mass flashing across the picnicking group. The incongruity of the scene was so bizarre, so surreal – the fascinated servants stealing a glimpse of this family in their distant northern landscape – that Morgan felt it must be trying to tell him something significant, but he could see nothing in it apart from incongruity. Moreover, he found such juxtapositions unsettling: he could almost feel the chilly Scottish weather, the clear scouring breeze, and the sudden ideal vision of Britain made him depressed, reminded him painfully of his current location.

As the scene changed to Windsor Castle he turned away, knowing that Feltham was just down the road. He walked with leaden feet back to the Commission building, weighed down with dissatisfaction and failure. He stopped at a bar and helped himself to a large whisky before continuing on his way. He went up to the first floor. On the landing was a small bathroom equipped with a bath, basin and WC, for, as well as the main offices being there, there was a suite of rooms for important guests. Morgan relieved himself and sat morosely on the edge of the bath. There was an old wall shower attachment which was dripping. He turned the tap tighter and it stopped. He fingered the plastic shower curtain distractedly, his mind far away. It was decorated with a motif of angel fishes, bubbles and seaweed fronds. A similar curtain covered the bathroom window. He pulled it aside and looked over the back lawn. The cinema screen burned with lambent colours like a jewel in the huge navy-blue night. The crowd of spellbound servants had been swelled by the soft arrival of their families from the nearby quarters. He saw the red and black pattern of a parade and faintly heard the tinny accompaniment of martial music. He drained his glass and set it down. For some reason the scene made him feel like weeping.

He splashed his face with water and adjusted his bow tie. He paused for a moment on the landing, wondering how he would describe the night's events to Fanshawe, before going slowly downstairs.

He had just reached the bottom when a woman's voice said, 'Oh . . . Hello.'

He gave a start of alarm as he had imagined himself to be quite alone. He looked round and saw Mrs Adekunle standing in the shadows of the large entrance hall, her headscarf removed and hanging from her hand. 'Hello,' he said. 'Couldn't you take the film either?'

'Made me homesick,' she said, stepping out into the light. Morgan saw she had mid-blonde hair, a little thin and lank, and a deep tan, which he hadn't noticed outside.

She held up the headscarf. 'This was coming off as well. And I needed the loo.' She unclipped her handbag, small and expensive-looking, and took out a packet of cigarettes. 'Cigarette?' she offered.

'No thanks,' Morgan said. 'Given up.'

'Mmm.' Celia Adekunle made an impressed noise as she lit her cigarette. 'Where is it?'

'Sorry?'

'The loo.'

'Oh. The official ones are back down that corridor. But why don't you go upstairs. The *un*official one's up there, bit plusher, second on your left on the landing.'

'My. I'm honoured. Thank you.' She moved towards the stair.

'I'd better warn you,' he said. 'For some reason it only locks from the outside. You have to clear your throat very loudly every five seconds or whistle a tune if you don't want to be interrupted.'

She laughed. 'Thanks,' she said. 'But I think everyone's engrossed out there.'

Morgan looked at his watch. 'Only another twenty minutes. I think I'll sit this one out.'

'That's not very British of you.'

'Nor of you come to that.'

'Ah. But I'm not British any more,' she smiled a little grimly. 'I'm Kinjanjan.'

'Oh I see,' he said. 'Then I'm the only guilty one.'

'What is it you do exactly?' she asked, 'Here, in the Commission?' She sounded interested so he told her.

'It's fairly routine in a small place like this. It's just a presence that's required really, in case of any problems and so on. But what I mainly do is take care of immigration. Vet the visa applications, issue them, keep up the records, that sort of thing. It's amazing how many people want to go to the UK, even from somewhere like Nkongsamba. There's a lot of paperwork and documentation. Not a very exciting life, unless it's enlivened by occasions like this.' He pointed in the direction of the back lawn, but she ignored his irony.

'I see,' she nodded. 'So you get to decide who goes?'

'That's about it.'

'Right,' she said brightly. 'I'll go and practise my whistling.' She climbed the stairs. 'Second door on the left?'

'That's right,' he said after her. 'I'll keep guard down here if you like.'

She laughed. 'My goodness, special privileges.'

Morgan heard her walk across the landing and open and close the door. She seemed a nice sort of person, he remarked to himself, he wondered what it must be like for her being married to someone like Adekunle. He paced about the hall trying not to imagine her sitting urinating but found, to his vague self-disgust, that he did so all the same. He was thankful when he heard the noisy flush of the cistern.

She came down the stairs shortly after tucking up a fold in her remade head-tie.

'Looks nice,' he said. 'The clothes.' He thought she looked ridiculous.

'Nice of you to say so,' she said drily, clearly not believing him. 'Sam's made me wear them at these official functions ever since he became seriously involved in politics, though I still feel a bit of a fraud. I think you need a black skin for this style. I just feel I look weedy and washed out.'

'I think it looks nice,' he insisted, not very convincingly.

'You're very kind,' she said in cynical tones reminiscent of her husband. Just then there was a loud and prolonged burst of applause from the garden.

'Looks like you've missed the end,' he said.

'Yes, I'd better find Sam.' She seemed to have lost some of her poise. 'Listen,' she said suddenly. 'Do you really want to speak to him?'

Morgan was confused. 'Well . . . Yes, actually, I suppose I would rather, but . . . unofficially, you know.' He smiled shamefacedly. 'He didn't seem too keen.'

'He wasn't on his home ground. He's always more . . . difficult then. That's why you should come to his birthday party.'

'Birthday?'

'Yes. It's next week. Friday night at the Hotel de Executive.' She enunciated the name carefully, conscious of its pretensions. 'Do you know it?'

Morgan nodded. 'It's on the way into town from here.'

'Good,' she said. 'I'll send you an invitation. You can be my guest.'

'Are you sure he won't mind?' Morgan asked. 'I mean, I won't be intruding or anything, will I? Do I need to bring a present?'

She laughed out loud. 'No, no,' she said. 'There'll be about three hundred people there. But don't worry. I'll tell him you'll be there. Look, I must be off.'

Morgan felt mingled sensations of relief and gratitude. 'That's amazingly kind of you, Mrs Adekunle. I'm indebted to you. Very.'

'Not at all,' she said. 'See you on Friday.'

Chapter 5

The Commission staff waved goodbye to the last of the departing cars. Morgan stood on the steps beside Jones and Fanshawe; behind them, as though assembled for a photograph, were Mrs Fanshawe, Priscilla, Mrs Jones and her children and another expatriate couple Morgan didn't recognize. He glanced at his watch: it was just after ten, he was to pick Hazel up at eleven.

'Great success,' Jones opined, his Welsh accent seeming to Morgan's ears stronger than ever. 'Marvellous film, I thought, marvellous. So . . . so *relaxed*, wasn't it? How you imagine they must really be, you know, behind the scenes, like.'

Fanshawe grunted absentmindedly. Morgan said nothing, he was thinking about Hazel, now that Celia Adekunle had solved his more immediate problem. Jones moved off in search of more enthusiastic appraisals.

'How did you get on?' Fanshawe asked immediately, snapping Morgan out of his sex-dream. 'I tried to sound him out a little myself. Tricky customer I thought,' he said grudgingly. 'Surprisingly . . . I don't know – sophisticated. Very confident man.' He paused. 'So, how did it go?'

Morgan inspected his fingernails. 'Oh, not too bad,' he said modestly, extracting maximum mileage from his stroke of good fortune. 'He's invited me to a party he's giving next Friday – his birthday party in fact.'

Fanshawe's face lit up with delighted surprise. 'But that's absolutely marvellous, Morgan. Marvellous. Great progress. Where's the party?'

'Hotel de Executive, in town.'

'Splendid. Into the lion's den, eh? How did he react to your moves?'

'He's a wary sort of character,' Morgan said evasively. 'I

was just sounding him out really. He seems . . . approachable, anyway.'

'Going well though,' Fanshawe said. 'A good night's work, well worth setting the whole thing up.' He looked round. 'Do you know the Wagners?' he asked, referring to the couple Morgan hadn't recognized. 'He's from the American consulate in the capital. Come and meet them. We're all going over to the house for a drink.'

'Oh, I'll give it a miss if you don't mind, Arthur,' he said. 'Been a long day.'

'Fine, fine. Please yourself.' They joined the group gathered round the front door and Morgan was presented to the Wagners – the 'w' was not pronounced as a 'v'. Errol and Nancy Wagner had greatly enjoyed the film, it transpired. Mrs Fanshawe turned to Morgan, just as he was about to speak to Priscilla, and smiled at him, but only with her mouth. Her eyes remained suspicious and probing.

'Joining us for a drink, Morgan?' she asked unpersuasively.

'No, I'm afraid I'm . . .'

'Shame. Never mind.' She turned to the others. 'Come on everybody, let's go Geraldine? Are the children all right? . . .' The party moved off leaving Morgan alone with Priscilla. She had established the beginnings of a tan which was offset by a straight white and green sleeveless dress and white shoes. Morgan began by apologizing as he could sense she was a little upset by his neglect of her.

'I *am* sorry, Priscilla,' he said. 'But it was semi-official buttering up of a local dignitary.'

'Well, it wasn't much fun for me.'

He stole a look at the backs of the retreating group, almost invisible in the darkness now, and gave Priscilla a fraternal kiss on the cheek.

'It wasn't exactly fun for me either,' he said reproachfully. 'I'd much rather have been with you.' She was looking very fanciable tonight, he thought. If only she'd get rid of that sulky, hard-done-by expression.

'But why can't you come along now? Honestly, Morgie, I haven't talked to you all day.'

Every tendon and sinew in his body seemed to go into spasm, triggered by the revolting diminutive she'd recently adopted. Did he look remotely like a 'Morgie' he wondered, nauseated? Where the hell had she dug that up from? No one had ever called him that, ever. With an effort he controlled himself and tried to think of a reasonable excuse. He thought for a moment. 'Tell you what,' he said. 'Do you fancy going fishing next week? Make a day of it? Picnic and all that,' he improvised hastily, silently thanking the Royal Family for inspiring him.

'Fishing?'

'Yes. It's great fun. I've done it once or twice. A place about seventy miles away. Called Olokomeji.'

'Well . . . Yes.' She thought about it. 'Sounds lovely.'

'Great,' Morgan exclaimed, hugely relieved. 'Don't worry. I'll make all the arrangements.' He put his hands on her shoulders. 'See you tomorrow maybe. I'm really bushed. Sorry,' he abased himself again. He kissed her on the lips, allowing his own to linger there a moment or so, but he sensed that nothing more passionate was likely to ensue. He understood implicitly that in the rules of the game they were playing his behaviour had been less than satisfactory tonight – even though the prospect of the fishing trip had mollified her slightly – and he would have to take his punishment like a man.

Chapter 6

The road to Olokomeji was quiet and through thick rain-forest. They had made an early start, at around seven, as the river was a two and a half hour ride away from Nkongsamba. Every now and then they would pass a small cluster of mud huts and roadside trading stalls that marked a village. The fascinated stares Morgan and Priscilla attracted spoke of the curiosity value that still attended white people as soon as the main roads and towns were left behind. Morgan had got Moses to make up a picnic of a cold roast chicken and sandwiches and he had also filled a cooler-bag with fridge-chilled bottles of beer. They stopped at one of the larger villages to buy fruit: a pineapple, oranges and bananas. Priscilla said she was entranced by the primitive nature of it all but her subdued demeanour seemed to tell another story as she unexcitedly took in the naked children, women pounding cassava in wooden tubs and slack-breasted old mammies expertly chopping sugar cane. Priscilla wore a red polka-dot dress with large white buttons down the front. When she removed her sunglasses she had dark rings under her eyes.

As they approached the large bridge across the river that marked the fishing pool Morgan kept his eyes peeled for the secluded turning that would lead them down to the bottom of the gorge. He saw it at the last moment and had to reverse back. It was a rutted laterite track that wound gingerly down the thickly forested slope to a small clearing. There he stopped the car and got out. The great pale-barked trees towered above them screening the sun, birds and insects chattered and buzzed setting up a surprising volume of noise. A well-trodden path led down to the fishing pool.

Morgan pounded his chest, 'Aaah-ooah-ooah, ooah-ooah!' he bellowed, adding in a throaty basso profundo: 'me Jane.'

It wasn't very funny, any wood or copse prompted the

same display, but as expected, it made Priscilla giggle. 'You are a silly,' she said. That was better, he thought, she needed to cheer up a bit – she had probably never been forced to get up this early for ages. They unloaded the picnic gear and the fishing rods and walked down to the river. To their right, about two hundred yards upstream and almost obscured by a bend in the river, were the high arches of the road bridge. The river was about fifty yards across and the colour of milky coffee. Ten or fifteen yards out into the stream from where they were standing were some rock outcrops beyond which were the deep pools where the Niger perch lurked. The far bank rose in a steepish rocky cliff amongst whose boulders and crannies lived a colony of baboons. It was very quiet. The sky was a washed-out blue and the water was so sluggish it seemed hardly to be moving.

'Pretty spectacular eh?' Morgan commented proudly, as if he owned it. 'Real *Heart of Darkness* stuff don't you think?'

'What's that?'

'Real *Heart of. . .* nothing. Not important.'

'Are you sure it's all right to swim in that?' Priscilla asked. 'It looks filthy.'

'Of course it is,' Morgan said, putting his arm round her shoulders and pecking her on the cheek. 'All right to swim in I mean. Here, give us a hand to spread this groundsheet.' They laid the groundsheet on the narrow bar of greyish sand at the bank. Morgan opened a bottle of beer, put it to his lips and took a long swig.

'Right,' he said. 'Into the swimming togs.' He had marked this particular activity as being a significant pointer as to how the rest of the day would go and also to indicate the extent to which his intimacy with Priscilla had spread. In the case of his previous companion at this very spot, the Rubenesque moustachioed wife of the Fiat dealer, the untamed prim-itiveness of the scene had inspired her to abandon all clothing for the duration of their stay, and she and Morgan had splashed about, fished and fucked like a couple of beefy naked survivors of some nuclear holocaust. But for all their spontaneous noble savagery he had felt that their soft pampered bodies, their tender skins and sunburnt buttocks, their chilled Gancia and paper cups made them a shouting crude anachronism in the wild and uncultivated landscape. He expected no such transformation from Priscilla but he hoped that they would not, at least, need to observe the traditional modest conventions when changing into their swimming suits. However he was considerably disappointed when Priscilla unbuttoned her dress and stepped out of it to reveal her swimsuit already on underneath. It was navy blue, high necked, and its stretched nylon outlined a complicated armature of plastic boning around the bust: it was the sort of costume worn by the captains of girls' school swimming teams.

A little put out, and suddenly lacking the naturist fervour of a moment ago, he wrapped a towel around his waist and with difficulty lowered his underpants and eased up his swimming shorts, a pair of psychedelically patterned surfin' baggies imported from the USA and purchased at the local Kingsway stores. They fully covered his ham-like thighs and, he reasoned, the dazzling swirl of colours should distract attention from his overflowing gut.

'Goodness,' was all Priscilla could say when he whipped away the towel with a flourish. She seemed to be in an unresponsive mood so he set about making up and then baiting the rods with finger-thick worms dug from the garden compost heap that morning by Friday. Purple gunge and clotted pus-like oozings soon covered his fingers as he looped and skewered the worms on the large hooks. Priscilla turned away as he did this; it made her sick, she said. She was definitely moody today, he decided. They waded out to the largest of the rock outcrops. The water was bath-warm almost, the river bed yielding mud. Priscilla spread her towel on a large flat-topped boulder while Morgan sloshed back for the beer. That secured, he cast Priscilla's line out into the pool and wedged it in the rocks by her head.

'You're here to fish you know,' he mock-rebuked her, 'not sunbathe. You can sunbathe any day at the club.'

'Oh don't be such a bore,' she said, lying flat on her back, her eyes closed, her hands by her side, palms down. 'This is lovely.'

Morgan did a little dance of rage on his own adjacent rock, silently mouthing imprecations and waving v-signs at her. This was not how she was meant to behave. Still, there was plenty of time, he considered; it was only mid-morning. Olokomeji always had a calming effect on him. The sun beat down, a car buzzed by on the road bridge, the float on his line hung steady in the pool. He took a great throat-pulsing swig from his beer bottle, the chill bitter fluid sluicing down his throat, contentment spreading through his veins with the alcohol.

Two hours later the river and its banks swam in a pleasant alcoholic haze. Morgan had donned an old bush hat and draped a shirt across his shoulders to protect him from the sun's heat, which was becoming intense as it reached its zenith. He had recast his line several times, but the original worm still remained on its hook. He was about to suggest lunch and a siesta when Priscilla exclaimed without looking up.

'What's that rattling noise? Is it you, Morgan?' He looked over and saw her rod leaping and quivering in spastic rage, the fibreglass whipping and bending as though suddenly animate. He scrambled over.

'Christ. Bloody hell! You've caught a fish,' he shouted, grabbing the rod which bucked and tugged in his hand as he vigorously wound in her catch. Priscilla watched in fascination by his side.

'God . . . it's, it's quite a . . . big one, too,' he grunted in amazement. He had never caught a fish at Olokomeji.

The fish was shortly hauled thrashing into the shallows

around the rock outcrop. Morgan thrust the rod into Priscilla's hand and clambered down. Taking some loops of line around his hand he hauled the jerking fish out of the water. It was a Niger perch, looked to be about six pounds, a thick solid grey thing with a blunt face. He heaved it up onto the flat top of the rock where it flipped and quivered on the hot surface.

The fish's one visible eye seemed to stare hostilely as they looked down on it.

'Shouldn't you kill it?' Priscilla suggested. 'You can't just let it bake and, well, die like that.' Morgan agreed. The only problem was he had never caught a fish that large – two feet long and heavy – and had never considered how one should go about putting them out of their misery. Did successful fishermen carry guns for this purpose, he wondered vaguely, or electric stunning devices?

He pressed his palm down on the slippery object and with his other hand wrenched and levered the hook free from its mouth. This new agony prompted the fish to renew its efforts and it bounced and floundered wildly about the rock.

'Don't let it fall back in!' Priscilla squealed.

Morgan grabbed the perch with both hands, its bulk preventing his fingers from meeting on either side. It was like holding a disembodied thigh muscle, cut from a leg, yet still pulsing with life. The tiddlers he'd caught in his past had been easily dealt with: the tail between finger and thumb and the head flipped on a nearby stone. He thought he would try a variation on this method and still clutching the exhausted fish he kneeled towards some uneven projections at one end of the rock.

'Quickly,' yelped Priscilla. 'Put the poor thing out of its misery.'

Easier said than done you stupid bitch, Morgan swore under his breath, and tentatively slapped its head against the rock. The fish, inspired to one final effort by this blow, twisted and jack-knifed out of his hands and fell off the edge of the rock and down onto a sand bar that ran between this and the next outcrop.

Swearing vilely Morgan jumped down after it and seized the twitching fish for the last time.

'Right, you little bastard,' he snarled through gritted teeth. 'Now get this,' and he smashed its upper half against the rock side. Once, twice, three times. Bits of flesh and blood splattered onto his forearms and very soon the fish felt inert and limp.

'You haven't spoilt it, have you?' Priscilla asked in a trembling voice.

Morgan looked up. Priscilla stood on the rock edge above him. He turned the fish over; a doll's eye dangled from the pulp he'd made of its head. Silver scales glinted from the rock.

'No,' he said. 'It'll be fine.' He stood up, damp sand sticking to his legs; fish blood covered fingers and knuckles and trickled in thin rivulets to drip from his forearms. He leapt, with as much agility as he could muster, back up the rocks onto the flat surface.

'There you are,' he said huskily, his chest heaving from the effort. 'Your fish.'

Morgan and Priscilla ate their lunch in an uneasy silence. She had become quite subdued while he tore at a chicken leg with pagan gusto. His mind raced exultantly. Christ, he thought to himself, D. H. Lawrence couldn't have arranged or directed that episode any more skilfully: the violence, the blood, the male aggression, the admiring female – the very air throbbed with felt life. Furthermore, Morgan suddenly thought, if D H L was anywhere near right she should be a pushover now.

Priscilla lay back on her towel. 'Ouch!' she yipped almost immediately and sat up again craning her hand round behind her back. Morgan saw a stunned large black ant wobble uncertainly across the towelling surface.

'There's your culprit,' he pointed and watched Priscilla

flatten it with the heel of her sandal. Great, he thought, now we've both killed.

'God, that was sore,' she complained turning her back to him. He saw the bite, a sixpence-sized weal just to the left of the top bump of her vertebrae. He covered it with his lips and licked the swelling gently.

'There,' he said and took her in his arms. They kissed and he lowered her back down onto the towel. He leant on his elbow looking down on her face. Lovingly he brushed her fringe aside with his fingers, then kissed her again with a conscious display of passionate abandon.

This continued for a couple of minutes before Morgan stopped and re-adopted his elbow-leaning posture. He casually slipped the right hand strap of her bathing suit off her shoulder. 'You know,' he said in what he thought was the correct tone of childlike rebuke, 'I'm getting dangerously fond of you.' Priscilla lay back, her lips slightly parted. Perhaps she had had too much beer, Morgan wondered, hence her passivity. She ran her hand through his hair. He wished she wouldn't do that.

'Why dangerous?' she asked teasingly.

Morgan slid the other strap down as far as it would go and bent to kiss her collar bone. 'Because,' he looked at her seriously, and summoned up all his courage, 'I think I may be falling in love with you . . .'

'Oh Morgie,' she sighed and put her arms round his neck pulling herself up so she could kiss him, and, as she did so he hooked his fingers onto the back of her bathing suit and tugged it down. He felt the coolness of a freed breast against his own. He rolled her back onto the towel. A pale-pink nipple showed above the dark blue nylon of the swimsuit. Carefully he uncovered the other and slipped Priscilla's arms out of the shoulder straps as if he were undressing a child. Her conical breasts were unbelievably firm, girlish and gravity-defying, standing straight up from her chest. Morgan kissed them reverently, they were cold and flecked with tiny sand grains. Priscilla lay still with an uncertain look on her face and her shoulders hunched as if she wasn't entirely sure how she had come to find herself in this position.

Morgan knelt beside her. 'You're very beautiful,' he said in proper tones of awe. He undid the waist strings of his swimming shorts, stood up and jammed his thumbs into his waist band. 'Very beautiful,' he repeated, and pushed down his swimming shorts, noticing as he did so that Priscilla hadn't moved. He had eased them round his buttocks when Priscilla suddenly said,

'Morgan. For goodness sake what are you doing?'

He hauled his shorts back up and dropped down beside her again. He kissed her face and neck. Stupid of him, he thought, to get the sequence wrong. 'I'm sorry, my love,' he said, sliding his hand beneath her swimsuit which was now bunched around her waist. She drew up her knees protectively.

'No, don't, Morgan, please.'

'But why, my darling? I *am* in love with you, I told you.' He tried to keep the whine out of his voice. Priscilla sat up and fitted the front of her swimsuit to her breasts. Morgan looked on in empty disbelief. She smiled sadly at him and rested her forehead on his. She kissed his nose.

'I know you are, Morgie,' she said with a note of assurance he found irritating. 'But I *can't*. Not today. Couldn't you tell, you silly? It's my time of the month.'

They were back in Nkongsamba by early evening, several hours earlier than planned. Priscilla asked him to pull into the side of the road before they reached the Commission. She took his right hand in her two.

'It was a lovely day,' she said. 'You were so sweet. I'm only sorry . . .'

'No, *I'm sorry*,' he said. He meant it too. 'Stupid of me,

incredibly.' They left it at that and sat in silence for a while. Morgan felt faintly sick, as though he'd eaten a huge cream tea or five bars of chocolate.

'Mor?' she said tentatively.

More what? he asked himself, until he realized with a renewed attack of nausea that his name had been reduced even further.

'Yes?'

'Did you . . . did you mean what you said?'

'About what?'

'About me . . . about how you feel.'

He leant over and kissed her. 'Of course,' he said quickly. She hung on to him tightly for a second.

'Oh I shall miss you,' she said fervently.

'Miss me?' he demanded. 'Where the . . . where are you going?'

'Didn't I say? I meant to tell you. Mummy and I are going to stay with the Wagners for a few days.' She squeezed his arm. 'But I'll hurry back.' She kissed his cheek and opened the door. 'Don't bother to come in.' She got out and shut the door blowing him a kiss through the open window. 'See you in a few days.'

Morgan reached behind him for a soggy newspaper-wrapped bundle. 'Here,' he said, trying to keep the bitterness out of his voice. 'Don't forget your fish.'

He turned the car round and drove directly back to town to the hotel where Hazel was currently living. He impatiently tooted his horn for five minutes until the proprietor emerged to see what all the fuss was about.

'Hazel?' Morgan asked. 'I'm waiting for Hazel.'

The proprietor spread his empty hands. 'Sorry, sah,' he said compassionately. 'She no dey. Nevah come home last night.'

That was when Morgan decided he had to find a flat for her.

Chapter 7

Celia Adekunle's invitation arrived as promised and Morgan and Fanshawe discussed the impending party in some detail. Morgan had earlier pressed for some additional bait other than Britain's goodwill in an attempt to lure Adekunle away from a position that looked to be securely on the fence.

'It's just not enough,' Morgan was saying on the Friday morning before the party, 'to let him know that we're rooting for his victory. We need something else to make a more binding alliance.'

'True,' Fanshawe admitted, 'but we don't want the man to feel that he gets our support as a matter of course.'

'No,' Morgan agreed cautiously.

'If anything we want him to feel grateful to us for this early recognition. Indebted.'

'Yes. Well, I'm not so sure.' Not for the first time Morgan wondered if he and Fanshawe were thinking along the same lines.

'I was on the phone to the capital this morning,' Fanshawe told him. 'They're pleased with the way things are going, very pleased. It looks more and more like the KNP are favourites for the election and they want us to press ahead. They want to get Adekunle to London.'

'London!'

'Yes, some time before the elections. But only once we're sure of his attitude.'

'I'm not sure if we . . .' Morgan began dubiously.

'Nonsense,' Fanshawe waved away his reservations. 'Tell you what though. Offer it to him as a kind of reward: you know, first class tickets, couple of nights at Claridges. That should bring him into line,' Fanshawe said confidently. Morgan wondered if they were talking about the same Adekunle. Fanshawe's approach seemed to belong to another age, as if plane tickets and hotel reservations were an updated version of beads and blankets.

Morgan sat there, his face heavy with scepticism. 'Cheer up,' Fanshawe said. 'We're practically granting the KNP official recognition before a vote's been cast. He can't turn up his nose at that. Why man, he should be eating out of your hand.'

So it had been agreed. As a gesture of goodwill – once Adekunle's pro-British stance had been confirmed – he was to fly to London courtesy of the British taxpayer. Morgan was unhappy about this move. It seemed to take too much for granted, and that night as he drove into town he was in a considerable state of nervousness. Fanshawe was expecting great things of him but for all he knew Adekunle might chuck him out as a gatecrasher.

The Hotel de Executive was a four-storey all-concrete L-shaped block set some way back from the road in a high-walled compound. The kerb outside was thronged with parked cars and he had to drive several hundred yards up the road before he could find a gap for himself. He was surprised to find the hotel compound almost deserted. A few young men sat aimlessly around tin tables but he heard a thump of music and the din of conversation which seemed to be coming from around the back of the hotel. In the foyer he presented his invitation to a girl sitting at a table and was directed down a dark corridor. Emerging from this he found himself in a large courtyard formed by two sides of the L and squared off by a kind of raised, covered gallery. He stood at the angle of the L: on his left was a band and in front of them a concrete dance floor. All round this, tables and chairs had been set and opposite the band on the raised gallery was a long bamboo-fronted bar. Lights shone down from the side of the hotel, and coloured bulbs were strung around the courtyard.

The place was packed with guests. Morgan could see a few white faces but most of the guests were black and wearing vibrant Kinjanjan costume. He edged his way self-consciously towards the bar. Above the band stretched a huge banner with 'HAPPY B'DAY SAM!' written on it, and below that another saying 'ACTION TODAY! VOTE KNP! VOTE SAM ADEKUNLE!' As far as Morgan could see there was no sign of the man in question, nor of his wife. The heat was intense, what with the lights and the press of people, and the noise was almost intolerable. The band was blaring out brassy highlife music at conversation-stopping level yet the conversation went on, excited and shrill. He ordered a beer but his money was waved away. Free drink for this mob, he thought, impressed; Adekunle was certainly being generous. He sipped at his beer and surveyed the crowd. He saw a few familiar faces: the mayor of Nkongsamba for one, Ola Dunyodi – Kinjanja's most famous playwright – for another, and various of Adekunle's university colleagues. The whole scene was reminiscent of an American electoral campaign, Morgan thought, right down to the hookers. For, hovering round the bar, were a number of gaudily dressed girls in the latest Western fashions, with huge lacquered wigs and expensive jewellery. Probably imported from the capital Morgan thought, they looked too fast for Nkongsamba.

There was a touch at his elbow. It was Georg Muller, the saw-mill owner and West German chargé d'affaires. He was in his early fifties with a creased, tired-looking face. Sometimes he looked ill too, but tonight it was only fatigue. He had yellowy stained teeth and a straggly wiry goatee that reminded Morgan of leek roots. He was wearing an unironed white shirt and mustard coloured trousers that almost matched his smile.

'I like the suit, Morgan,' he said. He had a hoarse Teutonic drawl, as if he were just recovering from laryngitis. 'A business suit, yes?'

'No,' Morgan said feeling embarrassingly spruced-up beside Muller's rumpled ease. 'I'm going on somewhere. I just popped in.'

'I didn't know you were a friend of Sam's,' Muller said.

'I've met him once or twice . . . Celia invited me.'

'Aah. The lovely Celia.' Muller waved his glass at the courtyard. 'Quite a party. Have you seen the tarts? They say Adekunle flew some of them in front Lagos and Abidjan. He'll be impressing a lot of people tonight. Still, I wish him luck.'

'Is that official BRD policy?' Morgan asked.

Muller laughed. 'It won't make much difference to us whoever wins. No, I'm speaking as a businessman. Sam buys a lot of wood from me and if he wins – well, you know how these things work – business will boom.'

Morgan was curious. 'What does a Professor of Economics want with wood?'

'Hell, man,' Muller said. 'He owns the biggest construction company in the Mid-West: Ussman Danda Ltd. Where have you been living these last years, Morgan?'

Morgan blushed. There was nothing in the Kingpin file on this. He knew the name, there were even commercials on the TV for it. 'Is that common knowledge?' he asked.

Muller shrugged and stroked his goatee. 'A few people know about it,' he said. 'It's not a very great secret. I thought you would have heard it somewhere.'

Morgan changed the subject. 'Are these tarts on the house too? Like the beer?'

'Why don't you try and see?'

'No thanks.' A few people were out on the dance floor, shuffling rhythmically around in the pronounced stick-arsed fashion of highlife as the band thumped and perspired away manfully. Morgan glanced out of the side of his eye at Muller. His wife was long dead and it was rumoured that he slept with his cook's thirteen-year-old daughter. But Muller never gave anything away and Morgan suspected that the story – like most of the poisonous anecdotes floating round Nkongsamba – had its source in a vindictive, drunken midnight conversation. Muller looked too ascetic for sex, Morgan decided, like some life-long opium-toker, genitals withered and redundant. He found it rather disgusting that he should be speculating on the state of Muller's loins so he changed the subject.

A short while later there was a commotion at the door as a passageway was cleared through the crowd and Adekunle appeared, flanked by a praesidium guard, waving his short stick above his head. The band halted in mid-number and there was a great shout from the assembled guests and a burst of tumultuous applause. 'KNP. KNP. KNP,' they chanted.

Tonight Adekunle more than ever resembled an African Henry VIII. His already considerable girth was amplified by the voluminous folds of his native costume which was white, trimmed and embroidered with gold thread. He moved slowly among his guests shaking hands, waving and smiling broadly. Some people bowed, others genuflected, ducking down and brushing the floor in front of him with the fingers of their right hand.

'Of course,' Morgan whispered to Muller, 'he's a chief isn't he?'

'One of the biggest,' Muller replied, 'his father owned virtually all of Nkongsamba before the British took it away.'

'Did they?' Morgan said, astonished.

'Oh yes. Compulsory purchase, sometime before the war. I think they gave him about two hundred pounds for it.' He paused, an amused look in his eye as he saw Morgan digesting this information. 'Look,' he added. 'There's Celia.' Morgan looked and saw Celia Adekunle amongst the others in Adekunle's train. She was wearing a rich red and blue native costume, her thin face small under the hugely knotted head-tie. She was smiling in a strained unrelaxed way as she received and returned greetings from and to the party faithful. He suddenly felt very sorry for her.

Adekunle returned eventually to the centre of the dance floor where a small dais had been placed. He took up his position on this and raised his hands to still the applause.

'My friends,' his voice boomed out powerfully. 'My friends, thank you, thank you. I just have a few words for you tonight. As the saying goes, "Make sure you fit talk, fore dey drink all de beer."' The burst of pidgin English brought shrieks of delighted laughter and foot stamping. Morgan and Muller took this opportunity to withdraw to the bar where snatches of Adekunle's speech came to them over the packed heads of the spectators. There was a great deal of bellowed rhetoric and crude mud-slinging in it, and at one point Morgan caught a glimpse of the politician, his face distorted with emphasis, brandishing his stick, his broad shoulders heaving as he vilified the policies of an opponent. Morgan knew that for the sake of Project Kingpin he really ought to try and listen more closely but demagoguery seemed to switch off vital circuits in his brain. As the shouts of passionate agreement began to crescendo Morgan whispered in Muller's ear.

'He's a different man on a platform, isn't he.'

'They expect it,' Muller said. 'They think that if a man can't make his voice heard then his argument must be weak.'

Morgan was suddenly conscious of his almost total inexperience. 'How long have you been out here, Georg?' he asked.

'In Kinjanja? Since 1948. But before that I was in the Cameroons.'

'Think Adekunle's going to win?' he said as casually as possible.

'He'll win here in the Mid-West. And I should think the KNP will win overall. That is, if the Army let them.'

Morgan nodded sagely in agreement. What the hell did the Army have to do with it? he asked himself in confusion.

'I don't see any Army boys here tonight, do you?' he asked spontaneously, playing for time.

Muller scanned the crowd. 'You're right,' he said. 'Good point. Not even in mufti. Of course, politicians are very unpopular with the military just now.'

Morgan felt vaguely excited by his lucky observation, but

143

a little confused as to its ramifications. Still, he had actually gathered some information tonight. He could now say to Fanshawe, 'Do you know, there wasn't a single Army boy at Adekunle's party. Very interesting I think,' and Fanshawe wouldn't have the faintest idea what he was talking about, but he'd be impressed just the same. Following up on his good fortune Morgan recalled a headline in a local newspaper about recent Army promotions.

'Interesting reshuffles going on at the barracks,' he said to Muller out of the side of his mouth.

Muller nodded. 'Orimi–Peters is a Moslem, you know.'

'That's right,' Morgan said. 'Very interesting.' The opaque cloudy void of his ignorance seemed to stretch away in front of him. He decided he'd better stop talking before Muller realized he was a complete fraud. He felt suddenly rather ashamed of himself. Kinjanja was a mystery to him, he realized, he knew next to nothing about the way its inhabitants' minds worked, the way its colonially imposed institutional superstructure related with the traditional tribal background; he knew nothing of the ethnic, racial and religious pressures surreptitiously influencing events. He felt suddenly like leaving and was aware of an absurd resentment directed at Muller, with his assured range of knowledge and his calm experience. Perhaps that's what comes of sleeping with your servant's children, he observed cruelly, and was immediately further ashamed by his mean-mindedness. A prolonged cheering outburst signalled the end of Adekunle's speech at that point.

'Have another drink?' Morgan asked Muller, as if to make up for his pusillanimous thoughts.

'No thanks,' Muller said. 'Only one a night. Doctor's orders.'

'Not Dr Murray, I trust,' Morgan said scornfully.

'Alex Murray?' Muller asked. 'I wish it was, but you have to be in the university to get him.'

'At least he's consistent,' Morgan sneered.

'Oh he's very consistent,' Muller said, misinterpreting. 'A very consistent man.'

Muller left shortly after that, and Morgan chatted for a while to some people from the university he knew and wondered how he was going to get near enough to Adekunle to put his new proposition to him. He spent a fair bit of time actively building up his confidence which had slipped alarmingly low since arriving at the Hotel de Executive. He felt like some medieval underling trying to present a suit to a feudal lord or overweight bishop, or one of those minor characters in Shakespeare's Roman plays who intrude upon the principals with petty wrangles about legacies or property disputes. Adekunle's stature and prestige now impressed itself on him much more forcefully as a result of the massive adulation and respect the assembled dignitaries were offering up. He felt simultaneously the unreality, stupidity and ill-conceived nature of Fanshawe's 'mission' for him. He and Fanshawe were like a couple of retarded kids playing a game together as the real world rumbled by unaffected.

'Cheer up,' Celia Adekunle said coming up to him. 'Why so gloomy? It's meant to be a party, you know.'

'Sorry,' he said glumly. 'Lot on my mind.'

'Really?' she said. 'Anything I can do?'

Morgan laughed more harshly than he intended. 'I doubt it,' he said. Then, 'Sorry. Thanks for asking, but it's not that important. I must say that's a splendid . . . um, outfit you're wearing.' The cloth was heavy and the colours glowing, and she wore a lot of gold around her neck and wrists.

'Thank you,' she said without much enthusiasm. 'I don't wear this stuff all the time, you know, I'd hate you to think I'd gone totally native.' The surprising stress she put on this last word embarrassed them both. Morgan looked away.

'Big crowd,' he said. 'Is there any chance of talking to your husband, do you think? Or is that a vain hope?'

'You're very keen to see Sam, aren't you,' she said thoughtfully, lighting a cigarette. 'I told him you were coming. He's expecting you.'

'Oh,' Morgan said gratefully. 'That's very good of you.'

'That's O K ,' Celia Adekunle said, scrutinizing him through a cloud of smoke. 'Just wait until the official meeting and greeting is over.'

'Right,' Morgan said. 'Let me get you a drink in the meantime.' He replenished her glass and stood chatting to her for a while. He asked her where she and Adekunle had met.

'Sheffield of all places,' she said. 'Sam did his B A there. I was secretary to his professor. Sam had some trouble at one time with his bursary and so I saw a lot of him in the office one term, getting forms signed and letters written.' She paused. 'He was so different from the other students. Much older of course, very ambitious and somehow experienced, even though he was at a bit of a loss in Sheffield at first. It wasn't much fun being a black student in those days. We went out together a few times . . . got our share of strange looks.'

'When did you get married?' Morgan prompted, feeling mildly interested.

'Sam went off to Harvard to do his PhD. He came back suddenly after a year and asked me to marry him, and I did.' She shrugged. 'We had two years in the States. My first boy was born there. Then we came here.'

Morgan smiled awkwardly. The story had been delivered in a curiously dead-pan tone. He wasn't sure what to make of it. 'So you're a secretary by trade,' he said lamely.

'No, I started off as a nurse. But I couldn't stick it. My mother had been a midwife and I was rather forced into the profession. But it's not something you can just *do*. You have to be a certain kind of person. It just got me down. Sick people all the time, people dying.' She gave a brittle clear laugh. 'I should have been a midwife. Get people going, instead of meeting them at the end of the race.'

'So you became a secretary.' Morgan felt his line of questioning was uninspired to say the least, but she seemed happy to talk about herself.

'I was waiting round, undecided. It seemed a good stop-gap, but then I found I quite liked it, especially working in a university. Intelligent people all around you, all that. My boss was nice too.'

'Sam's professor,' Morgan suspected that there was another story there too.

'Yes. He was a kind man. He . . . Then,' she made a mock-dramatic gesture, 'Sam Adekunle walked into my life, needing a signature on a bursary form.'

Morgan saw it all: the bored, frustrated secretary; Adekunle – black, potent. A chief's son, no doubt hints dropped of great wealth and limitless tribal lands. The sense of failure prompting a spirit of rebellion: go out with a black man, show how free you are, how you spurn the conventions of your life . . .

'I know what you're thinking,' she said. 'But I can assure you it wasn't how you imagine.' Morgan protested vehemently. 'It's alright,' she said, 'I know what they say about the white wives of Kinjanjans out here, and it's probably fairly accurate. But with Sam it wasn't like that. He was quite a different person in those days.'

Morgan found himself blushing. 'Look,' he insisted, 'I wasn't thinking anything, for heaven's sake.'

'I believe you,' she smiled. 'Relax. Only it's just that I haven't spoken about me and Sam for ages. And I do know what the expats say, I've been on the receiving end of enough nasty gossip.'

'Please. Don't classify me as a typical expat. Anything but.'

'Sorry,' she said. 'But I became pretty good at recognizing that "look" in people's eyes.' She jokingly speared two fingers at Morgan's eyes. 'I thought I saw it flashing there.' She glanced over her shoulder, 'Oh good,' she said. 'I think Sam's available now.'

★

Adekunle steered Morgan into a corner of the courtyard. He muttered something to one of his aides. 'Don't worry,' he said to Morgan. 'We won't be disturbed.'

Morgan looked about him. 'Isn't there somewhere less . . . exposed?'

Adekunle's laugh boomed out. 'My dear fellow, it would attract far more attention if I were seen leaving my own birthday party with you.' Morgan realized he was right.

'I found your speech very interesting,' he said.

'Did you?' Adekunle asked sceptically. 'And how does the Deputy High Commission rate the KNP's chances?'

'Good.' Morgan drew the word out as if it were the product of long deliberation. 'If the Army let you.' Adekunle looked at him sharply. Morgan was gratified by the accuracy of his shot in the dark.

'What do you mean by that?' Adekunle said with more interest.

'I don't think we need to go into detail, do we?'

'As you wish,' Adekunle said. 'We'll take a rain-check on it, as the saying goes. Anyway, Mr Leafy, I believe you wanted to talk to me.'

Morgan took a deep breath. 'I'm here – unofficially – to convey the, how shall I put it? *less* unofficial nature of Britain's, um, interest in the fortunes of the KNP.'

Adekunle thought about this. 'I see,' he said. 'But you shouldn't be talking to me. I am only, as our French friends say, a *fonctionnaire*.'

'Ah yes. But an important one. Certainly in the field of foreign affairs.'

'Just a supposition, Mr Leafy. I don't even know yet if I will be a member of the National Assembly.'

Morgan smiled patiently. 'You have a point there. But, after all, a lot of diplomacy never gets further than supposition. And, on the strength of *this* one we . . . we would be interested in preliminary consultation with the, ah, putative Foreign

Minister.' Morgan finished, he was quite pleased with the way he'd expressed himself and with his neat ambiguities.

'Consultation?' queried Adekunle.

'In London,' Morgan said.

'I see. In London.'

'Yes,' Morgan said, suppressing his impatience. This dainty circumlocution was suddenly getting on his nerves. 'We will be happy to arrange the flight – first class of course – and your accommodation.'

'In Claridges, I assume,' Adekunle said with a broad grin.

'Well, yes, as a matter of fact.' Morgan was surprised.

Adekunle gave a loud laugh. 'My good God,' he said. 'You British are indeed astonishing. You still think that all you need to do to get an African politician eating out of your hands is to offer first class air tickets and bed and breakfast at Claridges.' He wheezed with laughter. A few people nearby looked round and started to laugh too.

'Thank you,' Adekunle said finally. 'Thank you for your offer. I will see if I can fit it into my itinerary.'

'Itinerary?' Morgan repeated, nonplussed. 'Do you mean . . . ?'

'Yes, my dear Mr British Deputy High Commission man. You are a very late bird to catch this worm, as the saying goes. Once I've been to Washington, Paris, Bonn and Rome I'll see if I can drop in on London. Thank you again, Mr Leafy,' he said still smiling. 'No wonder the Empire went. Yes?' He broke off and wandered away to speak to his waiting guests.

Morgan ordered a whisky and soda from the barman. The hot blush had left his face but he felt his ears were still glowing. That stupid old fool Fanshawe, he railed to himself, nothing but shame, disgrace and public humiliation had attached itself to this spectacularly misconceived piece of under-the-counter dealing, and most of it was particularly closely associated with him. He heard Adekunle's laugh above the hum of conversation and imagined him amusing his friends with the details of their recent conversation.

The barman put down his glass.

'What of ice?' Morgan asked tersely.

'Ice 'e dey finish,' the barman snapped back equally shirtily and turned away. Bloody rude black bastard, Morgan seethed to himself, this fucking country was determined to . . .

'Go all right?' asked a voice at his shoulder. It was Celia Adekunle.

'Oh fine,' Morgan said frostily. 'Listen, do you think you could tell this snotty so-and-so to get me some ice for my drink?'

Morgan lay back on the bed in Hazel's hotel room. He could hear the high-pitched whine of a mosquito around but he didn't care. He threw the sheet off his damp body, sweat slicked every crevice and fold. The neon lights on the façade of the cheap hotel filtered through the shutters, the tinny music from the bar competed with the honking and revving of the traffic outside. He peered at the luminous dial of his watch: twenty past twelve. Hazel slept silently beside him on the grubby bed. He felt itches spring up spontaneously all over his body. He needed to piss. He needed a bath. He felt dreadful in fact: he had drunk far too much, he was sweaty and uncomfortable and the vigour of his sex with Hazel had supplied him with a tingling electric ache in his penis. The details of the night's unsatisfactory events crowded in on him. He let out an apologetic sigh: he had been unpardonably rude to Celia Adekunle. On being informed that the bar had indeed run out of ice due to excessive demand he had loudly declaimed that it was exactly what he had come to expect of Kinjanja and was a small but cogent illustration of what was wrong with the country. He had then bidden her a curt good night and sniffily walked out of the party. He could still clearly recall the hurt and surprise that had registered on her face as he strode past her. He clenched his fists beneath the sheets and groaned silently to himself. It wasn't her fault that he had been made to look a complete fool: she had only been friendly and helpful. He buried his knuckles in his eye sockets in an agony of futile remorse.

He had driven straight to Hazel's hotel. To his astonishment she was in. He upbraided her for the filthy state of her room and had sent down to the bar for a bottle of whisky, half of which was still left. Silently, he swung himself off the bed. He stood and stretched. The room was warm and fetid. With his hands as paddles he fanned air around his genitals. His penis felt hot and sore from the two brutal couplings he had experienced with Hazel. His attempts to take out his bruised pride on her had rebounded as unsatisfactorily as ever; she had responded to his harsh gusto in kind, uncomplaining and unresentfully, with patience and as far as he could see no bad feeling whatsoever, falling into a deep and apparently untroubled sleep as soon as he switched the light out.

He pulled on his trousers and shirt. There was a bathroom of sorts along the corridor where he planned on heading. He pulled open the door a crack and peered out. There was no one in sight. He padded along the passageway and into the bathroom. Gagging from the stench, he flicked on the light. Two geckos levered themselves back into their crevices in the ceiling and a large moth went into a stall, careered into the cistern and fell fluttering to the floor.

He lifted the top off the cistern and, as expected, he found it empty. With finger and thumb he jiggled the ballcock but no water flowed. Cursing, he unzipped his fly and aimed in the general direction of the brackish toilet bowl. It was quite disgusting, this, he thought to himself. Why should he have to put up with these privations and disreputable surroundings? He had to get Hazel into a flat. Something had to change in his life, something revolutionary and drastic: it couldn't go on this way, it just couldn't. He thought fondly of Priscilla in this connection, emblem of a bright tomorrow, rather as a martyr would invoke an image of the Virgin as the flames licked round his knees. There, he told himself, there his hope lay, and he relaxed his sphincter's faltering hold on his straining bladder.

The burning sulphurous pain brought a shrill yelp to his lips and he did a high-stepping jig of surprise and agony, his urine stream carelessly playing across the lavatory seat and immediate environs. The initial sting died down fairly quickly and as soon as he was able to he leant weakly against the wall. Careful examination revealed nothing other than post-sex inflammation and heightened colouring – for a minute he had thought it might have been a vengeful bite from a lavatorial insect he had disturbed – and as he zipped himself up he put it down to the combined effects of latex rubber, heat and prolonged friction on what was – let's face it – a fairly sensitive organ.

Chapter 8

Morgan had forgotten about his diagnosis the next morning as he sat on his verandah in the grip of an averagely acute hangover. Something in Hazel's room had indeed bitten him later, and savagely too, along his right thigh, which area he now scratched steadily as he stared blearily at the Daily Graphic, one of Kinjanja's more literate papers, whose headline read: 'UPKP corruption probe demanded.' It wasn't clear at this range whether the UPKP were demanding the probe or being investigated themselves but his headache wouldn't allow him to bring the small print into focus.

He finished his boiled egg and shouted for Friday to bring him some more orange juice. He tightened the belt on his dressing-gown. He wasn't looking forward to going into work. Friday had told him that Fanshawe had phoned three times between nine and half past ten last night: he would be waiting on the steps of the Commission for Morgan's report. He finished his juice, said 'shit' at the light fixture above the verandah table, got up and went to his bedroom. Friday had laid out a clean, pressed shirt, socks and trousers on the bed. Morgan saw he'd forgotten to put out fresh underpants. He looked in the drawer he kept them in but could only find ones he'd abandoned because the rubber in the elastic waistband had perished, making them suitable exclusively for unfortunate creatures with four-foot girths. He frowned, unable at this stage of the day to comprehend this mystery. As far as he could remember he had three functioning pairs of underpants. Friday washed them every day. He had changed twice yesterday but that still should have left one clean pair at least for him to wear this morning.

In the corner of his room was a wicker basket into which he threw all his clothes that needed washing. He lifted the lid. Three soiled white underpants nestled in the bottom like some flayed rodent brood savaged by a ferret.

'Friday!' Morgan bellowed down the verandah.

Friday came panting up impelled by the violence in Morgan's shout.

'Underpants!' Morgan accused his cowering diminutive servant. 'No bloody underpants. Why you nevah wash 'im?'

Friday hung his head. '*Je ne peux pas le faire*,' he said meekly. 'I don't like wash dis one.'

Morgan picked a pair out and held it dangling from his hand. Friday reared back, a grin of alarm on his face.

'It's *not* bloody funny!' Morgan growled furiously. 'Just because you're so bloody fastidious I've got to go to work in dirty knickers. Big joke eh? You've been washing them for two years, why stop now?'

Friday gestured at them. '*C'est dégueulasse*. I don't like dis ting for inside. Nevah fit wash 'im like dis.'

Morgan was puzzled. What was he talking about? Skid-marks? Sweat stains? He took the offending pair and spread the waistband wide with the fingers of both hands. What was the silly bugger objecting to now, he wondered as he peered in?

Morgan sat in the car park at the university clinic telling himself to keep calm. His heart seemed on the point of retreating to its warm niche in his chest. He breathed out slowly: it had been a dreadful shock – that vile *stuff* – he had let the pants fall from his trembling fingers, reeling back, his eyes bulging with horror. He now wore one of his pairs with an expanded waistband secured with a safety pin. He held his hands out in front of him: they were still shaking slightly but they would do. He got out of the car and walked nervously towards the clinic. He noticed with surprise a long queue of students winding out of the waiting room. Inside there wasn't a seat to spare. He went up to the reception window. The same little clerk sat behind it. Morgan leant against the wall.

'Dr Murray here?' he asked tiredly, like a man who hadn't slept all night. He remembered his sworn promise to himself that he would never visit Murray again. That sort of brash statement was all very well when you were healthy, he told himself but it was a different matter when horrible oozings were coming out of your body.

'Yes, sah,' the clerk said. 'Excuse me, sah, but are you senior staff?'

'What? . . . Yes I suppose I am. Just tell Dr Murray that it's Mr Leafy here. And that I need to see him urgently.'

'I'm sorry, sah. Senior staff clinic is at twelve o'clock. If you can return then . . .'

'Good God,' Morgan said in angry despair. 'What's going on in this place? I'm not a car or something, I just can't be sick to some timetable you've dreamt up. Look, look,' he shooed his hands at the clerk, 'go and tell Dr Murray it's an emergency. I'm Mr Leafy, from the Commission. Got that? Now go on.'

The clerk protested, 'Doctor will tell you to come back.'

'Never you mind,' Morgan hissed. 'Let me worry about that. Just tell him.' The clerk grudgingly left his position. Morgan paced distractedly up and down, his hands in his pockets, trying to ignore the rude stares and hostile mutters of the students who objected to him blatantly jumping the queue in this way. Presently the clerk came back and in whispers told him to go round to the dispensary and wait. Morgan went outside and round the corner of the building to a small bottle-lined annex where a genial chemist directed him to a row of wooden chairs against the wall of the verandah. Two African women sat there already, one nursing a child, and he reluctantly sat down beside her, modestly averting his eyes. What in God's name was Murray playing at? he wondered, feeling hot and uncomfortable. Who did he think he was to park him out here like some welfare case? A little boy wearing only a shirt came round from behind the other woman and stood in front of him gazing at the large white man in frank curiosity. He had a streaming cold and grey phlegm covered his upper lip like a shiny moustache. Below the hem of his shirt a bulging domed navel protruded a good two inches. Morgan looked away, uncomfortable. The nursing baby slurped noisily at its mother's breast. The little boy's thin dark penis pointed at Morgan's shiny shoes. Realities hounded you unmercifully in Africa, Morgan thought; just when he needed a bit of unreflecting peace, here they were, crowding round him.

Twenty sweaty minutes later Murray came out. He looked capable and cool in his normal outfit, supplemented this time by a stethoscope round his neck. Morgan stood up and went along the verandah to meet him halfway.

'Ah Dr Murray,' he said. 'I'm so glad . . .'

'My senior staff clinic's not for another hour, Mr Leafy.' Murray was firm and unsmiling.

'I know that,' Morgan said impatiently, 'but this was important.' He paused and decided it would be wise to make his tone more amenable. 'I thought it was an emergency.'

'I'll give you five minutes,' Murray said. 'There are sixty students out there who've been waiting longer than you.' Morgan followed him into his consulting room. The man was impossible, Morgan thought, almost deranged. It was as though he was doing you some astonishing favour in deigning to treat his patients. Still, he decided to keep his feelings to himself; this whole business was far too serious and delicate to allow his personal dislike of Murray to get in the way. He remembered the frosty exchanges of his last visit with vague regret and resolved not to let the mood deteriorate like that today.

'What's the trouble?' Murray asked, taking up his seat behind his desk. Morgan paused, trying to find appropriate words to convey the intimate nature of his problem.

'Well, this morning . . .' he began. 'That is to say I've been noticing some pain – actually more like discomfort really, a sort of tingling, really.' He swallowed, his tongue suddenly dry as pumice. Murray looked on steadily, giving nothing away. Morgan wondered what he was thinking.

'What in fact is *wrong*?' Murray asked bluntly.

'Discharge,' Morgan blurted out the word as if it were some dreadful obscenity. 'This morning I noticed, well, what you might call, ah, discharge, on my underpants, that is.'

'Is that all?'

'Pardon? Oh no, as I was saying there's been some discomfort on, when I go . . . when I urinate.' Morgan felt exhausted, as if he'd been running for miles. He wiped moisture from his upper lip. 'Not always,' he said feebly. 'Just sometimes.'

'How long has this been going on?' Murray asked. The

156

man was incredible, Morgan thought, not a trace of sympathy, no preliminary chat to put the patient at his ease.

'Couple of days I suppose,' Morgan confessed. Murray pulled his chair round to the side of his desk.

'Right,' he said briskly, 'Let's have a look.'

'You mean?' Morgan cleared his throat. 'Off?'

'Aye. Breeks down, the lot.'

Morgan thought there was a good chance he might faint. With trembling fingers he undid his trousers and let them drop to his ankles. Too late he remembered his baggy, perished underpants. He felt his face blaze with miserable embarrassment as he unfastened the safety pin holding up his useless Y-fronts.

'I think I should say these are not my normal . . .' he began in a rush. 'My steward refused to wash . . . So I had to . . . I *do* have some perfectly good ones . . .' This was *appalling*, he screamed to himself. Murray looked on unmoved. Morgan could hardly breathe from the effort he was making to stay calm; the powerful urge to explain overwhelmed him. With intense care he placed the safety pin on the edge of Murray's desk. It was useless, he let his underpants fall and looked anguishedly at the ceiling. He felt giddy and weak. The average human body, such as the one he possessed, couldn't tolerate, he felt sure, the extremes of shame and humiliation that his had been subjected to recently. Perhaps this ghastly discharge was a sign that it was finally cracking up, falling apart at the seams.

He reached out and caught the edge of the desk to steady himself. He felt his genitals contracting in the cool air of the consulting room. He was sure his penis had shrunk to about one inch long. Murray probably couldn't even see it: he'd need a magnifying glass or a microscope.

'What do you think?' he croaked.

'Looks alright,' Murray said noncommittally. He reached into a drawer for something. Morgan squinted down: it was a wooden spatula, like an ice-lolly stick. Murray used it to raise Morgan's penis. His head reeled.

'Any chancres?' Murray asked.

'*What*?' Morgan squeaked in horror.

'Sores, crabs, lice, rashes?'

'Good God no!'

'Fine. You can put your pants on now.'

Morgan shakily pulled up and pinned his pants round his waist. He could feel huge sobs of frustration and despair building up in his chest, crushing his lungs against his rib cage, making it increasingly hard to breathe. He zipped up his trousers with numb and unresponsive fingers, like a man in sub-zero temperatures.

'What is it?' he gasped weakly.

Murray was washing his hands at a small sink. 'No way of telling at the moment,' he said calmly. 'It could be nothing. People often get discharges for no significant reason at all, a natural defence mechanism. On the other hand it could be a non-gonococcal toxemia.'

'*Jesus Christ!*'

'They're very common out here. But don't worry. You seem well, but I think we'd still better check. Go down to the sister at the end of the corridor. See if you can get some discharge on a slide. And we'll do a urinalysis as well.'

'Right,' Morgan gulped, trying to stop his throat from closing – his Adam's apple seemed three times its normal size.

Murray walked down the corridor with him. 'What do you think it is?' Morgan asked again. 'Is it serious? Am I . . . ?'

'I doubt it very much,' Murray said reassuringly. 'But it wouldn't be very clever of me to try and guess before we've got the tests back. Don't you agree?' They stopped at a door with 'Surgery' written on it. 'Come back tomorrow, Mr Leafy,' Murray said. 'But try and make it at the right time.'

Five minutes later a plump kindly sister in a gleaming and

rigidly starched uniform happily accepted the smeared glass slide and the squat brimming bottle from a wordless Morgan, whose face still glowed pinkly and who felt that if he dared to open his mouth only an insane gibbering chatter would emerge. He swayed unreflectingly out to his car and sat hunched over the wheel for a full ten minutes trying to exert some minimal control over the cartwheeling and tumbling emotions that were furiously rioting within him.

When he had calmed himself sufficiently he drove slowly down the road to the Commission where he sat quietly at his desk and methodically worked his way through his in-tray, his mind concentrated on the work in front of him, trying not to think, attempting to erase the morning from his memory.

Fanshawe, however, interrupted him and called him into his office for a report on his meeting with Adekunle, and seemed disappointed in the lack of immediate progress. Morgan told him that, as requested, he had put the proposition to Adekunle and that he had said he would think about it. It seemed safer to describe the disastrous events of last night in as unsensational a way as possible.

'*Think* about a free trip to London and a buckshee stay at Claridges?' Fanshawe demanded rhetorically. 'What is there to think about, for God's sake?'

Morgan tried to implant a tone of reasonableness and lied spontaneously: 'It seems he's got to refer this to his central office or the Emir or something. He can't just up and off without telling anybody.'

'Well I don't know,' Fanshawe said, obviously flabbergasted that anyone should have even to consider such a gilt-edged opportunity.

'It's not just a question of buying their good intentions,' Morgan cautioned, trying to initiate the complex process of bringing Fanshawe round to face reality. 'They're sophisticated politicians.'

'Think so?' Fanshawe said dubiously, sounding surprised at

the novelty of this idea. 'To be quite frank they seem more like a bunch of cowboys to me.'

'With respect, Arthur,' Morgan said. 'I think you're underestimating them. Especially Adekunle.'

Fanshawe snorted his disbelief. 'Well, keep at it Morgan. Follow it up in a day or so. We're doing well, but we don't want any hitches in Project Kingpin at this stage.'

Morgan stood up, his heart heavy in the knowledge that to all intents and purposes Project Kingpin had passed away in the night. Later he would have to feed Fanshawe some doctored story about American or French counter-pressure, but for the moment it would be best to let him carry on believing it was still underway.

He left Fanshawe's office and walked moodily back to his own. On the way he bumped into Jones.

'Hello there, Morgan,' said the little Welshman cheerily. 'Don't worry, man. Worse things happen at sea.'

'What?' Morgan said, irritation giving an edge to his voice.

'Cheer up. You look dreadful.'

'Do I?' he said, suddenly alarmed. 'What's wrong?'

'It's your chin,' Jones quipped. Morgan touched his jaw. Had one of Murray's chancres suddenly bloomed there like a septic flower?

'My chin?' he said, mystified, feeling its contours.

'Yer, it's dangling round your ankles. You'll trip over it any second.' Morgan did not find this funny.

Jones went on unperturbed. 'What's happened? Arthur chew you up for something?'

Morgan wished Jones would go away. 'No,' he said shortly. 'Things on my mind.'

'You want to relax a bit, my boy. Working too hard. Why don't you come to the dance tonight with me and Geraldine?'

'What dance?'

'The club dance. The usual monthly one. Come and have a meal first and we'll all go down later.'

Morgan was surprised at Jones's thoughtfulness. 'No thanks, Denzil. But it's good of you to ask. I've got other things on.' Dinner with Jones and his wife was the last thing he required. Why was Jones being so nice though?

'Well, don't work too hard,' Jones advised. 'Leave some of it for the new man. He'll be here next week.'

Morgan sat at his desk and stared out at the familiar view of Nkongsamba. The afternoon sun was filtered through a dust haze and the distant hills on the horizon were softened like an aquatint. He had visited the lavatory twice that day with no ill-effects or recurrence of his symptoms and some of his fears were beginning to recede. Perhaps Murray's supposition was correct: it was probably some horrible coincidence, the climate, his sex-life, a temporary malfunction of his meta-bolism. Christ only knew, it was easy enough to happen in this place. He decided he'd just have to look after himself a little better. He made up his mind to have a quiet evening at home tonight: a couple of paperbacks, get Moses to cook him one of his specialities. As he was feeling a little improved he allowed himself a wry smile at the thought of his fierce embarrassment in Murray's consulting room. The man was unbelievable, he thought, he couldn't detect a trace of com-passion in him, he ran that clinic as if it were a meat-processing factory or an army barracks.

The phone on his desk rang. He picked it up. 'Leafy,' he said.

'Morgie,' came a familiar voice. It was Priscilla, naturally. 'I'm back,' she informed him.

'Marvellous. When did you arrive?' He felt a surge of momentary elation. This was what he needed after his shocks of the morning.

'Late last night. We had a lovely time.'

'Good. Good.' To his mild surprise and annoyance he couldn't think of anything he wanted to say to her.

'I'd have phoned you earlier but I've been at the club with Mummy. We had lunch.'

'Uh-uh. Good. Good.' Morgan remarked. He was now a little alarmed. This total inability to converse with the girl he loved was absurd.

'Morgie, they've got a dance on there tonight.'

'Yes, I know.' He wished she wouldn't call him that.

'Honestly! What's got into you today?' she said impatiently. 'Let's go to it, shall we? It'll be fun.'

'What? Oh yes, if you like. Of course.' He paused, what was happening to him? 'I'm sorry Priscilla, I've been working all day. Not thinking straight.'

'Pick me up about eightish?'

'Sure. On the dot. Ah, looking forward to seeing you,' he added with grotesque formality.

'Me too. Miss me?'

'Pardon?'

'Miss me, silly.'

'Oh . . . terribly.'

'Oh *good*. See you tonight. 'Bye.'

Morgan put down the phone. He felt an immense lassitude descend on him, and he realized that he still didn't feel like going out tonight. And, what was more perturbing, he didn't particularly want to spend the evening with Priscilla.

Chapter 9

Priscilla was wearing a new dress, or at least one that Morgan hadn't seen before. It had a white bodice with thin straps tied in a bow at her shoulders, a red plastic belt and a navy-blue skirt. Her tan had deepened as a result of her days on the coast and she looked healthy and efficient, like a successful sales promotion girl or an air hostess. Tonight, also, she was wearing pinky-orange lipstick and pale-blue eyeshadow. Her cheeks and forehead were still red from sunburn and her nose was peeling slightly.

'You look great,' Morgan said, a sherry poised in his hand. 'Doesn't she?' he turned to Mrs Fanshawe for confirmation.

'She's always been fond of clothes, ever since she was a tiny baby,' Mrs Fanshawe declared proudly. 'I remember once when she was in her pram . . .'

'Oh Mummy,' Priscilla interrupted with a laugh, 'Please don't tell that story again. I'm sure Morgie isn't the slightest bit interested.' Everyone tittered politely. 'Morgie' took a sip of his sherry and placed the glass on the table beside his armchair as Mrs Fanshawe dutifully completed the anecdote. For the first time he sensed Priscilla's parents eyeing him as a potential suitor for their daughter and this realization brought with it its usual cargo of conflicting emotions. He glanced at Mrs Fanshawe, smoke curling from her cigarette jammed in its black holder, her teeth clamped on its stem, her wide pale face beneath the jet-black hair, the immense prow of her chest. He tried to imagine her talking with his mother and Reg at the wedding reception and panic fluttered for a moment in his belly like a trapped bird. Chloe Fanshawe would be his mother-in-law . . . He abruptly stopped that train of thoughts from going any further.

'We'd better be off,' he said with a nervous smile.

Priscilla ran up the stairs to fetch her handbag and Morgan stood alone in the centre of the room, like a slave at auction, conscious again of the Fanshawes' evaluating stares.

'Priscilla enjoyed her day's fishing,' Fanshawe said. 'Sounds like quite a place. Must take me up sometime, Morgan.'

Oh no, Morgan thought. 'Gladly,' he said. He felt the bosom of the family mushily enfolding him with slow inexorability. He should be pleased, he realized; he firmly told himself he was. Then Priscilla arrived and the Fanshawes walked them to the door and waved them down the steps.

'Have a good time, you two,' Mrs Fanshawe cooed at them as they got into his car.

When they arrived at the club Morgan and Priscilla kissed restrainedly for a while in the car park. Priscilla put her arms round him and squeezed.

'I *have* missed you,' she said. 'Mummy and I talked a lot about you when we were staying with the Wagners.'

'You did?' Morgan said uncertainly.

'They're both very fond of you, you know.'

'The Wagners? But I've only met them once.'

'No, dopey!' Priscilla poked him in the side. 'Mummy and Daddy.'

'Are they?' he said in considerable surprise, but then covered this with a hasty 'of course, I'm very fond of them too,' amazed at his ability to form the words without choking. Everything, he remarked to himself, seemed to be advancing with exceptional smoothness. Perhaps tonight would be fine after all. He kissed Priscilla again to remind himself why he was going through with this factitious exchange of vows. He put his hand on her knee and ran it up her thigh under her dress until his fingers met the cotton of her pants. To his astonishment the expected reproachful wrist-slap was not forthcoming, in fact her own hand applied gentle pressure to the small of his back. They broke apart, her eyes bright and smiling. The familiar suffocating feeling established itself in Morgan's chest; it was like having your lungs stuffed with cotton wool. The evening was shaping up in an incredibly good-natured, accommodating way. Tonight could well be the night.

They walked arm-in-arm into the club where the dance was underway. The club had a regular dance once a month. There was nothing special in this, it was simply a way of bringing people in, of injecting a faint sense of occasion into Nkongsamba's unremarkable social life, and giving a boost to the restaurant and bar sales. Sometimes they hired a band but tonight Morgan saw they were relying solely on records. The lounge area had been cleared, the chairs pushed back to the wall and the central lights switched off. The armchairs had been arranged in intimate groups around small tables upon which candles burned in old Chianti bottles. A young man – manager of Nkongsamba's Barclay's Bank and social secretary of the club – sat behind the table that held the record player, flanked by two large speakers, leafing self-importantly through a pile of LPs. Some indeterminate jazz was playing, a clarinet dominant. Morgan found the music soothingly melancholic. A few people sat in the armchairs and three couples danced stiffly on the loose parquet flooring that rattled gently beneath their feet like distant castanets. The bar was busier, surrounded by people who looked only slightly better-dressed than usual: a tie there, a dab of make-up here, a string of pearls; but the atmosphere was little different from the one that usually prevailed in the club. This came as no surprise to Morgan – the monthly dance, for all its aspirations, had never brought out the best in Nkongsamba's avid socialites – but Priscilla seemed to be disappointed.

'I thought there'd be a band,' she wailed sadly.

'There is sometimes,' Morgan apologized.

'But they're not even trying,' she protested. 'It's like a party in somebody's flat.' Morgan had to agree. He put the blame on the unimaginative social secretary, who, as if to confirm this adverse judgement, replaced the jazz with cha-cha and successfully cleared the dance floor.

'It gets better as Christmas approaches,' Morgan said in compensation. 'Honestly. Anyway, let's have a drink.'

Morgan and Priscilla danced. They held each other close and moved slowly to and fro as somebody sang 'Yesterday, love was such an easy game to play.' Morgan rested his cheek on Priscilla's head. He smelt her straight clean hair, shiny and fine. It seemed to him, a little fancifully he had to admit, to be a symbol of everything his life was shortly to become. He shifted his erection against Priscilla's belly and dropped his head to kiss her bare shoulder. She locked her wrists around his neck and pulled him closer to her. Her prim façade was rapidly falling away he realized; she was probably missing Chinese Charlie's attentions by now. She had drunk two large scotches and had been very flirtatious in her own way: he had quite enjoyed himself. He squinted at his watch: it was twenty to ten, they had been here just over an hour.

While standing at the bar shortly after they had arrived, Jones and his wife accosted them. Jones had seemed somewhat put out to find Morgan at the club after refusing his invitation, and the Welshman had accepted his excuses with bad grace. The bloody oaf, Morgan thought to himself as he swayed gently with Priscilla in his arms, it should be pretty obvious to him by now why his offers to dine *chez* Jones were so regularly turned down: the drab unintelligent wife, the squalling brats who always woke up, the inferior food. Poor Jones, he thought, poor bloody Jones. The inept social secretary again demonstrated his sensitive feel for the mood of a party by playing some loud rock and roll and the dance floor soon emptied once more. Morgan and Priscilla stood undecided between the lounge and the bar. Priscilla looked like she had just been woken up.

'Drink?' Morgan suggested.

'Oh let's not stay on,' she said suggestively. 'Can you wait a minute? I just want to go to the loo.' Morgan said that would be no problem. He watched her go, watched her firm-muscled calves, the shimmying buttocks beneath the blue skirt. He felt his heart begin to beat faster: the house was tidy, there was drink and food if necessary, by chance clean sheets had been placed on the bed only yesterday – all was in order . . . Apart from himself, he thought, acknowledging the inopportune nag of his conscience at the memory of his visit to the clinic and the dreadful affliction Murray had mentioned: non-gonococcal something. But surely not, he thought, persuading himself. Even Murray had been happy to suspend his verdict. Furthermore there'd been no repetition of the burning pain, not another besmirching drop of discharge either. It must be all right – just a scary coincidence. However, he told himself, to satisfy his own mind finally, and quieten his conscience, he'd make one last check. He slipped off, humming the catchy refrain of the rock and roll number that was still blasting across the empty dance floor, by-passed the crowd around the bar and strolled jauntily down the passageway that led to the lavatory.

He stood in front of the urinals and passed water without so much as a twinge. He smiled to himself: he'd squared up to his responsibilities, he couldn't be accused in any mental tribunal of evading the issue. He'd done all that could reasonably be asked of a man about to bed his loved one. He zipped up his trousers and washed his hands. He considered his reflection for a moment in the mirror, straightened his tie and cautiously touched his hair with his hands. He wondered cursorily if he ought to grow a moustache – one of those fashionable droopy ones: it would probably suit him. 'Narcissist,' he fondly accused his reflection, and turned away.

He stepped out into the dark corridor and bumped into someone. They both backed off apologizing. Morgan recognized Murray's accent before he distinguished his features. But this evening his benevolence could include anyone – even Murray – so he said pleasantly, 'Evening, Doctor. Here for the dance?'

Murray didn't reply straight away. 'No . . .' he said thoughtfully, as if remembering something. 'The library.'

'Didn't think you were a dancing man somehow, Doctor,' he observed facetiously, almost enjoying what he interpreted as the first signs of discomfort he had ever witnessed on Murray's face. 'Well, good night to you,' he said gaily, moving off.

'Mr Leafy,' Murray said, calling him back. 'I suppose it's all right for me to tell you now. We've had the results of the tests we ran. I'm afraid I was wrong in my preliminary diagnosis.' He looked over his shoulder to ensure they were alone. 'About the non-gonococcal toxemia.'

'Ah-hah,' Morgan said triumphantly. 'I thought you probably were. No more symptoms by the way. Everything tip-top, never felt better. But don't worry, Doc,' he added boldly, 'can't win 'em all.'

'I was about to say,' Murray went on. 'I'm afraid it's not *non*-gonococcal.'

'I . . . I don't quite understand,' Morgan said falteringly, doubt spreading through his mind like a rumour of war. 'What are you saying?'

'That it *is* gonococcal. I'm sorry to say this, but you have gonorrhoea, Mr Leafy. It's nothing to be alarmed about, but it's definitely gonorrhoea.'

When Priscilla came down the stairs from the ladies' powder room she commented on Morgan's flushed appearance and asked him if he was feeling all right.

'I'm just a bit hot,' Morgan said dazedly. In fact he felt his head was about to explode, as if primed by the fatal words he had heard. Murray had calmed him down after his initial hysterical reaction, telling him repeatedly that it was nothing to worry about and to come to the clinic the next day as planned. 'I wouldn't drink anything more tonight if I were you, Mr Leafy,' he had added. 'In fact just let abstinence be your watchword all round for a while.'

Morgan felt like a frustrated Samson chained between the two mighty pillars of his predicament. On the one hand was the frightful sentence of sexual disease, and on the other was the daunting prospect of the next hour or so. As he had stood there immobile, waiting for Priscilla to reappear all he could say to himself in futile repetition was 'What am I going to do? What am I going to do?' Somehow he managed to chat until they reached the car where, once inside, Priscilla flung herself on him, her tongue scouring the inside of his mouth, her teeth clashing painfully on his. He responded as best as he could, agonizingly aware of his total detumescence. My God, he screamed to himself in sudden horror, what if I become impotent? He thought of the swarming regiments of bacilli at this very moment billeting themselves throughout his body, searching out the most comfortable spots. And anyway, he moaned, what happened to you when you had gonorrhoea? Did your nose fall off? Did you go mad? Did your balls swell to bloated pumpkins? He felt like weeping hot bitter tears of rage and disappointment.

'Morgie, you're not listening,' Priscilla complained petulantly.

'Sorry, um, darling,' he said, with a crazy smile. 'What is it?'

'What are we doing now?'

'Shall I drop you off?' he said unreflectingly.

'Morgie!' she cried. 'That's not funny!'

'Sorry, sorry,' he insisted again. 'Dreaming, don't know what I'm thinking about.' He kissed her distractedly; whatever happened she must never know. 'Let's go to my place,' he suggested as he knew she wanted him to. He needed time, he thought, time to calm down, to think of some way out of this filthy dilemma.

They pulled out of the club car park and quickly drove through the seedy quarters of Nkongsamba, past the glowing fires, the bright youths, the screeching clubs. Car headlights flashed in his eyes, the tooting horns and booming radios assaulted his ears. It was like some African bedlam. He thought of black Bosch-like devils with long pincers and barbed tridents grabbing and prodding at his vitals.

Priscilla wound down the window and leant her head back against the seat. Her hot palm rested casually on his thigh.

'Gosh,' she giggled. 'I've had too much to drink. When I shut my eyes the car feels like a roller-coaster.'

Morgan didn't reply. As some semblance of order returned to his jumbled brain a single question obsessively edged its way to the forefront of his mind. If he had gonorrhoea, how, pray, how in the name of God had he contracted it in the first place? There was, he knew, only one possible answer which might have been emblazoned along the horizon in mile-high letters of fire it was so obvious. HAZEL! *Hazel*. The slut, the whore, the rancid filthy tart! It was her and her yobbo boyfriends – *she* had given it to him!

While they roared up the main road north Morgan plotted unspeakably crude and violent acts of revenge which he intended personally and lingeringly to visit on her corrupt body, but as they steadily approached his house his more immediate problems began to reoccupy his mind. As he turned into his driveway and parked his car in the garage the options that were available to him presented themselves and were discarded. One: be honest, tell her the truth, or as much of it as was necessary. But no, he thought almost at once, that was impossible. What if it got back to her mother? And also it would rule out any hope of marriage – people just didn't get these afflictions in her world. Two: forget it, simply go ahead as if nothing were wrong. He almost passed out as he considered the possible consequences of this course of action. Priscilla would get it, he'd infect his future wife, and then . . . he stopped thinking about that one. Three: lie. His old friend Mendacity, or its siblings Delay and Prevarication, however unlikely they might seem. He saw now that in reality his only hope lay in keeping himself and Priscilla out of the same bed . . . He thought suddenly and maniacally of a self-inflicted wound: perhaps he could slice his hand while making sand-wiches, or trip on the way back into the house and crack his head on the doorstep. But he knew he just didn't have the guts to carry it off. Maybe he could simulate some other more sympathetic disease, like epilepsy, dropsy or sleeping sickness . . .

'Come on, slowcoach,' Priscilla's voice was a little woozy. 'I'm not going to wait all night.' Morgan got out of the car and walked back to the house with her, his arm round her shoulders. She hugged herself to him and in this way they awkwardly shuffled to the door.

Fifteen minutes later Morgan fought himself free of Priscilla's embrace and stumbled over to his drinks trolley where, despite Murray's warning, he poured himself a huge measure of whisky. He hoped the alcohol would somehow inspire him, lend whatever feeble excuse he managed to dream up authenticity. He contemplated the idea of drinking himself unconscious but he realized with renewed despair that it would only postpone the inevitable crunch. Tomorrow would bring no escape: the problem would still be there as it was clear that, although Priscilla might accept drunken senselessness for one night, she was generally behaving in a way that suggested she saw sexual congress with him as a desirable thing in principle. This was no one-night stand, after all, and there was no telling how long he might have to abstain. 'Let abstinence be your watchword,' Murray had said in typical fashion, like some doom-laden sybil or prophetic crone in a morality play. Recalling his words, Murray's features swam into his mind: the unsmiling blue eyes, the stern accent. Morgan felt positively light-headed with hatred: it was Murray's fault, he accused with passionate illogicality – Murray's intervention had landed him in this wickedly, poignantly ironic situation. He'd been trying to get into Priscilla's pants ever since she had arrived, and, now that she was actively encouraging this move, he was the one who had to advocate restraint.

'What are you doing, Morgie?' he heard Priscilla ask. He wasn't sure now that he liked the effect alcohol had on her: it made her winsome, lewdly coy, like some depraved child-prostitute.

'Nothing, darling,' he said, putting down his glass and turning round. She had risen from the couch, her mouth bruised from their kissing, her dress rumpled. She held out her arms towards him. Reluctantly he took her hands in his. She tugged him in the direction of the bedroom.

'Let's go, Morgie.'

He applied gentle braking pressure. He willed the alcohol to percolate through his system. 'Darling,' he said, trying to imbue his voice with subtle gradations of regret, prudence and reluctant moral wisdom. 'Let's not. I think we . . . Well, we should just stay here . . .'

Simultaneously he tried to mould his features into a complementary amalgam of love, respect and sage sincerity. Somewhere along the line his conception of facial expressions and tones of voice and Priscilla's refused to coincide. A look of delighted sly adventure came into her eyes. He watched this transmogrification with all the horror of a scientist observing the first stirrings of a monster he's unwittingly created.

'Here?' she said. 'On the floor, Morgie? Oh Morgie.' In front of his dumbfounded face she turned to the sofa and with a vandal's relish flung its cushions on the floor, hastily piling them into a makeshift harem-bed. She quickly switched off all the lights but one, running around excitedly, paying no heed to Morgan's beseeching rejoinders of 'Priscilla, wait. No, I didn't mean . . . Priscilla, please.' She kicked off her shoes and slid onto the cushion pile, giggling tipsily as she stretched and pouted in cinematic sensual abandon. 'Come on, Morgan,' she simpered. 'Don't keep a girl waiting.'

Morgan felt he couldn't go on much longer. What had happened to her? He had always suspected she was something of a goer – she had hinted as much herself – but it could only be drink that was producing this ghastly parody of a Hollywood vamp. Of course, he thought, remembering Olokomeji, she had no reason to believe that he wouldn't be highly stimulated by these sexy cavortings. He groaned softly, looking wildly around his room as if the Medici Gallery prints on its wall held some encoded inspiration. His eyes swivelled reluctantly back to Priscilla and he almost screamed when he saw she was wriggling out of her pants. She slipped them over her ankles and flung them playfully at him. She smiled in his direction, her eyes a little glazed. She reached up and undid the bows of her dress. The front flap dropped forward to reveal a lacy strapless bra that needlessly supported her small breasts. Morgan's mouth opened wordlessly as she reached behind her to unclasp it, the joints in her shoulders bulging roundly, her bottom lip caught in her teeth in exaggerated concentration. The bra fell away and for a brief moment he saw the pink nipples, before, in mad spontaneity, doing the only thing that came into his mind, he leapt across the room, dropped to his knees beside her and frenziedly replaced the bra over her breasts, like some fervent sexual reformer at a burlesque show.

'No!' he gasped. 'Don't, Priscilla. For God's sake don't go on.'

Astonishment registered for a second in her eyes before she giggled again, drunkenly enjoying the game. He looked in appalled consternation as she tried to wriggle free, one breast pinging out of its ill-applied cup, and grabbed at Morgan's crutch.

'No!' he yelped, attempting to fend her off with one hand while still using the other to keep her bra roughly clamped to some portion of her body above the waist. Her dress had rucked up to her thighs in the struggle and Morgan caught a flash of her dark triangle which he promptly tried to cover up, maintaining his fight against nudity, with his one unencumbered hand, hoping to flip the skirt back in place. Suddenly unimpeded now, Priscilla's fingers fastened on his fly-zip and before he knew it the zip was down and her right hand was thrust energetically into the gap. Morgan felt her sharp nails on his thighs, felt her fingers slip beneath his underpants and close round his infected organ.

'Don't touch it!' he shrieked violently, as though to an innocent child about to pet an adder, and leapt immediately to his feet, backing away from the cushions, his hand groping along the wall behind him. He switched on the main light and stood panting in aghast dismay by the door to the front verandah.

The sudden illumination from the twin ceiling lights dazzled Priscilla and for a moment she looked about her uncomprehendingly, before the harshness of her exposure dawned on her: the knowledge that in fact it hadn't been a game, that, after all, there was no fun involved slowly penetrated her drink-befuddled mind.

Morgan looked at her in dismal misgiving, as if she were a bloodied corpse planted in his sitting room. Her dress girdled her thighs, the brassière lay strung over a cushion, her small pink-tipped breasts heaved from the recent exertions. He watched her pass the back of her hand slowly across her eyes like someone awakening from a sleep. Awkwardly, almost meekly, she pulled her dress down over her legs and covered her exposed breasts with her arms.

'You bastard,' she said softly and then, suddenly, she snatched up the bra and her shoes and crouch-ran past him through the screen door and up the passage to the bathroom. Morgan hung his head in shame and abject despondency. He experienced Priscilla's humiliation as if it had been his own: the defenceless prurience of her position on the floor, the retroactive embarrassment, the baleful unsympathetic light, him standing over her, shock written across his face. But he knew too, instinctively, and with an assurance gained from his own experience that, publicly at least, it wouldn't stay that way for long. The self-defence mechanisms of the human psyche would swing efficiently into action, shrouding the truth, reallocating the shame, imposing new guilts and transferring the disgrace to him, where, he confessed, it properly belonged.

Numbly he replaced the scattered cushions on the sofa. He wanted to bawl like a baby, cry his frustration to the world, but instead he drank some more whisky, sat down and waited for Priscilla to reappear.

Presently the sharp clicks of her heels on the concrete floor of the corridor told him that, as expected, more than fresh make-up had been applied in her absence. In glum trepidation he noted the frozen little smile on her face.

'Will you take me home, please,' she spoke as to a waiting taxi-driver. They walked out to the car in silence, Morgan wondering what he could possibly say to prevent this damage from becoming irreparable. Priscilla got into the car and sat stiffly erect.

'Priscilla,' he began. 'I can explain. You see I thought it would be best if . . .'

'Would. You. Just. Take. Me. Home.' There was no trace of dejection in her voice, just cold, emphatic hatred. He started the car and backed it out into the driveway. The return journey to the Commission passed without another word being exchanged.

As he drove along the road Morgan saw his future disappearing in front of him with the remorseless inevitability of a torpedoed liner slipping beneath the waves. Already, only the creases in Priscilla's dress, like the bubbling ripples of water, bore witness to their former intimacy. But then they too would be ironed out tomorrow. It would be like nothing had ever happened. Morgan found it hard to believe that such glowing possibilities − an actual breathing state of affairs − could be blotted out with such ease; that all the hints and talk of love, the moments of passion, his eminently realizable dreams, could be erased, as he surely knew they would be, so abruptly. But the bitter chill that existed in the car confirmed this fact unsparingly.

He pulled up outside the Fanshawes' house. He said immediately, pleadingly 'Priscilla, believe me, darling, there *is* an explanation for all this. I can explain. Please don't feel that because I didn't . . .'

She turned to face him. 'I feel sorry for men like you,' she said softly and venomously. 'What I can't understand is how I failed to see it in the beginning. It's so obvious. You're pathetic creatures, all of you, with your big talk, your sexy swaggering behaviour. Pathetic, feeble weak creatures. I don't hate you, Morgan, I pity you.'

As Morgan listened to this his faltering hopes turned on one wing and went into a howling death-dive. He was horror-struck at her version of his behaviour: she thought he'd chickened out, couldn't take the heat, hadn't the lead in his pencil, which was absolutely the last thing he wanted. He had been assuming that she would think he was too 'nice', too 'decent' to compromise their love with a bit of fornication, but he saw the utter vanity of his wishes. His assault on her at Olokomeji on the river bank made any connection between him and ideas of gentlemanly restraint singularly inappropriate. With a sudden sickening feeling he saw just how apt Priscilla's interpretation of his behaviour was. It was also clear to him that for all this talk of pity on her part what she really felt for him was seething contempt. Then he was shocked to see Fanshawe walk on to the verandah and beckon them inside.

'Goodbye,' Priscilla said quickly, and got out of the car. She ran up the steps towards her father. Morgan gave a casual wave and drove off promptly so as not to see them talking. He tried not to think what Priscilla might say, what explanation she would provide for her early return and his refusal to join the family inside. He tilted his head towards the window and let the breeze play across his face. He couldn't actually recall from his anthology of personal disasters a more traumatic and ruinous evening; and yet it had hovered so tantalizingly close to being perfect, to cementing firmly the first bricks in the new future he had planned to build for himself.

With a surge of faint hope he thought that it might, just,

be possible to salvage something from the wreckage: perhaps by dint of tears or lovelorn propositions convince her that he was truly sincere and hadn't wanted to affect or alter their relationship by making it sexual at this early stage. He tried out an impromptu draft apologia on himself, but it sounded irredeemably bogus and unlikely. And he saw too, with a soured midnight clarity, that it had all gone too far, that after what Priscilla had in fact done — ripping off her clothes, practically *begging* him — there was no chance of rewriting her version of the night's events. He saw himself cast permanently in the role of rugby club braggart, victim of his own preposterous life-guard conceit: the trumpeted exploits of the local stud exposed as sham, the empty, well-hung innuendoes of a redundant gigolo. He felt his face go red with anger as he saw the details of the portrait emerge. If only she knew what he was really capable of . . . but then his choler turned to shame as he saw the stereotype close in around him. He didn't care what people said. Women always held the last card — he couldn't win this one.

When he arrived back home he went straight to bed. Like a Napoleon at his Waterloo, he had briefly cast his eyes over the scene of his defeat — and had spotted Priscilla's pants lying in the corner of the room where she had hurled them in pert abandon. The thought that he had driven a pantless Priscilla home was just the final ironic straw. He picked them up, successfully resisting the impulse to sniff them. They were white with blue lace trim round the leg-holes. They rested now in the drawer of his bedside table, a sad trophy of what might have been. As he masochistically re-ran the evening in his mind he reflected that if he hadn't met Murray at the club, if he'd even decided to have a trial pee when he reached home instead, none of this would have happened: in fact he'd be lying in bed with Priscilla at this very moment. But no, the random events and occurrences of his and Murray's day *had* to, like the Titanic and the iceberg, converge outside the gentlemen's lavatory at that precise moment with finely adjusted timing. And equally, he thought malevolently, it *had* to be Murray too. The man was assuming a daemonic, fatal role in his life, it seemed to him. Murray's untimely collision had jolted his conscience out of that closet in his mind where only seconds before it had been securely enclosed for the night and Morgan strongly doubted if he could ever forgive him for that. One side of him grudgingly admitted that Murray couldn't ever have known the effect of his on-the-spot diagnosis but this was more than countered by the hateful aptness of him being the reminder, the catalyst that had set his rusty creaking sense of values juddering into action. For he knew that it had been his inclination to do the 'decent' thing by Priscilla that had landed him in this mess – but it was with no sense of comfort or self-congratulation that he acknowledged this was so. His moral niceties – he blankly calculated – had cost him Priscilla and all the bright tomorrows that queued entrancingly behind her. With a sudden flash of prophetic inspiration he felt he knew why there was so much evil in the world: the price you paid for being good was simply quite out of proportion, preposterously over-valued. And as prime consumers of the commodity of goodness the human race had decided that as far as they were concerned they were just not prepared to pay the going rate any more. He turned over in his bed and furiously punched his pillows, tears of frustration at his own weakness pricking his eyes. That is, he thought, except for a few silly mugs: except for a few soft, stupid bastards like himself.

Chapter 10

Morgan closed the book and thought he could actually hear the blood draining from his face. He leant against a nearby wall and felt a tremor of blind fear run through his body. With shaking hands he re-inserted the thick volume back in its slot in the medical section. The book was called *Sexually Transmitted Diseases*.

He had decided not to go into the office until after his appointment with Murray. An agonizing tear-jerking session above his toilet bowl this morning had forcibly reminded him of his condition and, also, he wasn't at all keen to confront Fanshawe. There was no telling what Priscilla might have related to her parents about the previous night. As a result he had killed time over a lengthy but morose breakfast during which he had made up his mind to face facts and be ruthlessly honest with himself. To this end he had driven up to the university bookshop to see what details he could establish about his ailment. After hovering around the medical section for a while, making sure no one was watching him, he had found the book he wanted and had uneasily opened its shiny, copiously illustrated pages.

He now gazed sightlessly out at the bright sunlit piazza of the administrative block which was visible through the windows at this side of the bookshop. His head was a glossy catalogue of frightful images, a rotten putrefying grocer's filled with deliquescing cucumbers, split tomatoes, rancid sprouts, slime-ravaged lettuces. Crumbling noses, perforated palates, grotesquely swollen limbs danced in front of his eyes like images from some carnival for the terminally ill. His ears rang with some of the most foul, potent nomenclature he'd ever encountered: 'Teeming treponemes', 'purulent meatus', 'macules', 'pustules', *trichomonas vaginilus, granuloma iguinale,* bejel, venereal warts, *candida albicans* – the bleak, muscular terminology of medicine.

Unthinkingly he touched the blackhead in a nostril cleft, traced the contours of his mouth with his tongue, checked the torsion of his knee joints. There had been an entire lurid chapter on vicious tropical strains. His eyes caught words like 'chancroid', 'giant herpes', 'phagedenic lesions'. There were bizarre afflictions called 'pinta', 'crab-yaws' and, with horrific aptness, 'loath'. A severe tic established itself in his right cheek and his eyes watered as he read on in despairing astonishment. How, he wondered, could such things exist? What dreadful plight had brought these hopeless mutations before the lab-technician's lens? How, even, did they haul their friable, exuding and bloated bodies from place to place? He swallowed, trying to coax his drought-stricken saliva glands into action. He looked down at his stocky frame, sent out cautious messages, twitching feet and fingers. He seemed to sense electric current surging down the branching neurones, the capillaries faithfully irrigating the out-of-condition muscles and tissues, the tendons and cartilege pinning the frail armature of his body together. Don't give up on me, he silently beseeched, hold up a bit longer, he pleaded, don't fall apart. He promised his body he'd keep fit, eat high-fibre foods, treat it well, cosset and cherish its individual parts. He'd become an athletic, Vegan monk, he swore – anything to avoid joining the shiny spot-lit wrecks in the medical illustrations. *Anything*.

He felt tremulous and abashed as he timidly knocked on Murray's door half an hour later. Murray looked up from his desk as he entered and said good morning. He was writing something on a sheet of paper.

'Won't be a minute,' he said. Morgan wondered how Murray intended breaking it to him: whether he would do it gently, leading up to the grim prognosis, or deliver it as a no-nonsense broadside.

'We did a culture on the specimen you gave us,' Murray said, signing his name at the bottom of the piece of paper. He looked up with a brief smile on his face. 'Many urino-genital infections turn out to be non-gonococcal, but, as I told you last night, yours hasn't.'

'How,' Morgan cleared his throat to bring his voice down from piping falsetto. 'How . . . serious is it? I mean, have you the facilities out here to deal with such cases? You see I'm worried about whether I'll have to be flown home.' He swallowed. 'And what about my . . . f-f-face . . . and the rest of my body?'

Murray scrutinized the blurred hieroglyphics on his blotting pad. Oh Jesus, Morgan thought, he can't look me in the eye.

'You've been reading books, haven't you?' Murray said resignedly.

'I've been what? Books? . . . Well, I may have glanced . . .'

'Let *me* do the diagnosing, Mr Leafy. You'll save yourself a lot of grief.'

Morgan resented the patronizing tone in Murray's voice. 'One's naturally concerned . . . to know. The worst, I mean.'

Murray looked at him intently. 'A few cc's of penicillin, Mr Leafy, and three weeks quarantine.'

'Quarantine! What do you mean? Isolation?'

'No, I mean going without sex. Abstinence.'

'That's all?' Morgan questioned, sudden relief mingled with an obscure sense of being somehow cheated. 'An injection and . . . only three weeks?'

Murray raised his eyebrows in mild amusement. 'Two injections actually, just to make sure. Why, what were you expecting? Sulphur baths and amputation?'

Morgan felt foolish, an emotion he was coming to associate with Murray more and more. 'Well,' he said reproachfully. 'One has no idea.'

'Precisely,' Murray said with some force. 'We get on average three or four cases of non-specific sexual diseases a day. And not all of them among the students or the workers. We inject a lot of penicillin into senior staff.' Murray's voice was studiously neutral but Morgan felt he was automatically being classed with a gang of mental defectives. Now that the prospect of a lingering piecemeal death had receded he found Murray was beginning to get on his nerves yet again.

'I need a few facts,' Murray said, and took up his pen. 'First the names of your sexual partners over the last two months.'

'Is that absolutely necessary?'

'The law requires it.'

'Oh. I see. Well, there's only been one.' He spoke Hazel's name with some venom, thinking how close he had come to adding a second. Murray asked her age and address.

'Now,' he said briskly. 'Have you and, ah, your partner indulged in oral or anal sex?'

'Good God!' Morgan said, reddening. 'This is absurd. You're not doing research, are you? What do you need to know that for?'

Murray's features hardened. 'She could get oral or rectal ulcers, Mr Leafy – if it's not treated.' Morgan gulped and muttered oral in a chastened tone of voice. He'd never thought about the other alternative. 'Right,' Murray went on, 'I have to pass her name and this information on to the Ademola clinic in town. It might be better if you personally made sure she went along there. She must be treated too, obviously, and her other sexual partners traced.' He smiled grimly.

'There aren't any other sexual partners,' Morgan said right-eously but without much confidence. He thought for a moment or two. 'Listen, Dr Murray,' he said. 'Do I, ah, need to get involved in this any further. I mean go to the clinic – have my name passed along. There is my . . . my position here to consider – it could prove a little embarrassing. Couldn't we on this occasion forego the absolute letter . . . ?'

'I'm sorry, Mr Leafy,' Murray interrupted unsympath-etically. 'It takes two to tango, as they say, and I'm afraid it's unwise to give too much thought to embarrassment under these circumstances. Why should you get treatment you'd deny . . . ?'

'All right, all right,' Morgan interrupted bitterly. 'Point taken. But at least can't she be treated here? Don't worry, I'll pay. I'm happy to pay for her as a private patient.'

'No,' Murray said. 'Absolutely out of the question.' He scribbled something down on a piece of paper. 'Take that to sister in the surgery. She'll give you your first injection. Come back in six days for the next.' He walked to the door and held it open for him. 'Remember, Mr Leafy,' he said. 'No sexual intercourse and no alcohol for four weeks.'

'*Four*? I thought you said three,' Morgan objected.

'I think in your case we'd better make it four.'

Sitting in his office an hour later Morgan calmly decided that currently he probably hated Murray more intensely than any other human being in his life, though as always, there were a few contenders for first place. He couldn't understand, though, why he was letting Murray persistently get up his nose like this. He was just a functionary, after all; someone with a temporary responsibility for his health who he was obliged to consult at the moment. One met lots of obnoxious people in this category – civil servants, bank clerks, traffic wardens, dental receptionists and so on – in the necessary course of one's life, but they didn't inspire this energy-consuming hate. What was it about Murray, he wondered, that made him want to dash out his brains, run him over with his car, hack him into dog meat with a machete? It wasn't simply his repeated unhelpfulness towards a fellow Briton, his refusal to acknowledge his diplomatic status, or the cynical enjoyment he seemed to take in his, Morgan's, discomfort. Thinking about it further he decided it must be something to do with the way that Murray implicitly set himself in judgement – as a sort of human rebuke, a living breathing admonition to others. It was as if he was saying, look how feeble, pathetic and pretentious you lot are. Certainly that was the dominant impression Morgan gained from his encounters with him. And it was the cast of his features too, he thought: the short hair, the wrinkled suntanned wisdom of his face, his clean clothes, his exclusive healer's knowledge, the apparent absence of doubt and uncertainty in everything the man said. That was it, Morgan thought: when you met Murray all the shabby moral evasions that made up your life, all the grey zones of questionable behaviour, the whole sad compendium of self-regarding acts suddenly stood up to be counted. But what was worse, what was particularly galling about Murray was that, having somehow brought this effect about, he didn't really seem to care any further, wasn't especially surprised to find out that there were so many. We all meet people from time to time who make us feel like shits, Morgan admitted, but Murray was different. He was like a hygiene inspector who points out the filth, the grease and the rat droppings in the condemned kitchen but then goes away, clears off without telling you what to do to get rid of the mess, quite unconcerned whether you clean up the place or not.

Morgan wandered over to the window and stared out at Nkongsamba baking in the heat of the afternoon sun. He was getting tired of the view, it brought no relief, provided no sensations sweet, afforded no glimpses into the life of things for all the hours he spent contemplating it. He was annoyed to find his thoughts dwelling so exclusively on Murray, he had more important problems that demanded all his attention, namely how he was going to repair the awful damage to his relationship with Priscilla, what he was going to do about Adekunle, and the nature of the retribution he was going to inflict on Hazel.

For this last item he contented himself, three hours later, with a ringing slap on her face, but when Hazel collapsed wailing on the bed he was stricken with remorse and apologized, comforting her and covering her face with kisses. He felt like hitting her again, though, when she admitted to three other part-time lovers. He raged up and down the room for five minutes fouling the air with his curses and threats. He then drove her up to the Ademola clinic, a mean and fetid building down a side street near the law courts. They sat in a grubby, finger-smeared waiting room filled with crying children and tired mothers while they waited for a harassed Kinjanjan doctor to attend them. Eventually they were called into a small room and the doctor took down the details of the case. Hazel gave her name and those of her three sexual partners in a quiet voice, her eyes fixed on her hands which fidgeted on her lap.

The doctor looked up at Morgan. 'I believe you are having treatment at the university clinic,' he stated. Morgan admitted this, reflecting that Murray hadn't wasted any time getting on the phone. 'And your name?' the doctor asked. Morgan was surprised, Murray had obviously not told him everything. 'My name?' Morgan said thinking fast, and applying a silencing pressure on Hazel's elbow. 'Jones,' he said. 'Denzil Jones. D,e,n,z,i,l. And my address is . . .'

Chapter 11

Five days later Morgan stood again in the small arrivals hall of Nkongsamba's airport. A sense of déjà vu impressed itself on him strongly. There was the same heat, the Dakota stood on the tarmac, its nacelle still shrouded. The sulky girl still sat behind her badly-stocked bar and the magazines in the revolving rack were unchanged. Only the well-dressed family were absent. Morgan looked at his watch: thirty-five minutes late. He'd made a point of ringing the airport in advance and had been assured that the plane was on time. He paced about the floor shaking his head in disbelief. He couldn't even rely on his precautionary measures in this country: all your prudent checks on projected actions turned out to be a waste of time too.

He was at the airport to meet the new man, one Richard Dalmire. He had brought his own car and was to take Dalmire to the university guest-house where he would be staying until his accommodation was fixed up, and then on to the Fanshawes' for a lunchtime welcome drink. Morgan had been invited too but was not looking forward to it. He had kept a very low profile as far as the Fanshawe family were concerned since his disastrous night with Priscilla, immersing himself in his work, and he wasn't at all sure what sort of reaction he'd get from mother and daughter in public. Fanshawe himself had been away in the capital for a couple of days, finalizing arrangements for Project Kingpin, about which he still enthused, and briefing the High Commissioner on developments in the Mid-West regarding the approaching election. Morgan had been busy cobbling together a report of sorts for him to deliver, based entirely on studious sifting through the previous month's newspapers and what gossip he could pick up around the bar in the club. It was wholly subjective and largely unverifiable but he'd peppered it with jargon and official-sounding language and he had to admit that it looked rather in-depth and professional. He had worried a little about its lack of objectivity but he was coming round to the opinion that it was an impossible ideal, and anyway, nobody else in the capital would know any more than he did about it all.

He spotted Dalmire immediately among the plane's passengers and was surprised to find him so young. He was wearing a light-coloured suit with a pale-blue shirt and, of all things, a straw panama hat. He didn't seem to be feeling the heat at all and Morgan thought he looked like a courier on an up-market package tour, confident, and primed with all the requisite knowledge.

'Hello,' Morgan said, going up to him. 'Dalmire, isn't it? I'm Morgan Leafy, First Secretary.'

Dalmire beamed at him and shook his hand energetically. 'Hello,' he said. 'Glad to be here. I'm Dickie by the way.' His voice had a high, perfectly accented pitch.

Morgan had a curious reluctance to address Dalmire so familiarly; he couldn't explain why, but it would seem somehow like giving in before a shot had been fired. 'Let's get your bags,' he said.

On the way to the university guest-house Dalmire told him how grateful he was to be met by Morgan himself, how pleased he was to make his acquaintance and how thrilling he found it to be sent out to Nkongsamba. 'I mean, just look at it,' he said indicating some flimsy huts and a small herd of goats by a railway crossing they were drawing near. 'Unique, isn't it. Africa. That heat . . . the life . . . It's all so different. We'll never really change it. Not deep down.'

Morgan averted his face to conceal the smile that had appeared on it. Jesus Christ, he thought, where do they dig them up from? He had romanticized about Africa too, once, but that had been back in Britain, before he'd left for it. His colourful images and fond illusions had lasted about five minutes. Dispelled by the furnace blast of heat, littering his path on the walk from the plane to the humming immigration shacks at the international airport. All his Rider Haggard, *Jock of the Bushveldt*, Dr Livingstone-I-presume, *Heart of the Matter* pretensions fell from him with the sweat from his brow. Dalmire's naivety was of a firmer more adamantine cast than his had been: he would give him about two weeks.

They booked Dalmire into the guest-house, deposited his luggage and set out, after a pause to freshen up, on the road again for the Commission. Dalmire was full of questions, like a new boy on his first day at school, and happily conceded the rightness of every opinion Morgan expressed.

'Fanshawe's a Far East man, isn't he?' Dalmire asked.

'Yes,' Morgan said. 'So they sent him to Africa.'

'Does seem a bit odd,' Dalmire agreed, still gazing entranced at the passing landscape. 'How long have you been out here?'

'Getting on for three years.'

'Ah well, I suppose that's why they could send Fanshawe – you'd know the ropes.' Morgan looked round sharply to see if Dalmire was joking, but he seemed serious.

'You may be right,' he said, turning into the driveway of the Commission.

Half an hour later Morgan stood with an orange juice in his hand watching sidelong as Dalmire talked with Priscilla. It had not been as bad as he had feared, Priscilla had greeted him pleasantly enough – no one would have guessed anything was amiss. Fanshawe had been bluff and hearty, needlessly reintroducing him to Dalmire and making some patronizing but flattering remarks about his value. Only from Mrs Fanshawe had a palpable chill emerged, her eyes narrowing slightly as she asked him if it was sherry as usual. Morgan had smiled as broadly as he could and said no, he felt like a soft drink if she didn't mind.

'Oh,' she said obviously surprised. 'Everything all right?'

'Oh fine,' Morgan said confidently. 'Spot of upset tummy, that's all.' The frosty smile on her face as she handed him an orange squash let him know that she wanted to hear nothing further of his intestinal complaints. He was astonished, though, to hear Dalmire's response to Mrs Fanshawe's fluted, 'Sherry for you, Dickie?'

'I'd rather have a G and T if that's no bother,' Dalmire had replied.

It only went to show, Morgan told himself, resignedly, that he had never really fitted in. He'd been drinking their wretched sherry for years because misguidedly he thought they'd like him better for it. He'd never asked for anything else, apart from today, thinking it would be impolite and pushy, and so it had come to be known as his drink. He was just a fool to himself, he decided sadly, looking enviously at Dalmire's clear bluey gin with its clinking ice cubes. He felt suddenly depressed. Fanshawe was wittering on at his elbow about Project Kingpin and how useful his report had been, but Morgan only half-listened. Dalmire was talking to Mrs Fanshawe, asking her intelligent questions about her furniture. Priscilla wandered over to them with a tray of canapés and soon all three were nattering earnestly and easily away in a manner, he instinctively sensed, that he had never achieved.

Later, on the verandah saying their goodbyes, the Fanshawes led Dalmire off to show him their potted plants and he found himself miraculously alone with Priscilla.

'Priscilla,' he began, feeling like an awkward teenager. 'About the other night . . .' She interrupted him with a smile of such seraphic brightness that he wondered if she'd suddenly gone mad.

'Morgan,' she said. 'Let's not talk about it. Let's forget it totally. I'm to blame as well – in a way – so we'll just pretend it never happened. OK?' She paused. 'He seems very nice, Dickie.'

Morgan ignored her. Hope was fluttering in his heart like a moth round a candle flame. 'Priscilla, would you . . . can you? . . . Well, what about coming out tonight. Just a drink that's all, only a quiet drink, we'll . . .'

The bright smile returned. 'Didn't you hear what I said?' she asked patiently. 'Nothing's happened. Nothing's going to happen. Let's just leave it at that. I think it's best. It was all a dreadful mistake. I think it's better that way.'

Morgan hung his head. 'Sure,' he said. 'Of course. But I just wanted to say . . .' He never got the chance because Mrs Fanshawe swept up at that moment with Dalmire and Fanshawe in tow.

On the way back to the university Dalmire said musingly, 'They seem very nice sorts. Very nice indeed.'

'Mmm,' Morgan said non-committally, thinking: there's

no hope for you, boy. But his mind was soon locked back on other matters, such as the utter wreckage of his prospects with Priscilla.

'. . . Priscilla too.'

'What?'

'I was just saying that I liked their daughter too. Very attractive girl,' Dalmire commented appreciatively.

'Yes. I've, ah, been out with her a few times myself since she arrived,' Morgan said possessively, adding subtle emphasis to the words 'been out'.

'Oh I'm sorry . . . I hope you didn't think. Really, I was just . . .'

'It's OK,' Morgan laughed without much conviction. Dalmire was genuinely confused. 'She is attractive,' Morgan went on in a worldly manner. 'As nice as you'll find out here.'

'I am sorry,' Dalmire continued. 'It's just that she's offered to take me down to the club tonight. Show me around. I would hate you to think,' he twirled his hands around each other, 'that I was trying . . . anything.'

Morgan forced himself to smile. 'I'd come with you,' he said, spreading unconcern over his features like butter, 'only I'm tied up with work.'

Chapter 12

It was mid-morning. A clear washed-out blue sky was visible in the top half of the window of Morgan's office. He had been at work since seven-thirty. The phone went.

'Leafy here.'

'Mr Leafy, this is Sam Adekunle.' Morgan almost dropped the phone in surprise. 'Mr Leafy?' Adekunle repeated.

'Hello,' Morgan gasped. 'Good to hear from you. Anything I can do?'

'Yes,' Adekunle admitted. 'There is actually.' His voice was confident and smooth. 'About our last discussion. I think it might be worth resuming it, if you get my drift, so to speak, as you British say.'

Morgan agreed. He said he would be very happy to resume discussions.

'Let's meet at my house then,' Adekunle suggested. 'Do you know where it is on the university campus? Ask at the main gate. Shall we say three-thirty this afternoon?' Morgan said that was fine with him. He put the phone down and sat there feeling excited. At last, the break he wanted. But what did it all mean? Fanshawe had been pestering him for progress on Project Kingpin and Morgan had barely managed to keep him satisfied with the endless sections of his file on Adekunle's party. He felt he could apply for the job of official KNP historian so thorough was his knowledge of its background, membership, power base and influence. And since Dalmire had arrived and taken over most of the routine immigration work, Morgan had had plenty of time to amass his quantities of pointless information. It had become obvious though, that the initial singling-out of the KNP had been the right one to make as far as Britain was concerned. It had an ostensibly liberal–democratic, capitalist base and represented a coalition of Kinjanjan tribal loyalties in contrast to the limited regional background of the ruling UPKP. Whether it would win, however, was another matter. Popular rumblings of discontent over the evident corruption and earnest graft of politicians was intense. Absurdly, Kinjanja was in the top ten of champagne importers worldwide; the rival party newspapers assailed the impoverished, bureaucratically harassed populace with scandalous stories of weekend shopping sprees in Paris and London, village-sized parties with the guests shuttled in by helicopter, forced requisition of Kinjanjan Airlines planes for private use, and so on. Morgan had pages of clippings on gross abuse of power. Clearly the UPKP had to go but it was not so clear that any unchallenged winner would emerge from any of the opposition parties. Ultimately these things were decided on tribal and theological grounds, Morgan had come to learn, and the ethnic and religious mix in Kinjanja seemed, as far as he could establish, to point to no majority government. Still, he thought, closing his file, if you've got to back one horse in this field you could do worse than bet on the KNP.

Adekunle's house was grand and looked twice the size of any other on the campus, probably built by Ussman Danda Ltd, Morgan thought. It was an imposing, square, two-storeyed building with a column-supported balcony running round the entire length of the first floor. Attached to the house was, on one side, a jumble of servants' quarters and, on the other, a three-car garage. It was set in a large well-tended garden which was surrounded by a high barbed-wire fence. It looked like the residence of a state governor rather than the home of a professor of economics and Morgan wondered what Adekunle's university colleagues thought of such conspicuous consumption. Two khaki-clad watchmen opened the iron gates and Morgan pulled into the drive and parked by the front door. Fanshawe had been beside himself with glee when Morgan informed him about the phone call and, not for the first time, wondered if his superior had told him about everything that was riding on the success of Project Kingpin. The plane tickets, apparently, were ready – just waiting for a date – and according to Fanshawe the beds in Claridges were turned down in expectation.

Morgan rang the front-door bell and was shown by a white-uniformed steward into an airy sitting room which like most houses in Kinjanja was open to the garden and the breeze on two sides. The floors were wooden, the furniture light and Swedish-looking. Fine examples of Africana – masks, beaten bronze panels, carved calabashes – hung on the walls. He wondered if this was Celia Adekunle's doing and suspected it was.

She came into the room 'Hello,' she said. 'Sam told me you were coming. I'm afraid he's going to be a bit late.' She was wearing a straight, pale, lime-green summery dress with a V-neck and no sleeves. Morgan realized it was the first time he'd seen her in European clothes. In the shade of the room and set off by the colour of her dress her tan looked very dark.

'Oh I see,' Morgan said. 'Is it all right if I wait?'

'Of course,' she said. 'Please do. Would you like some tea?' They had some tea and chatted aimlessly.

'Lovely house,' Morgan said.

'Do you think so?' she said without much enthusiasm. 'We were hoping to move. I can't stand the fence. Sam was going to build a house nearer town but,' she gave a slight laugh, 'he can't afford it – these election expenses are terrible. The only trouble is that if he wins we'll probably need a bigger fence,' she didn't look at all pleased at the prospect, 'and guards.'

'Don't you want him to win?' he asked.

She looked at him critically. 'It doesn't really matter what *I* want,' she said in a flat voice. She got to her feet and took a cigarette from a box on a coffee table in front of him. As she bent down to pick one out he saw the pale whiteness of her bra down the front of her V-neck. She raised her eyes and caught him looking.

'Cigarette?' she offered, then said, 'No, I forgot. You've given up haven't you.' She looked at her watch, Morgan checked his: it was past four. 'Would you like a drink?' she asked. 'It's a bit late for more tea.' She called for the steward. 'What'll you have?' she asked him.

'Ooh . . .' he tried to look as if he was thinking about it. 'I'll have . . . tell you what, I'll just have a Coke.'

'One Coke and one vodka and tonic,' she directed the steward. She looked back at Morgan, a smile on her face.

'Don't smoke, don't drink. Are you completely vice-free, Mr Leafy?'

'Please, Morgan,' he invited, then shrugged his shoulders. 'I have my share,' he said. She was a strange woman, he thought, there's something curiously aggressive about her. He watched her resume her seat. Her hair was dry-looking, pulled back carelessly in a pony-tail; her eyes had that bruised, half-shut, heavy-lidded look he'd noticed before. Her crossed legs were very brown – even her toes were brown, he saw, where they peeped from her sandals. Her skin had that overtanned look where it loses its gloss and sheen and becomes dull and matt. He wondered if she were brown all over.

'What are you looking at?' she said suddenly.

Morgan was a bit taken aback. 'I . . . I was admiring your tan,' he said, flustered.

'Well, I don't have much else to do,' she confessed. 'I can lie out on the balcony there all day. Follow the sun round. It's . . . quite private. The kids are away at boarding-school, there's nothing here for me to do,' she indicated the house. 'Sometimes I go to the club in town in the mornings just to get away from the university, and the university wives. Yap yap gossip all day.' She stabbed out her cigarette. 'I'm often down there between nine and eleven week-days,' she looked at him pointedly. 'Do you go swimming, Morgan?' she asked.

Good Lord, he thought, this isn't very subtle. 'Yes,' he said. 'I like swimming.' There was a pause. He thought he should depressurize the atmosphere a little. 'I shall have more time for it now,' he said breezily. 'Since the new man's arrived. Taken over all my routine work.'

She came over for another cigarette. 'Is that all your immigration, visa application stuff?' she asked nonchalantly.

'That's right. Shunted it over to Dalmire. Leave me free for other things.' He didn't mean that to be an innuendo and he hoped she wouldn't interpret it that way. His libido was in very poor shape these days and he still had a week and a half to run on his quarantine.

'But,' she casually blew smoke into the air. 'You, ah, no doubt still have overall control of that side of things.'

'Oh yes,' Morgan said patronizingly. 'Young Dalmire only does the routine stuff – doesn't really know the ropes yet. Anything problematic still has to come through me.'

'I see,' she nodded, then looked up suddenly. 'I think that sounds like Sam.' She got to her feet. 'If you'll excuse me, Morgan, I know Sam won't want to be disturbed.' She walked towards the stairs. Morgan stood up. 'I enjoyed our chat,' she said. 'Perhaps I'll see you at the club some morning this week.' She skipped quickly up the stairs as Morgan heard Adekunle come through the front door. He turned to meet him.

'My good friend Mr Leafy,' Adekunle greeted him jovially, looking trussed-up and sweaty in a three-piece suit. He dumped a slim briefcase on an armchair and strode across the room, a pale brown palm extended. 'How is everything going?' he asked. 'Has Celia been looking after you well?'

'He *what*?' Fanshawe squeaked in outrage, plucking at the tiny hairs of his moustache. 'My God, the bloody nerve!'

'Yes, definitely,' Morgan said. 'He wants two weeks at Claridges and a car with a driver.'

Fanshawe looked shocked. 'Good grief,' he said. 'Just who do these chappies think they are?'

'And,' Morgan went on. 'He wants an open ticket, two in fact, and he wants to be met officially at the airport.'

'*Officially*?' Fanshawe shook his head in disbelief. 'What did you say to all this?'

Morgan paused. 'I said it was OK . . .' Fanshawe looked up in alarm. 'Of course I said I'd have to clear it first – made no firm promises.'

'Thank God for that,' Fanshawe ran his hand over his head,

smoothing down the smooth hair. 'Just as well, as I'm not at all sure we can swallow all that, not sure at all.'

'It should do the trick though,' Morgan suggested. 'Adekunle said that if we could arrange all this he'd forget about the other invitations.'

'What other invitations?' Morgan had never told him.

'To Paris, Washington, Rome.'

'Oh my God,' Fanshawe went pale. Morgan wondered just what he'd been telling the High Commissioner, what he'd guaranteed the mandarins in the Foreign Office. He saw suddenly that the man was as desperate to escape as he was: Project Kingpin was his passport out of Nkongsamba too. He watched Fanshawe drumming his fingers nervously on his desk top. 'He'll forget about them, you say?' he asked.

'So he assures me,' Morgan said. 'He says that he's not prepared to sell Kinjanja round the globe at this stage.' Morgan went on, trying to reassure him, 'I mean, Adekunle apart, it makes sense. Kinjanja was a British colony: it's natural for him to come to us. And I think he's bluffing to a certain extent. He doesn't want the French influence to spread any more in West Africa, and the Americans are tied up in Vietnam.'

Fanshawe looked at him. 'Yes,' he agreed. 'But it wouldn't do at all for him to go swanning off to these other countries. Especially if we give him what he asks for – I mean, that has to be a condition we lay down. Wouldn't do at all,' he repeated, 'he hasn't even been elected yet.'

'I don't think he could even if he wanted to. If he's going to be in the UK for two weeks it doesn't leave him much time for electioneering. He's got to be on the scene here: polling day's getting closer all the time and he's a big man in the party.'

Fanshawe brightened at this. 'That's true,' he said. 'You're right.' Morgan felt pleased with himself: he liked talking about the French and Americans in this way, enjoyed his confident analyses of the political situation. Fanshawe was putting a lot of faith in him, it was obvious.

'I'll see what I can do about his various requests,' Fanshawe said, frowning with concentration. 'They're getting awfully important these elections,' he said. 'There are more oil finds in the river delta. Lots of British money in there now. New refinery being built.' He spread his palms on the blotter and smiled weakly at Morgan. 'Your reports have confirmed Adekunle as our man. The High Commissioner's most impressed with your work, but there's a lot riding on it, you know. More than a couple of weeks in Claridges. Oh yes, much more now.' He paused, his frown still buckling his forehead. Morgan began to sense worry in the atmosphere, it seeped in through his pores. He wondered for a moment if Fanshawe was trying to put the wind up him – but then he realized he wasn't that good an actor.

'I'm sure we've made the right choice, Arthur,' he said.

'Oh yes,' Fanshawe said, waving his hand as if to disperse a cloud of cigarette smoke. 'I'm sure you have.'

Morgan walked out of the men's changing room into the glare of the morning sun, suddenly conscious of the coruscating dazzle of his surfing shorts. Around his neck he had casually slung a towel, the ends of which hung down over his broad chest. He wasn't too enamoured of public swimming, it made him hyper-aware of the inadequacy of his tan, the considerable size of his body and the countless millions of freckles that were sprinkled over it. Standing in front of the waist-high mirror in the changing room, inspecting himself before venturing outside, he had been alarmed, on presenting a profile of his torso, to see how far his breasts projected and vowed again to resume dieting and exercise.

He strode with false confidence out onto the terrace, acutely aware of his breasts juddering beneath the slung towel. At the tables and loungers around the poolside sat the usual quota of bored wives, some with children too young for nursery school. There were no men apart from an old white-haired fellow who was relaxing in the water at the deep end, his elbows hooked over the guttering, his feet idly kicking beneath the surface. Morgan looked closely at him: he always and immediately suspected such immobile contentment to be a sign of a covert subaquatic piss, but on reflection decided that the old chap just seemed to be enjoying the sun. Morgan found two unoccupied loungers and removed his towel and watch. Celia Adekunle had said she would be at the pool by half past ten. She was usually prompt.

He walked over to the shallow end and dived into the cool blue water. He glided beneath the surface enjoying the sensation of the water flowing over his skin, then broke through into the sunlight and set off down the length of the pool in a powerful and splashy crawl, driving the old man away from his comfortable perch. One of Morgan's flailing arms thwacked him across a retreating leg.

'So sorry,' Morgan called, enjoying himself, 'can't seem to change course once I've started.'

'Aaagh! Christ!' Morgan shouted as a spatter of cold water landed on his hot back. He turned round and squinted into the sun and saw Celia Adekunle leaning above him wringing out her wet hair over his body.

'Sorry I'm late,' she said, flopping onto the lounger and flinging her arms wide as she faced the sun. 'Whew,' she gasped, 'Water's lovely.'

'Bloody hell,' Morgan said, drying his back. 'You could give someone a heart attack like that.' He smiled. This was their third meeting by the pool in as many days. One morning he had been driving across Nkongsamba en route for the Commission and had spontaneously decided to call into the club. As she had told him he would, he found Celia there. They met again the following day, Morgan equipped with his swimming trunks this time, and they had swum, sunbathed and talked. She had left just after midday, but not before setting up this third meeting. Morgan found he enjoyed being with her. As he had noticed at their first encounter there was an implied intimacy in their exchanges, an unspoken familiarity, as if they possessed some private knowledge about each other, sensed instinctively the shared motives beneath the banter, but enjoyed the subterfuge nonetheless. He couldn't define it any more coherently than that, or even explain why it should have arisen in the first place.

He watched her settle on the lounger. Her eyes were closed against the sun, so he could observe her openly. She was wearing a yellow bikini, her body was thin and very brown. Her breasts were small and her legs thin with prominent boney knees. One puckered inch of appendectomy scar showed above the top of her bikini pants. The skin on her stomach was loose, leathery, almost, from the sun and creased as the result of her two children, he suspected. Looking at her this dispassionately he had to admit that there was nothing that physically really attracted him to her, and this perplexed him somewhat.

He lay back on his towel, shielding his eyes with a forearm. This being the case, he wondered, why was he spending so much time with her? Well, he told himself, she was potentially a prime source for information on Adekunle and the KNP – which was the explanation he would offer if Fanshawe ever saw fit to question him about his mornings at the pool. He had, certainly, learned that a considerable portion of Adekunle's private fortune had gone to buy certain influential figures very expensive gifts, and had ascertained that Ussman Danda Ltd was becoming dangerously overdrawn at the bank. But otherwise he had discovered little that he didn't know already: Adekunle, it appeared, didn't talk much about his political business; in fact, so Celia said, he hardly spoke to her at all. It was, she stressed, virtually a token marriage now. This information had been supplied the day before. Morgan had accompanied her to her car after their swim. After she told him this there had been a pause. Morgan had said, 'Oh I see.'

'You know,' she had said abruptly, looking at him with disturbing directness, 'we needn't meet *here*. We could go somewhere else.'

'Somewhere else?' he had said artlessly. 'I'm afraid I don't quite follow.'

She had made a small grimace, as though it was a response she had expected. She hunched her shoulders. 'One afternoon,' she said frankly, 'we could go for a drive.'

He had felt touched and flattered by the candour of her approach, sensing vaguely the emotional effort required to make it. He was flattered because it was the first time this had happened to him – at least in daylight and under conditions of sobriety. He thought of his quarantine period, still with several days to run, and said with as much respect and gentlemanly understanding as he could marshal, laying his hand on her arm, 'No, Celia, I don't really think we should go for a drive, not now anyway.'

She had laughed with a hollow gaiety, and shook her hair. 'No, you're right,' she said. 'Silly of me. I must be getting all confused.' She paused. 'Thanks though,' she said earnestly and climbed into the car. She wound down the window. 'We can still meet tomorrow, can't we? Same time?'

As he lay back now he asked himself if he would have been so thoughtful and reticent if he hadn't been working the dreaded gonococci out of his system. He didn't press himself too strongly on that point, didn't insist on an answer: it was sufficient, surely, that he'd behaved commendably, taken care that there was no reason for Celia to think she'd done anything cheap. Out of the corner of his eye he watched her turn over and unclip her bikini top to present a bare back to the sun. As she awkwardly attempted to slip her arms out of the straps one breast suddenly hung free like a bell before it was resnugged in its bra cup. He knew, then, that he was kidding himself: his mornings with Celia Adekunle had nothing to do with information-gathering.

A while later, after a swim and some conversation, he ordered drinks and a sandwich. The steward brought the clinking tray over. Celia looked across her vodka and tonic at him sipping his Coke and said, 'I don't know how you do it, Morgan. You must be the only man in Nkongsamba who doesn't drink.'

Morgan tapped his stomach. 'I promised myself I'd lose some beef.'

Celia laughed. 'Well, drinking Coke won't help.' She had a point there, he thought. He was about to say that he reckoned he'd be packing it in soon anyway when he saw a sight that made his chest thump with apprehension.

'Oh Jesus Christ,' he swore. Emerging from the ladies' half of the changing block at the far end of the pool were Priscilla and her mother. Priscilla was wearing her reinforced Olokomeji costume while her mother favoured a short white towelling robe which blew apart as she walked to reveal an immense two-piece maroon swimsuit of the sort favoured by pregnant women or demure American matrons; the kind that has two loose theatre-curtain flaps hanging from the upper half that effectively retain the necessary modesty while allowing the wearer the freedom of a two piece – if she's pregnant – or the impression she's still young enough for one – if she's conceited. Through the gap in the curtain Morgan caught a glimpse of very, very white skin, and above the top half noted the razor-thin crease of compressed cleavage surrounded by a juddering jelly-sea of tightly packed and constrained bosom. Two sturdy blue-veined thighs completed this vision of an ageing Juno, a thickened, middle-aged and middle-class Botticelli Venus returning to the waves, clutching in her right hand a rubber flower-bedecked bathing cap.

As they drew near it became obvious to Morgan that they had seen him but were, independently or by mutual pact, going to pretend they hadn't. From sheer obstinacy he decided he wasn't going to let this happen.

'Chloe! Priscilla!' he hailed as they came closer, the joviality of his tones belying the nervousness he felt. He hadn't seen Priscilla since the day he'd bumped into her and Dalmire at the club: Dalmire genial and talkative, Priscilla proudly independent. Recognition made inevitable by his shout, he saw her adopt this no-hard-feelings pose again.

'Hello,' she said gaily. 'Thought I'd seen those trunks before.'

He looked down, suddenly conscious of how prominently his groin bulged. 'Yes,' he said, sensing the nervousness about to overwhelm him. 'They are rather crying out for attention, aren't they.' He hurriedly introduced Celia. 'You know Celia Adekunle I think. Chloe Fanshawe, Priscilla Fanshawe.' They agreed they did. Morgan sensed the eyes of Mrs Fanshawe burning behind the opaque discs of the sunglasses she wore, sizing up, evaluating, condemning.

'Day off?' she asked through smiling teeth.

He was furious at the implication. He turned to face her. 'All work and no play,' he said in a steely voice. 'Don't want Jack turning into a dull boy, do we.'

There was an uncomfortable silence as the hostility seemed to crackle between them. 'Well, we mustn't keep you,' Mrs Fanshawe said. 'Goodbye, Mrs Adekunle . . . Morgan.' They marched off, Morgan stared hatefully at her broad beam.

'Goodness me,' Celia said. 'What on earth did you do to offend her?'

'God knows,' Morgan said uncomfortably. 'Something to do with being alive I think.' He sat there in silence, seething and cursing at being witnessed like this.

'Morgan,' Celia said. 'What's going on . . . ?' For a horrible moment he thought she was going to ask about Priscilla, but the pause only came about because she was lighting a cigarette. '. . . between you and Sam? What's this great interest all about?'

He breathed a sigh of relief. 'Nothing really,' he said cautiously, though he felt instinctively he could trust her, 'just some footling idea of Fanshawe's. He thinks Sam's party's going to win the election so we're being very friendly.' His mind was still on Priscilla so he added without thinking, 'That's why we're giving him the flight.'

'Flight? Where?'

'To London. For two weeks.' He looked round. 'Oh Christ,' he said. 'Didn't you know? Shit, I'm sorry.'

Celia smiled grimly and took a long trembling drag on her cigarette. As she exhaled she shook her head. 'No,' she replied. 'I didn't know. To London?'

'Yes,' he said, wondering if he'd given something vital away. 'He asked specifically for two seats – I had the tickets delivered today – I just assumed he'd be taking you . . . Perhaps it's a surprise,' he added gamely.

She laughed harshly. 'Fat chance,' she said. 'You see, Sam's got this possessive thing about me. He doesn't allow me to leave the country. I haven't been home for three years. He thinks that if I ever get back to Britain he'll never see me again.'

Morgan swallowed. 'Is he right? I mean, would you run away?'

She seemed quite composed again. 'Oh yes,' she said. 'Like a shot.'

Chapter 13

It was 3.45 in the afternoon. Morgan's Peugeot was parked down a laterite track in the shade of a towering mango tree which stood somewhere in the middle of a half-grown teak forest. Slim twenty-foot teak trees stretched away on both sides of the track, their oversized soup-plate leaves hanging motionless in the afternoon's torpid dust-heat. Celia

Adekunle's Mini was parked just in front of Morgan's car which had all its doors open, as if the driver and passengers had suddenly abandoned it in the face of an ambush or air attack and run into the forest.

Celia and Morgan knelt naked facing each other on the towel-draped back seat. This seemed to be the point to which all their conversations and meetings had inevitably been heading. There was a sense of something final in the air, of something ended, reached. They had talked calmly, kissed and removed their clothes with no trace of self-consciousness. Beyond the pool of shadow cast by the mango tree the sun seemed to beat down on the growing forest with a metallic solid strength, like bars round a prison cell. Morgan felt a sweat-drop trickle down the side of his face. Celia's hair looked damp and tousled. She dragged it back and held if off her neck with both hands, causing her small flat breasts with their disproportionately large nipples to rise.

'Oh my God,' she said. 'It's too hot for sex.'

Morgan leant forward over his thickening penis and licked the shine between her breasts. He felt as though he were in some kind of tin sauna, every inch of his body was moist, warm and dripping.

'Oh no it's not,' he said.

'Most impressive,' Fanshawe said. 'They were most impressed in the High Commission. Most impressed.' He handed back the Project Kingpin file. Morgan tucked it under his arm. Fanshawe had just returned from an important meeting in the capital. He settled back in his chair. 'We've done well, Morgan,' he said. 'Exactly the results I hoped this little . . . exercise would bring. I can tell you that as a result of our assessment of the political future in Kinjanja there's talk of substantially increasing UK investment here. Going to buy more oil from them too.' He held his hand out across the table. 'Pat on the back time, I think.' Morgan shook his hand, feeling a little foolish. 'It's not over yet though,' Fanshawe went on, wagging a cautionary finger. 'Let's hope they don't lose the election.' He laughed 'Mwah. Mwah-hwah-hwah.' He was joking.

Morgan managed a cheesy grin, a chill dispersing the brief warmth of self-congratulation. He wished in a way that Fanshawe took him along to these meetings he had at the High Commission in the capital; without that check there was no telling what lies and embellishments he passed on. Fanshawe was still talking. Morgan heard the word 'ambition'.

'Sorry, Arthur,' he redirected his attention. 'What was that?'

Fanshawe frowned. 'I was saying that the one thing we want to know a bit more about is Adekunle's personal ambitions. Apparently there's some feeling that he's got his sights set higher than Foreign Minister. What do you think?'

'I'll see what I can dig up,' Morgan said efficiently. He would ask Celia. He was seeing her again at six in the teak forest. Adekunle was out of town for a couple of days. The thought crossed his mind that this was using her rather. It crossed his mind and kept on going.

'I hear you've got a source very close to our Mr Kingpin,' Fanshawe said slyly. His wife must have been talking, Morgan thought.

Morgan put on a stagily innocent look. 'Oh, I just keep my ear to the ground you know.'

Fanshawe chuckled, 'Good man,' he said and stood up. 'Well, I'm off to lunch.' Morgan deposited the file in his office and walked down the main stairs with him. They passed Dalmire's office on the ground floor. Eight document-clutching visa supplicants sat outside the door on wooden benches.

Morgan and Fanshawe stood in the shade of the portico and gazed down the drive like a couple of squires surveying their property.

'I see Kingpin hasn't got round to making his trip yet,' Fanshawe commented.

'No,' Morgan said. 'I sent him the tickets a couple of days ago. He wanted the dates left open.'

'I know,' Fanshawe said. 'It's just that I keep getting asked when he's coming. Trouble with the hotel apparently. Can't you tell him to get his skates on?'

'He's not that sort of a person,' Morgan explained. 'But it must be soon, what with the elections being so close.'

'Beats me,' Fanshawe said: 'I'd have thought these fellas would have jumped at the chance of a few days in London . . .' He paused for a few seconds, as if pondering the natives' curious behaviour. 'Young Dalmire seems to have settled in well,' he said, changing tack.

'Yes,' Morgan agreed. Now they were a couple of house-masters discussing a new appointee to prefect. 'Pleasant chap,' he added. He found the implied status and importance conferred by their conversation not at all unpleasant. For an instant he understood what it must have been like in the old days, as they scrunched onto the gravel on the driveway. The uniformed doorman saluted, the sweating gardeners in their tattered shorts stopped their hoeing and weeding to greet them with wide subservient smiles.

'We've got this official visit coming up soon too,' Fanshawe reminded him, gazing imperiously across the dusty brown lawn. 'Duchess of Ripon. It seems she'll be with us for Christmas now. Bit of a stop over before going down to the capital for the Independence celebrations at New Year.'

'Ah. Yes. I see,' Morgan nodded importantly; Fanshawe had already told him about this and he wondered what he could be leading up to.

'Thought it could be Dickie's pigeon.'

'Sorry? Who?'

'Dalmire, Dickie Dalmire, man.'

'Oh yes.'

'Thought I'd let him handle the arrangements. Turns out his mother knows the Duchess quite well.'

'Right.' Morgan was surprised and a little resentful. 'Best to keep it in the family I suppose. I didn't know there was this connection.'

'Neither did I,' Fanshawe said. 'He told us all about it at dinner last night.'

Morgan walked round the flat with Hazel. It was sparsely furnished but it would do for her. It was in a good part of town too, as far as he was concerned. It wasn't a slum, nor near one, and there were some shops around, which could explain his presence if he was ever seen in the street. And it was a district only rarely visited by expatriates. Their neighbours were the Lebanese landlord's brother with his fat monoglot wife, and an assistant producer from the KTV studios. If he was discreet – or more importantly if Hazel was – there should be no problems, and it would in any event be better than the sordid hotel she had been staying in.

Mr Selim, the landlord, was downstairs in his boutique and fabric shop waiting while Morgan looked over the premises. He wandered into the bedroom. There was an iron frame bed with a thin, pink and dubiously stained Dunlopillo mattress on it. Hazel came in and bounced up and down on the bed setting up a cacophony of shouting metal.

'Ah-ah,' she said in pidgin. 'Dis bed 'e done need oilo.' This allusion to the main purpose of establishing her in the flat was another example of her compulsive tactlessness, Morgan thought. There was a kind of recalcitrant primitive innocence beneath the European clothes and make-up, a sort of happy fatalism. She contracted gonorrhoea, she was unfaithful, she cajoled him into renting her a flat: it was all the same to her. He could fume and rant, posture and pontificate, her attitude seemed to say, but pretty soon he'd calm down – the next time he felt like getting into bed. Lately he'd been finding this refusal to pretend, this satisfaction with brute facts intensely annoying, but, at the same time, he rather envied it. He suspected that life might possibly appear a lot less complicated that way.

Hazel came over and put her arms round his neck. She was wearing a short orange dress and white-rimmed sunglasses. 'What do you think of it, Morgan?' she asked. She accentuated the second syllable when she pronounced his name. 'It will be good. Don't you think so?'

'Take those bloody sunglasses off,' he ordered crossly. She meekly complied. He looked around. 'It's a bit of a dump,' he said, 'but it'll do, I suppose.' Hazel gave a squeal of pleasure and kissed him. Morgan returned it. She took his bottom lip between her teeth and nibbled it gently.

Morgan broke away. He had not made love with Hazel since their quarantine period had ended. Something about the brazen health of her body was holding him back, also the obscure idea that he still had to punish her somehow, show he was maintaining his displeasure at her earlier conduct. He wondered if she appreciated the subtle vindictive motives behind his behaviour. No, he thought, she probably considered him an idiot. In compensation he reminded himself of Celia's worn, flawed body: the small sagging breasts, the dull over-tanned skin, the appendix scar, her accommodating thighs. At least there was somebody who – however amazing it seemed – liked him for himself.

He looked at Hazel's buttocks straining the orange fabric of her dress, her thin legs in their high heels, the false luxury of her wig. But he needed Hazel too, he conceded. The last time he'd met Celia she'd reminded him of the impending arrival of her two boys for their Christmas holidays; it would be hard to meet then, she'd told him, if not impossible.

He congratulated himself on his well-laid contingency plans; he felt the satisfaction of a food-hoarder in a time of hardship – how clever he'd been, how well-off he'd be. But he also felt the inward bite of lonely selfishness and he despairingly admitted to himself that he just wasn't the kind of man who could take the money and run; he always had to stop outside the bank and have a think about it.

'You haven't told Mr Selim who I am, have you?' Morgan demanded of Hazel. 'He doesn't know anything about me, does he?' Hazel assured him Selim knew no more than was absolutely necessary. Morgan hoped she was telling the truth. Selim was no fool, he'd guess what was going on – just as long as he didn't make the connection between him and the Commission. A scandal of those proportions would be disastrous and not even the good opinions he'd amassed over Project Kingpin could help him there.

He counted out a month's rent and handed the notes to Hazel. 'There you are,' he said. 'I'll look in tomorrow evening, see how you've settled down. Expect me around seven.'

Chapter 14

Morgan slipped his feet into his shoes and stood up. The sun had nearly set, he could see its orange syrupy light gilding the flat leaves at the top of the higher teak trees. He stretched and rested his side for a moment against the warm metal of the Peugeot. He was naked. He peered into the car and saw Celia dabbing at herself with a tissue.

'Just off for a pee,' he said. He strode a few yards into the teak trees, his shoes crushing the brittle leaf-carpet with resounding crackles, and drenched a column of ants with his urine stream. The column broke up in confusion, and he entertained himself picking off stragglers while the pressure lasted. He wondered what the ant-world would make of that little episode. Did it, he wondered, somewhere fit into the scheme of ant-things?

He made his way back to the car, ducking under branches, brushing aside some of the lower boughs carelessly. He felt a slight breeze on his naked body and felt his skin respond with goosepimples. He heard the moronic unvaried chirrup of crickets and the beeping sonar of a fruit-bat on the wing.

'One man against nature,' he said to himself in a deep American accent, 'nood, in the African farst.' For a second or two he tried to imagine himself thus exposed, a creature of pure instinct. The setting was right: dusk, heat, foliage, animal noise, mysterious crepitations in the undergrowth. But *he* was wrong. What would anyone think if they saw him? A naked overweight freckled white man pissing on some ants. He looked down at his feet. And, he added, wearing brown suede Chelsea boots.

As he approached the car he plucked off a teak leaf and held it over his genitals. Celia sat in the rear seat, her head resting in the angle its back made with the window. She had a dreamy, peaceful look on her face. She saw him and laughed.

'And they saw that they were naked,' he said in a sonorous voice, 'and were sore ashamed. Come on Eve, make thyself an apron of teak leaves.' He flung his leaf into the car and clambered in to join her. He pressed his face into her lap feeling the wiry moistness of her pubic hair on his cheek and nose. He smelt the spermy salty smell of their sex.

She ran her fingers through his hair. He wished she wouldn't do that.

He sat up and looked at her. He traced the areola of her nipple with his fingernail, watching it pucker and thicken. He pressed it as if it were some kind of fleshy bell-push.

'OK?' he said. She nodded, still smiling. 'Recovered?' he asked.

'Yes thank you, Adam dear.'

'It's God, if you don't mind. I've just drowned a few hundred ants out there.'

'Why God, you sod!'

He gave her a kiss. 'We'd better go I suppose.'

'There's no hurry,' she said, stroking his face. 'I told you, Sam's away until tomorrow.'

'Great,' he said. 'Why don't we go and have a drink somewhere then?'

They dressed, got into their separate cars and drove carefully up the track and on to the road. Morgan looked in his rear-view mirror and saw the lights of Celia's Mini close behind him. He felt stiff, tired and, remarkably, he thought, happy.

About two miles from Nkongsamba he pulled into the car park of a largish hotel at a major road junction. It was called the Nkongsamba Road Motel. In Kinjanja names moved between extravagant, metaphorical fancy or prosaic, no-nonsense literalness. There was no in-between. They went into the bar which was lit with green neon and decorated with soft drink and beer advertisements. There were a dozen tin tables with chipped and peeling chairs round them. On one wall was a large poster of Sam Adekunle, and the message 'KNP for a united Kinjanja' below it.

Celia smiled grimly at Morgan. 'Can't seem to get away from him, can I?'

'Do you want to go somewhere else?' Morgan asked feeling an acid sickness spread throughout his stomach at the sight of Adekunle's face.

'Don't be silly,' she said. 'I don't mind and there's no chance of anybody recognizing me.' She sat down to put a stop to any further argument and Morgan ordered two beers. The bar was quiet at this time of night; there were a couple of the inevitable sunglassed youths and a table of four soldiers. Morgan and Celia attracted curious but unhostile stares: the Nkongsamba Road Motel didn't entice many white clients.

They sipped at their beers in silence. Morgan felt ill at ease though, with Adekunle's face staring at him over Celia's shoulder.

'Relax,' she said. 'It's only a poster.'

But he's looking straight at me,' Morgan said only half-jokingly. 'It's uncanny the way his eyes follow you round the room.' He held up his beer. 'Cheers,' he said, 'here's to the Garden of Eden.' They clinked glasses.

'It's hot though, isn't it,' Celia said. 'Can't you do something about the weather, God dearest?' Morgan smiled, it was their first private joke, sacrosanct, like a code no one could crack.

'Bloody uncomfortable as well,' he said. 'I shall have to get on to Peugeot's design team. They've slipped up badly with their back seat, I must say. Real lack of foresight.'

'Oh for a bed,' Celia sighed.

'I'll drink to that.' He raised his glass again.

'Guess what,' Celia said, dropping her voice to a husky whisper. 'I can feel you slowly oozing out of me while I'm sitting here.' For some reason the unadulterated candour of this statement left him at a loss for words.

'Sorry,' was all he managed to come up with.

She reached over and laid her hand on his arm. 'Don't be sorry,' she said softly. 'It's lovely.'

They finished their beers and went back out to the car park. A nail-sickle of moon hung suspended over Nkongsamba.

'Morgan,' Celia said, 'why don't you come back tonight? While Sam's away.'

'Are you sure?' Morgan questioned seriously. 'Isn't it a bit risky?'

'Please,' she said. 'The kids'll be back in a week. It might be our only chance.'

He hesitated. 'Well, if you're sure it's not too difficult.' He paused. 'This sounds absurdly Victorian,' he said, trying not to smile, 'but what about the servants?'

She was not so inhibited and gave a high clear laugh. 'Don't worry,' she said eventually, 'I can easily take care of them. Come on.'

He lay on Celia's bed. His head was propped on some pillows. A glass of whisky balanced on his chest. He squinted at it hypnotically as it tipped and wobbled with the rise and fall of his breathing.

'Do you feel at all guilty?' he asked. 'About Sam?' It was a question he asked of all the wives he slept with. Celia put her drink down on the bedside table and slipped in beside him. Morgan steadied his glass.

'No,' she said bluntly, as they all did. Celia leant back against the headboard and drew her knees up. 'Why should I? He's been through all his so-called cousins and nieces who hang around the house. God knows what he gets up to when he's away from home.'

'Is this the first time you've . . . ?' He let the question hover unfinished in the air.

She looked at him steadily. 'No. But let's not talk about that.'

'OK,' he said. 'Sorry.' He wasn't sure how he felt about that admission. He had thought he was something of a liberator – exclusive. He put it out of his mind.

Celia had gone to the house in advance of him, told the servants they could go home and, as soon as the coast was clear, had driven back to where he had parked the Peugeot – three hundred yards down the road – and picked him up.

Bereft of the pragmatic necessities brought about by sex in the back seat of a car their love-making had taken on a new and unfamiliar character that Morgan had found strange and a little discomfiting. It had been passionate and emotional – largely on Celia's part – straightforward and humour-free. She had caressed him almost maternally, whispering endearments, holding him tightly to her and he had felt like saying 'Hang about, just stop there a minute. This is sex, mature pleasure, not a love affair.' But he hadn't, and to his consternation had found himself joining in, closing his eyes, gasping romantically, dabbing little kisses here and there.

When the lights went back on things had sobered down, and the loosed and soaring emotions had been wound in like kites. Morgan lay on his back thinking about it all, a frown on his face. He wasn't sure if this was the way he wanted his relationship with Celia to go.

'Penny for them,' she said.

'What? . . . Oh, not worth it,' he smiled. She snuggled up to him and he put his drink on the bedside table. The air-conditioner was on and the roof fan beat above the bed too. The sheet lay dry across their two bodies. Morgan relished the absence of sweat. 'It's been a marvellous day,' he said, half-meaning it.

She kissed his chest. 'Hasn't it,' she agreed with enthusiasm, 'hasn't it just.'

Morgan whispered goodbye as Celia let him out of the front door. It was nearly four o'clock and still quite dark. He cautiously walked up the wide drive, through the open unattended gates and along the road to where he'd left his car. He felt tired, mentally and physically. The prospect of work in four hours was singularly unappealing.

He fumbled in the dark for his car keys.

'Good morning, Mr Leafy,' came a deep voice at his shoulder. The shock was so great his heart seemed to leap from his chest and bounce off the inside of his skull. He whirled round in fear and appalled surprise, his pulse thumping wildly somewhere in the region of his throat. It was Adekunle.

'Oh my God. Shit. Jesus,' Morgan whimpered in frantic despair, the keys falling from his hand to tinkle on the road. Adekunle bent down to retrieve them for him. Morgan accepted them back with trembling fingers.

'Did you have a pleasant night?' Adekunle asked sardonically, no trace of anger in his voice. 'Did you "make a catch" with my wife?' His cultured tones accentuated the Kinjanjan expression, he seemed astonishingly calm.

'Listen,' Morgan began defensively, trying to control an overpowering urge to take to his heels. 'I don't want you to think . . .'

'Don't tell me what to think, Mr Leafy,' Adekunle interrupted, hostility creeping into his voice. 'I don't need your observations on that matter. At all.' He paused. 'No, we have a problem with you here; the cat is now among the pigeons, as the saying goes, don't you think?' At the word 'we' Morgan looked around and saw two dark figures standing some yards off. Adekunle allowed him to take this in before saying, 'I wonder what your Mr Fanshawe will say when I make my protest to him about the . . . ah, nocturnal activities of his staff.' He poked Morgan savagely in the shoulder. 'What do you think his reaction will be, Mr Leafy?' Morgan couldn't answer: he was trying to stop himself being sick all over Adekunle's shoes. Adekunle prodded him again. 'You are a very greedy man, Mr Leafy. Very big appetite. My wife *and* your black girl in town.'

Morgan felt his legs were about to collapse spastically beneath him. He leant shakily against his car. 'How do you know all this?' he asked faintly. 'About Hazel and . . . and tonight?'

'It's my business to know these things,' Adekunle said silkily. He said it 'beezness', emotion cracking his Western accent. 'I have some very loyal servants working for me. No small detail escapes them.'

Morgan strove to make out Adekunle's features in the gloom. He felt queasy with fear and terror-struck anticipation. Surely Adekunle wouldn't go to Fanshawe with this? he reasoned; the shame, the loss of face would be too acute. But then he remembered that Hazel was to be reckoned with too.

Perhaps it might be best if Adekunle simply set his hefties on him.

'Look,' Morgan, began desperately, 'I don't know what you mean to do but I think you . . .'

'One moment, Mr Leafy,' Adekunle broke in venomously. 'You are making an error there. It is a question of what *you* are going to do. For me.'

Morgan felt hysterical laughter rise in his throat. '*Me?*' he repeated slowly as if he were mentally retarded. 'For *you?*'

'You have hit the nail on the head first time, as the saying goes,' Adekunle congratulated him. Morgan saw with a sudden terrorized clarity the impossibility of his situation. If Adekunle went to Fanshawe that would truly be the end, there would be no conceivable way he could talk himself out of it. He groaned softly to himself. Sleeping with Kingpin's wife! Fanshawe would go mad. And he could imagine how Adekunle could play it up: Fanshawe would see it as the end of all his expansionist dreams – the oil refinery, the investment, his new posting – he'd take it as a personal affront. And there was Hazel too. Morgan felt the blood drain from his face. If he wanted his life to continue in anything like the way he'd planned he would have to do whatever Adekunle asked of him. The alternatives were too mortifying and disastrous to consider. Adekunle had him in the palm of his hand.

'What are you going to do?' Morgan croaked. He didn't care: as long as he could save his neck and his job.

'As I told you, Mr Leafy, *I* am going to do nothing. Absolutely nothing. In return for which you will do me a favour – nothing too difficult for a man like you.' He paused. 'We are both civilized people, men of the world, Mr Leafy. I think we can both benefit from this . . . this indiscretion on your part. You retain your job, your status and your reputation. While I . . .' He left it unsaid.

'What do you want me to do?' Morgan said tiredly. He

couldn't see how he could be of any benefit to Adekunle: he just wasn't powerful enough.

'All I want you to do is get to know somebody,' Adekunle said. 'That's all. Just get to know him.'

'Who is this somebody?'

'Dr Alex Murray. Perhaps you're familiar with him already?'

Chapter 15

Adekunle gave him other instructions that night. First, he was to stay away from Celia – their affair was effectively over. Adekunle, it soon transpired, was making his London trip in three days' time and under no circumstances was Morgan to approach Celia while he was away. He assured Morgan that he would know immediately if he made any attempt to get in touch. Second, he was never to tell her about their meeting tonight: Celia was to remain ignorant of Adekunle's knowledge of the affair. Morgan dolefully agreed to every condition – the only contact he was permitted to make was to be in the form of a brief note pleading a sudden increase in work or any other rational excuse he could think up.

As for Murray, Adekunle told Morgan that he wanted him to become an acquaintance, a friend if possible, but, failing that, someone who had social contact with him, moved in the same circles.

'That's all I'm asking you to do,' Adekunle had said, the creeping onset of drawn revealing the pale gleam of his teeth as he smiled. 'Not a very onerous task in return for an error as potentially damaging as yours. Starting from tomorrow I want you to . . . to cultivate Dr Murray, get to know him, let him get to know you. I don't think that will be such a difficult job.'

Good God, thought Morgan, if only you knew. 'But why?' he had asked wretchedly. 'Why Murray? What's he got to do with you?'

'Let us say that at this stage, it is a precautionary matter,' Adekunle had replied. 'I will tell you in good time.' He tapped the bonnet of Morgan's car to emphasize his words. 'What you do not know cannot hurt you, as the saying goes. And believe me, Mr Leafy, I do not want you to be hurt in any way.'

Morgan smiled edgily. He didn't believe him at all. What, to him, was just about as worrying as hearing that Murray was the target was the almost complete absence of cuckolded rage on Adekunle's part. It crossed his mind for a moment that the whole thing had been allowed to develop – with him and Celia unwitting players – precisely with this contingency plan in mind. Adekunle was behaving more like a man disputing a reserved parking place than an irate husband confronting his wife's lover, and Morgan found this reasonableness, this lack of justifiable wrath most disturbing. What did it all signify? he wondered, searching Adekunle's features for a clue. Either he didn't give a damn about Celia's extra-marital flings or else his pressganging of Morgan as temporary ally for purposes unknown greatly outweighed in importance any injured pride or anger which he might feel like giving vent to. Both might be true of course, but Morgan came down heavily in favour of the last explanation. He felt sure that if he couldn't have served any purpose Adekunle's revenge would have been swift, no-nonsense and severe. He felt his chest seemingly fill up with something hard and solid – like quick-setting cement – as he contemplated this and the testing time that surely lay ahead.

That had been ten days ago. Stricken with cowardice he wrote a brief note to Celia informing her about the bales of paperwork that had suddenly appeared on his desk. He had Kojo and

Friday intercept all his calls at home and office with stories of Herculean busyness and endeavour and soon Celia stopped trying to get through. He became wary of seeing Hazel too, suspecting Adekunle's agents in every passer-by, and only visited her twice. Hazel didn't seem put out by this neglect: there was a new sleekness and confidence in her, he thought, no doubt fostered by the move to her own apartment. He suspected she was entertaining her own friends there – against his strict instructions – but was too preoccupied to do anything about it.

Half-heartedly he set about trying to follow Adekunle's directives. He made some surreptitious inquiries amongst his university acquaintances about Murray and it soon became clear that, as he had instinctively sensed, Murray was not a social man, seldom visiting the university club. He did have some close friends but saw them privately. Short of bearding him at the clinic, ambushing his car as he drove home from work or gatecrashing his dinner parties Morgan could see no way of easing himself into Murray's life. He would sit and fret about his task at home woefully conscious that time was running out. Adekunle was due back from London in a matter of days and would be expecting him to have made progress. What, he kept asking himself all the time, could be the link between Adekunle and Murray? They seemed about as far apart as it was possible for two people to be.

He became a subdued solitary figure at work, dutifully adding charts, graphs and tables of statistics to the Project Kingpin file, restricting his discussions with his colleagues to business matters. He spent quiet lonely nights at home, aimlessly flicking through his paperbacks, watching egregious Kinjanjan TV, steadily depleting his drinks trolley. He caught concerned glances from Friday and Moses over this untypical melancholia and careworn brooding. Friday even went so far as to approach him one evening and ask him what was wrong.

'Masta 'e nevah well,' Friday stated.

'No,' Morgan admitted.

'Wetin dis trouble? Make you tell me.'

Morgan thought of ways he could explain the nature of his problem. '*C'est cafard*,' he said finally, the French word summing everything up admirably.

'*Ah bon*,' Friday said. '*Maintenant je comprends*.'

As his problems continued and he found he was powerless to alleviate them he turned to alcohol in dire need of its amnesiac properties. For the last three nights since his confession to Friday he'd drunk himself into a whimpering blob of self-pity, crouching in the corner of his sitting room, from time to time dragging himself across the floor to his drinks trolley to make lethal cocktails which he gulped down with all the relish of a Socrates draining his cup of hemlock. Occasionally he would break out into short periods of intense vein-popping rage. His face volcanic with fury, bellowing foul curses at all those who were conspiring to ruin his life, he would prance and fume around his house for a minute or two before it subsided, passing with the suddenness of a tropical storm.

With the dim logic of nauseous, gunge-encrusted mornings he would offer himself sound advice, tell himself to calm down, get back in control, and utter stern warnings about the possibility of cracking up.

Slowly but surely his own brand of aversion therapy seemed to be having some effect. He was sitting in his office one such bleary afternoon asking himself if he'd finally hit the bottom and could perhaps now contemplate the long climb back up, and wondering whether to get Kojo to make him another Alka-Seltzer to help him on his way, when there was a tentative knock on his door.

'Come in,' he said.

It was Dalmire.

'Have you got a minute, Morgan?' he said. 'There's something, ah, I'd sort of like you to know.'

'Sit down,' Morgan said, trying to keep the weariness from his voice. He massaged his temples. Dalmire was wearing his old-colonial outfit of white shorts and beige knee socks. Morgan thought he looked slightly apprehensive.

'I wanted you to be the first to know,' he said. Then, correcting himself, 'among the first to know.'

'Mmm? Know what?' Morgan said, raising his eyebrows politely, wondering why it was he could taste every filling in his head.

'Last night,' Dalmire said. 'I know that once . . . well, that at one time you and she . . .' he paused. 'It was just that I particularly wanted to tell you myself, wouldn't have liked you to hear it from someone else.'

What *is* he wittering on about? Morgan thought. 'I'm sorry, Richard,' he said, 'but I've got a rather lax grip on things today and I'm just not with you. Do you think you could spell it out in words of one syllable?' He pointed to his head. 'Touch of the morning afters.'

'Oh sorry,' Dalmire said with a prudent smile. 'Must say I feel a bit that way myself.' He illustrated a rapidly expanding and contracting head with his hands. 'All that champagne. Stronger than you think.'

'Champagne, you said?'

'Yes. For me and Priscilla.'

'You. And. Priscilla.'

'Yes,' Dalmire smiled modestly. 'We got engaged last night.'

There was a long pause. A car tooted on the Nkongsamba road.

Morgan rose unsteadily to his feet, his face set. He wasn't allowing himself to think. He'd switched on to remote control, automatic pilot. He wound his lips back from his furred teeth in what he hoped was the semblance of a congratulatory smile and cranked his arm across the desk.

'Congratulations,' he said, as Dalmire eagerly shook his outstretched hand. 'Mar-marvellous news.' He turned to his filing cabinet. 'What about a drink?' He held up the gin bottle he kept in the top drawer. Dalmire mimed enthusiastic assent. Morgan poured out two gins and added the remains of a tonic bottle. He handed the glass to Dalmire.

'Good man,' Dalmire said, gratefully accepting the gin. 'Oh, good man.'

PART THREE

Chapter 1

Fanshawe and Morgan looked down at Innocence's body. Morgan replaced the cloth. He felt tired, dirty, hungry and suddenly very sad. He couldn't understand why Fanshawe had asked him to remove the cloth and looked scathingly at him as he stood there, his hands clasped behind his back, thoughtfully chewing his lower lip.

'Mmm. Uh-uh,' he said after a while. 'So she's still there.' Morgan gazed up at the clear morning sky in wonder at the man's astonishing grasp of the facts. 'Nasty business,' Fanshawe went on. 'Very nasty business.' He turned away, making little whistling noises between his teeth. The small crowd of onlookers was reduced to mainly women and children; nearby a mammy was setting up her stall in blithe unconcern. On the ground by the body were little juju tokens: a pile of stones, two feathers and a leaf, an upended tin with a stone on top.

Morgan moved away and joined Fanshawe.

'What do you suggest we do?' Fanshawe asked.

'Me?' Morgan said, astonished to be still singled out.

'Yes, Morgan, you,' Fanshawe said firmly. 'I'm putting you in charge of sorting out this whole unfortunate affair. I'm completely tied up with the Duchess's visit and besides,' he waved his hand disdainfully at the body, the onlookers, the tokens, 'All this is a mystery to me. Never could have happened out East,' he said shaking his head in sorrow at the folly of African ways.

Morgan swayed on his feet from tiredness. He glared at a naked child who had been staring at him and Fanshawe as they conversed. The child backed off but didn't go away, obviously intensely curious to see what these two white men would get up to next. Morgan looked about him. People strolled to and fro: labourers bought food from the traders' stalls, mammies weaved by with brimming water buckets on their heads, children gambolled about on the verandah. It was quieter than usual, as if out of respect for Innocence, but, Morgan saw, that was the only concession they were making. In fact the mood was more one of indifference, resigned imperturbability, in strong contrast to the brain-racking that he and Fanshawe were going through.

'Damn it,' Fanshawe said abruptly. 'I've just thought. It can't be here when the Duchess arrives.'

'Don't worry, she's not going to see it anyway,' Morgan said. He noticed the gender change. 'See *her*,' he added defiantly.

'No,' Fanshawe agreed. 'But that's beside the point. It just won't be right, if you see what I mean, knowing that there's a dead body somewhere in the grounds. Not good enough I'm afraid. You'll just have to get rid of it. That's all, Morgan. I'm relying on you.'

Morgan felt the retort form in his mouth but clenched his teeth to keep it back. He looked at Fanshawe's thin face with its preposterous moustache, and if he could have arranged for a second thunderbolt would have directed it at him there and then.

'The problem is,' Morgan said reasonably, 'that no one will remove the body until certain rites have been performed. Lightning strikes are very expensive, apparently, because it's a rare sign of Shango's displeasure. It costs, so I'm told, about sixty pounds but then there's the special funeral after that — which is extra.'

'I see,' said Fanshawe. 'What about her family?'

'There's only Maria.'

'Hasn't she got the money?'

Morgan was amazed at the thick-headedness of the man. 'She has fifteen pounds,' he said flatly.

'Oh,' Fanshawe said, as if it were the result of a deliberate policy of spendthriftness on Maria's part.

Morgan rubbed his forehead. 'I asked Murray to help last

might. But he wouldn't lift a finger.' He looked to Fanshawe for support. 'Very bad show I thought.'

'You can't blame Murray,' Fanshawe said at once.

'Why on earth not?' Morgan asked belligerently.

'He's not allowed to set foot outside the university gates, that's why. Kicks up no end of trouble apparently with the Nkongsamban health authorities. Seems there's a lot of friction between the municipal workers and those at the health service. I believe it's some sort of jealousy over their pay and conditions.'

'He never told me this,' Morgan protested.

'It's common knowledge, old chap. Probably thought you knew all about it.'

Morgan sighed: that bit of information didn't exactly help. 'Well,' he went on doggedly, 'the Ademola clinic say they'll take her body if only we can get it down to them.'

Fanshawe looked at his watch, and then glanced finally at Innocence. 'I'll leave it all in your capable hands, Morgan. I must dash off now. Great shame,' he said, 'great shame.' Morgan wondered if he was referring to Innocence's horrible death or the way it was inconveniencing him.

'By the way, did the poet chappie ever turn up?' Fanshawe asked.

'What!?!'

'Priscilla said something about a poet gone missing.'

Morgan reminded himself of his spontaneous excuse of the previous night. He cursed silently, remembering that it wasn't entirely fiction. There *was* a poet and he had invited him to stay at the Commission. He wondered when precisely he was due – he couldn't recall the exact dates. The last thing he needed now was a poet turning up out of the blue looking for a bed. He'd check later; meanwhile he played for time.

'Oh yes. British Council man. Don't worry Arthur, everything's under control.'

'Good,' Fanshawe said, taking a final look at Innocence.

227

'Let me know how you get on.' He turned away and walked briskly back to the house.

That evening Morgan came back to stare at Innocence's shrouded body. He shooed away a sniffing dog and tried to imagine the lump as a large cheery woman, but his tired brain saw only its lumpiness. It was half past nine. He had driven up to the Commission on an impulse, with a mad hope that something might have occurred in his absence to spirit Innocence away, but her stolid materiality rebuked him as he stood there, effectively dispersing his wild fancies. During the afternoon he had telephoned two other firms of undertakers who had readily agreed to remove the body, but both had evidently been repulsed, or more likely had been persuaded of the extreme consequences of getting on the wrong side of Shango.

He had sat on by the phone for a further half hour deliberating whether to ring Adekunle and inform him of the disastrous turn his 'friendship' with Murray had taken. In the end, he had decided it would be safer for him to play a waiting game. Events were so totally beyond his control now that there was no telling what might happen next.

Today was Tuesday. He had intended playing golf with Murray on Thursday and Adekunle had requested a meeting before then. Morgan shuddered at the maze of complexities ahead of him and again cursed his irresoluteness, his shilly-shallying, the protracted moral dithering he indulged in. He made Hamlet look rash and hot-headed. He turned away from Innocence and walked dejectedly back across the laterite square towards the Commission, followed as ever by a small squad of curious children. Around about him hens pecked and goats chewed in the darkness, pungent cooking smells filled his nostrils from the charcoal braziers that glowed on the verandahs on either side. The night was hot and sultry, the constellations clear in the black sky above his head.

'Good evenin', sah,' a voice called from one side. Morgan

turned in its direction. Sitting on packing cases around a lantern were Isaac, Ezekiel and Joseph. They were wearing cloth wraps and were bare-chested with the exception of Isaac who wore a ragged vest. They were drinking what Morgan took to be palm wine.

'Evening,' Morgan said, approaching the verandah. There was a pause as if they were expecting him to say something. He thought for a few seconds and then added lamely, 'She is still there.'

'Dat's correct,' Isaac said. 'Please, sah, save your time. Don't send undertaking man for here again. Dey nevan go take her. Dis he be Shango killing. Dey no fit totch 'im.'

There were grunts of agreement from Ezekiel and Joseph. There was no animosity in Isaac's tone; he was a patient teacher instructing a particularly backward child.

'But I have to try,' Morgan protested. 'Mr Fanshawe is not happy. The Duchess is coming.' There were tut-tuts of commiseration at his plight. Morgan looked at the three men sitting in front of their houses with their palm wine and confidence and suddenly felt lost in this sense of apartness.

'Don't you mind?' he asked them suddenly. 'That Innocence is lying out there?' He pointed in her general direction. 'What do you think is going to happen?'

The three looked at each other as if they found it hard to understand him. 'There is no problem,' Ezekie. said finally. 'Make you bring one fetish priest, then you can take her.' There were amused chuckles at this. Things will take whatever course Shango has assigned, they seemed to be implying.

Morgan bade them good night and made his way back to his car.

Chapter 2

The next morning Morgan drove to work earlier than usual and found to his surprise a small demonstration outside the Commission gates, which were firmly closed. There were about thirty or forty young men who looked like students, a few of them carrying hastily made-up placards. Morgan tooted his horn and they cleared the road obligingly with a few jeering cries and a brief chant of 'UK out. UK out.' As the gate was being opened a head appeared at his window and Morgan recognized the serious unsmiling features of Femi Robinson, the Mid-West representative of the Marxist-Leninist People's Party of Kinjanja.

'Mr Leafy,' Robinson said. 'We wish to protest with sincere vigour.' Robinson had a permanently worried expression which had furrowed deep inverted-v creases in his brow, and of course the thin sprinkling of pubic beard and swelling afro hair-style favoured by black American radicals. Morgan wondered how Robinson knew his name, as he took in the flimsy banners and placards. UK STAY OUT OF KINJANJAN POLITICS, they read, NO UK IMPERIALISM IN KINJANJA.

'What the hell is going on?' Morgan asked in astonishment.

'We are protesting against the, ah, destabilizatory tactics of the British Gov'ment in the internal politics of Kinjanja.'

Morgan tried to work a species of mystified smile onto his face that would suggest he hadn't the slightest idea what Robinson was talking about, even though his brain was twinkling with warning lights like the console of a crashing airliner. Robinson flourished a copy of the *Daily Graphic*. Morgan saw a large picture of Adekunle at the foot of some aeroplane steps shaking hands with a morning-suited Foreign Office representative. The banner headline read: ADEKUNLE VISITS UK. Morgan felt his stomach swirl and tilt.

'Doesn't mean a thing,' he asserted quickly and firmly. 'Pure nonsense. KNP propaganda obviously. Now, if you'll excuse me, I have work to do.' He set his car in motion and swept through the gates hearing Robinson's final shout of 'Is that official?' dying away behind him.

Dry-mouthed he raced up the stairs into his office and snatched all three copies of the Kinjanjan daily papers off a startled Kojo's desk. Each front page told the same story. Adekunle on official visit . . . invited to attend . . . greeted by Under-Secretary of State . . . Consultations with Foreign Office . . . Morgan sat down, his head reeling. The elections were less than two weeks away; the whole tone of the reports emphasized the rightness of the KNP to rule Kinjanja in the considered opinion of the British Government.

Morgan urgently took stock of this frightful new development, contemplated the ramifications of this breach of confidence, tried to work out Adekunle's motives. Clearly it gave the KNP a vital boost of status and responsibility – equated them, no less, with the UPKP – the resident government. Such official fêting would be vastly impressive to the average undecided and literate Kinjanjan voter – but no doubt word would be swiftly conveyed to the grass roots. Nobody, after all, was consulting any other political party. It would also, of course, offend the others, especially the vocal minority – Femi Robinson and his ilk – but Morgan assumed that Adekunle would hold this a negligible price to pay for this coup in pre-election publicity.

He himself felt curiously distanced from it all: it could either be a catastrophic turn in events or quite insignificant. Project Kingpin was out in the open, but who cared? He realized too that he and Fanshawe had been successfully duped by Adekunle – manipulated and exploited with consummate ease. It didn't surprise him that much: Project Kingpin had been bumbling and amateurish from the start, blown up out of all proportion by Fanshawe's extravagant dreams. It seemed somehow fitting it should now be exposed for what it was. But his heart was still racing from the unprecedented suddenness of its dissolution. He wondered how Fanshawe would react. His thoughts were interrupted by Kojo appearing in the doorway.

'Excuse, sah,' the little man said. 'The porter says there is a Mr Robinson at the front door requestin' an urgent meeting.'

'No no no!' Morgan shouted. 'Tell him to see Mr Fanshawe.'

'Mr Fanshawe is not here.'

'Oh Jesus Christ,' Morgan theatrically smote his brow. 'All right, send him up.'

Robinson soon arrived. Morgan noticed that he was wearing a black woollen polo-neck, black leather gloves and had put on a pair of cheap wire-framed sunglasses, every inch the black power activist. Morgan could see the sweat beading his nose and forehead.

'Mr Robinson,' he said. 'What can I do for you?'

'We demand an explanation,' Robinson began officiously, rapping Morgan's desk with a gloved finger. 'By what or whose rights has the British Gov'ment the power to summon *un*elected political leaders to London for consultatory po'poses?'

'I've no idea,' said Morgan, genially passing the buck. 'It's as big a surprise to me. I'm afraid you'll need to talk to Mr Fanshawe on that one. But then,' he added fairly, 'he may know nothing about it either.'

Robinson seemed to be preparing himself for a mighty explosion of scoffing disbelief but his fervour visibly collapsed before Morgan's eyes, as if he'd been punched in the belly. 'Mr Leafy,' he said resignedly, taking off his gloves and wiping his dripping hands on his trousers, 'whatever you are doing you are playing a very dangerous game. We have a saying here: "If you are cleaning a room you don't sweep the det under the carpet . . ."'

'Sorry. The debt?'

'Yes, the det, the rubbish, the dust.'

'I see. Go on.'

'As I was saying: "you don't sweep the det under the carpet because somebody can easily come and lift it up and find the det beneath." This is what has been going on in Kinjanja for these last five or six years. The carpet is now raised from the floor!' The old passion returned for an instant.

Morgan nodded sagely, as if considering the gnomic trenchancy of Kinjanjan folklore. 'Well that's all very interesting, Mr Robinson, but there's nothing I, or even the British Government can do about . . . about the shoddy housework, if you see what I mean. It's a Kinjanjan problem.'

'If it is a Kinjanjan problem why are you consulting with the KNP?'

'Are we, Mr Robinson? Are you absolutely sure of that?' Morgan said, diplomatically avoiding the question by asking another.

Robinson practically erupted with frustration. 'It is written here!' he shouted, jabbing at the newspapers covering Morgan's desk. 'Here, here and here!'

'Ah, but you don't want to believe everything you read in the newspapers, especially at election time.'

'In that case issue a denial.'

'Pardon?'

'Deny it. Expose the KNP if they are lying as you say.'

Morgan felt a flutter of worry. He smiled, 'No, we can't do that. We don't issue denials, as a matter of policy. We find it has the habit of conferring a certain dignity on accusations and, um, inaccuracies which only deserve to be ignored.'

'Jargon!' Robinson asserted fiercely, his arms windmilling around in exasperation. 'This is diplomatic jargon. If one man says you killed his wife,' he pointed at Morgan, 'do you keep your silence? If they accuse you of thieving, do you not deny it?'

'Mr Robinson, please,' Morgan said, rattled by the cogency of the man's argument. 'Those are quite spurious examples. Really, I think you need to get this newspaper thing in perspective. It's an electioneering ploy — vote-catching.'

Robinson slumped in his chair. 'From a British perspective it may be nothing. From a Kinjanjan perspective it is very serious indeed.' He paused. 'I will tell you why. If the KNP win because of this, or even if the UPKP are returned, there will be very serious problems.'

'I don't quite follow,' Morgan said.

'Do you know,' the finger prodded at his chest again, 'that Kinjanja is the seventh largest importer of champagne in the world? Do you know that last year over two hundred Mercedes Benzes were purchased for government officials?' He sat back. 'They will not allow such corruption to continue. Then we are in dangerous trouble.'

'Who?' Morgan asked. 'Who won't allow it?'

'The Army of course,' Robinson said, flinging his arms wide. 'There have been mutinies in the North already. All troops have been recalled to barracks. They will take over.'

Morgan frowned sceptically. 'Are you sure about that?'

'Everybody knows it,' Robinson declaimed scathingly.

'But what about the voters? What if they vote a party in?'

'You go to one village. You pay the chief. You say vote for me and you get your votes.'

'But in the towns, surely . . .'

'Even in the towns it is the same.'

Morgan shrugged helplessly. 'But I don't quite see what I can do about any of this.'

'Expose the lie,' Robinson said with ardour. 'It is simple. If the KNP are lying you must say so.'

Morgan gulped. He thought he should change the course of the questioning. 'But why here? Why Nkongsamba? We're not important. You should go to the High Commission in the capital.'

'We have gone,' Robinson said. 'We are there at the gates at this very moment. But, as you know, Adekunle is a chief in Nkongsamba; there is a strong connection with the town.'

'Well, look I'm sorry,' Morgan apologized. 'But there's absolutely nothing I can do. I'll tell you what though, I'll pass your message on to higher echelons – I'm sure they'll pay close attention to it.' He rose to his feet to signify the meeting was at an end. Robinson smiled sarcastically.

'That is no good,' he said. 'You must act now. There is very little time.'

As soon as Robinson had gone Morgan raced out of his office and bumped into Mrs Bryce on the landing. She was carrying a bundle of sheets in her hands.

'Ah Mrs Bryce,' he said breathlessly. 'Just the person. Where's Mr Fanshawe?'

'He's away,' she said simply.

'I know that,' Morgan said slowly, with forced reasonableness. 'But where?'

'The capital, meeting the Duchess of Ripon. She arrives today. Weren't you informed of all this?'

Of course, Morgan remembered now: the wretched visit.

'He'll be back tomorrow,' Mrs Bryce continued. 'Anything urgent?'

'Ah no. No. It can wait. Keep until tomorrow I suppose.' He looked at Mrs Bryce again. 'I hope you don't mind me asking, Mrs Bryce, but what are those sheets for?'

'Making up the beds in the guest suite,' she said, marching off towards it across the landing. 'The Duchess is spending Christmas night here.'

Morgan wished grievous septic inflammation on her mosquito-bitten legs and thoughtfully retraced his steps back into the office. Kojo sat at his desk, one hand covering the mouthpiece of his telephone.

'Mr Fanshawe on the line, sah,' he said. 'From the High Commission.'

'Oh Christ, no,' Morgan muttered. He picked up the phone in his office. He took a deep breath.

'Arthur?' he said breezily. 'Hello. How's everything with you?'

'Seen the papers?' Fanshawe squeaked in fury down the phone. 'It's a disaster, man. Grade A disaster!'

'Sorry Arthur . . . I don't quite . . . I mean . . .' his stomach hollowed. He felt the blood drain from his face.

'There are about two thousand demonstrators outside the High Commission here raising merry hell. Phones've been going all day. H.E.'s been summoned to Government House. The UPKP are hopping mad. Hopping. It's dreadful, Morgan. Dreadful.'

'God,' was all Morgan could find to say.

'And. And the Duchess is due to arrive here this afternoon. What's she going to think when she finds the High Commission surrounded by rioters?'

There was a silence. It seemed to Morgan that Fanshawe was expecting an answer. 'I don't know,' he began. 'I suppose . . .'

'She'll think it's quite disgraceful, that's what,' Fanshawe told him. 'I mean, really Morgan, what's Adekunle playing at?'

Morgan thought quickly. 'It might not be that bad – in the long term. What if he wins?'

'Well there has been talk of that,' Fanshawe conceded, his voice calming down. 'That would make a difference. Our pundit-chappies here think the prestige he's bought with this visit will outweigh any damage. But, and this is the main thing, Project Kingpin wasn't meant to work out this way at all. The whole thing's been handled very badly. Very badly.'

Morgan felt anger flare up inside him as he sensed the gun barrels of blame swinging ponderously around to point at him. '*We* could have had no idea he was going to do this though, could *we*, Arthur? It is a breach of trust on Adekunle's part, not ours. What do you suggest *we* do?'

'Yes, well . . .' Fanshawe said, obviously taken aback. 'The official line is say nothing, do nothing. The elections are not far off, everything may work out for the best, if the KNP emerge as victors. But, if the UPKP get back in, Anglo-Kinjanjan relations are going to be decidedly rocky.'

For a moment Morgan wondered whether he ought to pass on Robinson's dire warnings, but then thought better of it: Fanshawe had enough on his plate as it was – as did they all. 'It's been fairly quiet up here. We had a small demo but nothing to write home about: the PPK mob.'

'And who in God's name are the PPK?' Fanshawe demanded impatiently. 'I can never get these initials straight.'

'The Marxists: People's Party of Kinjanja, Femi Robinson and his merry band.' He craned his neck to get a view down the drive. 'But they've all gone home now, more or less.'

'That's something at least,' Fanshawe said ungraciously. 'But how about our other problem?'

'Innocence? Ah. Yes. I'm afraid not much progress there. I had a couple more undertakers out, but they wouldn't touch her.'

'Damnation,' Fanshawe swore angrily. 'Everything's going wrong. Listen, Morgan, I want two things from you: some sort of denial or apology from Adekunle, and Innocence out of the way before the Duchess arrives.' He spoke of her as though she were a tree that had fallen down and blocked his drive.

Morgan cursed at him under his breath. 'You won't get a peep out of Adekunle, I can tell you that right now,' he said harshly. Then, 'Sorry Arthur, lot on my mind. I'll see what I can do.' He thought: you horrible, revolting little shit.

'Very well,' Fanshawe said in a hurt offended voice. 'Try and come up with some results for once.'

He hung up, swore at Fanshawe again, and thought grimly how fragile loyalty was. He gazed emptily at his desk top. Disaster was mounting on disaster. What was he going to do?

There was a cocky rat-a-tat-tat on his door and Dalmire came in. He looked smart and fresh and annoyingly cheerful.

'Sorry I'm late,' Dalmire said. 'Got held up by a demonstration at the university. Then I arrive here and guess what? We've got one of our own. What's it all about?' Morgan sullenly indicated the newspapers. Dalmire glanced at them. 'God,' he said. 'He's got some cheek, hasn't he?'

'Well, yes and no,' Morgan said ambiguously. He didn't feel like explaining the intricacies of Project Kingpin to Dalmire at the moment. 'Were they demonstrating about this,' he indicated the newspapers, 'at the university as well?'

Dalmire had moved away to the window. 'No,' he said. 'Something quite separate. Apparently there's some threat to close down the university by the government. They say they won't reopen after the Christmas holidays because of general student bolshiness,' he smiled, as if his mind was on other matters. 'I've no idea what it's all about, but there were hundreds of students all round the admin block. It seems they intend staying up, occupying the rooms over the holidays. One of these sit-in things or whatever they're called.'

'Christ, typical,' Morgan said in disgust, but thankful at least it had nothing to do with Kingpin.

'Ever been skiing?' Dalmire asked out of the blue.

'What? No, doesn't appeal. Why?'

'We were thinking about skiing – me and Pris – for our hols.' A dreamy look lit up Dalmire's eyes.

'Honeymoon, don't you mean?' Morgan said, trying to keep the resentment and impatience out of his voice.

'No, no. That comes later.' Dalmire paused, he seemed slightly embarrassed. 'Didn't I tell you? We're going on holiday. Leaving after Christmas. I thought it might be fun to go skiing. New Year on the slopes, a welcome in the mountains, that sort of thing.'

'HOLIDAY?' Morgan exclaimed, appalled. 'But you've only been out here for a couple of months. Christ, my last leave was in March.'

'I'm taking it off my leave, don't worry,' Dalmire said

hastily. 'It was Priscilla's idea actually. Arthur said it would be fine.'

Morgan felt he was about to splutter inarticulately with rage like some gouty brigadier, but with an effort he composed himself. The lucky bastard, he thought, envy mixed with outrage at the gross injustice. That was what came of marrying the boss's daughter. Dalmire, however, appeared quite oblivious of his resentment.

'So what do you think?' he said. 'About skiing?'

'Sounds great,' Morgan said, thinking: maybe he'll break his leg. Maybe he'll break his back. An evil idea edged its way into his mind. 'By the way, Richard,' he asked, 'did you hear what happened to Innocence?'

Three little boys watched as Dalmire sat down heavily on the verandah. He had turned quite pale. 'Oh my God,' he said dully, holding the back of his hand up to his mouth. Morgan blanched himself and threw the cloth back over Innocence's body, disturbing the cloud of flies that hovered above it.

'Pretty gruesome, isn't it?' Morgan said.

Dalmire swallowed and puffed out his cheeks, 'My God,' he said again. 'That's repulsive. Revolting. To think . . .' he paused and then added in explanation. 'It's the first dead body I've seen.'

A small fire had been lit near Innocence in a little charcoal brazier onto which leaves and green twigs were occasionally flung. A smudge of bluey smoke hung about this end of the compound, meant, Morgan assumed, to drive away flies and overlay any smell.

Dalmire got to his feet and walked unsteadily away. Morgan felt a little sorry for him: it was a mean sort of revenge but it was intensely satisfying nonetheless to see him so shaken up.

'Oyibo, oyibo,' a little naked girl shouted in delight, dancing on the verandah and pointing a stubby plump finger at the trembling Dalmire.

'The kids,' Dalmire said. 'What about these kids just running about? It's unreal.'

'Yes,' Morgan agreed, walking over to join him and looking back at the scene: Innocence's covered body, the wash-place, the juju spells, the smoking fire, the wandering semi-nude children, hens pecking in the dust. He didn't feel as mature and dispassionate as he was trying to sound. 'But it's Africa.'

They were walking slowly back to the Commission in thoughtful silence, when a shrill call came across the lawn.

'Morgan. Oh, Morgan.' It was Mrs Fanshawe. She was standing by the edge of her drive beckoning him over.

'Bloody hell,' he said crossly. 'What does she want?' Then, remembering she was Dalmire's future mother-in-law, added apologetically 'Sorry, Richard. Bit unsettled.' Dalmire, however, was too preoccupied with intimations of mortality to take offence and waved his excuses away.

'Morning, Chloe,' Morgan said as he approached. Mrs Fanshawe was wearing a tight-waisted, sleeveless dress in a brilliant ultramarine that contrasted strongly with her almost ethereally pale skin and raven hair. It also made her look twice her normal size, somehow.

'Just been over to see Innocence,' he said, like some charitable WRVS helper. 'Unfortunately no one'll move her.'

'She's still there?' exclaimed Mrs Fanshawe raising her hands to her temples. 'Oh it's too ghastly.'

'Yes, it's been quite a day so far,' he said ruefully, 'what with our demonstration. Did you see it?'

'It's still going on,' she said scornfully, 'if you can call it a demonstration. I've just come back from town and there are still three of them loitering by the gate. This funny little man with some sort of beard and a huge head of hair shouted at me as I drove in.' They walked towards the house. 'He was wearing a black polo neck and leather gloves. Looked miserably hot.'

Morgan was wary about the friendly chatter: she wanted

something. 'That'll be Femi Robinson, urban guerrilla,' he said. 'Got to wear the authentic anarchist gear you know.' They chortled together patronizingly over this as they entered the sitting room.

'Drink?' Mrs Fanshawe asked. 'You must need one. Surely you're not still on orange juice.'

'No no,' he laughed falsely. 'I'll have a gin and tonic if I may.' Anything Dalmire can do, he thought.

Mrs Fanshawe looked at him appraisingly. 'Always thought G and T was more your drink, you know? Could never understand your lust for sherry.'

Morgan was startled. What had come over the woman? he wondered, she'd never been so familiar. He was asking himself what could be behind it all when he was served a gin and tonic by a red-eyed Maria. He thought suddenly of her mother cooking slowly in the hot sun.

'She insisted on working,' Mrs Fanshawe whispered guiltily as Maria left the room. 'Wouldn't take any more time off.'

'Priscilla home?' Morgan asked unconcernedly, trying to alter the images in his mind.

'No,' said Mrs Fanshawe. 'She's at the club. Consolidating her tan. She and Dickie are off on holiday, you know.' He did know. Mrs Fanshawe paused to screw a cigarette into its holder. 'I want you to come upstairs, Morgan,' she said. 'I've got something to show you.'

Morgan warily followed the large turquoise globes of her buttocks up the stairs wondering again what was going on. The ubiquitous chinoiserie of the house was more muted on the first floor, confined to pictures and curtain material. Mrs Fanshawe led him into a small room with a low divan, and a table, upon which stood a sewing machine. In the corner was a dressmaker's dummy. Morgan took a spine-bracing gulp of the gin which he'd brought up the stairs with him. Mrs Fanshawe deposited her cigarette and holder in an ashtray and unhooked something from the back of the door. It was red. 'What do you think?' she asked.

'Looks suspiciously like a boiler suit to me,' he ventured.

'It is, or rather was. It's an ordinary white one I dyed red. I've made the sleeves short too. I thought that would make a nice tropical Santa. Mmm? What do you say?'

'Mmnng . . . sorry. I . . .'

'Of course I'm going to put some spangly stuff on it. I picked some up in town.' She beamed at him. 'Thought I'd get you to try it on first though,' she frowned, looking him up and down. 'I didn't know your size. We may have to let it out a bit here and there.'

'Looks OK to me,' Morgan said, offended at this casual reference to his bulk.

'No,' Mrs Fanshawe said firmly. 'Try it on now, let's make sure.'

'*Now?*' Morgan yelped. 'Can't I take it away? And tell you later?'

'Of course not,' Mrs Fanshawe said professionally. 'Just step into it now.'

Morgan felt suddenly light-headed and giddy. With numb fingers he accepted the horrible red garment from Mrs Fanshawe. He took off his shoes and was about to insert his left foot into the appropriate leg hole when Mrs Fanshawe uttered a bright trill of laughter.

'Don't be so prim,' she mocked. 'You won't be wearing shirt and trousers on the day. How on earth am I meant to get a proper fit?'

Unable to speak Morgan hesitantly removed his tie, shirt and trousers and stood motionless in his boxer shorts and socks, slightly bent over, his shoulders unnaturally rounded as though he had a bad back.

'Come on then,' Mrs Fanshawe ordered, like a hearty games mistress encouraging a flagging hockey team.

Inflating his chest Morgan stepped into the overalls, pulled them up, slipped his arms into the sleeves. He was trying not to think what he had looked like standing there in his loose baggy underwear and brown socks, trying to ignore the acid smell of fresh sweat that seemed to billow noxiously from his armpits. Mrs Fanshawe busied around him tugging and pulling as he slowly did up the buttons on the front.

'Not bad,' she said. 'Not too bad at all. Might have to let it out around the tummy a little, that's all. Want to see yourself in a mirror?'

Morgan shook his head emphatically.

'Super,' she enthused. 'I'll make a beard out of some cotton wool, I'll attach a hood and that'll be that. The kiddies'll love it.'

Morgan thought he was going to be sick as he struggled to get out of the tight overalls. His nervousness, discomfort and profound embarrassment had caused sweat to pour forth and he had to wriggle and squirm his shoulders and hips free of the clinging material. Mrs Fanshawe was humming to herself as she rummaged through her sewing basket. Morgan bent down, picked up the boiler suit and handed it back to her. He avoided her eye but as she turned to take the suit from him her humming ceased abruptly and she said, 'Oh!' in a tone of perplexed surprise.

'What about gum boots?' Morgan said as though in a trance, his eyes fixed on a crack in the wall. 'I suppose I'll need those too.' He groped for his shirt on the divan.

'Oh . . . yes. Yes.' Mrs Fanshawe said, suddenly confused, gathering the red suit up into a bundle and hugging it to her chest. 'Um. Look . . . I'll, erm, see to that. Yes yes. That's what I'll do.' Morgan shot a glance at her. She'd suddenly gone most peculiar, he thought, seeing her gazing intently out of the window.

'I've just remembered something,' she blurted. 'Something I must do at once,' she said, scrambling for the door. 'Let yourself out, won't you?' She was gone.

A very, very strange woman, Morgan thought, his churning addled brain beginning to return to normal. What an odd family the Fanshawes were, he considered, but what had got into her? He sat down on the divan. It was covered in a coarsely woven bedspread. He felt the rough tickle of the material on the back of his thighs and, he suddenly realized, on a portion of his anatomy that should have been unexposed. He mouthed a silent horror-struck 'Oh no!' and slowly looked down at his lap. From the simple slit in his boxer shorts that passed for a fly, his penis protruded, long, pale and flaccid. It must have popped out during his struggles to remove the boiler suit. Now he knew.

Chapter 3

Morgan drove down to the club. There was a curious fixed smile on his face as though he was under deep hypnosis or, like some cartoon character, had been hit very hard on the head. With all the skill of a Zen master he had emptied his mind of thought. He was a bundle of reflexes driving down the road, a dazed refugee mindlessly fleeing the mushroom cloud of shame and embarrassment that towered over the Commission.

It was lunchtime and the pool was quiet. He changed, stepped out onto the rough concrete surround and with the zeal of a born-again baptist on the banks of the river Jordan hurled himself into the pool. He swam powerfully below the surface, thrusting himself through the cool blue water, his eyes mistily focused on the shifting dappled light patterns on the pool-bottom. He imagined the sweat, the dirt and disgrace sliding from his body like a slick of sun-tan oil.

He hauled himself from the pool, sat down in the shade of an umbrella and drank two icy bottles of beer in quick succession. Gently, patiently, he began to come round. After an hour of careful self-counselling and analysis, and a thorough survey and methodological setting-out of his problems, the jumbled perspectives of his life slowly reformed and sanity resumed something like its rightful place in the order of things.

Calmer and pleased with this massive act of self-discipline he changed back into his clothes and walked through the club on the way to his car. As he was passing the noticeboard in the vestibule his eye was caught by the red lettering of the GRAND BOXING DAY GOLF TOURNAMENT and he noticed – as instinctively as if it had been his own – Murray's name among the list of those who wished to compete. Morgan was forcibly reminded of his aborted golf-match and he felt the millstone of his worries resettle itself comfortably around his neck.

The childish idea came to Morgan that if he just sat still for long enough, if he didn't trouble anyone, didn't draw any attention to himself, all the hideous traumas currently rampaging through his life would get bored and rumble on past him like a marauding army off to lay waste to the next village up the road. Accordingly, he crept into his office and sat quietly at his desk for three quarters of an hour filling his blotting pad with tiny doodles of spirals and concentric circles. But then a wide jaw-cracking yawn made him realize that total quiescence, utter passivity, held out no hope and precious few charms. Besides, he just wasn't that sort of person: he *had* to do something, even if it was only to cock things up further. He looked quizzically at his ink-darkened blotting pad, and wondered if, for the last couple of hours, he'd been having a minor nervous breakdown, if this was what it was like when you started to go mad.

'Hey man,' he said in a fruity drawl, 'when the going gets tough the tough gets going. Right?' He thumped his desk with his fist, his face breaking out into a piratical leer. '*Damn* right,' he told himself. 'It's not the size of the man in the fight, it's the size of fight in the man.' His gung-ho homilies elated him for a moment but then his spirits collapsed with the suddenness of a fountain being switched off. He picked up his pen and fitted a minute spiral into a gap at the corner of his blotting pad.

Kojo's face appeared round the door.

'It's all right, Kojo,' Morgan said sadly. 'I was talking to myself.'

'Excuse, sah. There is a man on the phone. He will not give his name and he is abusin' me because I will not connect him to you. He says to tell Mr Leafy it is Sam.'

'Oh Christ,' Morgan said gloomily. There was no respite. 'Put him through.'

Adekunle came on the line. 'Good afternoon, my friend. I thought, as the saying goes, discretion was better than valour, under the circumstances.'

Morgan was getting tired of Adekunle's bloody sayings. 'We're all very annoyed with you here,' he said boldly. 'To put it mildly, as the saying goes.'

Adekunle's hearty laugh echoed tinnily in his ear. 'Is that so?' he said. 'As I'm sure you'll agree, Mr Leafy, all is fair in love and politics. But,' he said, the levity gone from his voice, 'I've not called to discuss these matters. You have your "meeting" with Dr Murray tomorrow. I must speak with you about it before then.'

'Ah well,' Morgan said, suddenly not caring. 'There's a bit of a problem there. I'm afraid . . .'

'There is no problem,' Adekunle said harshly. 'For your own sake, I hope not.' Morgan swallowed, his mouth dry. 'Do you know the fish-pond on the university campus?' Adekunle asked. Morgan said he did. 'Then let us meet there at half past five this afternoon. Yes?'

*

The fish-pond was another example of Kinjanjan literalness, but this time so extreme that it almost returned to metaphor. There were doubtless fish in it and it was, just, in the general class of ponds, but, more truthfully, it was a large and impressive artificial lake at the south-western edge of the university campus. Morgan sat in his car looking at it, waiting for Adekunle. Normally a tranquil scene of great beauty, today Morgan's half-creating mind saw only stark primitive nature, hostile and unwelcoming, feral and unsafe.

The fish-pond formed an attenuated oval, roughly half a mile long and three hundred yards wide in the middle. A large stream poured sluggishly into it at one end but there was no obvious channel for the waters to escape. Perhaps the earth just seeped it up, Morgan thought, for the pond had the solid unnatural stillness of stagnancy and the huge pale-trunked trees that bordered it on the far bank were perfectly reflected in its mirror-like surface.

The beige-grey light of approaching dusk softened edges and blurred contours. Over to his right Morgan could see the white roof of a senior staff house, but apart from the tarmac road his car rested on, everything else was untouched and unchanged. He would not have been surprised if a pterodactyl had hunched itself into the air from the darkening trees, or if some squamous prehistoric beast had plodded out of the tall rushes onto the mud beach below the road. He felt his depression icily grip his brain as he stared moodily across the neutral uncomplaining lake.

His gloomy reverie was interrupted by the sound of Adekunle's Mercedes. Morgan got out of his car as Adekunle drew up behind him. Adekunle was smoking a large cigar but Morgan sensed that his normal mood of cynical joviality was absent.

'Mr Leafy,' he said at once. 'You have made me a worried man with your talk of problems and difficulties. What has gone wrong?'

Morgan kicked a pebble off the road. 'I had an argument with Murray,' he said flatly. 'Under the circumstances there's no way we can play a friendly round of golf tomorrow.'

'No, this will not do,' Adekunle said sharply. 'You cannot slip out of this so easily, my friend. You must put our . . . offer to Dr Murray before the twenty-ninth of this month. I have decided that I must know my position before then.'

'I'm telling you we had a blazing row,' Morgan protested. 'I shouted at him. I insulted him. Honestly, he must hate my guts.'

'A very poor joke, my friend. I see how you are trying,' Adekunle wiggled his hand, 'to snake your way out of our agreement. It will not succeed, I warn you. You will only force me to take my complaints to Mr Fanshawe.'

Morgan was almost sobbing with frustration. 'It's true I tell you. It happened on Monday night . . . Oh, never mind.' He picked up a twig and flung it savagely at the glimmering fish-pond. It was nearly dark. The crickets sawed away, the bats dipped above their heads. Something in his tone must have made Adekunle realize that he wasn't joking.

'All right,' Adekunle said grudgingly. 'OK. You have a set-back. But it must be overcome at some point before the election. I don't care how. It is mandatory that this business with Dr Murray is secured before then. You must arrange it,' he waved his cigar aggressively at Morgan.

'But why me?' Morgan complained. 'Why don't you just ring him up? Put it to him straight?'

'My good friend Mr Leafy,' Adekunle chuckled. 'How very naïve you are. Is it not better to be offered a . . . a financial inducement by one of your own people? By one who you would normally assume to be above this sort of transaction. A representative of the British Crown furthermore.' He took a satisfied puff at his cigar. 'Believe me it is very hard to remain honest when the standards of the highest are in question.'

Morgan reluctantly conceded the acuteness of his logic. If,

by implication, the Commission staff were on the make, why should anyone else worry about soiling their hands? *Quis custodiet* and all that. He wondered again how Murray would respond.

'Would you like to see what we are going to all this trouble about?' Adekunle asked.

Morgan said he might as well, and followed Adekunle up the road, away from the senior staff house and along the side of the fish-pond. At the end of the lake the road ascended a small hill and then curved round to rejoin the campus. Up at this slightly higher altitude Morgan could see behind him the lights of more staff houses.

'There you are,' Adekunle said. The ground in front of them dipped down into a shallow marshy river valley then rose suddenly on the other side to meet a small plateau. In the gathering darkness Morgan could make out a line of trees.

'This is the land I own,' Adekunle said. 'Up as far as those trees. This is where they want to build the hall and cafeteria. As you can see it is ideally placed.'

'Where's the dump going to be?' Morgan asked unfeelingly.

'Beyond those trees. Far beyond them. I sold all that land several years ago. The refuse lorries and the night-soil trans-porters are already bringing the rubbish out here,' he added sadly. He paused. 'Here we are ten minutes away from the lecture theatres, ten minutes' walk from the university centre.' He looked at Morgan and then at the end of his cigar. 'If not for Dr Murray,' he said bitterly, 'they would write me the cheque *today*!' He almost shouted the last word. 'He has postponed the Building Committee three times already while he pursued his investigations. I know he intends to give a negative report. And so now I am driven to these desperate measures.'

Morgan didn't try too hard to sympathize with him. 'How much are you selling the land for?' he asked.

'Two hundred and seventy-five thousand pounds,'

Adekunle said with feeling. 'For a ten-thousand pound invest-ment,' Morgan said. 'Not bad.'

Adekunle came up to him and seized his arm. Morgan could smell his cigar smoke. 'This is why, Mr Leafy, you are going to help me, otherwise I take my complaints about your behaviour to the *High* Commissioner,' he threatened. 'I will not need to go to Mr Fanshawe: I will go to the top man.' He released his grip. 'Your kind offer of a visit to London was most useful. I have some good friends there now. Believe me, Mr Leafy, if I so wish I can make serious trouble for you. Find your own way to approach Murray. That is all. And before the twenty-ninth.' His voice was harsh and angry again.

Morgan tried to coax some saliva into his dry mouth. 'But how?' he wailed. 'Jesus Christ, I told you I . . .'

'I don't care!' Adekunle spat out suddenly, trembling with rage. 'I certainly won't give one bloody damn shit for the career of a junior diplomat!'

'All right,' Morgan said weakly. 'Alright. I'll think of some-thing.' He felt very tired, overcome with weariness. He turned and set off back down the road to his car. Adekunle caught up with him.

'Forgive me for losing my temper,' he said quietly, 'but as I told you the financial costs of an election campaign are high.' He added in a surprisingly meek tone, 'You don't know what this . . . this obstruction by Murray means. I have my own concerns.' Morgan said nothing. 'There is no reason,' Adekunle went on, 'Why we should not *both* benefit from this, ah, how shall we say it? partnership.'

'Thanks,' Morgan said hollowly. He would do it, he knew: primarily to save his own tattered skin and secure his piddling job. But there was another reason. Something in him made him feel that Murray would accept the bribe this time, and he desperately wanted to be there the day his feet turned to clay and his pedestal was kicked out from under him. And he wanted to be the one to apply the boot.

He stopped in his tracks. He had an idea.

'Do you know the golf professional at the club?' he asked.

'No,' Adekunle said. 'What's his name?'

'Bernard something. Bernard Odemu I think.'

'Is he a Kinjanjan?'

'Yes.' Morgan paused. 'Do you think you could "persuade" him somehow to partner me with Murray in the Boxing Day golf tournament? I should think he's the man responsible for the draw. Would that be possible, do you think?'

'Is that all?' Adekunle asked, amused. 'Then of course.'

Power, Morgan thought, an amazing thing.

Chapter 4

There was, Morgan decided, a distinct smell now coming from Innocence's body: a sort of sour-sweet smell. Which wasn't surprising, he admitted, as she had been lying out in the sun for nearly four days. It was the morning of 24 December – Christmas Eve – clear, bright, the sun shining, the temperature in the high eighties. He was waiting for Fanshawe.

Fanshawe had summoned him to the servants' quarters to, as he put it, 'sort out this Innocence-problem once and for all.' The Innocence-problem lay – as it had always done, unmovingly, stoically – beneath its garish shroud. As each day had gone by so the juju tokens had multiplied and now there were twenty or so little cairns or assemblies of leaf, twig and pebble clustered around the body.

He saw Fanshawe stride into the compound. He could tell from the quick no-nonsense pace that his superior was not in the best of moods. He sighed quietly to himself.

'Morning,' Fanshawe said brusquely. 'How are things going?'

Morgan felt strangely composed and lethargically in control for some reason. His meeting with Adekunle seemed to have jolted him out of his incipient crack-up, shaped the random nature of his various problems, given him a direction to follow. At least he had to act now; however unsavoury those acts might be. He also had the feeling that things couldn't get much worse – but that, he knew, was a dangerous assumption to make.

'Well,' he said with a shrug in response to Fanshawe's question, indicating at the same time Innocence's body. 'Not much change as you can see.' He was quite pleased with his insouciance; he decided it was a pose he should strive to adopt more often in future.

'Damnation!' Fanshawe swore, his brows knotting fiercely. 'Intolerable bloody country,' he seethed. 'They just go about their business – without a care in the world, as if it was an ordinary day – stepping over dead bodies without a second thought . . . Savage, unfeeling brutes.'

'Well,' Morgan said thoughtfully. He liked beginning his sentences with 'well': it gave them a pondered, considered tone. 'That's only from our point of view you know, Arthur. Shango's a fairly top-notch deity out here and we have to respect . . .'

'I'm not interested in this hocus-pocus rubbish, Leafy,' Fanshawe hissed through clenched teeth. A drop of spittle flew out of his mouth and landed on Morgan's sleeve, but he charitably decided not to draw attention to it by dabbing it away with his handkerchief. He was cool. He had also noticed the pointed use of his surname: Fanshawe was really heating up, he thought, it was all getting on top of him.

'This bloody juju claptrap gets right up my . . . For Christ's sake, man, the Duchess of Ripon is coming here tomorrow. The Queen's personal representative! It's impossible.' Fanshawe shook his head vigorously. 'It *can't* be here.'

'Well . . .' Morgan began.

'I do wish you wouldn't keep beginning all your remarks with "well", Leafy, it's most irritating,' Fanshawe burst out temperamentally.

'Sorry I'm sure,' Morgan said, his eyebrows raised in surprise. 'I was just going to say that the Duchess is hardly likely to wander over to the servants' quarters.'

'That doesn't make the slightest bit of difference,' Fanshawe expostulated. 'It's the principle of the thing. For heaven's sake, this is Commission property, you just can't have it littered with decomposing bodies. And,' he added contemptuously, 'if you can't see that then I'm sorry for you. Very sorry indeed.'

A strained silence ensued. With his thumb-nail Morgan pushed back some encroaching cuticles.

'I suppose we'd better get it over with,' Fanshawe said suddenly and marched towards the body. 'Come on,' he called to Morgan. Morgan joined him, wondering what he planned on doing.

'What are you going to do?' Morgan asked, looking round apprehensively at the audience of children and mothers that had gathered.

'I'm going to have a look of course,' Fanshawe said, the points of a blush appearing on his cheek-bones.

'Why?'

'Ah, to see for myself,' he said, smoothing his moustache, adding vaguely, 'check up, you know.' Morgan realized that Fanshawe was fascinated: he felt the cloth was keeping something from him.

'It's not a pretty sight,' Morgan cautioned.

'Please, masta,' a voice called from the crowd. They looked round, it was Isaac. He advanced a few paces. 'I beg you, sah, nevah totch 'im one time. Make you go leff am, sah. Dis no respec'.'

'I am only going to look,' Fanshawe declaimed pompously. 'Now don't worry, Isaac.' He whispered to Morgan, 'Pull

back the cloth.' Morgan felt like saying pull it back yourself. He was beginning to resent the assumption that he was
some kind of mortuary assistant. However, he obeyed the
order.

Fanshawe lurched back as if he'd been punched in the chest.
His eyes bulged. 'God,' he said hoarsely. Morgan breathed
through his mouth. The crowd edged forward to catch a
glimpse. Morgan threw the cloth back over Innocence's body.
He stepped away carefully.

'Phew,' he said to Fanshawe, dabbing at his face with a
handkerchief. 'It's amazing how quickly . . . you know, how
fast everything . . .'

Fanshawe was pale and obviously shocked. He led Morgan
unsteadily a little way down the compound.

'That does it,' he said vehemently. 'She's got to go. She has
to. It's . . . It's obscene, that's what it is. I'd no idea that sort
of effect . . . well, happened. Get rid of her. That's all. Away
from here. Get rid of her, Morgan. Any way you can.'

Morgan felt the anger of the subordinate who always gets
the dirty jobs. 'But *how* Arthur?' he protested. 'Just tell me
how and I'll do it. Be reasonable for God's sake. You can see
how impossible . . .'

'I don't care!' Fanshawe almost shrieked. 'I'll give you
twenty-four hours. It's been days now since I asked you to
take care of everything. If you had just handled things properly
the first night we wouldn't be in this frightful mess now. Get
an armed guard, anything. Just get rid of that body before the
Duchess arrives.' He stared furiously at Morgan for an instant,
his jaw clenched, the muscles and tendons standing out on his
neck. Then he turned abruptly on his heel and marched off
back to the Commission.

Morgan stood in the compound, rigid with bile–churning
rage. Fuck you! you stinking little shit! he mouthed at Fanshawe's retreating back. He made twisted vampire claws with
his hands and savaged the air in front of his face. He turned

and glared at the crowd, slowly dispersing now. They might have been waxworks, moon-men or zombies for all the understanding their minds shared with his. But there again, he thought, the same could be said about the gulf that existed between him and Fanshawe.

Morgan had to confess that the Innocence-problem seemed insoluble. His one good idea was swiftly quashed by Fanshawe. Morgan had gone down to the Commission's front door and consulted Isaac about the juju ceremony. If he had the money now, Morgan asked, how long would it take to pacify Shango? Isaac thought about it. If the fetish priest could come this evening, if the goat, the beer and the other accessories were purchased forthwith then the whole ceremony might possibly be contracted into two days. But, he warned, tomorrow being Christmas Day the fetish priest might demand extra money for working on a public holiday. Fine, Morgan said, thanks.

Back in his office he had phoned Fanshawe.

'I think I've found a way out of it, Arthur,' he said.

'Yes. Go on,' Fanshawe snapped.

'What we do is do it their way. We've been swimming against the tide so far. So, now we get the juju man, slaughter the goat and get him to exorcize the demon or whatever. I can't see any other alternative.'

'I thought there was some kind of money problem.'

'Yes, there is. But only as far as Maria is concerned. But I thought we could pay for it.'

'Out of the question,' Fanshawe said immediately. 'We don't want to establish that precedent.'

'Hold on,' Morgan said, losing patience. 'Give it some thought. Couldn't we lend it to her at least?' Mean bastard, he said under his breath.

'Well, perhaps. We could consider it. But tell me, how long will this "exorcism" take?'

'Couple of days. I can get on to . . .'

'No! No!' Fanshawe jammered. '*Impossible*. Don't you listen to anything I say? It's *got* to be away by tomorrow. The Duchess . . .' Morgan let him rant on. His scalp crawled with hatred at the man's intransigence. '. . . and remember, Morgan. I'm making this top priority. Forget Kingpin, forget the elections. I just want that body away. I'm making it your sole responsibility.'

And very handy for you too, Morgan thought bitterly, replacing the phone on the receiver, but where did that leave him?

At four that afternoon he decided to go home. At the gate stood Femi Robinson on his own, holding up a placard that read, NO SUEZ IN KINJANJA.

Morgan stopped his car and leant out of the window. 'Isn't that a little extreme?' he called. Robinson approached the car. He was still in his polo-neck and gloves. Somehow he'd managed to pull a beret down over his afro. His BO preceded him like a cloud of mustard gas. His worried face shone with moisture, rivulets of sweat slid down his jaw-bone. A bleb hung from his chin.

'Don't you think,' Morgan indicated the placard, 'that it's also, well, a bit subtle?'

'The message is directed at you British,' Robinson said belligerently. 'Not at my own supporters.'

'And where are they, if you don't mind my asking?'

'They are both buying beer from the trader down the road.' Robinson scowled when he saw Morgan laughing. 'You can laugh,' he accused, 'but soon it will be on the other side of your face.'

'I'm sorry,' said Morgan, suppressing his grin. 'But what you said . . . it's a joke, quite well known.'

Robinson suddenly relaxed. He smiled. 'I admit their fervour is not so great today, but there will be more soon. You must beware. I believe your High Commissioner has apologized. But it is not sufficient. The diplomaticization of the problem is a smoke-screen. And,' he banged his fist on the window sill, 'if the KNP win?' He sucked air in through his teeth and shook his head sadly.

'Thanks for the warning,' Morgan said. He put the car in gear. Robinson took a pace back and brandished his placard.

'I shall remain,' he said, 'to ensure you are not forgettin'.'

As soon as he returned home Morgan showered and crawled into bed for a siesta. He shut his eyes and told himself to relax, ordered every sinew and tendon in his body to ease off, advised his heart to slow its pace. But Fanshawe's hysterical commands seemed to bounce around the inside of his head like a series of powerfully struck squash balls: 'You're responsible . . . top priority . . . twenty-four hours . . .' He supposed it was some form of indirect punishment for the embarrassment he had suffered over Adekunle's effective PR job for the KNP. Morgan wondered if Adekunle had fixed the craw yet. He felt suddenly weak and helpless: an impotent Sisyphus who's just been informed there'll be two rocks from tomorrow – a fagged-out Hercules with a gross of labours to complete. He wanted to weep and blub. It wasn't fair, it wasn't fair . . .

There was a ring at the doorbell. Dispiritedly, remembering Friday and Moses didn't come in until later, he pulled on his dressing-gown and shuffled grumbling down the passageway to see who it was.

Standing there was Kojo, his wife and their three children. Kojo was wearing a shiny black suit, gleaming shoes and a bright red tie. He was carrying a large enamel basin containing something covered by a cloth. His wife, a tiny smiling woman with a creamy caramel skin and huge dangling earrings, was in a lacy blouse, luxuriant black velvet wrap-around and head-tie. The three boys were miniature replicas of their father with small black short-trousered suits and red ties, closely shaven hair and serious-nervous faces. Confronted by such daunting spic-and-spanness Morgan was suddenly aware of his exposed hairy shanks and bare feet, his shabby dressing-gown and tousled hair.

'Kojo,' he said. 'Hello . . . yes, what um . . . hello.' He was very surprised to see them.

Kojo smiled at his confusion. 'Good afternoon, sah, how are you? I have brought my family to greet you.' He paused, waiting to see if comprehension would dawn on Morgan's face. 'For Christmas,' he added finally. Morgan understood. Such courtesy visits were annually paid by employees and servants. Tomorrow he was expecting the nightwatchman, the gardener and the man who cleaned his car once a week, but Kojo had never been before.

'Of course,' Morgan said. 'Go inside, please. Sit down. I'll go and put some clothes on.'

Cursing with irritation he went back to his bedroom and pulled on his clothes. He returned to his sitting room to find the tiny family occupying the edges of two chairs and a settee.

'Yes,' he said stupidly, rubbing his hands together in a bad imitation of a genial host. 'I don't think I've met your wife and sons before.'

Kojo stood up. 'This is my wife Elizabeth.' Elizabeth half rose to her feet as Morgan shook her hand and she gave a demure curtsey. 'Yes, sah,' she said.

Kojo led him on to the three boys. 'And these are my sons: Anthony, Gerald and Arthur.'

'Named after Mr Fanshawe?' Morgan asked curiously.

'Yes, sah. I requested his permission.'

'Good,' Morgan said, his mind empty of conversational gambits. 'Good good good. Yes,' he said abruptly. 'I know. What'll you have to drink? Gin, whisky, some beer?'

'Please, a soft drink. But before, please, I have this gift for you.' Kojo pushed forward the enamel basin on the carpet. Morgan scrutinized the dark cloth covering its contents. For some reason he was reminded of Innocence's shroud. He thought his eyes must have been playing tricks on him because he was sure he could detect a tremor of movement below it. Then, from underneath the cloth, came a faintly musical croak. Morgan leapt back in alarm, causing Kojo's boys to giggle softly to themselves.

'Jesus Christ!' Morgan exclaimed, then wished he hadn't used the profanity. 'It's alive!'

Kojo drew back the cloth to reveal a large turkey, its legs securely trussed. With an effort he lifted it up by its roped legs and held the bird out, upside down, to Morgan. 'Merry Christmas, sah,' Kojo said. The turkey's stumpy wings were also tied together and it vainly tried to flap them. Its pink wattles hung over its startled face. Between the dangling combs its glaring maddened eye seemed to stare in accusation at Morgan. Feeling slightly queasy he reached out and grasped its scaly stick-like ankles. As he took the weight, the turkey twitched its head, parted its beak and gave a sotto voce 'gobble-gobble'. Morgan promptly released his hold and the terrified bird dropped heavily to the floor where it gave a great gobbling shriek and shat greenily on his carpet. Kojo's family fell about in delighted mirth at his feebleness, Mrs Kojo with her arms folded across her stomach, politely bent over to hide her face, the three boys laughing and slapping each other on the shoulders.

Kojo picked up the panicking bird. 'Sah,' he said considerately. 'If you don't like it I can remove it.'

Morgan grinned sheepishly. 'Yes,' he said. 'I think you'd better handle things.'

Kojo took the turkey out to the garden and tied one of its legs to a bush with a long piece of string while Mrs Kojo expertly cleaned up the mess and Morgan served up the soft drinks. They chatted politely for five minutes or so but soon Kojo rose to his feet and announced their departure. Morgan rushed into his study and wrote out a cheque for ten pounds which he sealed in an envelope and slipped into Kojo's hand at the front door.

Kojo tucked it away in his suit pocket. 'T'ank you, sah,' he said simply.

Morgan watched the little family wander away up his garden path in the soft late-afternoon light, the small boys looking curiously back at him. He heard them chattering excitedly. He wondered what they would be saying about him, what they thought of the stupid fat white man who was too frightened to hold a turkey. He walked out into his garden and strolled round to the back near the kitchen. The turkey stood at the extremity of its bit of string tugging futilely with one foot while it tried to peck at the ground just beyond its reach. It was a big bird, in good condition. He wondered how much it had cost: not ten pounds anyway, he told himself unkindly; at least Kojo got what he came for.

Dusk was advancing and he heard the insect and animal orchestra begin to strike up. He went morosely back into the house. It seemed huge and empty and he felt its vacant rooms and dark corners whisper with melancholy and depression.

'Come on,' he said out loud to himself, striding to his hi-fi to select Frank Sinatra's *Songs for Swingin' Lovers*, 'you're not a bloody Romantic poet.' As the music boomed out he heard the turkey gobble outside in the garden and he looked at the dents and hollows Kojo's family had made in the cushions of his armchairs and settee. Their absence seemed more absolute despite the evidence of these shallow templates of their bodies. He felt suddenly angry at his mean-minded interpretation of their motives in visiting him. Kojo had never come before and now Morgan felt obscurely pleased and flattered that he had brought along his family. He thought that, in fact, Kojo probably liked him for some reason. This cheered him up and he began to hum along with Frank. He smiled to himself remembering how he'd dropped the turkey and the bird's reaction as it had hit the floor. What had Kojo said? Typical Kojo: tact itself – 'If you don't like it I can remove it.'

'If you don't like it I can remove it . . .'

Friday bounced into the sitting room. '*Bon soir*, masta,' he said cheerfully. 'Dis na fine bed for garden. *Extra*.'

Morgan looked at him, a mad idea taking shape in his head. He would show them. Yes. He would show the bastards.

'Tell me, Friday,' he asked ingenuously. 'What are you doing tonight?'

Chapter 5

'There she is,' Morgan whispered, crouching behind the trunk of a dwarf palm. He pointed fifteen yards in front of him to the dark bundle that was Innocence's body, just distinguishable in the moonlight. Friday squatted beside him.

'Ah-ah-ah,' he croaked. 'I go see 'im.'

They were hiding in the small grove of trees and ill-tended yam and cassava allotments that stood behind the wash-place at the northern end of the servants' quarters. It was half past three in the morning. To his left Morgan could see the straggling line of tall nim trees that bordered the Commission grounds – and separated the servants' quarters from the garden – and beyond them the unlit mass of the Fanshawes' house. There was a clear three-quarter moon in the sky which palely illuminated everything and caused the buildings. trees and bushes to cast dagger-edged impenetrable shadows. Twenty yards behind them the Peugeot was parked on a dusty track, its boot gaping in expectation. With some effort he and Friday had pushed it up from the main road to a point as close as possible to the servants' quarters.

Beside him Morgan could sense Friday's fear coming off him like perfume.

'I thought you weren't frightened of Shango,' he whispered angrily.

'*Comment?*'

Christ almighty, Morgan swore to himself, wondering what sort of an accomplice he'd chosen. He tried again. 'You say me you nevah fright for Shango. *Tu n'as pas peur de Shango,*' he translated as an afterthought.

'Is true, masta. But I dey fear for os if dis people livin' for here catch os one time.' He gestured at the dark lines of the housing blocks. He had a point there, Morgan had to admit. Up to now it had been the dogs that he was most concerned about but so far they hadn't met any. There had been the odd bleat from a tethered goat and a heart-stoppingly strident cock-a-doodle-doo from an irate rooster, but as everyone knew Kinjanjan cocks crowed at any time except dawn no one, apparently, had deemed it anything out of the ordinary.

Morgan had cajoled, threatened, bullied and finally bribed Friday to come along on this escapade. First, he had established that Friday, being a Dahomey man, didn't even know about Shango, far less worry about offending him. Religious objections out of the way it had only taken some earnest pleading, followed by threats of instant dismissal and/or GBH and finally a promise of a five-pound bonus to secure his participation in operation body-snatch.

Morgan felt himself tingle with uneasy excitement. Admittedly, he was very nearly drunk, but he didn't feel as nervous as he'd expected. This was the marvellous thing about action, he thought; at least he was doing something about his problems instead of sitting at home and fretting about them. He planned simply to bundle Innocence's body into the boot and drive her down to the morgue at Ademola clinic. He didn't really care who he upset: as far as he was concerned he was merely following Fanshawe's explicit instruction. 'Get rid of it,' he had said. 'Use an armed guard if you have to.' Well, Morgan thought, there was no need to be quite so dramatic as that.

'*Allons-y,*' he hissed at Friday, and they scurried closer, hunched like two commandos behind enemy lines. They slid into the moon-shadow cast by the gable end of the block nearest the Commission, pressing their backs against the wall. Innocence's body lay a few yards away from them across the gap between the block's verandah and the raised concrete floor of the wash-place. The moonlight coming through the leaves of the towering cotton tree dappled the ground with shade. Not far off the smudge fire gave out lingering wreaths of smoke from the pile of greenery that had been placed on top of the charcoal. But the smell of the smoke wasn't sufficient.

'*Oh là là,*' Friday whispered. '*Ça pue.*'

Morgan smelt the rotting sweetness flow through his nose and down into his lungs like water. He felt his stomach heave and saliva pump into his mouth. He leant his head against the rough wall behind him. Suddenly he wished he wasn't there. What had possessed him to do such a thing? How could he . . .

'*Ça va,* masta?' Friday asked in concern.

'*Oui,* I mean yes.' He swallowed. Now or never. 'Come on,' he said. They crept out to the body. The laterite square was deserted and everything was quiet, bathed in the grey-blue of moonglow. Quickly Morgan flicked back the cloth from the now familiar body. The smell seemed to billow out like an explosion. Friday gave a little whimper when he saw Innocence. Dappled moonlight lay across her face; a patch of light on her mouth made her teeth gleam. Morgan dry-retched and gagged.

'*Vite,*' he whispered huskily. '*Prends la main et . . .*' he couldn't remember the French for pull, '. . . pull 'im!' Without thinking he gripped Innocence's bloated forearm with both hands and he saw a recoiling Friday hesitatingly do the same. The skin was like no skin he had ever touched before – like thick rubber. He thought it bitterly ironic and singularly peculiar of him that this very afternoon he had been unable to bring himself to hold a turkey's legs. He tugged and Innocence shifted. Despite the illusion of balloon-lightness she was alarmingly heavy. And stiff. He saw that the arm which he was pulling remained unnaturally bent. He gave a little sob.

'Pull, Friday,' he whispered, '*Pull!*'

They pulled and with a scrape of dust and gravel dragged her back into the secure shadow cast by the gable end of the block. Morgan found he was panting loudly. Friday looked as if he were facing a firing squad. Morgan didn't dare let go of Innocence's wrist in case he wouldn't be able to bring himself to grip it again. Over the rasping sound of his breathing he heard the horrible buzzing of disturbed flies. With a shudder he locked away his imagination for the night. He looked back at the spot where Innocence had been. The cloth lay like a dark puddle of water, surrounded by the small piles of votive juju-tokens. He wondered what the Commission servants would think when they woke up in the morning. Was this what it had been like when they found the stone had been rolled away?, he asked himself in a bizarre impulse of heuristic theology. But his speculations were interrupted by a thin chant of fear coming from Friday's lips.

'Shut up!' Morgan hissed. 'Come on!'

With difficulty they dragged Innocence up the path a few yards into the allotment grove. Morgan was amazed at the rigidity of her joints and wondered how long they could withstand the strain. He didn't like to think what might happen if they gave. They paused for a few seconds to get their breath back, their chests heaving, without talking. Was this what it was like with Burke and Hare? he wondered: silence, guilt and horror? Why, he asked himself, was his mind insisting on working in this exegetical and pedantic way? Friday looked straight ahead of him, his hands on his knees, his eyes half-focused on the Commission garden.

Suddenly his mouth dropped open and his eyes widened in terror.

'Masta,' he stuttered, a shaking arm pointing towards the Commission, '*Mais non . . .* !'

Morgan snapped his head round, his heart jumping some-

264

where at the back of his throat. Beyond the nim trees the wide expanse of the Commission garden lay illuminated in the calm moonlight. And there Morgan clearly saw a tall white shape moving slowly to and fro. He heard a faint noise carry across the garden, '. . . oooh . . . owe . . .'

'Mmnngrllggrrk,' was the only sound that issued from his petrified vocal chords.

Friday had leapt to his feet, stark terror written across his incredulous features. '*Shango!*' he gasped. 'Shango 'e done come,' he bleated helplessly, stepping back from the body as if controlled by an alien force. '*Je m'en vais.*'

Ghastly calamities spontaneously reared up in Morgan's mind. He jumped up and fiercely grabbed hold of Friday's shirt-front, hauling the little man up on his tiptoes. 'You bloody stay here,' he whispered brutally, 'or I'll kill you.' Friday's eyes rolled at the savagery of this threat. Morgan pushed him back down onto his knees by Innocence's body.

Friday covered his face with his hands. 'Masta,' he whimpered. 'I go beg you don't leaf me wit dis dead woman . . .' He pointed suddenly again. 'Ah-ah! Shango is comin'.'

Morgan's scrambled brain registered the presence of the pale spectre roaming about the garden once more. Without thinking he dashed towards the line of nim trees. Pressing himself to a thick trunk he peered out across the moonlit lawn.

It seemed to be a person; tall and dressed in white, holding something in one hand. He strained his ears to try and make out the noises it was uttering.

'Hello-oo,' he heard. 'Anyone at ho-ome?'

In a sudden blind boiling rage, incoherent with terror, relief and fuming anger he charged off in a wild arm-flailing sprint across the lawn towards the figure. The man – as Morgan swiftly approached he recognized the person as such – looked round when he heard the sound of Morgan's thundering footsteps, paused for an instant, and then, patently transfigured by shocked alarm himself, began to run away – a difficult operation this, for he was encumbered by a suitcase. Morgan's hell-for-leather momentum soon brought him within range of the lumbering lanky Shango-impersonator and like a plucky full-back bringing down a try-scoring three-quarter, he launched himself at the man's knees.

The man in white came crashing to the ground with a shrill cry of pain and surprise. Morgan bit his lip to prevent his own pain – two badly bruised knees from the concrete-hard lawn – expressing itself in a whoop of anguish. He leapt to his feet still spitting with anger. The man remained groggily on all fours, searching the ground for something.

'Who . . . the fuck . . . are you?' Morgan demanded breathlessly in a stage scream-whisper. 'What the hell . . . do you think you're doing . . . prowling around at this time of night disturbing . . . making a bloody nuisance of yourself?'

The man found and put on a pair of round gold-rimmed spectacles and rose unsteadily to his feet. He was very tall and thin. In the moonlight Morgan could make out longish fair hair, a middle parting, prominent nose and shadow-hollowed cheeks. Morgan flashed a glance back over his shoulder at the servants' quarters. No lights were showing; he only prayed Friday was still with Innocence. He looked back. The man was muttering something about a dildo.

'Dildo?' Morgan repeated in furious incomprehension, anger still coursing through his body. 'What have bloody dildos got to do with this?' He saw the man's suitcase on the ground and for a crazed unreal moment thought he'd felled a travelling salesman for a sexual-aids firm who was trying to whip up some West African business.

'No,' the man said in a whimper. 'Bilbow. My name. My name's Greg Bilbow.' He had a weedy Yorkshire accent.

'I don't give a damn what your name is. What are you doing prowling around here in the dead of night? That's what I want to know.'

The man seemed on the point of breaking down but

Morgan was unrelenting. He had more important things to worry about than the sentiments of some nomadic Yorkshireman.

'I've had a nightmare trip,' his victim continued dolefully. 'A nightmare. I've just paid out forty-five pounds on a taxi fare. Forty-five pounds! I think I've been to Timbuctoo and back.' He sniffed. 'I got off the train at Nkongsamba at seven-thirty this evening. I found a taxi and asked to be taken to the British Deputy High Commission.' He peered at his watch. 'We've been driving around for over eight hours,' there was a barely suppressed sob in his voice.

'Well, you've arrived,' Morgan said harshly, thinking that they really shouldn't let such innocents out in the world. 'You've been conned. The station's about twenty minutes away.'

'Thank God,' the man said, seemingly happy only to have made it. 'Oh thank God!'

'But you'll have to come back tomorrow,' Morgan said unsparingly, agonizingly conscious of the time he was wasting. 'Everything's closed up until the morning. There's a hotel half a mile down the road. They'll put you up.'

'But I've got no money,' the man whined. 'I spent it all on the taxi.'

'That's your problem, old son,' Morgan laughed cruelly, drained of human kindness. 'Now push off.'

The man was flapping a piece of paper about. 'But I've got a letter here from someone called Morgan Leafy who says I can stay at the Commission.' His shoulders slumped in desperation. 'Please,' he added feebly.

Cogs began to click and spin in Morgan's brain. 'What did you say your name was?'

'Bilbow. Greg Bilbow.'

'What is it you do exactly?'

'Me? I'm a poet.'

★

It was surprisingly easy for Morgan and Friday to drag Innocence the remaining few yards and then, with the strength of desperate men, heave her into the boot. Morgan closed the lid and locked it. He felt like the driver of a runaway car hurtling down a mountain road: nominally in control, but only just. Ruthlessly suppressing the urge to fall to the ground, scream and beat the earth with his fists, he quietly explained the true nature of the ghostly apparition to Friday in demotic pidgin French. Friday stood there taking it in, nodding his head and muttering to himself, '*Jamais . . . jamais de ma vie . . . non, non . . . jamais.*' Normally Morgan would have commiserated with him: his solitary vigil in the dark over Innocence's body, the stink, the flies, Shango, a disappearing accomplice who threatened him with violent death all must have tested his mettle considerably.

They pushed the car back down the track to the road and then drove down to the Commission entrance where Bilbow stood waiting as he had been instructed to. Morgan had offered to put him up for the night. He climbed into the front seat.

'I'm tremendously grateful,' he began. 'Amazing coincidence that you should be out and about at this time.'

'Yes, isn't it,' Morgan said, thinking quickly. 'I'm just driving my houseboy back from taking his wife to hospital,' he jerked his thumb at Friday in the back. 'I was going past the Commission when I thought I saw somebody wandering around in the garden.'

'You gave me a right turn,' Bilbow said cheerfully. He seemed to have settled down. 'The way you charged out of those trees, your arms all waving, the look on your face – I almost died . . .' the Yorkshire accent drew the vowels out interminably. Morgan felt an extreme tiredness descend on him, then they drove over a pot-hole and Innocence's body thumped in the boot. Friday gave a squeak of alarm.

'He's very upset,' Morgan explained in response to Bilbow's

surprised face. 'Just married.' Bilbow nodded understandingly and turned to an uncomprehending Friday.

'Sorry to hear about your wife,' he said. 'Hope she gets better soon.'

Morgan drove on. There was no point in taking the body to Ademola morgue tonight, he thought. It would just have to wait until tomorrow.

'Hey,' Bilbow said jovially. 'I've joost realized. It's Christmas Day. Merry Christmas everyone!'

Chapter 6

Bilbow wore an old green towelling shirt with short sleeves and his white cotton jeans which still displayed the dirt scuffs from his encounter with Morgan the night before. At first glance he looked ridiculously young with his tall lean body, blue eyes behind the round spectacle frames and the overall blandness of his near albino colouring – longish straight platinum hair, invisible eyebrows and lashes, pink starlet lips. But a closer inspection revealed the graininess of his skin, the thin lines stretching down from the corners of his nostrils, and others forming brackets round his mouth. His voice, which his panic and distress had made whiny last night, had settled into its normal deeper timbre, and for all its comic book Yorkshire tones it had a genuinely friendly and quietly relaxed quality.

'Merry Christmas,' he said as Morgan shambled through the screen door onto the verandah. He was sitting at the verandah table with the remains of his breakfast in front of him. He gestured at the sunlit garden. 'Quite bizarre,' he said. 'Here I am in a short-sleeved shirt eating – what's it called? – paw-paw in a temperature of eighty degrees while everyone at home's wrapped up warm watching the telly.'

'Yeah well,' Morgan said surlily through his hangover, thinking of last night's events, 'that's what it's like in Africa: out of the ordinary.'

'I've got a present for you,' Bilbow said. 'Well not so much a present, more of a thank you for last night. Saved me life.' He held out a slim book. Morgan took it. *The Small Carafe and Other Poems* by Greg Bilbow.

'Thanks,' Morgan said gruffly. 'I'll, ah, have a look at it later.' He sat down in front of his bowl of cornflakes. He rubbed his eyes. Merry bloody Christmas. He felt hellish, like the survivor of some week-long battle. Surely things would calm down now? He looked across the table at Bilbow – the fine, centrally-parted blond hair, the pinched bespectacled face. He didn't seem to suspect anything about last night, seemed quite happy to accept Morgan's version of events. That, at least, was something.

Morgan pushed his uneaten cornflakes to one side and thought about his Christmas Day ahead. First he had to get rid of the decomposing body in his car boot, then dress up as Santa Claus and hand out presents to kids: the contrast seemed ghoulishly obscene.

'Here,' Bilbow interrupted his thoughts, 'talking about presents, there's a cracking big 'un arrived for you. It's in t'sitting room. Bloody heavy it was too.'

Lying on the sitting-room carpet was indeed a huge brightly wrapped present about five feet long. Falling to his knees beside it Morgan savagely tore away the wrapping paper.

'Christ,' Bilbow said admiringly.

Morgan looked on aghast. It was a massive mustard and black golf bag, the sort carried by champion American golfers, or rather by their tottering caddies. Fumbling at the buckles and catches Morgan unzipped the hood. A complete set of gleaming golf clubs was revealed, newly minted, like lethal weapons.

'Here's a note,' said Bilbow, picking a card from the torn

and shredded pile of wrapping paper. ' "Have a good game. Sam." Jesus, who's Sam?'

'My uncle,' Morgan lied, his throat dry. 'He's an eccentric millionaire.'

'You're not kidding,' Bilbow observed 'There's about four hundred quid's worth there.'

'Is there?' Morgan replied blankly. He'd forgotten about Murray. This was Adekunle's way of telling him the draw had been rigged. Morgan sat cross-legged on his sitting-room floor, his head in his hands.

'Here,' Bilbow asked. 'Are you all right, Morgan?'

The phone rang. 'I'll get it,' Bilbow said agreeably. He went over to the phone. 'It's for you,' he said. 'Someone called Fanshawe.'

Morgan shuffled over.

'Leafy!' Fanshawe screamed down the phone. 'Get over here. *Now*!'

Femi Robinson gave a clenched fist salute as Morgan swept past him into the Commission drive. He noted there were no guards at the gate but thought nothing of it. It was Christmas Day after all: a holiday for everyone – except for Robinson. You had to admire the man's stamina, Morgan thought as he stepped out of his car, he could do with a dose of it himself.

Fanshawe was pacing up and down on the Commission steps, his face white and drawn with anger.

'Merry Christmas, Arth . . .'

'It's gone!' Fanshawe exclaimed shrilly. 'Gone. Disappeared in the night. Vanished!'

'Of course she has,' Morgan said calmly. What was the little cretin so upset about? he wondered to himself impatiently. Wasn't that exactly what he wanted?

'What do you mean "of course"?' Fanshawe's face was very close to his own. Morgan backed down the steps.

'For God's sake, Arthur,' he protested. 'You told me – no,

you *ordered* me to get rid of Innocence's body. Top priority, sole responsibility, remember? Well I've simply followed my instructions that's all.' He folded his arms across his chest and looked hurt and offended.

'Oh *no*,' Fanshawe groaned. 'Oh God no! Don't tell me she's in the morgue. Disaster. Utter, utter disaster.'

'Well no,' Morgan said, surprised at his vehement chagrin. 'She's not in the morgue, she's in the boot of my car.'

Fanshawe stared very hard at him – as if his face had suddenly turned bright green or smoke was belching from his ears.

'What?' Fanshawe demanded hoarsely.

'In my car.'

'That one?'

'It's the only car I've got.'

'Oh my God.'

'What's the problem?' Morgan asked, quickly losing such small reserves of patience as he had left.

'You've got to put her back.'

Morgan gazed out of his office window at the lone defiant figure of Femi Robinson. Surely there was some sort of lesson for him in the man's stupid perseverance, his stubborn isolation? He looked down at his Peugeot standing in the empty car park full in the glare of the afternoon sun. He winced. The boot would be like a pressure cooker: Christ alone knew what was happening to Innocence in there. He turned away, stoking up the fires of hatred for Fanshawe. If only the stupid bastard had followed his advice, he thought angrily, but oh no, you couldn't have a decomposing corpse anywhere near the Duchess. So flunky Leafy had removed the body as instructed and what had happened? Every Commission servant had gone on instant strike, had refused to stir from their quarters except to announce their action to a startled Fanshawe over his Christmas breakfast.

Fanshawe had sniffed round the boot of Morgan's car like

a suspicious customs officer searching for drugs, stopping every now and then to stare at Morgan in disbelief. The smell and the hovering flies soon convinced him that the body was indeed there.

'You've got to put it back,' he said weakly. 'I almost had a revolt on my hands this morning. A riot. It was frightful.' He leant against the boot of the car and then leapt back as if the metal was boiling hot. 'How can you drive around,' he said with distasteful curiosity, 'with . . . that in your car?' He looked uncomprehendingly at Morgan. 'Doesn't it upset you?' Morgan ignored him. 'Put it *back*?' he said incredulously. 'What are you talking about? How, for God's sake, how?'

'I don't care,' Fanshawe insisted stridently. 'This strike you've landed us in is an absolute catastrophe. The Duchess is arriving here after lunch and there's not a single Commission servant on duty anywhere.' He looked wildly round the garden as if he expected to see them crouching defiantly behind the trees and bushes. 'And tomorrow,' he went on, 'tomorrow there are two hundred people coming here for a buffet-lunch reception. It'll be a farce. A total disgrace!' He rubbed his forehead vigorously as if to disperse the images of milling, unfed and unwatered dignitaries. 'At least,' he said, 'you haven't delivered her to the morgue. That *is* something in your favour. We have a chance of salvaging some shreds of our reputation. You've *got* to have Innocence back where she was by tomorrow, that's all: it's the only way the servants will come back to work. That's all there is to it. We can just cope today, but tomorrow we simply must have everyone back at their posts. It's quite impossible otherwise – we'd never live it down.'

'Hold on a sec,' Morgan said, controlling the urge to seize Fanshawe by his scrawny throat. 'I can't just drive up to the servants' quarters and tip her out of the boot. They'll lynch me, for Christ's sake! What exactly do you expect me to do?'

'I'm having absolutely nothing more to do with it,' Fanshawe exclaimed, his voice getting higher as he grew more excited, waving his hands about in front of his face. 'Nothing. Nothing at all. It's all your doing: you sort the wretched mess out. Get her back, that's all I care. That strike's got to be over by tomorrow.' He flinched visibly at the memory. 'It was positively horrific this morning,' he said. 'There we were sitting happily at breakfast, exchanging presents, when this mob turns up outside. Isaac, Joseph, all these men normally quite agreeable pleasant types. They were most aggressive and insulting. Chloe was terribly upset, really distraught. She had to go and lie down and . . .'

'They don't think I did it, do they?' Morgan asked, suddenly worried.

'No. At least I don't think so. But they're convinced we had something to do with it. That's why they're going on strike, until we return the body. Those were the conditions.' Fanshawe scuffed at the gravel with his feet. For a moment Morgan saw him as a perplexed and worried man, not sure if he could cope. Then before his eyes he saw him change: the shoulders stiffened, the jaw was set, the pompous light gleamed in his eye.

'Things have got themselves into a pretty fair mess all round,' he stated accusingly to Morgan. 'The Kingpin Project's a shambles, we're having to kow-tow to the present government in apology which is the last thing we wanted. Then there's this appalling death: bodies littering the compound. And now you've landed us with a total strike just when the Duchess is arriving. The whole Nkongsamba part of her visit is going to be one long saga of inefficiency and shoddiness. How do you think our record's going to look after this, eh? I'll tell you: absolutely fifth-rate, totally and unacceptably non-British. Now,' he continued, 'I'm leaving it up to you to rectify things as best as you can. There's nothing we can do to salvage Kingpin at this late stage but we can at the very least make sure the Duchess leaves Nkongsamba with happy memories and no horror-stories to tell the High Commissioner when she gets down to the capital.' His voice dropped a register. 'I'm deeply disappointed in you, Morgan. Deeply. I thought you were a man of experience and ability. Someone I could rely on. But I'm sorry to say you've let me down shockingly on every count, so, let's see what you can do to make amends.'

Morgan had watched him walk away. The black splenetic fury that would normally have erupted had been replaced this time by bleak cynical resignation. The injustice was so towering, so out of proportion that no rage could hope to match it. Fanshawe was scum, he had decided, not worthy even of his most scathing contempt.

He turned away from the window and went back to his desk. There, folded on his chair, were his Santa Claus overalls and a large cotton-wool beard. Beneath the seat were shiny black gumboots. On his desk was a note from Mrs Fanshawe outlining his duties and itinerary.

His stomach rumbled with hunger. He had not returned home but had stayed on at the Commission and moped. Around lunchtime he had telephoned his house and spoken to Bilbow.

'Shame you're tied up,' Bilbow had said. 'Your boys have given me a great loonch. Whopping roast turkey, all the trimmings.'

Morgan's saliva glands surged into action, but 'leave some for me' was all he said. Bilbow was due to take part in some festival of poetry and dance at the university arts theatre on Boxing Day, co-sponsored by the Kinjanjan Ministry of Culture and the British Council as part of the nationwide Independence anniversary celebrations. Morgan vaguely remembered the letter he had signed several days previously telling him the Commission could provide accommodation. Under the circumstances, he thought, it was scarcely surprising it had slipped his mind. He told Bilbow he could stay on with him if he wanted, and to his relief the poet accepted. Morgan thought it as well to keep him away from the Fanshawes.

He looked at his watch: 3.45. According to the timetable he had to be at the club at 4.00, where a Land-Rover would be waiting, laden with the presents he was to distribute. Weighed down with self-pity he began to change into his Santa outfit. He took off his shirt and trousers and put on the red overalls. Mrs Fanshawe had added gold tinsel trimmings and a hood. He put on the gumboots and hooked the beard over his ears. For a second or two he thought he might pass out. There was no let-up, he bitterly reflected, no relief from the succession of Job-like torments he was inflicted with. He wondered what on earth he looked like and went through to the landing bathroom to find a mirror.

Mrs Bryce had clearly been at work. A scrap of carpet had been laid on the scuffed parquet of the landing and flower-filled vases were placed on every window ledge. Morgan peered into the guest suite. All was clean and fresh in readiness for her Grace. In the bathroom the porcelain gleamed from energetic Vimming; small tablets of soap and neatly folded towels were laid out as if for kit inspection. The only tawdry element was the plastic shower curtain with its faded aquatic motifs; obviously Fanshawe's budget didn't stretch to replacing that.

Morgan regarded his reflection in the mirror of the medicine cabinet. He did look suitably Christmassy he thought, though the too-short sleeves seemed an absurdly rakish note, his broad shoulders and thick arms making him appear an aggressively youthful and somehow faintly yobbish Santa. He sighed, causing his spade-like beard to flutter: the things he did for his country.

Passing through the hall on the way out to his car he heard the buzz of an incoming call on the untended switchboard. He hesitated for a moment and then decided to answer it.

'Deputy High Commission.'

'Morgan?' It was Celia. His heart sank. She was crying. 'Thank God it's you.'

'What's wrong?' he asked, trying to keep the resignation out of his voice.

'I tried to ring you at home, someone told me you were here.' She sniffed. 'I have to see you. It's urgent. I'm so unhappy, so miserable.'

Join the club, he thought ungraciously. 'Celia,' he said in a despairing tone, 'look, I don't know. I've got a hell of a lot on. Christ, I'm even dressed up as Santa bloody Claus at the moment.'

'Please,' she wailed. 'It's terribly important. You've got to help me.'

No! he screamed inwardly. *No.* He couldn't help anybody else, not now, not any more; he was fully employed helping himself. No, no, a thousand times no. But all he said was, 'I can't talk now, Celia. Give me a ring tomorrow sometime, OK?'

'Gareth Jones . . . There you are, Merry Christmas . . . Bronwyn Jones. Hello Bronwyn, Merry Christmas . . . Funsho Akinremi? Merry Christmas Funsho . . . Trampus McKrindle. Ah, Trampus? Where's Trampus? . . . There you are, Merry Christmas . . . What have we here? I can't read this . . . Yes, Yvonne and Tracy Patten. Merry Christmas, girls . . .'

It took him almost an hour to distribute the presents from the two immense sacks that were sitting in the open back of the Land-Rover. It was parked on the lawn in front of the club. On the grass below the terrace were long tables where the scores of children had eaten their Christmas tea and which were now covered with the incredible detritus all children's parties seemed to leave behind them. The tables reminded Morgan of unscrubbed surgical trestles from some Crimean War dressing-station, covered in blobs and shreds of multi-coloured jelly, flattened cakes, vivid spilt drinks, oozing trifle mush, deliquescent ice-cream. Morgan had called each child out to receive two presents – one donated by their parents expressly for this purpose, the other a tin of sweets ostensibly provided by the Duchess – reading their names out from the cards in a booming ho-ho-ho Santa voice. His cheeks and jaw-bones ached from the effort of smiling. Despite the disguise of his beard he had found it impossible to convey an impression of geniality with a straight face. On the terrace overlooking the children, the parents and other interested onlookers stood clutching drinks. Morgan could see the Joneses and Dalmire and Priscilla. On a low podium to the right of the Land-Rover sat the Duchess of Ripon herself, flanked by the Fanshawes.

After all the presents had been handed out Dalmire strode onto the lawn, clapped his hands for silence and without the least trace of anxiety gave a short speech thanking the Duchess for hosting the party, honouring the Nkongsamba club with her presence and called on everyone to give three cheers.

As the last hurrah died away Morgan clambered down from the back of the Land-Rover, snatched off his beard and made for the bar at a brisk trot. He saw Fanshawe, however, imperiously beckon him over to their group. Reluctantly he changed course.

'This is Mr Leafy, our First Secretary,' Fanshawe introduced him to the Duchess.

'You made a splendid Santa, Mr Leafy, I'm most grateful.' Morgan looked into the hooded, deeply bored eyes of a stumpy middle-aged woman. She had frosted blond-grey hair curling from beneath her straw turban and lumpy unpleasant features that shone with decades of insincerity, arrogance and bad manners. As he shook her damp soft hand he noticed the way the loose flesh on her upper arm jiggled to and fro.

'Not at all, Ma'am,' he said. 'My pleasure entirely.'

Mrs Fanshawe led her off to the official car while Fanshawe lingered behind. He clutched at Morgan's wrist.

'Luckily, we're dining with the Governor tonight,' he

hissed, unyielding still in his displeasure. 'But what's happening with Innocence?'

'Ah, I'm working on that, Arthur.'

'Where is she?'

'Ooh, about fifty yards away.'

'Not in your . . . ?'

'Yes. I'm afraid the car's the safest place until I can work out a plan.'

Fanshawe had gone pale again. 'I'll never understand you,' he said hollowly, shaking his head. 'Never. Just get her back. That's all. Get her back in place tonight.' Morgan said nothing, all he could think about was the drink that was waiting for him at the bar.

'Nothing else must go wrong, Leafy,' Fanshawe threatened. 'Everything must be settled by tomorrow. I'm warning you,' he added grimly. 'Your future depends on it.'

Morgan watched the last lights go out in the servants' quarters. He sat in his car hugging the gallon-can of petrol to his chest trying to stop the car's interior tilting and swaying like a boat on a rough sea, attempting to get his eyes to focus on objects for more than two seconds at a time. He had stood at the club bar and had drunk steadily all evening, still clad in his Santa costume, looking like some cheap dictator from a banana republic with his rubber jack-boots and tinsel epaulettes. He had been the butt of much good-humoured ribbing and had smiled emptily through it all, happily allowing people to buy him drinks. Around eleven o'clock his pickled brain had finally come up with an idea, a way of replacing Innocence's body, and he was now waiting to put the first phase into effect.

At ten past twelve he finally grew tired of sitting around so he left his car and stumbled across the road, correcting his course several times, and made his way in a series of diagonals towards the servants' quarters. He was approaching them from the main road side. Between the road and the first block of the quarters lay a ditch, a patch of scrub waste-land and the sizeable mound of the quarters' rubbish heap. Morgan fell into the ditch, hauled himself out and crossed through the scrub patch as quietly as he could, holding the petrol can in both hands. He was glad he was wearing gumboots as they would protect him from any snake or scorpion he might encounter. He awkwardly scaled the crumbling gamey slope of the dump. He heard things scuttling away from his feet but he tried not to think about them. When he reached the first of the old car-hulks that rested on the top he stopped and crouched down beside it to get his breath back. He was about thirty or forty feet away from the first block of the servants' quarters. All the windows facing him were shuttered. To his left he could just make out the tin roof of the wash-place. The moon obligingly cast the same light as it had done just twenty-four hours or so before. Morgan thought wryly that he had not expected to be back quite so soon. He sat down carefully and listened for any noises. He suspected that Isaac, Joseph and Ezekiel would be far more vigilant tonight, hence the need for the diversion he'd planned. He heard nothing unusual. The moon shone down on the corrugated-iron roofs of the quarters, the smell of rotting vegetables and stale shite rose up sluggishly all about him. Unthinkingly, he unscrewed the cap from the petrol can and poured its contents over the floor of the rusty chassis and across the torn and gaping upholstery of the seats. Stepping back he struck a match and tossed it into the car. Nothing happened. He inched closer, struck another, threw. Nothing happened. Tiring of this game he went up to the car and dropped a match directly onto the remains of the back seat. With a soft *whoomph* the car seemed to explode in a ball of fire before his face. He felt the flames scald his eyeballs and he fell back in fearful horror. The car blazed away furiously, touching everything with orange. Morgan forgot about his face.

'*FAYAH*!' he yelled with hoarse abandon at the servants' quarters. 'YOU GET FAYAH FOR HEAH!'

As he scramble-sprinted back to his car he could hear doors slamming and the first shrill screams of alarm. He jumped into his car and drove speedily up the road a hundred yards before flinging it round in a sharp right-hand turn onto the laterite track up which he and Friday had laboriously pushed it the previous night. He roared up to the end of the track, throwing caution to the winds, assuming that everyone's attention would by now be fully concentrated on the fire. Switching off the lights and crashing the gears, he reversed as far as he could into the allotment grove. Through the trees he could see a tall column of flame shooting up from the blazing car and see dark shapes of rushing figures silhouetted against the glow. Fumbling with his keys he opened the boot and flung it open.

The smell leapt out and hit him with almost palpable force, as if it were some powerful genie suddenly released from the dark recesses of his car. Morgan thought he was going to faint: he gagged and spat several times on the ground. Then with the strength and singlemindedness of a drunk and demonically-inspired man he levered and hauled Innocence's body from the boot. The cloying smells seemed to seize his throat like boney fingers as she thumped heavily to the ground. He grabbed her rigid arms and dragged her along the path. He felt his face tense and contort into a twisted sobbing grimace as he heaved and strained at his ghastly burden. He stopped for a moment behind a tree to wipe his sweating hands on his overalls, sour vomit in his throat, his heart thumping timpanically in his ears. He darted into the gable-shadow of the nearest block. People wailed and ran across the laterite square, some carrying buckets of water but most seemed to be around at the back of the far building fighting or observing the blaze. Morgan dashed back to Innocence's body, seized it for the last time and dragged it down the path and into the shadow, leaving it only a few yards from where she had originally been struck down. He glanced at her inflated shape-less corpse.

'Here we are again,' he said with a mad note in his voice, then, like some nameless fiend or apprentice devil, he scurried back from tree to tree to his car.

Morgan stopped the Peugeot some distance up the road and watched the wreck quickly burn itself out. He felt tears trickling from his eyes but put that down to the searing they had received when the car went up. His hands were caked with dust from the verge where he'd rubbed them in a demented Lady-Macbethian attempt to drive the clinging feel of Inno-cence's skin from his palms. He felt very odd indeed, he decided: a freakish macédoine of moods and sensations, still high from the alcohol, his nostrils reeking with the smell of putrefaction, a fist of outraged sadness lodged somewhere in the back of his head, his body quivering from the massive adrenalin dose that had flooded its muscles and tissues. He resolved not to move an inch until everything had calmed down.

A short while later he heard the astonished shout and clamour of excited voices as the body was discovered. And when he drove by after a further ten minutes he saw briefly a cluster of lanterns beyond the wash-place. He drove a couple of hundred yards past the Commission gate then parked his car at the side of the road and walked cautiously back. He wanted to change out of his ridiculously festive Santa uniform and he was also desperately keen to wash his hands. He was glad to see the Commission itself was completely dark, though he noticed Fanshawe's house was brightly lit. He assumed the Duchess was being entertained there as he saw several cars parked in its drive. He wondered if they had been aware of the blaze on the dump.

He quietly let himself into the Commission and crept through the hall and up the stairs. On the landing he decided

282

to clean up first before he changed back into his clothes. He tiptoed into the guest bathroom and softly closed the door behind him. He switched on the light and gave a gasp of horror-struck astonishment when he saw his reflection in the mirror. His face was black with dirt and smoke and scored by tear-tracks. One eyebrow had been singed away leaving a shiny rose stripe and the sparse hair of his widow's peak had been heat-blasted into a frizzy blond quiff, like an atrocious candy-floss perm. His startled eyes stared blearily back at him in angry albino pinkness.

'Oh Sweet bloody Jesus,' he wailed in dismay. 'You poor bloody idiot.' Was it worth it, he asked himself, was it worth it?

He had only begun to wash his hands when he heard the voices in the hall. He heard Chloe Fanshawe's loudly yodelled goodnights and the sound of two people coming up the stairs. He felt panic clench his heart into a tiny pounding ball. He switched off the light in the bathroom and stood nailed to the middle of the floor wondering what to do until some faint instinct of self-preservation steered him towards the bath. He stepped in and drew the shower curtain around him, seeking some form of safety however flimsy.

He heard modulated English voices. Someone said, 'Did you unpack everything, Sylvia?' and Sylvia replied, 'Yes, Ma'am.' Ma'am would be the Duchess, he reasoned, wondering who Sylvia might be: probably a lady-in-waiting, chaperone or first companion of the bedchamber or whatever it was, he decided. He thought hopelessly that perhaps no one would need to use the bathroom . . .

The light went on. Morgan froze behind his shower curtain.
'. . . Ghastly little man I thought,' he heard the Duchess say. 'And his wife! Good Lord, what an extraordinary . . . oh I don't know, the people they send out here.' Morgan's instinctive dislike was strengthened by this general slur. The door was shut and he smelt cigarette smoke. He tried not to

breathe. Through the semi-transparent plastic of the curtain he could make out a dim grey shape. He heard a zip being run down, the rustle of a dress being lowered. He saw the shape sit down on the WC, heard the straining grunts, the farts, the splashes. Ah, he thought to himself, a manic giggle chattering in his head, so they do go to the toilet like everyone else. There was the noise of paper crumpling, the flush, clothes being readjusted, the running of water from the taps. He heard the Duchess mutter 'bloody filthy', at the state he'd left the basin in, then the water stopped. The door was opened.

'Sylvia?' came the voice more distantly from the passageway. 'When exactly are we leaving tomorrow?'

Morgan breathed again, perhaps he might make it after all. He wondered if he had the time to clamber out of the bathroom window and make his escape across the back lawn. Maybe Sylvia would only have a pee as well and that would be it. He felt so tense he thought his spine might snap. But he had no time to dwell on the state of his body as there were more steps on the landing outside. Christ, Sylvia arriving, he thought. Some obscure need for disguise made him reach into his pocket for his cotton-wool beard which he quickly put on. He heard the door click shut, smelt cigarette smoke and he knew the Duchess had returned. Please God, he prayed with all the intensity he could muster, please just let her clean her teeth. I'll do anything God, he promised, *anything*. He held his breath in agonized anticipation. He heard a rustle, a snap of elastic, the sound of something soft hit the floor.

He saw a shadow-hand reach for the shower curtain. With a rusty click of metal castors the curtain was twitched back. Morgan and the Duchess stared at each other eye to eye. He had never seen dumbfounded surprise and shock registered on anyone's face quite so distinctly before. After all, the thought flashed through his brain, it's not every day you find Father Christmas in your bath. The Duchess stood there slack and squat, quite naked apart from a pale-blue shower cap and a half smoked cigarette in one hand. Morgan saw breasts like empty socks, floppy-jersey fat folds, a grey Brillo pad, turkey thighs. Her mouth hung open in paralysed disbelief.

'Evening, Duchess,' Morgan squeaked from behind his beard, stepping from the bath with the falsetto audacity of a Raffles. He flung open the bathroom window, lowered the lid of the W C, stepped up and slung his legs over the window-sill. He glanced back over his shoulder. He didn't care anymore. Her mouth was still open but an arm was across her breasts and a hand pressed into her lap.

'Listen,' he said. 'I promise I won't tell if you won't.'

He dropped down six feet onto the tar-paper roof of the rear verandah, crawled to the edge and hung down, falling onto the back lawn. As he tore across the dark grass towards the gate he felt curiously exultant and carefree as he waited for the Duchess's screams to rend the night air. But nothing disturbed the impartial gaze of the stars and the convivial silence of the scene.

Bilbow stuck his head out of the spare bedroom when Morgan let himself into the house twenty minutes later.

'Bloody hell,' Bilbow said, looking at Morgan's face. 'What happened to you, Santa? Reindeers crash? Sledge get shot down in flames?'

Morgan didn't bother to reply – he was too busy pouring himself a huge drink.

'By the way,' Bilbow said, wandering into the sitting room. 'Some chap called Adekunle's been ringing all day. Says you *must* phone him as soon as you get in, doesn't matter what time it is. Make any sense?'

It didn't. So he went to bed.

Chapter 7

Morgan stood next to the caddie cage – a kind of miniature POW camp where the caddies lounged – waiting for the caddie master to select him a boy. A Boxing Day sun shone in the clear pale-blue sky and it was already hot for ten o'clock. He was due on the first tee by 10.30 but had come down early as he wasn't keen to remain in the house. He had not phoned Adekunle as requested, neither had he made contact with Fanshawe to see what the reaction had been to the miraculous reappearance of Innocence. The phone had gone twice while he was eating his breakfast but he had ignored it. On his way to the club he had been held up by a big election march on behalf of the UPKP weaving its way through Nkongsamba's twisted streets en route for a rally at the football stadium. So eventful had his life become of late that he had forgotten that voting commenced tomorrow.

A young boy in a grubby Hawaiian shirt hefted Morgan's clubs onto his shoulder. He had transferred some of Adekunle's gleaming beauties into his own well-worn plastic and canvas golf-bag as he had been unwilling to attract amused comment on speculation over Adekunle's monstrosity, which was of such generous proportions that it could have functioned happily as a great-dane's kennel or motorbike garage when it wasn't being transported round a golf-course. Besides, he was sure it would have taken at least two caddies to lift it anyway, and he wanted as little company as possible today. He moved slowly over towards the first tee. Many golfers had made an early start as the tournament was intended to wind up around lunchtime. In fact, he and Murray were driving off third from the end. Morgan nodded and smiled at those he knew, and he received many curious glances in return. He was aware that he looked a little peculiar, what with his frizzy teddyboy quiff (flattened for two minutes with a water-loaded comb, springing perkily back up as it dried), one eyebrow replaced by an oblong of elastoplast, red eyes and a shiny pink nose. He slipped on a transparent green sun-visor to protect his tingling sensitive face from the increasingly hot glare. Half-heartedly he rehearsed his bribe speech like a nervous best man at a wedding, but the words refused to form themselves into any convincing order, and when they did he thought he sounded like some oily dockside pimp: 'hey meester, you want feelthy peectures.' That sort of approach would never work with Murray. Generally speaking he was finding it increasingly hard to concentrate on what he had to do later in the course of the morning. The trauma of Innocence's death, the body snatch, the . . . whatever the opposite of body snatch was – the body drop, the mind-blowing confrontation with the Duchess, had robbed him of any satisfaction he had planned to derive from this symbolic act of corruption. It had now become a simple exercise in self-defence, in skin saving, because he knew – more than ever now – that in order not to lose control irretrievably of his life he had to hold on to his job.

Also he felt terrible. The tensions of the last two nights plus the strenuous drinking had combined to produce a hangover of mythic proportions. It seemed as if his entire body had been tenderized by one of those jagged wooden mallets used for bashing steaks. His tongue felt twice as large as normal, as though it was striving to loll out of the side of his mouth like a dog's and he had a neuralgic headache that loosened every tooth in its socket and made his sinus passages hum like tuning forks.

He swished a golf-club around experimentally. He hadn't played golf for three months or more and he heard his back and shoulders creaking and clicking under the unfamiliar strain. Checking up on his backswing he suddenly saw Murray walking past the caddie cage towards him and felt his heart lurch with nerves and panic. Then he saw Murray's son and the sickness turned to irrational anger. Why had he brought his wretched kid along with him?

Murray came up. He smiled evenly.

'Merry Xmas, Mr Leafy. I see we've been drawn together.'

'Yes, quite a coincidence, don't you think?' There was a pause. 'Ah . . . look, by the way, I wanted to apologize about the other night . . . the phone call. I was a bit upset. You know, the dead body and, well, everything, generally. I didn't realize your position exactly.'

'Don't worry about it,' Murray said. 'I haven't been.'

'Good. No hard feelings then.'

'No feelings at all, Mr Leafy.' He looked closely at Morgan. 'Your face all right?'

Morgan laughed. 'Slight accident with my gas cooker. Blowback I think they call it. Ha-ha.'

'I see.' Murray looked closer. 'Gives you a curious expression.' He paused. 'I hope you don't mind my son coming along – playing some of the shorter holes?'

'Not at all,' Morgan forced a smile in the boy's direction. 'Have a good Christmas?' he asked.

Morgan played very badly. The fairways were burnt almost white from the sun and were as hard as a road. He developed out of nowhere a curling fading slice on almost every shot including his putts. The small greens, known as 'browns' because of their tar and sand surfacing – proved elusively hard to hit, the balls skittering over them again and again, refusing to slow down on the baked ground. Murray agreed to call him Morgan, chatted amiably enough and coached his son with a professional brevity and acuteness. Because of the boy playing some of the shorter holes they waved through the twosomes that were coming behind and soon they were at the tail-end of the tournament, which, Morgan thought, actually suited him quite well.

They completed the first nine holes by midday and paused

at a fairway drink-shack to slake their thirst. Morgan had scored a dire 63 on the outward nine – Murray a useful 37 – and it was shaping up to be his all-time worst-ever round of golf in more ways than one. He had imagined that, after everything he had been through, bribing Murray would turn out to be a piece of cake, but as ever the physical presence of the man unsettled him. He felt nervous, adolescent and drained of self-confidence.

The first nine holes had sent them up one side of a river valley and back down the other. The second nine branched out into the thick forest that surrounded Nkongsamba. There was a sharp dog-leg after the eleventh, and they wouldn't see the clubhouse or the outskirts of the town again until the sixteenth. Morgan watched Murray drive off easily and fluently. The ball sailed a straight two hundred yards and bounced another fifty leaving him within easy range of the brown. Morgan squared up to his ball. He decided to give it everything he'd got, show this old man how to hit a golf-ball, pretend it was Fanshawe's head he was striking. He took a prodigious swing and cracked the ball with all his force: it shot off and out in a steady curve to his right, plunging into dense and thorny rough.

'*Shit*!' he swore, then apologized for the boy's sake.

'You shouldn't try to hit it so hard,' Murray advised. 'Relaxation's the key to this game.'

'That's the fiendishly annoying thing about golf,' Morgan complained, knowing relaxation was just about the last state he could achieve at the moment. 'It's such a, you know, *controlled* game. Everything's held back, sort of restrained. You can't thrash away at things, soak up the aggression, tire yourself out like you can in other sports. Every time I wind myself up for a massive effort I know it's going to be disastrous.'

Murray looked at him quizzically, as if this admission held the key to his character. 'But that's what it's all about though, isn't it? Knowing when to hold back. Staying in control. Using the head and other wooden clubs.'

Morgan laughed uncomfortably: he didn't welcome the implied criticism. 'I suppose I'm just the wrong personality for the game,' he said ruefully.

'Don't give up so easily,' Murray said as he walked over to the rough with him. 'Keep at it. It may come right one day.'

They poked around in the tangled thorny bushes looking for Morgan's ball. They threw up thick clouds of dust, flies, tics, grasshoppers, uncovered a calcined coil of human faeces, but no ball.

'Do you like it out here?' Morgan asked Murray as he hacked at the undergrowth with his club head. 'Dust, heat, stink . . . impenetrable jungle.'

'Well enough,' Murray said. 'I probably like it as much as I'd like anywhere. It has its advantages as well as its disadvantages.'

'You're quite content then,' Morgan established a little belligerently.

Murray released the bush he was pulling back. He smiled. 'Is anybody *quite* content?'

'Well I know for a fact *I'm* not,' Morgan confessed. 'But you seem to be – of all the people I've met.'

Murray pointed his club at him. 'There you go,' he said, 'telling me how I feel. A piece of advice: don't confuse seeming with being. You can never know anything for sure, of course, but it's a pretty safe maxim.'

'Goodness. Quite a philosopher. So you're not happy then?'

Murray laughed. 'This has taken rather a serious turn for a harmless game of golf, hasn't it? I think we'd better give your ball up. Play another?'

'No thanks. I'll just walk this one through.' He watched Murray play his ball up to just short of the brown.

'Are you going to stay here all your life?' Morgan asked conversationally as they strolled after it.

'No,' Murray said. 'I shall leave when I can.'

'Aha,' Morgan said in triumph. 'So you don't like it here.'

'What exactly are you trying to prove?' Murray asked with

an amused smile. 'It's got nothing to do with liking the place, it's just that there are other things I want to do with my life apart from working in Africa.' He eyed his chip shot, played, and ran the ball onto the brown five feet from the hole.

'Such as what?' Morgan inquired. 'What do you want to do next? Go back to Scotland?'

'No,' Murray said, sighting along his putter. 'I've not planned anything really.' He putted the ball into the hole. 'What I'd like to do is go somewhere warm – I don't think I could survive another British winter – Portugal maybe. Go swimming, sailing, play a bit of golf, read a bit more, watch my family grow up . . . that sort of thing. Fairly average and unremarkable ambitions, I'm afraid.'

'And that's it?' For some reason Morgan felt a sense of disappointment.

'What did you expect,' Murray rebuked him jokingly, 'that I wanted to be President of the World Health Organization? I'll be "content" enough, thank you, if I can manage the other things.'

They played the next two holes. Morgan's nerves returned and the sun shone down with uncomfortable force as they hit their way further into the forest. The fairways became enclosed on both sides by tall trees and dense undergrowth. Thin paths broke out from one green wall, meandered across the golf-course and disappeared into narrow openings in the jungle on the other side. If your shot was inaccurate there was virtually no hope of ever finding your ball. Morgan lost another three, Murray kept to par, even the boy played better than he did.

Morgan knew that if he didn't approach Murray soon it would be too late and he grew progressively more unhappy about the task ahead. The game of golf, he now saw, had been a bad idea. Perhaps if Murray had shown resentment at his rudeness the other night, if he'd been sniffy and stand-offish, made it clear that he didn't like him that much, found the idea of a round of golf in his company distasteful, it would have been less of a problem. He had been expecting something like that, he supposed: the Calvinistic cold shoulder. But Murray had been amicable and considerate, and he realized that his dreams of destroying him held no appeal, were non-existent really because, he saw, the Murray he detested lived on only in his mind – had little or nothing to do with the man walking by his side. There would be no satisfaction in watching this Murray crumble now: he just didn't hate the man enough; in fact, surprised as he was at the admission, he almost liked him. Murray was right, he thought: he *had* confused seeming with being. He'd established an idea about the man in his head on the basis of a couple of incidents and had never really bothered to check its veracity. With a depressingly acute flash of insight he realized that he did the same with almost everyone he met . . . But all these speculations were academic: Murray still had to be bribed and that was that – his own survival depended on it. He was only sorry that this new-found knowledge about his victim made the success of his venture almost inevitable: Murray was as human and fallible as he was.

He allowed his thoughts to switch to Fanshawe and the reception for the Duchess that would be going on at this very moment. He hadn't troubled to inform anyone that he wouldn't be present. It was just as well, he considered. He was sure Duchess wouldn't object – he knew with a strange certainty that no one would hear about their meeting in the bathroom. Shivering slightly at the memory, he recalled the stark unappealing nudity. Another example, he suddenly realized, of the old seeming/being gulf: just another middle-aged lady – nothing regal, nothing remotely special or different there.

They walked down the fairway of the fourteenth hole. It was a long one, par 5, and represented the extremity of the golf-course's thrust out into the jungle. They turned back towards the town after this. Morgan felt an unfamiliar weakness in his knees, a quiet roaring in his ears, his heart beating strongly in his head. He checked that Murray's son was out of earshot.

'How . . .' he cleared the squeak from his throat. 'How would you fancy ten thousand pounds?' he asked suddenly.

'Pardon?' Murray looked round in surprise.

'Ten thousand pounds. How would you like it?' he repeated with leering cupidity.

'You offering?' Murray said with a smile.

'No, I mean . . . You could do a lot with ten thousand. I mean *one* could . . .' He back-pedalled a little. 'You know, I was just thinking it's a . . . sort of *handy* sum. Not like winning the pools but . . . useful just the same.'

'Yes,' Murray said non-committally. 'I suppose you're right. Very useful. Why?'

Morgan's fortitude seemed to collapse in upon itself like a dying star. 'You can have it if you want,' he said quietly.

Murray stopped in his tracks. 'Sorry?' he said frowning. 'I can have what?'

'Ten thousand pounds. You can have it.'

'Is this some kind of a joke?' He waved away his son who was walking back towards them to see why they'd stopped. 'What do you mean, I can *have* ten thousand pounds?'

Morgan swallowed. He felt the heat hammering down on his head. His singe marks stung with sweat. 'I will give you ten thousand pounds,' he said slowly. 'If . . . if you do something.'

'Come on, Dad,' the boy shouted.

'I see,' Murray said. He looked serious and saddened. 'If I do something. And what is this something?'

'You have to put in a positive report on the new hall of residence and cafeteria site,' Morgan said in a rush.

Murray's eyebrows shot up in surprise. He fixed his penetrating gaze on Morgan's sweating face. 'The hall site? *You* want me to change my mind. How do you know . . . ? Wait, wait a second . . . What has the University of Nkongsamba's building programme got to do with you, for Christ's sake?'

Morgan removed his sun-visor and wiped his brow. He felt he was about to die. Desperation mounted in his body like flood-waters behind a flimsy dam. He tried to keep calm.

'Well, not *me* so much. I'm acting for someone.'

'Who?'

'I . . . I can't tell you that, obviously.'

Murray gripped Morgan's arm. 'What the hell have you got into? You stupid bloody fool.' Morgan felt his head spin. Everything was going wrong. Why was Murray interrogating him like this? He saw Murray thinking hard.

'Who's behind it?' he said again.

Morgan tried to pull himself together. 'I'm not at liberty . . .' he began pompously, but Murray interrupted him with an upraised palm.

'Let me guess,' Murray said. 'It's Adekunle isn't it?'

'No!' Morgan said hastily, realized he'd countered with give-away swiftness, said 'Who?' in a futile attempt to regain lost ground. He saw there was no point in denying it. 'Yes,' he admitted in a low voice.

Murray released his grip. 'I thought so,' he said as though to himself, 'I'd been suspicious . . .' He returned his attention to Morgan who stood there looking at the ground. 'I'm sorry, Morgan,' he said feelingly. 'Very sorry. But I just can't let this one go. You can understand my position. I have to report it.'

That was it. The weight was too much for the hurriedly assembled collection of twigs and branches. The flood-waters burst through, sweeping everything away. Morgan felt the prickle of tears on his eyelids, brimming behind his lashes. Too late he closed his eyes, squeezed them tight shut but the tears seeped through, fat and hot, trickling down his fat hot cheeks as his legs gave way beneath him.

Murray's son stood aimlessly with the two caddies some dozen yards off. He looked puzzled and angry, Morgan thought, watching the boy throw stones into the bush. Morgan was sitting propped up against a tree at the edge of the fairway. He wondered if he'd passed out or if his brain had simply refused to record events, so embarrassing had they been – a kind of merciful amnesia to spare him further torments.

Murray stood beside him looking down. 'All right now?' he asked considerately.

Morgan scrambled to his feet rubbing his eyes. 'Christ,' he said shakily. 'Sorry I fell to pieces.' He took a deep breath. 'But if you knew what I'd been through the last few days you'd be amazed that I can still function normally at all.'

'Adekunle?'

'No. Not entirely. Other things as well. I'll tell you about them some day: they'll make your hair curl.' Morgan dusted the grass off his trousers. 'All things considered, Adekunle's been quite reasonable under the circumstances.'

Murray handed him his sun-visor. 'I think we'd better call it a day,' he said. 'Head back to the clubhouse.' Morgan agreed, and they walked off in silence back up the fairway, Murray's son and the caddies remaining a discreet ten yards behind. Morgan shot a glance at Murray's face. It was set firm in concentration, his brow lowered in a frown. Morgan rubbed the back of his neck, massaging the knots of tension his muscles had twisted themselves into. Paradoxically, he felt better: one problem at least was over – resolved – however unsatisfactorily. He wouldn't have to bribe Murray again.

'Look,' Morgan said, keen to break the silence. 'I'm sorry. I . . . I was acting under instructions.'

'I take it he's threatening you with something?'

'God yes. You don't think I'm his partner, do you?' Morgan looked offended.

Murray apologized. 'What has he got on you?' he asked.

Morgan let out a long breath. 'I think it's probably better if I keep that to myself. Let's just say he knows something that

I'd rather my boss didn't. Nothing criminal,' he added hastily. 'More in the scandal line – if you know what I mean.'

'I see.' Murray ran a hand through his hair. 'It sounds like a real mess to me.' He paused. 'What would happen to you if Mr Fanshawe found out about whatever this scandal is?'

Morgan shrugged. He told himself it didn't matter so much now. 'Oh I don't know. Disgrace. Sent home. I'll lose my job for sure. Fanshawe and I aren't exactly best buddies anyway at the moment.'

Murray didn't say anything to this and they continued their walk in silence. Back at the clubhouse they paid off the caddies and put their clubs in their cars. Morgan slung his in the back seat. He wasn't ever going to use his boot again.

He suddenly felt the familiar panic seize his heart as he contemplated the results of Murray reporting him. He had been lying to himself earlier: losing his job did matter – more than anything, and the thought of an ignominious return to Britain made him feel sick. Somehow he had to persuade Murray to go easy; the man seemed to like him, perhaps he'd agree to help if he knew how he really felt. He walked over to Murray's car and overheard his son ask, 'Dad, why was that man crying like that?' and he wished the poisonous little brat would clear off.

'Alex,' Morgan called. 'Can I . . . can I have a word?' Murray came over.

'This is incredibly embarrassing for me,' Morgan said, 'But I have to ask. Please don't report this to anyone.'

'But I've told . . .'

'I'm begging you,' Morgan said earnestly. 'Please, I *will* lose my job, you see, and it's the only thing in my life that means anything to me, that's any good at all. Please.'

'What are you asking me to do?' Murray said. 'Pretend all this never happened?'

Morgan squirmed. 'Well . . . yes.' But he saw immediately that it wouldn't be enough. 'Couldn't you just forget about making that negative report on the site? You see, if you do veto the project Adekunle will go to Fanshawe anyway. That was the deal: I had to stop you from doing that.'

Murray lowered his voice. 'So in fact you want me to give the all-clear for the hall project. But why should I?'

'For *me*,' Morgan pleaded. 'Otherwise I'm finished. I mean that. Not just my job. Everything.'

'Why is this project so important to Adekunle? Is he bidding for the contract through Ussman Danda?'

'No,' Morgan said quietly. 'He owns the land.'

Murray looked up at the sky. 'Jesus Christ,' he laughed sardonically, 'no wonder he'll pay ten thousand pounds.'

'That's still available, by the way,' Morgan interjected.

'I'll forget you said that,' Murray responded harshly. He paused. 'You're asking me to let that hall project go through for your sake alone – so that you can keep your job.'

Morgan looked at the ground. 'Yes,' he said ashamedly. 'I know I'm a bloody fool, that I got myself in this mess but . . .'

'No,' Murray said flatly. 'I'm sorry, Morgan, but no. I just can't – won't – go that far.'

'But why not?' Morgan beseeched unreasonably, 'Why not? What's so important about the University of Nkongsamba, Adekunle, this country? What does it matter to us – people like us? In the end there's absolutely nothing we can do; the Adekunles of this world'll win through eventually. Let them build the bloody hall there.' He felt like a man seeing the end of his tether twitch beyond his grasp.

'It's got absolutely nothing to do with the University of Nkongsamba,' Murray said patiently.

'Then why won't you do this one little thing?' Morgan asked despairingly. 'I'll go down on my knees if you like.' He felt the familiar sensations of intense Murray-hatred returning. 'Is it because it's "wrong"?' he asked sarcastically. 'You don't want to do the "wrong" thing, is that it? Can't you see that life's just not that simple? Good/bad, right/wrong. It just doesn't work that way any more.' He spread his hands. 'You're way out of touch Alex, out on a limb: nobody else is playing by those rules, so why you? Why is it so important for me to lose my job?'

Morgan saw Murray's jaw muscles tighten. 'Frankly I don't give a damn about your job,' he said in his steely Scottish voice. 'If you're a big enough bloody fool to get entangled with people like Adekunle then that's your problem. As for your simple reading of how my mind works, that's off-target too. I'm not concerned about "good" and "bad" as you put it either; if I'm interested in anything it's in seeing a bit of fairness in the world, and I just don't think it's fair that some greedy bastard like Adekunle should cheat his way into several hundred thousand pounds at other people's expense. And I'm afraid for your sake that I can't just sit back and let him get away with it. And now that I'm in a position to see that he doesn't, nothing's going to stop me. I won't worry too much about whether it's right or wrong but at least I'll be secure in the knowledge that some justice has been done, that one fat bastard hasn't had it all his own way. I'm sorry, but I can't see my letting you keep your job, and thereby allowing the University of Nkongsamba to build a hall of residence on a rubbish dump and provide Adekunle with a small fortune, as being remotely just or fair. It may sound stupid but I couldn't forgive myself.'

Morgan's shoulders slumped. He felt exhausted. He felt angry because there was no response he could make: he agreed with everything Murray had said.

'Look,' Murray continued in a less passionate tone. 'I'll tell you what I'll do. I won't make any report until January the third which is the day my committee meets again. Adekunle's had it now. I'm not naïve enough to believe I can ever prove he owns the land, but nothing he can do can stop my negative report. That gives you time to sort things out yourself – and

I promise I won't mention your name in connection with this.'

'But Adekunle will, don't you see?'

'That's why I'm giving you the time. Pre-empt him. Go to Fanshawe yourself: tell him everything before Adekunle can.'

Morgan groaned. 'No, it won't work. I could never tell Fanshawe these things. You don't know him, don't know his expectations. He'd go raving mad.'

'It's your only option,' Murray said. 'You never can tell about people, what they'll think, what they'll do. You may be surprised.' He waved at his son. 'See Fanshawe,' he advised, 'lay things on the line. But remember: January the third and I make my report to the Buildings, Works and Sites Committee.' He paused and touched Morgan fleetingly on the shoulder. 'I'm sorry,' he said. 'But I've got to do it.'

Morgan watched him go to join his son.

Chapter 8

Morgan lay on Hazel's bed staring up at the ceiling, his hands behind his head. Hazel had gone out to buy him more beer as he had drunk his way through the six bottles in the fridge during the course of the afternoon. He had come to the flat straight after his catastrophic round of golf with Murray, gone into hiding like a fugitive, lying low. Before he'd left the club he'd phoned Bilbow, told him to make himself at home and said that he didn't know when he'd be back.

'That Adekunle chap came round this morning just after you'd left,' Bilbow had said. 'Seemed very keen to see you. Oh yes, and if that Fanshawe character rings up once more I

299

think I'll blow me top. He's phoned half a dozen times today already. What've you done to him?'

Morgan's heart sagged. What were Fanshawe and Adekunle after? 'Never mind,' he'd told Bilbow. 'Just keep telling them you don't know where I am.'

'As you wish, squire,' Bilbow cheerily acknowledged.

Morgan had passed the day in a perplexing succession of moods: deep Stygian gloom, devil-may-care indifference, throat-tightening self-pity and his usual apocalyptic universe-hating rages. The sole alteration in the pattern was that Murray did not appear as major target of his vengeful fury. It was no longer the same between him and Murray now, he realized; the old clear-cut division had been replaced by something more complex and puzzling. The front-line had disappeared. This was a turn in events that he found distinctly off-putting, for it seemed to take no account of the fact that Murray had bluntly told him that he was not going to change his mind about the negative site report – the pivot upon which the future hinged as far as he was concerned. He just couldn't understand why he was letting the man off so lightly.

The next morning he lay contentedly in bed watching Hazel get dressed. The sun shone through the slats in the shutters. The traffic sounds came up fuzzily from the street below.

'Where are you going, by the way?' he asked her.

'To vote of course,' she said.

'Christ yes!' he exclaimed. 'That's right, it's election day today. God. Do you know I'd completely forgotten. Who are you going to vote for?'

Hazel picked up her handbag and adjusted her wig. He wished he hadn't asked: he knew what she was going to say. She looked round. 'KNP,' she said simply. 'For a united Kinjanja.'

Morgan's benign morning mood disappeared. He thought suddenly of his fate and the grim alternatives in front of him

– either *he* told Fanshawe or Adekunle would. He sat up in bed, a serious look on his face.

'I think there is something you should know, Hazel,' he said. Hazel stopped at the door. 'I'm afraid things may be changing soon.'

'In what way?'

'I think I might be leaving. Going back to the UK.' He scrutinized Hazel's face for her reaction. She appeared to be considering the news, her bottom lip thrust out, her almond eyes narrowed.

'For why?'

'Well . . . I'm in a bit of trouble you see, and they'll send me back home as a punishment,' he said. Hazel shrugged. 'How . . . How do you feel about that?' he asked, beckoning her over to the bed. She sat down beside him. He put his arm round her shoulders. 'Will you be sorry?' he asked.

'Oh yes,' she said. 'I don't want you to go.' But he couldn't see any tears in her eyes.

Morgan stayed in Hazel's flat for the duration of polling day – the twenty-seventh. On the morning of the twenty-eighth he drove back to his house and found Greg Bilbow packing his bags.

'You off already?' Morgan asked.

'Yes,' Bilbow said. 'I'm getting a plane back down to the capital in a couple of hours. Where the hell have you been anyway?' Bilbow inquired with amusement. 'I've never known anyone so in demand. Phone going like the clappers. Your pals Adekunle and Fanshawe as per, and also some female called Celia.'

'Oh Gawd,' Morgan groaned, exaggeratedly rolling his eyeballs. He'd forgotten about Celia's frantic message on Christmas Day.

'You in some kind of trouble?' Bilbow asked sympathetically.

'To put it mildly.'

'Sorry. Anything I can do?'

'No, no. You've been great anyway, acting as my answering service.'

Bilbow smiled. 'No problem. Except for that Fanshawe. I think he thought I was you, you know, putting on a Yorkshire accent. He kept saying "Come on, Leafy, I know it's you." "Stop playing these childish games, Leafy." ' Bilbow had Fanshawe's pompous accusations off to a tee.

Morgan laughed uneasily. 'Bloody typical,' he said. He looked at Bilbow's thin face. 'Here,' he said. 'Tell you what. I'll give you a lift to the airport. Don't want you getting in any more taxis.'

To his amazement Morgan managed to purchase two bottles of beer from the sulky girl at the Nkongsamba airport bar. They were unchilled, but you couldn't have everything. Morgan and Bilbow sat down at a table to wait for the plane which was reputed to be fifty minutes late. They drank their beers and chatted. To his surprise Morgan found he warmed to Bilbow, and discovered him to be a loquacious, wry character and wished he had been able to spend more time in his company. He bought two more beers and told him this.

'Yes, I'm sorry I've been behaving so mysteriously since you came,' Morgan said. 'I could have shown you around a bit. Anyway I thought you were due to stay on a while longer. Wasn't your Anglo-Kinjanjan do meant to last a couple more days?'

'It was,' Bilbow said. 'But the whole thing's been stopped because of the student unrest at the university. There were big demonstrations yesterday. The riot police were called in. Had all the signs of turning out very nasty indeed. I thought it was something to do with the elections but I was told it's because of some threat to shut down the university next term.'

Morgan punched his palm. 'God, the elections,' he said. 'I

keep forgetting about them.' Vote-counting would be going on today; they should know the result by late afternoon. He wondered if a KNP victory could possibly help him now.

There was the crackle of a loudspeaker announcing the imminent arrival of Bilbow's plane.

'Only an hour and ten minutes behind schedule,' Morgan observed brightly. 'Things are looking up.'

Morgan had just got out of the bath when the phone went later that afternoon. Pulling his dressing-gown around him he padded wetly down the corridor to the sitting room.

'Hello,' he said tentatively. 'Leafy here.'

'Ah, my good friend, you have returned from your travels.' It was Adekunle. Morgan leant weakly against the wall.

'Yes,' he said. 'I was going to ring you. I . . .'

'To congratulate me I hope.'

'Sorry?'

'My dear Mr Leafy. Are you not listening to the election returns? We have won, my friend. Victory is ours!' Geniality and good-fellowship oozed from Adekunle's voice.

'Oh.' Morgan felt no excitement. He was unsure whether this was good or bad news. 'Congratulations.'

'Such enthusiasm,' Adekunle said cynically. 'Still. It looks like being a small majority but a majority nonetheless.' He paused. 'I have been trying to phone you. I assume you went ahead with the other matter. Dr Murray and our agreement.'

'Ah. Now, yes. That was something I . . .'

'Did you or didn't you?'

Morgan thought fast. 'I didn't,' he said, instinctively seeking safety in a lie. 'I . . . I was assessing his mood and, um, the conditions just weren't suitable.'

'Good,' Adekunle said. 'Good.'

'What did you say?'

'I said good. You have put my mind at ease. This was what

303

I was trying to contact you about but you were nowhere to be found. I was going to tell you not to do anything on this occasion.'

Morgan sat down on the floor. 'Why?' he said in a shocked whisper.

'I have made other plans. I will tell you about them tonight.'

'Tonight?'

'Yes. At my house. A little victory celebration before I take up my new duties with the government. Shall we say eight o'clock?'

'Well it's very kind of you to ask but I . . .'

'My good friend,' Adekunle said. 'Let us eat, drink and be merry, as the saying goes. I count on seeing you. Goodbye.'

Chapter 9

Innocence had been dragged back to her original position. The juju spells had multiplied around her, the same cloth shrouded her body. Morgan thought it was as though nothing had ever happened, as if those two dreadful nights had never taken place. He returned the torch to Ezekiel. The warm African night enclosed them: to the west a thin gash of livid orange, some greys, rose pinks and metallic blues lingered on, edging the rain clouds on the horizon.

'So,' Morgan said to no one in particular. 'She is still there.' Isaac, Joseph and Ezekiel nodded in agreement.

'Some person done move her tree days ago,' Isaac informed him in a deeply suspicious voice.

'I know,' Morgan said. 'Mr Fanshawe told me. Bad business that. However I'm very glad to see she was brought back.'

'Dis 'e no respec',' Ezekiel affirmed.

'Well,' Morgan said, suddenly making up his mind, 'you

can tell Maria to bring the fetish priest tomorrow. I will pay,' he announced. There were mutters of astonishment.

'You will pay, sah?' Isaac confirmed.

'That is what I said. I will pay. Everything.'

'Fun'ral as well?' Joseph asked.

'Yes yes. Let's get the whole thing sorted out. Over. Finished.'

'Dis 'e very good ting,' Ezekiel declared. 'Very very good.'

'Isaac,' Morgan said, 'if I give you money tomorrow will you buy the beer and goat et cetera for Maria? Is that OK?'

'Orighti,' Isaac agreed. They made their arrangements. Morgan noticed how the cost had jumped to eighty pounds now he was footing the bill. It would be an especially large celebration they assured him, to which he was cordially invited. He didn't begrudge it. If anyone deserved a decent send-off, he thought, it was poor Innocence. He'd get it all back out of petty cash, somehow, before he left.

They strolled to the edge of the compound. Cooking smells came from the charcoal braziers. A toothless mammy passed in the dark, her flat black breasts swinging in the light of the lantern she balanced on her head. The child she was leading by one hand pointed at Morgan and called out 'Oyibo, oyibo.' White man. Morgan wondered if they ever stopped noticing.

He sniffed the air. 'Is it going to rain tonight?' he asked.

'I think we get small rain tonight, sah,' Isaac said. Morgan was about to make a remark about lightning never striking twice but thought better of it. He said he would see them in the morning and walked across the lawn to his car.

He drove home to change for Adekunle's party. As he was pulling on his shirt he shouted for Friday to bring him a whisky and soda. Friday brought the drink and established that he would not be requiring any supper. Morgan decided against his dinner jacket and put on a pale grey suit. As he reached into the wardrobe for it he noticed Friday still lingering by the door.

'Yes, Friday? What is it?'

'Please, sah. Let me warn you something.'

'Warn me? About what?'

'Nevah go for Nkongsamba tomorrow. I beg you, sah.'

'Why, for God's sake?'

'The soldiers will be there.'

'Soldiers? What are you talking about? A coup? Do you mean *a coup d'état*?'

'*Ah oui. C'est ça. Un coup d'état. Demain.*'

'How do you know?'

'Everybody is knowing.'

'OK, Friday, thank you.' The little man left. What nonsense, Morgan thought, as he knotted his tie. That night with Innocence must have addled his brain.

As he set off for Adekunle's house at ten to eight he felt he was like a man living on borrowed time. The news that he need not have bothered to bribe Murray after all had been a particularly cruel and ironic blow. All that humiliation, all that soul-searching need never have occurred – at that point anyway. Adekunle had seemed only to speak of a post-ponement, a temporary change of plan. In any event it was over now, and he thought that wasn't necessarily bad. For the first time in several weeks he sensed a modicum of composure entering his life, probably due to the fact that there was little he could do now to alter or influence events. He decided, there and then, to take Murray's advice and tell Fanshawe of his indiscretions and thereby deprive Adekunle of the satisfaction of fulfilling his threat. Fanshawe of course would still sack him – or recommend his dismissal – but it would be far better than allowing Adekunle to breathe slanders in his ear. In fact, he made up his mind, he wasn't going to allow Fanshawe to derive any pleasure from firing him either. He would resign – tell Fanshawe everything, then hand in his resignation. He smiled at the thought: yes, that would be best. He was setting his house in order at last, and now Innocence too was tidied up, so to speak – everything set in motion for the wake. The only small unresolved cloud on his horizon was Celia. He felt a glow of affection spread through his body as he ran through the memories. Celia, the one true love affair of his life, he realized with astonishment, or at least the relationship that came closest to it. Now that he didn't care about Adekunle he must try to see more of her, he told himself, before he booked his passage home.

Driving up a hill on the way to the university his headlight beams picked out a familiar black-clad figure. It was Femi Robinson, trudging up the slope with a bundle of placards under his arm. Morgan pulled into the verge. Robinson trotted up.

'Can I give you a lift?' Morgan asked. He felt generous and he had nothing against Robinson: in fact he sympathized with him. 'I'm going as far as the university,' he added. Robinson gladly accepted, flung his placards in the back seat and got in beside him. Morgan caught a glimpse of one that read PEDAGOGY YES! DEMAGOGY NO! He pulled the car back on to the road and set off on his way once again. They obviously shared the same destination.

'You've abandoned us then?' Morgan said, indicating the placards and winding down the window as far as it would go. Robinson could have ideally played Sweat in some allegorical deodorant ad.

Robinson scowled. 'Since the election has been won according to your plans there is no point in warning the people. So tonight we are protesting at the presence of riot police on the university campus and the planned closure next semester.'

'But won't the new government make any difference?' Morgan asked.

Robinson laughed scornfully at this display of naïvety. 'I assume you are making the joke. I told you: UPKP, KNP – they are just the same. They don't like students making them trouble.'

'So you are off to lend your support.'

'It is my duty, while I can. I expect the PPK to be banned very soon.'

Morgan looked at Robinson with some admiration. He seemed always to be searching for a new set of hopeless odds he could pit himself against. 'Well,' he said. 'I'll put in a good word for you with the new Foreign Minister.'

Robinson looked round sharply. 'You are going to meet Adekunle already?'

Morgan laughed. 'Don't worry. It's unofficial – a victory celebration I believe.'

'Fanshawe will be there I suppose,' Robinson sneered, 'to congratulate his puppet.' He spat out the last word with some venom.

Morgan hadn't considered this possibility. He hoped Robinson was wrong. 'Adekunle Fanshawe's puppet?' he scoffed. 'That's a bit ridiculous, isn't it?'

Robinson folded his arms across his chest. 'This is how we see the Anglo-KNP collusion prior to the election. How do you want us to interpret it otherwise?'

Morgan couldn't think of anything to say. He hoped he hadn't blundered in telling him of Adekunle's victory celebration.

He stopped the car outside the university's main gate. 'I'll let you out here, Femi, if you don't mind,' he said. 'I'm not sure if it would be wise for me to be seen delivering revolutionaries to their demonstrations.'

Robinson collected his placards. 'Thanks for the lift,' he said. 'I enjoyed our conversation. It was most interesting.'

As Morgan drew near Adekunle's house he was waved down by a uniformed guard and told to park his car some distance away. The roads nearby were lined with vehicles but as he approached he saw that the area immediately in front of the house had been left clear and the building itself was lit up with floodlights. He saw loudspeakers rigged up on the first-floor balcony and a dozen or so KNP supporters standing outside the gate. It looked as if Adekunle was planning to deliver a post-election victory address to the party faithful at some point in the evening. The front gate was opened once Morgan had established his credentials and he stepped through and walked down the drive. At the bottom down by the garages were several official-looking limousines and it was with a sinking feeling that he recognized Fanshawe's black Austin Princess parked alongside Muller's rather dirty Mercedes. Both cars were also sporting their national flags on the bonnets.

Peter, the Commission driver, snapped out an extravagant salute as Morgan came by. 'Evenin', sah,' he called. Morgan went over.

'Hello Peter. Mr Fanshawe here?'

'Yes, sah. I go bring them all.'

'All?'

'Yes, sah. Mrs Fanshawe, Mr Dalmire and Miss Fanshawe also.'

Morgan looked towards the house. The downstairs rooms seemed crowded with people. A little victory celebration, Adekunle had said.

'Are there many people here?' he asked.

'Oh yes,' Peter said. 'Plenty plenty, sah.'

Morgan edged his way through the crowded sitting room towards the bar. The atmosphere was hot and frenetic and there was a mood of euphoria in the air rather like a New Year party. He kept his head down. He didn't want to see anyone, he was only here because Adekunle had ordered him to attend. He fought his way to the bar.

'Large whisky please. And soda.'

'Hello *you*,' he heard, and looked round. It was Priscilla. 'Good Lord!' she said. 'What's happened to your face? And your hair?'

'Christmas pud,' he explained. 'Too much brandy. Never

realized the stuff was so combustible.' He thought she looked breathtakingly desirable, from the neck down: tanned and glowing with health in a creamy scoop-necked dress.

'So that's why we haven't seen you,' she said, popping an olive into her mouth. 'I think Daddy's been trying to get hold of you for days.'

'Really?' Morgan said, touching his elastoplast eyebrow with one hand and trying to control the featherlight cilia of his quiff with the other. 'I've been convalescing,' he added in explanation. He changed the subject. 'I thought you and Dickie were going on holiday after Christmas. Skiing, wasn't it?'

'We are,' she said. 'In fact we shall have to be off soon as we're driving down overnight to the capital. Plane leaves at some ungodly hour in the morning. Peter's taking us in the big car. Oh look, there's Dickie.'

Dalmire approached looking young and clean-cut in a white dinner jacket. 'Well,' he said. 'The prodigal returns. What on earth have you been doing to your face?' He bent over and whispered in Morgan's ear. 'Arthur wants to see you, Morgan. I think he's in a bit of a bate.'

'What about?' Morgan asked.

'Innocence mainly, I think.'

'That's all taken care of now.'

'And something to do with the Duchess too.'

'Oh Christ. I suppose I'd better get it over with. Where is he?'

'Over on the other side of the room. Under that mask thing on the wall.'

Morgan began to ease and weave his way through the packed bodies across the room in the direction Dalmire had indicated. He was half way there, wedged between an enormous Kinjanjan lady and a gesticulating KNP official when he felt a tug at his sleeve. It was Denzil Jones.

'Hello, Denzil. Some other time. I've got to see Arthur.'

'Just a word, Morgan,' Jones wriggled himself closer. He looked downcast and serious. Perspiration gleamed on his blue jowls. He shot a nervous glance around the room. 'Do you know anything about this?' he asked, shoving a piece of paper into Morgan's hand. It was a bill from the Ademola clinic for Hazel's treatment which it clearly specified along with the penicillin dosage.

'Doesn't mean anything to me,' Morgan said innocently. 'Have you been overcharged?' He cursed under his breath: he'd given Hazel money to pay that bill.

'It's not bloody true, man!' Jones yelped. 'It's not your idea of a joke, is it? Because if it is, it's not very funny. Not funny at all.' He looked miserable. 'Geraldine went mad. She refused to come here tonight.'

'Sorry, Denzil. Probably some of the buggers at the club.' He patted Jones's shoulder. 'Cheer up, old son.' He'd always wanted to say that to Jones. He pushed his way on through the crowd.

'Hello, Arthur,' he said. Fanshawe was in full regalia: bum-freezer DJ, cummerbund, medal ribbons.

'Morgan! Where the hell have you been?' he demanded. 'And what in God's name have you done to your face?'

'A slight accident. I've been, ah, convalescing. Needed a bit of peace and quiet.'

'Oh marvellous,' Fanshawe said with heavy sarcasm. 'Marvellous. And what about Innocence eh? Just leave her to rot.'

'I got her back, didn't I?' Morgan said petulantly. He explained the new arrangements he'd made and Fanshawe seemed to calm down somewhat. 'All the servants came back on time, I assume?' Morgan said. 'Did the function go all right?'

Fanshawe put his hands on his hips. 'Good question. It did actually. But why weren't you there?'

'I wasn't well, I told you. Listen Arthur . . .'

'You were missed you know,' Fanshawe said. 'Particularly by the Duchess. For some reason she kept asking where you were. Got in a very bad mood when you never appeared.'

Fanshawe thought some more about this. 'Curious woman
. . . very pleasant though, mind you. Seemed especially put
out by your absence.' He looked suspiciously at Morgan.
'Make any sense?'

'Beats me,' Morgan said. 'Look, Arthur, I want to talk to
you about something important.'

'Still,' Fanshawe said, completely ignoring him and clapping him on the shoulder, 'water under the bridge and all
that.' He gestured at the party. 'All's well et cetera.' He
dropped his voice. 'Kingpin looks like paying off. Lucky for
all of us.'

'That's actually what I want to talk about, Arthur, I . . .'

'Good *grief*!' It was Chloe Fanshawe, brushing aside a couple
of guests to intrude upon their dialogue. 'What's happened to
your face? Your hair?' She was wearing a shocking pink dress
encrusted with silvery threadwork and had a triple rope of
pearls around the soft folds of her neck. She must have re-dyed
her hair, Morgan thought, its blackness was so dense, giving
her skin the edible texture and whiteness of marshmallow.

'My Christmas present,' Morgan improvised. 'Cigarette
lighter. Turned the flame adjuster the wrong way. Lit a cigarette and whoomph.'

'Dear me. Shame . . . Arthur, come along. I want you to
meet . . .'

Morgan clawed his way back to the bar. Obviously he
wasn't going to be able to break the news of his resignation
to Fanshawe tonight. He replenished his drink. He noticed
Dalmire and Priscilla chatting cosily and the old envy returned
to him for a minute. He turned away and saw Georg Muller
and his daughter Liesl coming over. Morgan raised his hand
in salutation. He knew her well, she came out every year for
Xmas.

'I want to give you a kiss,' Liesl said flirtatiously, 'But I
don't want to cause you pain.'

'Haha,' Morgan said. He was getting tired of explaining about his face.

'What happened?' Muller asked, looking as smart as he ever did in a rumpled green safari suit.

'Well there was this baby trapped in a burning house and . . . oh never mind. How are you, Liesl? You look fit.'

'I'm fine,' she said. On her high heels she was at least three inches taller than him. 'I wish I could return the compliment. Kinjanja seems not to be agreeing with you.'

'You're telling me,' Morgan said with feeling.

'The British are out in force tonight,' Muller observed wryly. 'You must all be very pleased about the election.'

Morgan shrugged. 'It all depends on your point of view.'

Muller laughed. 'You are a sly fellow, Morgan. I haven't forgotten the last time we met.' There was an uncomfortable pause. It suddenly struck Morgan that Muller somehow resented him, thought he'd done something clever and underhand with Adekunle and the KNP.

Liesl broke the ice. 'The new government has its first crisis anyway. I hear the students have occupied the administration block. The riot squad have been called in again.'

'I was just talking to the Vice-Chancellor,' Muller said. 'It has quite spoiled his Christmas.'

'I know how he feels,' Morgan said. Just then he saw Adekunle approaching, the guests parting obediently in front of him like the Red Sea before Moses. Morgan felt a tremble start up in his right leg.

'Georg, my friend,' Adekunle boomed. 'Can I steal our bruised and battered Mr Leafy for a moment?' Muller bowed his acquiescence and Morgan followed Adekunle's flowing robes across the room and into the hush of his study.

Adekunle carefully placed his bulk on the edge of the desk. 'Well?' he said.

'Sorry,' Morgan found it hard to concentrate. 'Congratulations on your victory.'

'Thank you,' Adekunle said graciously. 'But I was thinking more about our own agreement. You said that you decided in the end not to put our proposition to Dr Murray.'

'That's right,' Morgan lied, deciding to pacify Adekunle until he'd had a chance to speak to Fanshawe. 'It was just all wrong. His mood . . . he just wouldn't have been amenable. I could sense it instantly.'

Adekunle lit a cigarette. 'You are sure of that? You said nothing to him? Because we have other plans now. To have to pay Murray would be most inconvenient.'

'He still intends to give a negative report on the site,' Morgan said, telling the truth for once. 'I assume,' he added.

'Good.'

Morgan was perplexed. 'Why good?'

Adekunle looked at him. 'Let us just say that I have discovered a . . . a "cousin" in the Senate office. It now becomes simply a matter of misplacing the minutes of the Buildings Works and Sites Committee meeting when Murray vetoes the site.' He puffed smoke into the air, a smile of satisfaction on his face. 'A simple, effective, and, as it turns out, a far cheaper method. I am only sorry I could not have arranged it earlier. Saved you some, what shall we say? . . . heartsearching, some worries perhaps.' Adekunle tapped ash into a thick-bottomed glass ashtray. Morgan felt like burying it in his head. So Murray's report would be intercepted. And now Adekunle was Foreign Minister he couldn't see Murray pressing any effective charges either. A bit of dirt might be stirred up but knowing Kinjanjan politics it wouldn't make any difference. He felt suddenly sorry for Murray and his lone struggle for 'fairness'. He was just too small a man. The Adekunles of his world always came out on top.

'Ah, what about me then?' he asked in a feebler voice than he had meant.

'Yes, what about you, Mr Leafy. I think we shall let you, as the saying goes, lie doggo for a while. You are still under a considerable "obligation" to me as I'm sure you will acknowledge. I can foresee some time in the future when you might be able to repay that debt.'

Morgan knew then that his job was finally gone. There had been some faint hope that Adekunle might have let him off, in a post-victory amnesty now that everything had turned out so well for him. He was glad then that he'd decided to resign. He couldn't linger on as Adekunle's man in the Commission, not any more. He felt an odd sensation of relief mingle with his general despair. In a way he'd be glad to get the whole farce over and done with – extricate himself from the enfolding net of lies and complicity. You'd better get a move on, you fat bastard, he swore at Adekunle under his breath, because I won't be around much longer.

The phone on Adekunle's desk rang. He picked it up. 'Yes,' he said sharply. 'What? . . . These damn fools! . . . OK, OK, send them in . . . This has to be finished tonight, you understand.' He put the phone down.

'These students,' he said. 'Setting fire to cars, destroying documents. It can't be permitted.'

'No, quite,' Morgan agreed. 'Disgraceful.'

Morgan looked blearily out of the bathroom window on the first floor trying to see beyond the glare of the floodlights. He had just been sick in the toilet bowl – the result of the two gins, a buck's fizz, a whisky and a drambuie he had drunk, one after another, on emerging from Adekunle's study, snatching drinks from passing stewards as if he were challenging some inebriate's world record. Celebrating the end of his life, he had told himself.

As usually happened after a drink-induced vomit he felt both better and worse. He borrowed a toothbrush and cleaned his teeth. The crowd outside had scarcely grown at all and was still quiet and docile. Hardly a sweeping popular victory, he thought, wondering when Adekunle would be giving his speech. He opened the window and strained his ears: he thought he could make out a distant chanting that seemed to be getting louder – the grass roots support arriving, he assumed.

He left the bathroom and shakily advanced towards the stairhead. He had to go and drink some more, try to blot out the dismal future that lay inevitably ahead of him. Priscilla, Adekunle, Fanshawe, Kingpin, Innocence and Murray: it had all been too much. He had tried, he had fought, but he couldn't stand the pace any longer. The odds had always been too great: it was time to surrender.

'Psst, Morgan.'

He looked round in surprise. Celia appeared for an instant in a doorway. She beckoned him into the room. Celia! She closed the door behind him and they kissed. He was glad he'd cleaned his teeth. They stood in a guest bedroom as far as he could make out. Celia had left the light off.

'Where have you been?' he asked a little slurringly. 'I didn't see you downstairs.'

'That was what I was going to ask you. You told me to phone you, remember?' she said in wounded accusation. 'I kept getting this Yorkshireman who said he didn't know where you were.'

'I . . . I was out of town,' Morgan said. He stroked her hair and kissed her cheeks. 'I had something to clear up.' He pulled her to him. 'I've missed you, Celia,' he began, but she pushed him away.

'It's Sam,' she said despairingly. 'I've decided. I'm leaving him. You've got to help me.'

'Celia, Celia,' he complained gently. 'Don't start that again. I know he's a bastard but how can you leave him? What about the boys?' She had raised this topic of conversation on a couple of occasions before, but he had always managed to stop it before it had gone any further.

'No, I mean it!' she said in a shrill whisper. 'I've got a plan.'

He peered nervously at her, a little alarmed at her vehemence: she seemed to be on the verge of cracking up.

'But I can't help you, Celia,' he said patiently. 'Not any more. I'm not in a position to. I won't be . . .'

'What are you talking about?' she said irritably. 'You're the only person who *can*. You're the only one with the authority.'

He felt vaguely flattered at this reference to his masculine resourcefulness. He tried to put his arm round her again but she shrugged it off. 'Celia, darling,' he said. 'You have all my support and my . . . affection.' He had almost said 'love', but not while she was in this mood. 'And you're a very special person to me.' He gave a bitter chuckle. 'You're the best thing that ever happened to me in this bloody country. No,' he held up his hand with drunken insistence as she tried to interrupt. 'No. I mean it. I've felt closer to you than to anybody. Honestly,' he said sincerely. 'That's what's so hellish. That's the only thing that upsets me about leaving, my darling. I don't want to leave you.'

'*Leaving?*' she gasped. 'What do you mean, "leaving"?'

He tried to smooth down his candy-floss forelock. 'I've got myself into serious trouble,' he said, still thinking it wise to keep Adekunle out of it. 'My fault. My stupidity, but it's very serious. I'd lose my job. So I'm resigning. Tomorrow. I'm going back home.'

Celia gave a stifled cry. 'But you can't.'

'Can't what my darling?'

'You can't resign your job.'

He smiled at her tenderly. 'I have to,' he said. 'I'm in a terrible fix. If you knew, you'd see it was the only way. There's no alternative.' In the dark of the room he saw her cheeks streaming with tears. He felt his heart swell. She was loyal: she cared for him.

'*No!*' she said in a mad tearful croak. 'No. You can't resign. You can't,' she repeated. 'You can't, not yet. I need you. I need you for the visa. You're the only one who can get me the visa.'

'Visa? What visa?'

She beat at his chest with her small fists. 'You've got to get me a visa for Britain,' she sobbed, her face contorted with grief and dismay. 'I'm a Kinjanjan. I have a Kinjanjan passport. I can't fly home without a visa. You've got to get me one. I need a visa to get home and only you can get me one.' Slowly she fell to her knees on the floor.

Morgan stood there. It was as if everything in his body had stopped moving for a second. Brief suspended animation. His mind flashed back to his early meetings with her. He recalled now, how almost from the first there had been innocent inquiries about his job and responsibilities: the momentary alarm when Dalmire arrived, relief when she found out he was still in control. He let out a long quivering breath as the truth hit him with agonizing force: he had just been a part of her escape plan – an important one, but a part nonetheless. She couldn't get free access to Britain with her Kinjanjan passport: she needed a visa. So she found somebody who could supply one without her husband knowing.

Morgan looked down at her crying on the floor. Used again Leafy, he said to himself. You bloody fool. He felt angry at his conceit, bitterly furious for convincing himself that there was something special here, something different. It was just like everything else, he said to himself with sad cynicism, exactly the same. But what did it matter to him, really? He was an aristocrat of pain and frustration, a prince of anguish and embarrassment. He moved to the door.

'I'm sorry, Celia,' he said. 'But it's too late now.'

Out on the landing he wiped his eyes, took a few deep breaths and flung wild knockout punches at some invisible opponent. Funnily enough, he found he didn't hate or resent Celia. He just felt angry with himself for failing to see the facts. Murray was right: it was the old seeming/being trap again, and he fell into it every time. Where was that penetrating insight he prided himself on? he asked. Where's the gimlet eye that strips away duplicity and pretension, that uncompromising assessor of human motives? He heard a dull roaring in his ears. He leant against the wall and shut his eyes but it didn't go away. He opened his eyes and it dawned on him that it was coming from outside. He ran to a window and looked out. The crowd seemed suddenly enormous. A dark mass beyond the floodlit garden pressing up against the barbed wire fence and filling the road. They were chanting something rhythmically. He saw a small figure in black leading the shouts with a loudhailer. He listened. He couldn't believe his ears.

'FAN-SHAWE,' the crowd roared. 'FAN-SHAWE, FAN-SHAWE, FAN-SHAWE.'

Morgan dashed down the stairs. The guests had spontaneously backed up against the wall furthest away from the demonstration. There was a hum of uneasy discussion, but people were more occupied casting wary glances about them searching for emergency exits, as if in a basement night-club with a notoriously fallible sprinkler-system. The Commission staff stood to one side looking increasingly uncomfortable. Morgan joined them.

'What's going on?' he asked.

'We were just about to go,' Fanshawe spoke up nervously. 'Dickie and Pris had to drive down to the capital for their plane.' He gulped. 'Peter had brought round the car to the front door. We saw this huge crowd had turned up. We thought they were KNP supporters, but as soon as I stepped out they went mad. Shouting and jeering.'

'Yer,' Jones chipped in. 'Like some kind of signal. FAN-SHAWE, FAN-SHAWE.'

'Thank you, Denzil,' Fanshawe snapped. 'We know what they're saying.' He turned to Morgan. 'What's it all about, Morgan?' Everybody looked at him.

'Why are you asking me?' he protested. 'I don't know

anything.' But before another word could be said there was a crash of breaking glass from upstairs and screams from the women guests. There then followed a hail of stones directed at the house. The party broke up in confusion, people running, screaming, crawling under tables, huddling in terrified groups as stones and rocks came flying through the open French windows, thudding and skittering onto the carpet. Chairs and sofas were upturned to form flimsy barricades behind which terrified guests crouched.

Morgan rushed to the front door and opened it an inch. He was in time to see Peter abandon the Commission car and take to his heels. At the top of the drive some thirty yards away Morgan saw a line of Adekunle's uniformed servants manning the firmly closed gates. And beyond them, clutching a megaphone, the small dark figure of Femi Robinson.

'UK OUT,' he bellowed verbosely. 'NO EXTERNAL INTER-FERENCE WITH KINJANJAN AUTONOMY.'

Unable to chant this the crowd satisfied themselves with shouts of 'FAN-SHAWE, FAN-SHAWE, FAN-SHAWE.'

A stone thudded into the door. Oh my Christ, Morgan thought, I told him we'd be here. Robinson must have convinced a good few of the demonstrating students that their protests would be more effectively directed at Fanshawe than at the university authorities. It must have seemed a golden opportunity: the conspirators caught celebrating. Morgan felt sick. He looked round and saw the object of the mob's abuse equally whitefaced with fear.

'How did they know I was coming here tonight?' Fanshawe whimpered. 'Morgan, this is ghastly. You've got to do something.'

'Me?' There were more wails and screams from the guests as another volley of missiles spattered against the house's façade. Morgan saw Adekunle and Muller striding towards them.

'Is this your doing, my friend?' Adekunle hissed at Morgan.

'Me?' Morgan repeated, dumbfounded that he should be so singled out in this way. 'For God's sake no!'

'ADEKUNLE IS A PUPPET OF UK,' Robinson screamed outside.

'FAN-SHAWE, FAN-SHAWE, FAN-SHAWE.' agreed the crowd.

'Students,' Adekunle spat out the word. 'Phone for the police,' he ordered an aide.

Muller peered out of the door. 'That gate is going to go soon,' he observed calmly. 'Look. They are burning a Union Jack now.' Morgan looked over his shoulder and confirmed it.

'FAN-SHAWE, FAN-SHAWE,' the crowd chanted tirelessly. It was a very chantable name, Morgan thought.

'My God, what if they break through?' Fanshawe squeaked in terror to his wife, Jones, Dalmire and Priscilla, who had joined the group in the hall. They all ducked as another window shattered somewhere above them.

'KNP IS A BRITISH POLITICAL PARTY,' boomed Robinson's amplified voice.

'This is disgraceful, intolerable,' Adekunle ranted. 'My house is being destroyed. My reputation ruined. I am meant to be giving a victory speech. There will be journalists and TV here in an hour.' His words were almost drowned by the thumping beat of FAN-SHAWE, FAN-SHAWE from hundreds of straining throats.

'It seems to me that it's only you British they want,' Muller stated coldly. 'They've no argument with the rest of us here. If you go maybe they'll leave us alone.'

'*Well!*' Mrs Fanshawe expostulated, her eyes roasting Muller's thin body.

'Typical bloody Hun remark,' yipped Fanshawe from her side.

'Yer,' Jones added patriotically. 'Who won the war boyo, eh? Answer me that if you damn well please.'

'Daddy, Daddy, what'll we do?' Priscilla whined. Dalmire hugged her to him reassuringly.

'FANSHAWE IS A FASCIST IMPERIALIST CRIMINAL,' Robinson trumpeted, setting up a blood-curdling yell of accord from the mob.

'You have to get out!' Adekunle shouted suddenly. '*Get out!* Get out of my house. I'm ordering you.' His eyes were wide with panicky alarm.

'Hold on,' Morgan countered angrily. 'We can't just wander off. They'll stone us to death.' As if to illustrate this point forcefully more stones clattered against the door.

'I don't care!' Adekunle proclaimed. 'Muller is right. They only want you. Go to your own houses. Fight your battles on your own ground.'

As the saying goes, Morgan thought sarcastically. He thought he'd never seen a more pathetic craven bunch. 'Listen,' he said. 'I've got an idea.' All heads turned to face him. 'They want Arthur, right? So let's give them Arthur.'

'*Leafy!*' Fanshawe squawked, swaying back on his heels. 'Are you out of your mind? What are you saying, man?'

'Not *you*, Arthur,' he said, a surge of confidence flooding through his body, '*Me*. I'll go in your place as a decoy. I'll lead the crowd away and then the rest of you can make your escape.' There was a sudden silence in the hall as they considered this idea. Morgan wondered what had made him suggest this course of action. Drink, yes. Guilt too. But above all a desire to get out, *do* something.

'But how will they know it's me and not you?' Fanshawe asked, hope flickering in his eyes.

'I'll take the car,' Morgan said. 'You lot can take mine, it's parked back up the road. Head straight for the capital and the High Commission. Dickie and Priscilla can even catch their plane.' He thrust his car keys into Fanshawe's hand. 'And,' he said in a flash of inspiration, 'let me change into your suit.

Tell the guards to fling open the gates and I'll drive out hell-for-leather.'

'It might work,' Muller said.

'Do it!' Adekunle commanded.

As quickly as they could Morgan and Fanshawe swapped clothes, the females present modestly turning away. Fanshawe's jacket and trousers fitted Morgan like a second skin; bracing his shoulders back, forcing his chest out, the sleeves stopping in mid-forearm, a two-inch gap of leg visible between his turn-ups and socks.

'It's a bit small, isn't it?' Mrs Fanshawe said, raising her voice to be heard above the relentless swell and crash of her husband's name being shouted outside.

'I'm only after the effect,' Morgan panted, hastily knotting the bow-tie. 'They'll just see someone in black and white dash into the car.' Adekunle meanwhile gave orders to a servant to inform the guards at the gate of the plan and the man slipped unwillingly out of the front door and sprinted up the drive to pass on the instructions.

'OK?' Morgan asked, wanting to be off before second thoughts could catch up with him.

'We need a moustache,' Dalmire suggested and Priscilla rummaged in her handbag for an eyebrow pencil. She drew a thin moustache on Morgan's upper lip.

'How do I look?' he asked, and everyone laughed nervously. 'Right,' he said. 'Let's go. As soon as the crowd break away, get into my car and head off. They may besiege the Commission tomorrow for all we know.' He stood poised by the door. He felt surprisingly calm. He was glad to be getting out of the house. He was fed up pissing about in this country.

'Wait,' Mrs Fanshawe suddenly announced. 'I'm coming with you. It'll be far more convincing if we both go. Arthur's hardly likely to make a dash for it without me.'

'No, Mummy,' Priscilla cried.

'Chloe. I can't allow it,' Fanshawe piped up.

'Nonsense,' Mrs Fanshawe exclaimed. 'When you leave here go to the Commission and we'll try and meet you there. Don't wait long. If we're held up go on down to the capital. There are plenty of people I can stay with until things calm down. I'll be in no danger.' She would hear of no arguments in opposition. 'Don't you agree, Morgan?' she asked.

'A brilliant idea,' Adekunle contributed.

'Well it'll certainly be more realistic,' Morgan admitted. 'But are you sure . . . ?'

'Of course I'm sure.' She said goodbye to her family: Fanshawe like some woebegone derelict in an outsize Salvation Army suit; Dalmire and Priscilla proud and young (Priscilla sniffling a bit but probably glad she wouldn't miss her ski holiday, Morgan thought). Adekunle and Muller stood behind them – Adekunle fierce and outraged, Muller looking quite unconcerned. Beyond them Morgan saw Celia hunched miserably on the stairs.

Jones slapped him on the back. 'Good man, Morgan,' he said. 'You give 'em 'ell.'

With a nod to each other Morgan and Mrs Fanshawe paused briefly at the door then flung it open and dashed down the steps to the car. There was a great shout from the multitudes behind the fence as the objects of their venom appeared and a fresh salvo of stones was launched. Morgan leapt into the driver's seat and slammed the door, Mrs Fanshawe doing the same beside him almost simultaneously. Peter, thankfully, had left the key in the ignition and Morgan started the engine. Stones pinged off the bodywork of the car. The crowd surged forward against the fence screaming and shouting.

'Get down,' Morgan yelled. 'Here we go!' He put the car in gear and accelerated up the drive, hunched over the wheel, his hand jammed down on the horn. Taken aback at this sudden blaring charge the crowd at the gate recoiled in terror, unwilling to be mown down. The guards dragged wide the gates and in seconds the large black car thundered through, people flinging themselves madly out of the way. Morgan swung the car fiercely onto the road, all the windows simultaneously shattering as a barrage of sticks, bottles and stones was hurled at this new target. He glimpsed Femi Robinson extricating himself from a bush, brandishing his megaphone in frustrated rage. Elbowing a hole in the fragmented windscreen, Morgan gunned the motor and sped down the road away from Adekunle's house. On both sides the massed demonstrators pelted the car as it flashed by. A small stone came in through the right window and glanced off Morgan's head. Reflexively, he swerved the car and it ploughed off the road lurching into the shadowy ditch. Morgan snatched a look back out of the window and saw the mob streaming after him in hot bellowing pursuit, the leaders a mere twenty or thirty yards away. Frantically he changed down, rammed the accelerator to the floor and the car leapt out of the ditch, its rear wheels spinning furiously, sending up great gouts of dust and gravel. Without thinking of where he was going Morgan took the first turning that presented itself, drove until another road branched off, turned down it, took a left, a right, another right. Very soon all sounds of pursuit died away. He motored steadily along the narrow tree-lined campus roads, the panic seeping from his body, bungalows lying sedately on either side, the wind whistling through the shattered windows, cool on his face.

'I think we made it,' he said huskily to Mrs Fanshawe.

'Yes,' she said in a quiet voice, sitting upright again. 'Do you . . . do you think the others will have got away?'

'I should think so, we caused enough of a distraction. And anyway I think it was clear that their argument was with us . . . that is, with Arthur.'

'Poor Arthur,' Mrs Fanshawe said, putting her hand up to her mouth. 'He'll be so terribly upset about all this.'

Morgan made no reply to that. He peered ahead of him.

He had no idea where he was. The residential areas of the campus were a maze of these quiet dark roads. He looked quickly at Mrs Fanshawe. She had hardly spoken, hadn't screamed or made any kind of a fuss, just sat clinging to her seat. He was impressed. They came to a crossroads and he stopped the car.

'Any clue which way?' he asked, turning to face her.

'Oh Lord, you've got blood on your face,' she said. Morgan touched his forehead above his right eye. His fingertips came away dark and wet.

'I was hit by a stone,' he said. 'Probably looks worse than it is. Just a scratch,' he added bravely.

'I think if you turn left here it should take us to the main gate.'

Morgan did as she advised. He noticed the roads were strangely empty. They had seen no other cars and many of the staff houses showed no lights. Everyone battening down the hatches with a campus revolution on their hands, he thought. He heard a heavy rumble of thunder. The promised rain was approaching.

'Thunder,' he commented, just wanting to say something. 'That should damp their spirits a bit.'

They drove round a sharp bend. As they did so the headlights picked out the lone figure of a man standing at the corner of a road junction. Morgan drove past and then slammed his foot on the brakes.

'Why have you stopped?' Mrs Fanshawe asked, surprised.

'That was Murray.'

'Who?'

'Murray. Dr Murray. That man standing by the road there.'

'So what?'

'I . . . I've got something to tell him. Won't be a sec.' Morgan got out of the car and jogged back up the road.

'Dr Murray,' he called. 'Alex. It's me, Morgan Leafy.' Murray was standing at the roadside in his usual outfit of grey flannels, white short-sleeved shirt and tie. He looked closely at Morgan in the dark.

'What the hell happened to you?' he asked in tones of real astonishment. Morgan realized suddenly what kind of outlandish figure he must cut in his shrunken formal clothes, his scrawled moustache, elastoplast eyebrow and bloodied forehead. He told Murray about the riot outside Adekunle's house.

'Mrs Fanshawe and I made our escape,' he concluded. 'Drew the mob away, I think.'

'Quite the hero,' Murray said drily. 'I wouldn't carry on much further up this road though if I were you,' he went on. 'There's a pitched battle going on between the riot police and the students occupying the administrative offices. You'll run right into the middle of it. Listen.' Morgan heard above the shrill of the crickets in the grass and hedges a distant shouting and a kind of firework-popping effect.

'I'm told the riot police are blazing away at anything that moves and there's tear gas everywhere.'

'Oh Christ,' Morgan said. 'What do we do now?'

'There's only one other road out of the campus but it's miles back in the other direction. I doubt you'll be able to find it.'

'What are you doing out anyway?' Morgan inquired. 'If you don't mind me asking.'

'I don't mind,' Murray said. 'I'm waiting for my ambulance to come and pick me up. Apparently my clinic's full of injured students. Broken heads and broken bones. And some gunshot wounds.'

'Oh.'

'If you want to stay at my house you're very welcome. It's just up the road there.'

'Thanks,' Morgan said. 'But we've got to try and reunite Mrs Fanshawe with her family and get them down to the High Commission. I think we'll try and skirt round the riot, sneak out of the main gate.'

'Well, be careful,' Murray warned. 'Those riot squad boys are not the most amenable characters.'

'We will,' Morgan said. There was a pause. 'Look,' he said a little awkwardly, 'the reason I stopped was that I wanted to tell you that I've decided to resign my job tomorrow. I'll be leaving soon — so you don't need to worry about me when you make your report. Just as well,' he shrugged. 'You were right. It's better to face up to it.' He tried to grin in the darkness but it didn't really come off. 'I feel it's the right thing, you know. This place and me . . . well, never really got on. I think in a way I'll actually be quite glad to be shot of it all. So,' he spread his arms, 'give Adekunle the works. There's nothing he can do . . . you know, that's going to foul things up for me. I've, ah, beaten him to it. Ha ha.' The hollow laugh died away.

'I shall,' Murray said. 'Don't worry.'

There was a silence. It seemed to form like a wall between them. There was so much that he suddenly wanted to say to Murray: vaguely articulated ideas, half thought-out notions, old apologies, explanations.

'One more thing,' Morgan said. 'I almost forgot. I found out tonight that Adekunle's got some chum in the Senate who plans to "lose" your committee's minutes. I'd take a few copies if I were you.'

'I will,' Murray said. 'Many thanks. They'll never buy that land from him, don't worry.'

'Great,' Morgan said, patting his pockets like a man searching for matches. 'Good,' he noted. 'Sure we can't give you a lift somewhere?'

'No thanks. The ambulance will be here any minute.'

'Right.' He looked round. 'Well,' he breathed out loudly. How could he say what he felt to Murray? 'I just wanted to see you . . . tell you about things.' He let his eyes rest on Murray's face but it was too dark for him to distinguish his features clearly. He held out his hand and Murray shook it briefly. He held the dry cool hand for a second. 'Well, I'll, ah, see you, Alex. Maybe next week? Perhaps I could look by . . . before I go. I just wanted to put you in the picture now.'

'Fine,' Murray said. 'Thanks, Morgan. It was good of you.'

Morgan gave a half wave, muttered something indistinct and walked away. Thunder mumbled in the sky overhead. In the car he looked back and saw Murray standing there, saw the faint gleam of his white shirt.

Chapter 10

'What shall we do?' Mrs Fanshawe asked, looking at the line of riot police that effectively cut them off from the main gate and safety. Morgan could think of no reply at the moment so he kept his mouth shut. They were hiding behind a dense bush some fifty yards away from the administration block which looked as if it had been the target for an air strike. Three cars blazed furiously in front of it casting a flickering orange glow over the white walls of the arts theatre, the bookshop and the senate offices. Every visible window had been smashed, makeshift barricades of office furniture blocked walkways and entrances and thousands of sheets of paper blew across the piazza and around the foot of the clock tower. Ahead of them stretched the dual carriageway that led to the main gate and across which now stood a three-deep line of fully equipped riot police who were slowly advancing towards the occupied administrative offices. From the darkness came screams, shouts and cat calls from marauding students who occasionally crept close enough to the regrouping riot police to pelt them with stones and any other missiles that came to hand. The air tingled with dispersing tear gas, making their eyes water and their skin itchy. From time to time an edgy policeman loosed off a warning round into the air.

Morgan thought the atmosphere reminded him of the fateful lull before a battle. Like melodramatic stage effects the thunder grumbled distantly and lightning flickered along the western horizon. It looked as though the centre of the storm was passing Nkongsamba by, but a few fat drops of rain had fallen to add to their discomfort.

After leaving Murray they had driven on up the road going slower and slower as the noise of the tumult ahead increased. They thought about retracing their steps and looking for the back gate, but their ignorance of the route and the prospect of bumping into frustrated rioters made them decide eventually to abandon the battered car and try to skirt round the trouble, leaving the roads and cutting through several gardens to reach their present position behind the bush. Morgan looked at Mrs Fanshawe. Her pink dress was torn at the hem and looked grubby, the pearls round her neck individually trapped the flames of the burning cars. She showed no signs of flagging yet.

Morgan, however, felt exhausted, the tensions of the drive knotting and cramping every muscle in his body. He felt morose and uncaring too, troubled by his strange meeting with Murray . . .

'Morgan,' Mrs Fanshawe hissed. 'If those men keep walking in this direction they're going to stumble right over us.'

'Oh God. Christ yes, you're right. What do you want to do, Chloe? Shall we go back to the car? Perhaps we could hide in one of the houses?'

'Let's just get out of this lunatic asylum,' she said. 'If we cut back into the gardens again,' she pointed to the gardens of the houses that lined the dual carriageway, 'surely we can work our way round to the main gate.'

'Yes,' he said, complimenting her on her presence of mind. 'Good idea.' He felt a sudden compulsion to lie down and go to sleep. He watched the advancing riot police fire half a dozen canisters of tear gas at the besieged administrative offices. Two of them exploded prettily on the piazza sending thick orange-tinted clouds of gas spreading among the trampled flower-beds and ornamental fish-ponds.

'Morgan!' Mrs Fanshawe rebuked him. 'Let's go, for heaven's sake!' He looked up and saw the line of police about thirty yards in front of him, some with round shields, gas masks and long truncheons, some with rifles carried at port arms. An icy douche of raw terror sluicing through his veins, he seized Mrs Fanshawe's hand and, keeping in a low crouch, they scurried from the shelter of their bush and dashed across a patch of open ground making for the high hedge of the nearest garden.

An immediate shout went up from the police, and from the corner of his eye he caught the muzzle flash of rifles as they were fired. He didn't hear the sound of the shots, just a curious slapping noise in the air around his head which he half-registered as the effect of bullets passing close by. He gave a heaving sob, straightened up and dragged Mrs Fanshawe on behind him. He heard the pounding of heavy boots as some of the riot squad decided to give chase.

'Hurry!' he yelped in panic. 'They're coming after us!'

The hedge loomed up in the dark. He didn't check his pace, merely bent his head down, raised a forearm and charged through. A branch caught him a winding thwack in the chest, but he burst clear and stumbled into the tranquil space of a large garden. Ahead of them lay a dark and securely shuttered house. He heard the noise of more guns firing, a flat undramatic retort and heard bullets thunk into the boles of trees, shred leaves and twigs from the branches. They're mad, he thought wildly, they'll shoot at anything, they don't care.

'Come on,' Mrs Fanshawe gasped, already half way across the garden tottering along awkwardly in her elegant shoes. Morgan started after her, spurred on by the cries of the riot police clubbing their way through the hedge.

They ran through into the next-door garden, past a chicken coop that erupted with startled caws and cluckings, on through another hedge, tripping and falling over roots and undulations in the ground. Morgan seized Mrs Fanshawe's hand again and dragged her on, his heart punching its way through his ribcage, the blood roaring in his ears, stitches buckling both sides, his legs crude instruments of torture.

'Stop,' wheezed Mrs Fanshawe. He stopped. They fell to the ground behind a tree, coughing and gasping from the effort. No one seemed to be following them any more. There was a dull explosion and a barrage balloon of flame sailed into the night sky above the administration offices. Another car gone up, Morgan thought; the petrol tank. Or perhaps the riot squad have called in the artillery, he suggested to himself. He wouldn't have been surprised.

By the time they reached the campus perimeter fence it had started to rain. Not a downpour, just a steady drizzle. Morgan held the barbed wire strands as wide apart as he could but Mrs Fanshawe still tore her dress badly squeezing her bulk through. They crawled up a slope onto the main road. It was like another world. Opposite them was a small village, lantern lights gleaming peacefully in doorways, blue neon over a roadside drinks bar. They sank down on the verge. Mrs Fanshawe removed her shoes. Both heels had snapped off. In the distance behind them came the shouts and poppings as the riot police pressed home their attack.

'Thank Christ we got out of that,' Morgan said. A quarter of a mile down the road he saw the lights of the university's main gate. Several lorries and what looked like an armoured car were parked outside.

'They *were* shooting at us, weren't they?' Mrs Fanshawe confirmed in an awed voice, massaging her feet.

'I'm afraid so,' Morgan admitted, sensing delayed shock

about to pounce on him like a wild beast. He got to his feet. He had to keep moving.

'Let's get you to the Commission,' he said, helping Mrs Fanshawe up. They limped across the warm tarmacadam to the roadside kiosk. Behind it stood a youth in a baseball cap, his face bizarrely tinted from the fizzing blue fluorescent strip above his head. On the front of the kiosk was written SISSY'S GO-WELL DRINKOTHEQUE. The boy in the cap looked up in astonishment as Morgan and Mrs Fanshawe appeared out of the darkness.

'Ow!' he exclaimed, rubbing his face. 'Wetin go wrong here? Jesos Chrise!' He shook his head. Morgan looked at Mrs Fanshawe. The rip in her hem had split up to her thigh, her pink dress was tattered and filthy, and her negotiation of the barbed wire fence had somehow torn a triangular flap from her bodice exposing several square inches of her reinforced nylon long-line bra. Even her normally immovable hair hung in damp tangles over her forehead. She carried a heelless shoe in each hand. Morgan knew all too well what he looked like in his soiled circus-clown outfit. Self-consciously he tried to rub away the pencilled moustache on his upper lip. From the mud huts beyond the roadside bar a few curious faces peered. A small boy ran round the corner of a house and said 'Oyibo' but the sound died on his lips as he looked at these strange white people.

'Good evening,' Morgan said to the youth. 'You get car for this village?'

'You want car?'

'Yes. I go pay you ten pound if you take us to UK Commission.'

'Ten poun'?'

'Yes.'

'Make you give me money now.'

'No,' Morgan said firmly. 'First you drive us, before I pay.'

The youth left his kiosk and went back to one of the mud

huts where a shouted argument ensued. After a few minutes an older man appeared in ragged shorts and a singlet.

'Good evening, sah,' he said. 'My name is Pious. I have a car. I can take you.' He led them down a muddy stinking lane to where an old black Vauxhall Velox was parked. Morgan got into the back with Mrs Fanshawe. The interior smelt vaguely of animals, as if it had been used for transporting sheep or goats, but he didn't care any longer.

After several attempts the bronchitic engine finally started and they set out on the journey to the Commission. Again Morgan noted the untypical quietness of the roads.

'Why are there no cars tonight?' he asked their driver.

'Ammy comin',' Pious said simply.

'Army? What do you mean? For the riot at the university?'

Pious shrugged. 'I don't know. Plenty Ammy lorries passing tonight. Plenty.' Morgan sat back. He remembered Robinson's hints and Friday's warning about a coup. He gave up. It was conceivable that the population knew something that the politicians didn't. Anything could happen here, he now realized.

The Commission was dark and unbesieged. The Fanshawes' house was locked up and empty. There was a note from Fanshawe saying they had seen Morgan and Mrs Fanshawe evade the mob, safely escaped themselves from Adekunle's house, had left the campus by the back gate and after waiting for an hour had gone on down to the capital. The Joneses, it appeared, were going to put up Mrs Fanshawe in her family's temporary absence.

'Well,' Morgan said, on hearing this, 'we'd better get you to the Joneses. It seems as though everything went OK.' He paused. 'You could stay here if you want. I can go and get the servants . . .'

'No,' Mrs Fanshawe said, re-reading the note. 'I don't feel like staying here on my own. But do you think I could clean up a bit at your place first? Perhaps Denzil could come over and collect me.'

'Sure,' Morgan said. 'Fine.'

Pious dropped them at Morgan's house. Morgan ran in to get the money to pay him off. It was worth every penny. He looked at his watch. Half past eleven. He felt like he'd been on the run for weeks. But, he reasoned with a wry smile, in a way that was true enough. Pious drove off noisily and for a moment or two Morgan stood alone in his driveway, the light rain falling on his head. Small rain, Isaac had called it. For a second he thought he could hear the pop-gun effect of distant shooting. He wondered what was going on: everybody shooting at everybody else tonight. He shivered at the memory. Thunder mumbled and lightning flashed away to the south-west. He smelt the musty attic odour of damp earth and listened to the bats and toads, the creek-creek of the crickets starting up again.

He went back into his house. Mrs Fanshawe stood in the middle of the carpet examining the rents in her dress. She gave a tired laugh when he came in.

'My God, Morgan,' she said. 'What on earth must we look like?' Morgan smiled. She looked very strange with her small bare feet, her thigh gaping from the slit in the dress, her hair tousled, half her underwear on show; like a survivor from a plane crash. Only the three strings of pearls belonged to the Mrs Fanshawe of earlier in the evening.

'I feel I should thank you, Morgan,' she said.

'What for?'

'For everything you did tonight. You were splendid.'

Morgan bowed his head. 'Thanks,' he said, adding awkwardly, 'you did all right yourself.'

This mutual congratulation made them feel embarrassed and they both scrutinized the weave of the carpet. Morgan moved to the drinks table.

'Do you want a drink?' he asked. 'Or would you rather have a bath first?'

'Oh a bath I think,' she said. 'Lovely.' Morgan led her

up the corridor and into his bedroom. He showed her the bathroom.

'There are plenty of towels,' he said. 'I'm afraid we can't rise to a new dress.'

'Don't worry about that,' she reassured him.

He went back into the sitting room and poured himself a whisky. He sat down in an armchair and took a sip. Outside in the dark the rain pattered gently on the leaves of the trees and dripped into the gutters. He felt tired. He knew the recriminations and problems ahead of him: the resignation, Adekunle's wrath, the exposure of Celia. Her name made his features tighten as he remembered the scene at the house. What the hell, he thought with sudden generosity. She could have her visa: it didn't matter to him really. She was just desperate, in a jam: he'd have done the same in her circumstances – or worse. He'd see she got one tomorrow.

He got up and poured himself another whisky. He felt let down and demoralized. Everything he'd done had been in vain, he considered. He hadn't even held on to his job. He heard the creak of the swing door and Mrs Fanshawe came in. She was wearing his blue towelling dressing-gown and was carrying her dress.

'Have you got a needle and thread?' she asked innocently. 'I'll try and patch up these tears before I call Denzil.'

Morgan rummaged around in a few drawers and found what she wanted. Mrs Fanshawe sat down and began to sew up the dress. Morgan found the domestic scene strangely unsettling. It reminded him uncomfortably of that hot afternoon in her house, fitting the Father Christmas costume, the day he'd . . . He excused himself saying he was going to have a shower.

In the bathroom he stripped off his clothes and washed his dusty sweaty body clean beneath the cool water. He bent to pick up the soap from the side of the bath and found it wet and slippy. As he worked up a lather he thought it strange to consider that minutes earlier the soap had followed a similar course over Mrs Fanshawe's considerable frame. He noticed a sprinkle of talcum powder on the bathroom floor, he saw some black hairs stark against the white enamel of the bath. For some reason he felt a little apprehensive, a ball of air seemed to lodge itself in his throat. He and Mrs Fanshawe had been through a lot together tonight, he told himself. They had shared considerable danger, been shot at . . .

He pulled on a fresh shirt and a pair of trousers and padded back through to the sitting room. Mrs Fanshawe sat on the sofa, the repaired dress beside her. Her face looked clean, her black hair was combed back from her white forehead, still slightly damp.

'Have you phoned Denzil yet?' Morgan asked, an unfamiliar catch in his voice.

'No,' she said deliberately, allowing a silence to fall before adding, 'I've decided I'd rather stay here tonight, if that's fine with you.'

Oh my God, Morgan thought as he unbuttoned his shirt. No God, no. What was he doing? he asked himself hysterically. What did he think he was playing at? Across on the other side of the bed from him Mrs Fanshawe removed her dressing-gown, her eyes never leaving his face, a strange relaxed smile on her lips. Morgan's gaze was locked on to hers, and he was only dimly aware of the large white body in its sensible underwear, caught an unfocused glimpse of the white breasts tumbling free of the nylon cuirass that supported them, sensed vaguely the stooping pant-removing gesture that revealed momentarily the patch of dark amidst the creamy plains of her thighs, before she slipped into his bed pulling the sheet up to her neck.

Morgan lowered his trousers. After she'd asked if he'd mind her staying, she had risen to her feet and walked over to him.

'Let's have a look at that cut on your forehead,' she commanded, and obediently he lowered his head so she could examine it better, bringing their faces to within a close six inches of each other. Morgan gulped. Suddenly they were kissing, her thin lips pressed to his, her hands running up and down his back. And now she was lying naked in his bed. He eased off his underpants and slid under the sheet to join her. She pulled him close. Hesitantly he allowed his hand to rest on her side, somewhere safe. Her skin felt unbelievably soft and pampered.

She edged closer. He felt the cushiony weight of her breasts flatten between them. She cupped his face with her hands.

'Morgan,' she said. 'We've been through too much tonight not to . . . not to be with each other now.'

He nodded wordlessly. He felt his fear and surprise slowly yielding to arousal. He trickled his fingers across her wide thighs. He remembered suddenly that Priscilla's pants lay in the drawer of the bedside table. What a peculiar world it was, he thought helplessly, where this sort of fateful irony could occur.

'Do you remember that day you came to try on the Santa Claus outfit?' she asked softly.

He nodded again.

'I've been thinking about you since then,' she said. 'A lot.'

Surely, Morgan asked himself indignantly, she didn't think he let it happen on purpose? She must credit him with a seductive technique marginally more refined than . . . *that*? As if to prove his point he nuzzled her breasts, touching his lips to a nipple, while she gave an appreciative sigh into his ear.

The phone rang beside the bed.

Morgan looked up. 'I'd better answer it,' he said. 'I'll take it in the sitting room. It might be . . .' They both knew who it might be. He pulled on his dressing-gown and ran down the corridor.

'Yes?' he said, picking up the phone.

'Mr Leafy?'

'Yes. Speaking.'

'First Secretary at the Commission?'

'That's right.'

'This is Inspector Gbeho here. Nkongsamba police head-quarters.'

'Hello, Inspector,' Morgan knotted his dressing-gown cord. 'What can I do for you?'

'I phoned Mr Fanshawe at the Commission but there was no reply. You are the next senior British official in Nkongsamba according to my records.'

'That's correct,' Morgan said a little impatiently. 'What's the trouble exactly?'

'It's just a routine call, sir, whenever there is a death. To pass on the information.'

'A death?'

'Of a British subject.'

Morgan felt his heart begin to beat faster. He took a deep breath. He shut his eyes, a tremor passing through his body.

'I see,' he said. 'Who is it?'

'A man. A Dr Murray. Dr Alexander Murray. From the university . . . Hello Mr Leafy. Are you still there?'

'He's dead?'

'Yes, sir.'

'How . . . What happened?'

'I believe he was transporting injured students to the Ademola clinic in the university ambulance. The ambulance skidded and crashed. From the rain on the roads. Dr Murray was killed in the crash.'

'Anybody else?'

'No. Some cuts and bruises. Oh yes, the driver broke his leg.'

'Have you told Murray's family?'

'Yes, sir.'

'Thank you for phoning, Inspector. I'll be in touch in the morning.'

Morgan gently replaced the phone. Murray was dead. He tried to come to terms with the fact. It was hard. He walked out onto the verandah. Dead. Like Innocence. All sorts of ideas and images crowded into his mind. He covered his face with his hands.

'Who was it, Morgan?' Mrs Fanshawe called from the bedroom door. She had wrapped the sheet around her. 'Was it Arthur?'

'No. It was the police. Murray's dead.' He controlled his voice. 'Dr Murray.'

'Dead? That chap we saw tonight?'

'Yes, that's the one.'

'What happened?'

'Crash. In his ambulance of all things. Something damn bloody silly anyway.'

'Oh . . . Are you coming to bed?'

'Yes. Just give me a second.'

It was still raining, pattering softly on the roof. He stood on the edge of the verandah and looked out into the night. The thunder passed on towards the coast. The sheet lightning flashed over the jungle to the south. Shango was angry. He thought vaguely that he'd have to see Murray's family and as he did so he felt his throat contract and thicken and tears press for a moment in his eyes. Why Murray? he asked himself in despair. A good man like that: there weren't many of them around – Kojo, Friday, Murray. Why not Dalmire, why not Fanshawe? Why not me?

'Morgan,' Mrs Fanshawe called. 'Come on, Morgan.'

He turned to go. Adekunle wouldn't weep, for one. His land was as good as sold now. Murray wouldn't like that at all, he thought. In fact Murray would expect him to do something about it. And perhaps he would too, now that he had nothing to lose. Perhaps. He thought about it. Innocence could get buried. Celia could have her visa. Maybe Murray deserved his fairness. But what was Morgan Leafy left with?

Very little, he answered himself. Very little. No job and no future. Mrs Fanshawe in the bedroom. And Hazel. Hazel who told him she didn't want him to leave . . . but no, he wasn't sure about Hazel.

He opened the screen door and walked slowly up the passage towards the bedroom and Chloe Fanshawe. He wondered what Murray would think of this. Not much, he was certain. Alive or dead Murray somehow managed to barge his way into his life as persistently as ever. And suddenly he didn't want particularly to go on with it: two large white bodies heaving and grunting in an absurd parody of love

He paused at the bedroom door. Chloe Fanshawe lay on the bed, resting on one elbow, the sheet twisted around her large body. She flung it aside.

'Here you are at last,' she said. 'What kept you?'

'Listen, Chloe,' Morgan began haltingly. 'I've been . . . giving things some thought, and I'm not so sure . . .'

Outside the rain fell softly in the dark, the toads and crickets made their noises and all sorts of insects began to test and spread their wings in anticipation of the rain stopping. The riot was over, the piazza deserted, smoke wisps curled from the burnt-out cars. Elsewhere in the country units of the Kinjanjan army surrounded Government House, took over the radio and TV stations, and began arresting prominent political leaders. Innocence lay in the muddy compound of the servants' quarters, and Murray lay on a marble slab in the Ademola morgue. The thunder passed on towards the coast and, somewhere, Shango, that mysterious and incomprehensible god, flashed and capered happily above the silent dripping jungle.

He just wanted a decent book to read ...

Not too much to ask, is it? It was in 1935 when Allen Lane, Managing Director of Bodley Head Publishers, stood on a platform at Exeter railway station looking for something good to read on his journey back to London. His choice was limited to popular magazines and poor-quality paperbacks – the same choice faced every day by the vast majority of readers, few of whom could afford hardbacks. Lane's disappointment and subsequent anger at the range of books generally available led him to found a company – and change the world.

'We believed in the existence in this country of a vast reading public for intelligent books at a low price, and staked everything on it'
Sir Allen Lane, 1902–1970, founder of Penguin Books

The quality paperback had arrived – and not just in bookshops. Lane was adamant that his Penguins should appear in chain stores and tobacconists, and should cost no more than a packet of cigarettes.

Reading habits (and cigarette prices) have changed since 1935, but Penguin still believes in publishing the best books for everybody to enjoy. We still believe that good design costs no more than bad design, and we still believe that quality books published passionately and responsibly make the world a better place.

So wherever you see the little bird – whether it's on a piece of prize-winning literary fiction or a celebrity autobiography, political tour de force or historical masterpiece, a serial-killer thriller, reference book, world classic or a piece of pure escapism – you can bet that it represents the very best that the genre has to offer.

Whatever you like to read – trust Penguin.